save me

Vickie
Choose wsely!

Natasha Preston

BOOKS BY NATASHA PRESTON

THE SILENCE SERIES

Silence
Broken Silence
Players, Bumps, and Cocktail Sausages
Silent Night

THE CHANCE SERIES (STAND-ALONE SERIES)

Second Chance
Our Chance

STAND-ALONES

Save Me
With the Band
The Cellar
Awake
The Cabin

NATASHAPRESTON.COM

save me

NATASHA PRESTON

Visit my website at www.natashapreston.com
Cover Designer: Dalliance Designs
Editor and Interior Designer: Jovana Shirley, Unforeseen
Editing, www.unforeseenediting.com

This book is a work of fiction. Names, characters, places, and
incidents either are products of the author's imagination or are
used fictitiously. Any resemblance to actual persons, living or
dead, events, or locales is entirely coincidental.

ISBN-13: 978-1500962135

For Kirsty Moseley.
Kirsty, this one could only ever be for you!

Tegan

I SAT IN THE SMALL family room with my mum and older sister, waiting to hear if our worst nightmare—the one we didn't speak aloud in case we jinxed it—was about to come true.

Dad's parents and brother were on their way, but at the minute, it was just us three. I needed more people here, more to focus on, so I could pretend the surgeons weren't fighting to save my dad's life right now.

The room we were in was all wrong. It was light and welcoming with bright flowers in a tall vase on the coffee table. It was cheerful and gave false hope. Not everyone who came in here was going to leave happy.

Ava sniffed and wiped her nose. She and Mum clung to each other. They were close. I was close to Dad. Whenever anything bad happened, it was just assumed that Dad would comfort me, and Mum would comfort Ava. I wanted—

needed—the support they were offering each other, but I knew the only person who could do that was in emergency surgery.

"What's taking them so long?" Ava said.

She already knew the answer. The surgeon was fighting to stop a pretty serious bleed in his brain. I was terrified that they wouldn't be able to. Tugging my blonde hair as I wound it around my finger, I tried to block out the negative thoughts.

"He'll be fine," Mum said, nodding more to herself than anyone else.

I tensed my body, stupidly telling myself that, if I just stayed as still as I could, he'd be fine. That was ridiculous though. If I sat as still as a statue or did cartwheels around the room, it would make absolutely no difference in the outcome of the operation. That was all down to Dad and the surgeons.

We'd only been here for forty-five minutes, but it felt like hours, days even. Dad had already been in surgery when we received the call. I didn't know how long it would take to fix him up, and I didn't know if it was a good sign or not that we hadn't heard anything since we arrived.

"Alison!" Nan said, bursting through the door. Tears streamed down her face, taking her mascara with it.

Mum stood up and hugged her tight. They cried together for a minute before Nan pulled away and sat in Mum's seat between me and Ava, putting an arm around each of us. Her son was in surgery, but she was doing her best to comfort us.

Ava cried harder, turning to sob on Mum's shoulder on the other side of her now. I couldn't cry at all. I didn't want to. It would be like accepting there was a possibility that my strong dad wouldn't make it. Deep down, of course, I knew there was a chance that could happen. He was going to make it though.

Next in the room were Grandad and Uncle Sam, just minutes behind Nan. I watched them talking, exchanging comforting words almost animatedly, but I didn't really hear a thing.

"Tegan, are you okay?" Mum asked softly. She knelt down in front of me, concern etched on her tear-stained face.

save me

How long has she been there for?

I nodded—at least, I thought I did. I didn't want her worrying. "I'm fine," I replied. *Fine* wasn't how I felt at all; *petrified* was a much better fit.

She smiled and sat back on her chair, wrapping her arm around Ava again.

Waiting was excruciating. *What if they come with bad news? What if they couldn't stop the bleeding? His car had been hit by a lorry. What chance did he really have against that?*

"Mrs Pennells?"

At the doctor's words, I leapt up with everyone else. My world stopped. The doctor's face was blank, giving nothing away. I could feel my heart racing at a hundred miles an hour.

"I'm so sorry. We did everything we could—"

I spaced out, muscles locking in position, hearing only the ringing in my ears, as I tried to think of a way that I'd misheard that. Black spots danced in front of my face. My lungs burned; I couldn't get enough oxygen. Then, I was falling.

When I came around, the doctor was kneeling above me with my mum at the other side, sobbing hysterically.

It hit me like a bus. *Dad's gone.*

A crushing, stabbing pain pierced through my body as I lay on the rough carpet. *No. No, he can't die. He* can't. I wasn't ready to lose him. I should be in my sixties when that happened, not fucking seventeen.

I opened my mouth, but the suffocating pain stopped any sounds from coming out. I was plunged into ice-cold water, sinking lower and lower, while the doctor tried to get a response from me.

I couldn't lose him. It already felt so painful. I could barely breathe. *How can I go on without my dad?* The thought of getting off the floor made me want to curl up in a ball and stop existing.

"Tegan…" Mum sobbed.

In a trance, I sat up, falling straight into her lap. Her arms curled around me, and we cried together. It was the first time Mum had really held me since I was a little kid.

"Mrs Pennells?" the doctor said once she knew I was okay. "I'm sorry to have to bring this up now, but I'd like to talk to you about organ donation, if that's okay?"

I froze again and felt Mum nod against the top of my head.

"Simon would have wanted that. Do you need me to sign anything?"

"No, he carried a donor card. I just wanted to make sure you were aware that your husband would be doing an incredible thing for others."

My mind finally pieced together exactly what that meant. His organs were going to be cut out.

No! I wanted to stand up and scream, but I couldn't move an inch.

They couldn't cut him apart and take anything out of him.

His heart? Are they going to take his heart? That belongs to us.

My dad was a person, not a body they could just take things out of. He was my dad, and I wanted him whole. I wanted him back.

"Would you like to stay here and say good-bye when he's out of surgery?" she asked.

When he had his organs removed, she meant. I didn't want to see my dad dead.

"Yes, I need to see my child," Nan said between heavy sobs.

"Of course. I'll come back soon."

Nothing was said as we waited for the surgeons to remove God knew what.

Is there a limit to what they can take? Dad would have had his wishes listed, but what if they take everything anyway? No one will know.

save me

I didn't even know he was a registered donor. Why didn't he tell me that, so I would have had some warning?

Mum and Ava didn't look at all surprised. They must have known.

I stayed curled up on Mum's lap the whole time they were cutting his organs out. Mum must have been uncomfortable, as I was, but neither of us had the energy to move.

"Mum," I whispered, barely recognising my own voice.

"Ye-yes?"

I didn't know what I wanted to ask. I needed her to tell me that they had gotten it wrong. I needed her to tell me that Dad was okay and would walk into the room at any second. I wanted my dad.

"Shh…we're going to be okay," she whispered.

Liar.

Dad was the heart of our family. Nothing was going to be okay.

Time passed, but I didn't know how much, and then the doctor came back for us.

"Mrs Pennells? If you'd follow me, you can come through now."

I looked up through blurry eyes and shook my head. I didn't want to see him like that.

Mum took a deep breath and stood up, lifting me with her. "You need to, Tegan. You have to say good-bye."

No, I didn't. I didn't want to tell the most important person in my life good-bye. "I don't want to," I replied, sitting down on a chair.

"Are you sure, sweetheart?" Nan asked, kneeling in front of me.

"I don't want to say good-bye." *Why the fuck can't they understand that?* My stomach turned, and bile burned my throat. Sobs racked my body as I tried to stop crying. It hurt so much. I needed it to stop.

Nan nodded. "Okay, I'll stay with you."

"No, you go. You want to, and I want to be alone."

There was no way I was going to be the reason Nan didn't get to say bye to her son. I sat on the chair, painfully gripping the seat, as I forced myself to take a breath.

It's going to be okay. Everything is going to be okay.

I was fooling myself, but I couldn't help it. I desperately wanted to believe it would be okay, that I would get through it. I was scared for the upcoming few days, weeks, and months. I didn't want to miss him. *How will I deal with not seeing or speaking to him again?*

I breathed deeply through my nose, clenching my stomach muscles, just trying to stop from curling up and dying, too.

"Are you okay?" someone asked.

I jerked and looked up. A tall guy, maybe a few years older than me, with ash-brown hair towered over me. He looked down, eyes full of concern.

"No, I don't…I…" *I'm drowning.*

I wanted it to stop. I wanted my heart to stop hurting. I wanted to shout and scream and hide. I felt like I itched all over, like my skin was crawling, like I was being held down and bugs were crawling all over me. I was too hot, too cold, too empty, and alone.

He sat next to me, drawing my attention back to him, while who I assumed was his mum, brother, and sister sat over on the other side of the room. They all looked alike—the same shade of light-brown hair and light-green eyes.

"I'm Lucas," he said, giving me a warm smile. His voice was deep but friendly.

I didn't want to talk to him, even as nice as he seemed. I didn't feel that I could even hold a conversation right now. I wanted to be far, far away. The others didn't say anything. They just sat there and twiddled their thumbs or started clock-watching.

"Tegan," I whispered, clearing my sore throat.

"Are you here alone, Tegan?"

I shook my head. "No, they're saying…good-bye."

I didn't see his reaction, but it took him a minute to talk again. "You're not?"

"Can't." Out of the corner of my eye, I saw him nod his head.

We fell into silence, which suited me fine, but I could tell he was searching for something to say. Maybe he needed to keep busy to pass the time.

"Are you okay?" I asked.

He nodded even though his eyes told me otherwise. "Yeah. Do you want to talk about it?"

No. I didn't want it to even be happening, so I certainly didn't want to talk about it.

I shook my head and wrapped my arms around myself.

"Okay," he said.

We sat mostly in silence until Mum and Ava came back, clinging to each other and crying. Nan, Grandad, and Sam were just behind them. I didn't move.

Lucas's mum, who'd tried to talk to me a few times, stood up. "I'm so sorry for your loss," she said.

They knew I'd lost my dad. They'd managed to get that much out of me.

"Thank you," Mum whispered, frowning and taking my hand.

"I'm Emily. Your daughter told us what happened. Is there anything we can do? A lift home?"

"Alison. Thank you, but I've got my car." Taking a composing deep breath, Mum asked, "Are you okay, Emily?"

"I'm not sure. I should be. I am. I'm scared. My husband's needed a heart transplant for six months, and he's finally getting it."

I sank deeper into the water.

Tegan

I WOKE UP, AND the pain of missing Dad hit me hard again, same as every morning since he'd died. Getting out of bed took a hell of a lot of effort, and I could quite happily stay curled up under the covers all day.

It'd been four days since his funeral, and I hadn't been able to cry. Something was wrong with me. Dad meant everything to me. He was the person I'd turn to, the one who'd make sense of the world, and the one who'd teach and guide me. He would've told me how to handle losing someone I love, but he was gone, and I didn't even know how to grieve. I was a zombie.

When I got to the bottom of the stairs, I heard Mum and Ava talking and crying together in the living room. That was the same every day, too.

I turned the corner and saw them huddled up on the sofa together. They helped each other so much. Mum was to Ava what Dad had been to me. She would be okay. Mum was holding her up. She was trying to do that for me, too, but I just felt disconnected. All I knew was, it hurt so much more than words could describe, and nothing was helping to ease it at all.

Dad's things were all over the house. I wanted to hide every single thing that reminded me of him, but Mum and Ava wanted them around. They wanted to feel close to Dad, and I wished I could forget.

"Tegan," Mum said, holding her hand out. "Come here, sweetheart."

My stomach turned. I didn't want to sit with them, hear them talking about him and crying. I hated when my mum cried. She was the strong one. My parents had always been solid as rock for me and Ava. Mum didn't normally cry in front of us, but right now, she was a mess. Every time I saw that look in her eye or heard her sobbing, I'd feel like I was being ripped open all over again. It wasn't enough that I lost my dad, but my mum also had to be in pain, too. It wasn't fair.

"I-I need a drink," I said, spinning around and making a run for the kitchen.

Breathing heavily over the sink, I took deep breaths to try to calm my queasy stomach.

On the counter was another frozen meal defrosting. People had brought us food. Since he'd died, Mum's friends had been coming every couple of days with meals. Everyone was too nice. I wanted things to be normal, not for people to look at me with sympathy.

"Tegan, you okay?" Ava asked.

I turned around and looked into her tear-stained eyes. "I'm fine."

I wasn't fine. I was drowning, but the person who could tell me how to stop was gone.

"I'm thinking of going out today. There's only so long I can spend looking at the same four walls. You want to come? It might be good for all of us to get out of the house and take our minds off everything."

save me

That was what I wanted. I wanted my mind somewhere else, somewhere my dad hadn't died, somewhere I didn't feel like I was so completely lost and alone.

"Yeah, I'll come."

I regretted it the second we got into town. The people who knew what'd happened stopped to offer their condolences, or they pretended like they hadn't seen us because they didn't know what to say.

My friends were in Starbucks, and I watched through the window as they laughed and messed around, throwing wadded up napkins into empty coffee cups. A few weeks ago, that had been me, too. Every one of them had tried calling or coming over, but I'd ignored them or sent them away every time. I couldn't do it.

My best friend, Sophie—the one whom I did still speak with because she wouldn't mention Dad, knowing I didn't want to talk—looked over and stood up.

Shit, I don't want any of them to see me.

I felt like running to the bookshop next door to find Mum, but Sophie was already halfway to the door, and I didn't want to hear Mum having a conversation about my dad with the lady who owned the shop.

"Tegan, hey," Sophie said.

"Hey."

"You want to join us?"

"No, thanks. I'm here with Mum and Ava."

"Okay, cool. You up for a party at Adam's tonight? His parents are on their annual South of France holiday."

I didn't want to say yes, but I kept thinking about what Ava had said about getting out and taking my mind off of what'd happened. "Sure, I'm in."

"Great! I'll get Adam to pick you up, too."

"It's at Adam's house."

"I know, but I don't like to walk, and he's too nice." She laughed and tucked her short dark blonde hair behind her ear. "Pick you up at eight."

"Thanks, Soph."

She grinned. "No worries. Bye, hon."

Mum and Ava came out of the bookshop a few minutes later.

"Lunch now?" Mum asked.

"Sure. Is it okay if I go to a party at Adam's tonight?" I asked.

"Of course. I think it'll be good for you to spend some time with your friends."

"Thanks. Where are we going to eat?"

"That place Dad loved?" Ava suggested.

The positivity I'd felt before was replaced with dread.

"Not there," I said, practically snapping. "Um, what about the pizza place? Mum, you said you wanted to try that pesto base next time we were in town."

Mum put her arm around me, and I hated it. I wanted the comfort, but I didn't want it to hurt. When she hugged me, she cried, and I felt even guiltier for not being able to do the same.

Adam's annual parents-are-gone party was the same every year. People would drink far more than they could handle and end up passed out on the floor, sofa, or bed. I'd have a few every time but never to that extent. But, this year, I was on my sixth, and the alcohol combined with not being at home with my grieving family and seeing Dad's stuff everywhere meant I was feeling good.

I sat on the bench outside, getting some fresh air. My head felt fuzzy but in the best way possible. Nothing hurt; nothing was hard.

Adam's older brother, Ian, sat beside me. "Hey, how are you doing?"

"Good. You?" I replied.

He nodded, swigging on his bottle of brandy. Down on the lawn, some girl I didn't recognise slapped another girl and chucked her drink on her. That didn't usually happen at Adam's parties.

"What happened there?" I asked.

He shrugged. "She doesn't like that Sammy has the same shoes or some shit like that. They were bitching each other out about it earlier."

They were wearing the same shoes, but so what? "She's a bit of a bitch," I said.

"Yeah, but that's intentional. No one can hurt the bitch."

No one can hurt the bitch.

"What are you looking all pissed off over?"

"Nothing," I replied. I was going to be okay now. "I need more to drink."

He handed the bottle over, and I took a swig. It was the most disgusting thing I'd ever tasted, but that didn't stop me from going back for more.

"Keep drinking," Ian said. "It makes everything ten times better."

"I never believed that before now." I took another long swig and winced.

"You want to know what else helps?"

"Sure." I would do anything to stop from hurting so much.

Smiling, he leant in, and I was completely unprepared for his lips. Stunned, I sat still for a second until I felt the comfort I craved with none of the feelings. Ian meant nothing to me, and I clearly meant nothing to him because he didn't even take me to his room. I let him kiss me. I let him take me to his car at the side of the house. I let him pull up my skirt.

It hurt. It was my first time, and he either didn't know that, or he didn't care, but it didn't matter. I was close to someone without hurting—emotionally anyway. I closed off, shut everything away, and for the first time since Dad had died, I felt absolutely nothing at all.

Ian was right. Alcohol and sex took the pain away.

I leant against the bar and downed the shot. In the thirteen days since I'd lost my virginity and learnt how to feel fuck-all, I was free. Sex was entirely overrated—pleasure-wise anyway. What it did, however, was take me to a place where I didn't have to think about anything.

Sophie loved the new me. She was promiscuous, and now, she had a wingwoman. I hated the new me. Hated what I did to my body and hated how my relationship with Mum and Ava had so many cracks that I didn't think there was enough glue in the entire world to fix it. But I did love how I didn't feel like I was standing in a roomful of people screaming for help but not being heard.

"No one can hurt the bitch."

Since Sophie had left me half an hour ago to dance with some guy, I was left alone at the bar to drink until I passed out or was picked up. Either was fine by me. I'd never be clean again, so what was the point in worrying?

A guy with eyes the colour of dark chocolate and tattoos that'd make any woman swoon leant on the bar beside me. "Hey," he said.

Hello. Jesus, he is gorgeous. His just-fucked hair made me want to jump him in the middle of the club.

"Hi."

"I'm Kai Chambers."

I smiled. His name was just as hot. "Tegan Pennells."

"Can I buy you a drink?" he asked, looking so deep into my eyes that I wanted to tell him to do one.

I smiled again. He saw more. I didn't want him to see me.

"Thanks," I replied. "I'll have a vodka and lemonade."

Kai was different. The other guys—eight to date—hadn't given a shit about me at all. They hadn't asked if I wanted a drink or made any attempt to even learn my name. I wasn't convinced that it was better this way, but I couldn't make myself walk away after that second drink or the third.

He was funny and a huge pervert. But he wasn't a sleaze.

When he took me into a bathroom stall, for the first time since I'd lost my virginity, I wanted sex. Normal sex. When he kissed me, I ached for a whole new reason. He kissed wherever his lips could reach, touched wherever his hands could reach. It wasn't purely selfish. He wasn't in a race to get off and then leave. He made sure it felt good for me, and I realised that sex wasn't overrated. Kai was the first person to make me come, the first person to kiss me after, the first person to ask for my number, and the first person to take me back to a table and continue talking to me for the rest of the night.

Lucas

Dad lay on the sofa with two bottles of water, a cup of tea, all the medication he needed, and a sandwich wrapped up for lunch on the end table beside him. Mum had had to go back to work part-time yesterday, so Dad was alone for a lot of the day, but plenty of people would pop in to make sure he was all right. It had only been three weeks since the transplant, and I was shit-scared of leaving him in case something happened. He was going to need regular visits to the hospital and six weekly blood tests for the rest of his life. I wasn't a religious person, but I fucking prayed to everything that could be out there to make him okay.

As the last person who left the house every day, I had the responsibility of double-checking he had everything he'd need for the first hour until my aunt and Nan arrived.

"Lucas," Dad said, "I'm fine, and if I need another drink, I'll get up and get it. That much, I can do for myself. Go to work before you're fired."

I did another check of the table. "You sure you don't need anything before I go?"

"I'm fine."

"You're not in any pain?"

"No more than usual. I've got my tablets right beside me, ready to take in half an hour. Get going."

I nodded. "Right. Okay. Nan and Leanne will be here soon."

"I know. Now, go."

I was terrified of leaving him. Dad had congestive heart failure, and it had been getting progressively worse until the point when we had been told that he would die very soon if he didn't have a transplant.

I walked out of the house and forced myself to get in my car and drive to work. I'd never wanted to blow off work and just drive so much. I'd thought things would get better after the operation, thought I'd worry less, but now, we were faced with Dad's body rejecting the heart and having some pretty serious side effects from all the medication he was on.

The garage I worked at was a mile down the road, so I knew I could make it back in a minute if Dad needed me. I just didn't know, if something bad happened, whether a minute would be quick enough.

"Morning," Malcolm said, scratching his beer belly. Mal was the boss, but he acted more like a dad, always looking out for me and my colleague, Leon. "You ready to spray the Merc?"

"Yeah, gimme five, and I'll be out back."

I chucked my phone on the desk and grabbed a mask.

"Hey, how's your dad?" Leon asked, coming out of the bathroom.

"He's doing all right."

"Good. And the girl you've been obsessing over?"

Tegan Pennells, daughter of the man who had donated his heart to my old man. You probably couldn't get much more complicated than that. She wouldn't leave my head though. I couldn't stop seeing that look on her face. Her dad had died, and she'd been devastated.

I wanted to help her, but I had no idea how. Mum and Alison had been keeping in touch, and I knew my twin sister, Grace, and Tegan's sister, Ava, talked, but Tegan never reached out, and I wasn't sure if she wanted to. Couldn't blame her. I didn't think I'd want to talk to the people who were still a complete family because mine wasn't.

"I'm not stressing over her, and I don't know." I rubbed my forehead. "I wanna do something. We owe her whole family so much."

"Her dad made a choice. It's not one you have to pay for, Lucas. That's not how it works."

"Yeah, I get that. He did it to help someone else. It's selfless and an incredible legacy, but to me, he saved my dad's life, and I want to do something to help his daughter."

"All right, I get it. Just be prepared for her to not want your help. Anyway, we'd better get this car sprayed fucking pink." He turned his nose up. "I swear, if I didn't need to eat, I'd refuse to fuck up cars this way."

I grabbed my spray gun and mask and headed back out.

Leon's words stuck around. Tegan might not want or need my help, but from what Grace had said, Alison and Ava were doing as well as they could under the circumstances, but Tegan was all over the place.

No matter what anyone said, I owed it to Simon to try.

Tegan

I WAS PROBABLY BECOMING immune to alcohol because, when I woke up, I didn't want to saw my own head off. That suited me just fine. I wanted the freedom from thinking, and being drunk gave that to me, but I was totally fine with not having a hangover in the morning.

I drained the bottle of water I'd left on my bedside table. It tasted foul, being warm, but I didn't care. I didn't care about anything anymore.

Heading downstairs for dry toast, tea, and painkillers, I could hear the hushed voices of my mum and sister.

They were doing okay. The funeral had been a turning point for them. They cried a lot and missed him like crazy, but they also spoke about him and smiled. I had absolutely no idea how they could do that without grief consuming them. I couldn't stand it.

They would say things like, "Remember when..." or, "He loved this..."

All past-tense stuff.

In a short space of time, I'd learnt how to successfully shut myself out from everything going on, and there was no way I was coming out of that.

Mum and Ava sat at the kitchen table, drinking tea. I could tell Mum had been crying by the light-red tint around her eyes, slightly hidden by concealer.

"Morning," I muttered as I opened the medicine cupboard.

"Good morning, honey," Mum whispered.

My heart squeezed at how sad she sounded. I clenched my jaw and concentrated on popping the little white pills out of the packet. *Don't care.*

I wanted to be empty. It was simpler.

The funeral was three weeks ago to the day. Up until then—for the six days before that—all Mum and Ava had done was cry and hold each other.

The funeral was the second worst day of my life. I'd felt like I was on the edge of drowning the whole time, and I didn't know how to get out of the water. I was lost. My family had all come together to say good-bye. They'd all thrown dirt onto his coffin and whispered their good-byes. I'd stood still, staring into space and trying not to fall apart. Almost everyone had encouraged me to say good-bye, too. But I couldn't. I wanted him back, not to throw mud at him and walk away.

The house was painfully silent now. Before, it had been filled with music and laughter. The piano was always being played by one of us. Now, I couldn't even go into the music room.

"I spoke to Emily yesterday," Mum said.

My hand tightened around the glass of water. Why she wanted to keep in touch with the family of the man who had gotten Dad's heart, I didn't know.

"Carl's doing well, and they've asked us to visit one weekend."

"What?" My heart fell into my stomach. *Is she fucking serious?*

save me

I knew they all spoke, but I didn't know my family wanted to see them.

That was a doubly horrible day. Mum had stayed at the hospital, talking to Emily and her family for a little while, taking comfort in the knowledge that she knew where her husband's heart was going.

Mum smiled. "Tegan, I know it's a difficult and an…unusual situation, but I think it would be good for us all."

"I'm not going," I said.

"We're all going, Tegan. We need this." She got up and left the room.

We didn't need a visit to the Daniels' house. We needed Dad.

I narrowed my eyes and shoved the pills in my mouth.

"You're being really selfish, Tegan," Ava said. "Can't you just do this for her?"

"Shut up, Ava. Why do you want to go there? What good could it possibly do?" Tears pricked my eyes. *I will not cry. Push it away.* Breathing deeply, I managed to distance myself, returning to the safety of what felt like my dungeon.

"They're good people, and we have a connection to Dad."

That was my limit. I couldn't hear any more without screaming at her. I fled the room and went back upstairs.

Screw everything.

I just wanted to sleep all day. I wanted—*needed*—to forget. I needed to get so drunk that I wouldn't even remember my own name.

Grabbing my phone, I texted my friend Adam.

What's happening tonight? Kai's?

His reply came minutes later.

Yeah. Pick you up at 7?

K. Thanks.

Okay, seven o'clock was eleven hours away. I'd need to kill nine hours until I could start getting ready.

What the hell am I going to do for the next nine hours?

Keeping busy was the key.

"Tegan, do you want to look through some photos with us?" Mum called, her voice echoing upstairs.

"No!" I yelled back.

Why do they want a reminder that we can only see him in a fucking picture anyway? I wanted no part in any of their reminiscing. He was gone, and we were still here. That was just how it was.

Groaning, I flopped back on my bed as I heard footsteps coming up the stairs. *Here we go.*

Mum stopped at the threshold of my room. "Honey, are you sure?"

"Yes," I snapped. *Stop pushing, and just leave me alone!*

She nodded, her face plagued with pure sadness. I looked away.

"Okay. Do you have any plans today?"

"Going out."

"Where?"

"Sophie's. Adam's picking me up."

She probably didn't believe me, but it wasn't like she was going to stop me.

"Did you want anything else?"

"No," she replied quietly.

I kept my eyes firmly on an old magazine on my desk, refusing to look at her.

Why did he have to leave and break her heart?

As soon as she turned away and left, I breathed a sigh of relief and closed my eyes.

Kai

My MIND WAS STUCK on a certain blonde that I had pretty serious mixed feelings for. On the one hand, I wanted to spend as much time with her as I could—exclusively—but on the other, I knew she was nowhere near ready for anything like that, and I had only just gotten through my own shit.

"Kai," Dad said, letting himself into my office and closing the door behind him. "Can we have a chat?"

I scratched my forehead. "What have I done?"

He sat down, which didn't look good for me. "There's nothing wrong at work."

Yeah, I worked for my dad, but then when you ditch school from the age of fifteen to drink, smoke, and break the law, it didn't leave you with many options.

"Then, what's this about?"

"We've not heard from you in a few days. Your mum's worried, and Eloise said she's tried calling a few times."

"Not been in the mood for an Elle lecture."

My eldest sister was Little Miss Perfect, and although she never looked down on me or anyone, I couldn't help feeling that little bit more of a failure around her. She was the type of person who gave great advice and took it herself. Out of the four of us siblings, she was the most together, and when we'd dropped to being three of us six years ago, she'd stepped up big time. She had been able to help my other sister, Carly, but I was beyond anything. Hadn't helped that I was high a lot of the time.

"She's not going to give you a lecture. She just wants to know how you are."

"I'm fine, Dad; you know that."

I'd been fine for a year, but would they let it go? If I missed a call or didn't go over for a couple of days, it was always because I was back in my pot-smoking, pill-taking, bike-riding hole.

"I do know, but we'll never stop worrying."

I ran my hand over my face, clenching my jaw.

Will I always be the messed up one, even after getting my shit together?

I didn't want them to worry unnecessarily. It'd been a year since I came out of the other end of the tunnel, but apparently, that was not long enough for them to trust that I'd accepted that Isaac's death was out of my hands. His words still haunted me, but I knew he wouldn't have blamed me for not being able to save him. I wasn't a match—none of us were—and there wasn't a single thing I could ever do to change that.

"Try."

He laughed. "We'll try. What are you doing after work?"

"Taking Tegan out on the bike."

"Hmm."

The fuck does that mean?

"What?" I asked, glaring.

"Her name keeps coming up. Has been for a little while now."

"And?"

"And nothing."

"Bullshit. Spit it out, Dad."

"I was just wondering what was going on there."

Or Mum, Elle, and Carly were wondering and had nominated Dad to find out.

"We're *friends*. There's nothing to tell, so you can report that back to the three witches and tell them to keep their noses out."

Chuckling, he stood up. "Will do. If you need anything…"

Nodding robotically, I replied, "Thanks."

Dad left, and I looked at the time on my laptop. I needed to get out on my bike and blow off some steam with Tegan. I wanted to go now. But I had another two hours.

"Where are we?" Tegan asked, running her fingers through her mass of long blonde hair.

I'd taken her to a place I came to often when I wanted to ride without many other people around getting in my way. It was peaceful out in the country and gave me time to think.

"Not too far out of town; don't worry."

"I'm not worried."

Good.

She'd been on my bike a few times before. I loved having her arms wrapped around my waist, clinging to me, with her chest squished to my back.

"So, Kai, why have you brought me to a bunch of fields on the edge of a forest?"

I smiled and took my helmet off. "I like riding down the winding country roads, much better than looking at miles and miles of grey on the motorway. It's peaceful out here."

I used to ride my bike in the country a lot, passing around the edge of the barriers to cruise along the forest roads you weren't supposed to go down. I liked that I would be the only one there.

"It is."

"There's no one around for miles. No cars can get down here."

"Other than vehicles where the driver has the keys to the gates. Say employees of the Forestry Commission," she said, raising her light eyebrow.

"True, but it's six o'clock in the evening and just starting to get dark, so I doubt any foresters will still be working."

"Hmm…why did you really bring me out here, Kai?"

Smiling, I took a few steps closer to her. "What are you suggesting?"

"That you brought me here for some alfresco loving."

I laughed and caught her wrist, pulling her perfect body against mine. "You've got a dirty little mind, Princess. I brought you here to admire the view."

She pressed herself against me, hooking her fingers through the belt buckles on my jeans. "Lie."

"Not saying I won't, but that wasn't my plan."

"Is it your plan now?"

My mouth watered. *Fuck yeah, that's my plan now!*

"Have you ever had sex on a bike?" I asked.

She blinked in shock and slowly shook her head.

I grinned. "Let's change that."

"Have you?" she squeaked.

I leant closer, nipping her ear. "No. We're changing that, too."

"H-how? We'll fall off."

"I wouldn't let you fall, but I won't be on the bike." I pulled back and spun her around, dragging my greedy hands over her stomach, heading south. "You're going to be over it, and I'll be behind."

I heard her quick intake of breath, and my dick hardened. Slipping my hand below her waistband, I growled with need. It'd only been three days since I last had her, and that was much too long. I was addicted.

Tegan moaned, her head dropping back against my shoulder, as I reached her damp heat. I wasted no time in

save me

dipping my finger inside her, earning a hiss of my name and a roll of her hips.

I removed my finger, and retracting my hand just arched her back.

"What are you doing?" she asked, glaring over her shoulder.

I might have stopped, but I hadn't let her move yet, and I didn't plan to.

"This," I replied, shoving her trousers down.

She gasped but didn't try stopping me. The late sun shone on her bare legs, and I had to fight the urge to drop to my knees and wrap them around my shoulders. I needed to be inside her far too much for that right now.

She stepped out of the trousers and looked over her shoulder again.

Shit, I really did need her soon. I was uncomfortably hard. "Bend over the bike."

"Won't we knock it over?"

"Right now, I don't give a fuck. Bend over, Tegan."

She did as she had been told, bending over and placing her hands on the seat in the most delicious way. I groaned at the sight of her. She was fucking beautiful, so full of light that she'd shoved below the surface. I wanted to break through it and show her that she could get over whatever had happened, but she was the only one who could do that.

I unzipped my jeans and let them fall to my feet along with my boxers. My erection sprang free and throbbed at the image before me.

Tegan's heavy breaths matched my own as I pressed the tip of my cock at her entrance. Impatient as ever, she pushed her hips back, forcing me in a centimetre more. I closed my eyes, gritting my teeth. She was tight, and the feeling of being inside her was out of this world.

"Kai," she panted. "Please."

I was done. I couldn't hold off when she begged. Gripping her firmly so that she wouldn't fly forward and take my bike with her, I rammed hard, filling her with one thrust. We both

29

cried out loudly. *Fuck, that feels good.* Her walls gripped me with every thrust.

I wanted more, wanted to go harder, faster, but I knew I couldn't if I didn't want to knock the bike over. And I told her I wouldn't let her fall. She didn't have a lot of faith in anyone right now. I was determined she'd at least have it in me.

"Shit, Tegan," I groaned, slowly pulling out and pushing back in at the same agonisingly, perfectly slow pace. I felt her tighten and ripple around me.

"What are you doing?" she panted.

She was close, and I'd slowed down, but it felt too good. I wanted to savour the feel of her, the warmth.

"Kai!"

"I know." I was balancing on the edge, too. I could feel it building right down to my fucking toes.

She pushed back, trying to force me to go harder. I let go of her hip with one of my hands and captured her clit between two fingers, squeezing gently. She bucked beneath me, fingers gripping the leather seat.

"Fuck, Kai. Fuck!"

"You're so sweary when I'm inside you," I said, hissing, as she sharply pushed back.

Jesus, that felt incredible. Shit.

I felt Tegan fall over the edge, clamping hard around me and crying out my name. I followed straightaway, exploding inside her, moaning deeply. This was exactly where I wanted to be. I was sure of that after knowing her just three and a half weeks. It was either going to end really good or really bad for me. I wasn't sure how long I could do in-between for.

Tegan

TAKING ONE LAST LOOK in the mirror, I frowned. *What the hell have I become?* I looked older, more like twenty-one rather than seventeen. My dress was too short and revealing, not the old me at all. But I wasn't really me anymore, so what did it matter anyway?

I turned away, not wanting to see myself. After going for a ride with Kai, he'd dropped me off at home, so I could get ready for his party.

Mum looked horrified as I walked into the living room. She didn't recognise me either.

Good.

"Tegan, what on earth are you wearing?"

"A dress," I replied.

"It's very short. I don't think it's appropriate."

I shrugged. "So?"

"Honey, if you go out with so much on show and drink the amount you have been, anything could happen."

I didn't care about that. I already felt cheap and dirty most of the time now, so some guy copping a feel would mean nothing. And I didn't care if something worse happened. *How can I be scared to die when I feel so guilty for living?*

"Don't you think you should stay in tonight?" she said.

A suggestion, not a demand. It was so infuriating. I wanted her to ground me and mean it. I wanted her to shout and get angry. I wanted her to fix this whole situation. I knew that was selfish—she'd lost her husband—but I needed her to fix me. I couldn't do it on my own. I didn't even know how.

"The dress is fine. See you later." I waved my hand over my shoulder as I walked out of the room, ending the conversation there.

As I'd thought, she didn't try to stop me. Since the funeral, she'd half-given up on being the parent. I could do whatever I wanted, and she wouldn't do a thing about it. Well, she might occasionally shout, but nothing would come of it.

Slamming the front door in frustration, I walked to Adam's car that was parked at the side of the road.

Showtime.

"Hey," I said, plastering on my perfected fake smile.

His eyes flicked down to my outfit and almost bulged out of his head. He wasn't used to seeing me in short dresses either.

"Hey. Everything okay?" he asked.

I nodded and unscrewed the top off the vodka hidden in my handbag. Taking a swig, I winced as the alcohol burned my throat. I didn't like the taste, but it did the job.

"Fine," I said.

Adam sighed and shook his head but said nothing. That was about as bad as it got. He and Sophie never mentioned what had happened, and I was so thankful for that. They knew I didn't want to talk about it. They were pretty much the only friends I saw from school now. The rest of them had kept shoving sympathy at me. I didn't want sympathy. I wanted my dad, but that couldn't happen, so fuck it all.

save me

We stopped at Sophie's, and Adam beeped the horn. Soph walked out seconds later. Her short bob whipped across her face as she skipped toward us. Her pale eyes shone with excitement for the night ahead. I envied her that.

"Good evening, ladies," she said, grinning at Adam.

Choosing to say nothing, he rolled his eyes and pulled out of her drive.

Sophie was an awesome friend. I could always count on her, and she knew exactly how to handle every situation, which was why she never mentioned the accident. We'd known each other since the start of high school six years ago. Adam, on the other hand, had only been friends with us for two years when he moved out of London. But I was still equally close to them both.

Ten minutes later, after listening to Sophie ramble on about how she was getting some with a guy called Greg, I was *really* ready to get out of the car. I was more than relieved when Kai's detached red brick house came into view.

I got out of the car literally as soon as Adam stopped. As much as I loved Sophie, I couldn't stand her cheeriness for much longer. Thankfully, Kai had something going on at his house almost every night even if it was just having a few friends over. We would hang out when he finished working, too, so I was never home much anymore. Weekends were reserved for parties, and tonight was going to be a drunken one.

The door was open as a few people trailed inside behind a guy carrying a big speaker. Kai was lucky his neighbour was a little ways down the road—or the neighbour was. The motorbike that Kai had made me scream over a few hours ago was safely tucked away in the garage. He usually left it out if it wasn't meant to rain. My cheeks heated just from me looking at the garage door, knowing the bike was behind it.

I left Adam and Sophie talking to a couple of people by the front door and went to find Kai. The living room had a fair amount of almost drunk people already. I recognised a few, but I didn't really know them.

Kai wasn't in the kitchen either, and no one was outside. I couldn't be bothered to wander upstairs, so I decided to grab a drink first since I was in the kitchen and all. I poured Southern Comfort in a plastic cup and added a little Coke.

"Planning on getting drunk?" Kai said into my ear, pressing his chest against my back.

Looking over my shoulder, I gave him a shy smile. "Absolutely."

"Hmm, I do enjoy a drunk Tegan."

"I'll bet," I replied sarcastically.

He smiled, but it didn't reach his eyes. "I prefer you sober though."

I didn't.

"Sorry, no can do." I took a sip. "This is a party, and you've supplied a lot of alcohol."

He raised an eyebrow. "So, it's my fault you're going to get wasted?"

"Correct," I replied, turning on the spot so that we were chest-to-chest. "You just said you enjoy a drunk Tegan, too."

"I did. I do." He was holding something back.

The longer he looked into my eyes, the more I worried he was seeing right through me, seeing the real, painfully unhappy, completely lost me. I held his gaze, refusing to back down. I didn't want anyone to see that vulnerability. I would rather they thought I was a heartless cow.

"Good," I said before taking a long sip of my drink.

Kai's dark brown eyes continued to delve down to what seemed like my very core.

Stop. Seeing. Me.

"Want to dance?" I asked.

With a small half-smile, he nodded, stepping back and holding his hand out. "Sure, princess."

That was better. I'd rather him be normal and call me that stupid nickname. I was the furthest thing from a fucking princess, in any form.

I put my drink down and took his hand, walking back into the living room where a few people were dancing around the

save me

DJ. The addition of the third speaker made it a lot louder, and the people who had been talking had moved outside.

Kai pulled me against his chest, and I gripped his tattoo-covered upper arm. I hadn't been close enough to really see every part of the intricate tattoo yet. Well, I had been close enough, but I was usually too distracted to check the ink out. I loved what I saw though—all clouds and stars and a clock that I wasn't sure what it meant. I needed to see it properly.

Kai was a good dancer, but I knew that already. He'd do this sexy thing where he stared into my eyes, gripping my hips and holding me tight against him. It'd get me every time, making my blood simmer.

He was the best distraction. When I was with him, I wouldn't need to try to forget. I just would.

We moved perfectly together, as if we'd practiced a thousand times over. I let him take everything away, take me away, so there was no more running or hiding. I was free from the crippling need to make everything disappear.

Kai's lips moved, but I couldn't hear what he'd said over the sound of Usher saying, "Yeah," a million times. I pulled his head down, capturing his lips in a hot and heavy kiss. As good as he was at dancing, he was even better with his mouth. Kai quickly took over the kiss, the way he usually did. I didn't mind. It was too good to fight over who was in control.

His fingertips, still on my hips, pinched my flesh through my skintight dress. I loved it when lust would start taking over. The foggy haze of all things Kai overwhelmed me completely, and I wasn't broken or drowning anymore.

"Kai," I said over the music.

Nuzzling my neck, he replied, "Hmm?"

"Take me upstairs and make me forget my own name."

His hand left my hip and wrapped around my wrist. I was practically dragged up to his bedroom.

Tegan

I WOKE UP TO A mildly thumping head. Light burned my eyes through the curtains. *Shit, it's morning!*

I groaned.

"Hey," Kai whispered from beside me, "I made you some toast. You should eat something."

He handed me a plate, and my stomach turned. *Can I eat it without throwing up?*

"Thanks, Kai." I took the plate, grabbed a slice, and bit into it. My stomach screamed for food, but I wouldn't be able to handle much. "You feeling okay?" I asked between mouthfuls.

I didn't dare look at my phone. Mum would probably be worrying. She was *definitely* worrying. But it wasn't like I hadn't stayed out all night before, and I was with Adam and Sophie, so she would most likely assume I was at Soph's.

"I'm good. Are you?"

I got the feeling he wasn't just asking about my hangover.

"I am now, yeah."

Lie.

"Your mum's been calling and texting. I phoned Sophie to ask her to text your mum and let her know you stayed at hers. She might not believe that though."

Didn't matter if she believed it or not. She wouldn't do anything about it. "Thanks, Kai."

"Want me to take you home after you've eaten?"

"Trying to get rid of me?"

"No, just trying not to get you in too much trouble."

"I won't be in trouble," I said.

I looked away from his dark eyes.

At that moment, he was completely an open book, eyes saying, *You might not care now, but you'll regret it later.*

Maybe I would, but what was the point in planning or worrying about the future?

Dad had had hundreds of things he wanted to do, like worrying about a big presentation at work, but then he'd died, and none of it mattered.

Nothing matters.

At twelve o'clock, just thirty minutes after I'd woken up, Kai drove me home in his car. He did our usual—stopping a few houses down, so Mum wouldn't see him.

As I reached the end of my drive, my phone beeped with a text from Kai. I smiled at his eagerness.

Wanna come out tonight?

I typed a quick reply, agreeing, and shoved my key in the lock. The door flew open before I could even get a chance to open it.

save me

Ava stood in front of me, her face almost red with anger. "Why are you being so fucking selfish?" she snapped.

"Why are you such a dramatic bitch?" I pushed past her and headed upstairs.

"Think of Mum, Tegan!" Ava shouted after me.

Think of Mum? I could barely think of anything. I liked it that way.

I dumped my bag in my room and left to go to the bathroom for a much-needed shower. Showers used to make me feel better, the water washing away whatever drama was going on. Now, it just made me wet.

Mum had *promised* that, after his funeral, things would start to get better. She'd said we'd be fine. Stupidly, I'd believed her. Nothing was even remotely better. I still felt like I was treading water, so close to drowning.

I had a quick steaming hot shower and got out, wrapping a large towel around my body. After getting dry and dressed, I left, not bothering to do my hair or makeup. Looking in the mirror was hard; I didn't recognise the person staring back at me.

"We're going to Nan and Grandad's for dinner," Ava said as I passed her in the hallway. Her voice was clipped; she was still angry.

"That's nice," I replied, dodging into my room and curling up under the covers.

She followed.

I miss her. I miss me.

We were fairly close, I supposed. When I was little, I'd followed her around, wanting to be just like her. I wouldn't mind being more like her now. She was dealing the way everyone expected you to when someone you loved died—cry and miss them but take them with you while you carried on.

I stayed under the covers, waiting for whatever lecture was coming.

"You're not coming, Tegan, really?"

"Nope. Busy."

She turned her nose up. "Fine, suit yourself."

I jumped as she slammed the door behind her.

About two hours after Ava had left my room, Mum knocked on the door and let herself in. "Tegan, come with us. Please."

I could hear the hurt in her voice, and it made my stomach clench. I wished I had some magical cure to make her feel better, too, but I knew there was nothing I could do for her. She had Ava to comfort and to comfort her. They were more like best friends than mother and daughter. Sometimes, I wished Mum and I could do some of the things she did with Ava, but I guessed we just had a different relationship. I was Daddy's girl, and Ava was Mummy's.

"Mum, I'm going out with Adam and Sophie."

I watched as fight passed through her eyes. It was gone as quickly as it'd appeared. She wanted to make me; she wanted to set the rules and force me to follow. I half-wanted that, too. We both knew she wasn't going to.

"Right," she replied with a heavy sigh. "Okay. Don't be too late."

I nodded, but my agreement meant as little as her order.

"Honey, why don't you practice the piano? We could reschedule your exam."

"No," I replied. I didn't even want to look at a piano, let alone play the fucking thing.

"But—"

"No, Mum. I don't want to play anymore," I said.

It was something I had done with Dad. Now that he was gone, it meant nothing.

"Tegan, I—"

"No," I said, slightly more stern than before.

"All right. Well, remember, tomorrow, we're leaving right after lunch."

See? She knew I wouldn't be home early enough for her to give me the rundown of tomorrow's events later.

"Yep," I replied.

save me

I was so not looking forward to visiting the Daniels. Carl was doing well, and as much of a bitch as it made me, I couldn't quite be jumping for joy over it.

At half past seven, I started to get ready. I curled my hair and put on a little makeup. My outfit was a short dark denim skirt and hot-pink camisole that showed off a small amount of cleavage. Again, I looked older and like a stranger.

Just as I was finishing up, Kai beeped his horn. Knowing that I was going to be with him again tonight made me relax a bit. Tomorrow was going to be a nightmare, so I was determined to shove everything away for as long as I could. No one did that better for me than Kai.

I left the house, feeling optimistic—for the night anyway.

He stared at my legs, not even bothering to hide his ogling, as I got in his car.

"Eyes are up here, Kai," I said sarcastically.

He grinned, unashamed. "Sorry. You look…my mouth is actually watering."

"Thanks." *Mine is, too.*

He looked drop-dead gorgeous in dark jeans and a black shirt. The top two buttons were undone, giving a peek at the dog tags he wore around his neck.

"So, cheesy new club then?" he asked.

"Sounds shit, but I'm sure the company won't be."

He smirked. "I'll make sure you have a good night."

I didn't doubt it for a second.

Kai

TEGAN WAS STILL FAST asleep at ten thirty, and I wasn't sure if I should wake her or let her sleep. When she'd been off her tits on vodka, she'd mentioned something about going somewhere she didn't want to go. I didn't know what time this thing she didn't want to do was.

Last night, I'd also found out why she looked like she was in constant pain. Her dad had died. That was fucking rough. You expected your parents to go first but not until you were all old.

I wished it were Tegan who'd told me what'd happened, but as much as I'd wanted it to come from her, I'd just wanted to bloody know. Sophie, thankfully, had a big mouth. Soph didn't say when, but I could tell it hadn't been too long ago.

It was weird. Back when I had been exactly where Tegan was, I had thought I was the only one in the world who couldn't deal with death in the normal way. I could see the same thought in her eyes.

Breathing deeply, she stretched her back, arching her naked body into mine. Two bright leafy eyes locked on me, and she smiled. Tegan's eyes were an incredible shade of green with brown around the iris and yellow around the pupil. As amazing as they were, they were also pained and withdrawn.

She'd done a bloody good job of alienating the people in her life and building a wall around herself, much better than I had. I still gave a fuck, and that pissed me off and made me retaliate even more. Right now, Tegan was made of stone.

"Hey," I said, running my hand down her back and across the top of that peachy arse.

"Hey." She traced one of the waves tattooed on my arm. "You got any painkillers?"

"Sore head, have we?"

She smirked. "Not too bad, but I want to take something just in case."

"I'll get you some in a minute. What time do you need to go home?"

Her eyes flicked to the alarm clock on my bedside table. "I have an hour," she said, tracing the tattoo across my shoulder and then leaving it to head lower. "Do you have anywhere to be?"

I licked my dry bottom lip and pulled her flush with me. "I do now."

She tilted her head back when I planted the first kiss at the base of her throat. Rolling her onto her back, I kissed down between her breasts.

"Will you let me take you back on my bike?"

"That depends," she replied.

I took her nipple between my teeth and flicked the tip with my tongue. "On what?"

"On how good this is going to be."

Pulling away, I smirked at her. "Are we running a reward system right now?"

"Yes. Do the thing with your fingers and mouth, and I'll consider it. Do the thing where I'm on your lap and you're using those fingers, and it's a dead cert."

save me

As if I wasn't already hard, I was aching now. I laughed. "Like that, do we?"

She nodded, pulling her lip between her teeth. "I more than like that."

I sat up and pulled the covers all the way off her, shoving them onto the floor. "Stand up, Tegan."

"Huh? That's not how we do that."

"I know. Stand up."

I watched her rise up in front of me and couldn't keep my hands off her toned legs. No one had ever managed to get to me the way she did.

"Why am I standing?" she asked, looking down at me.

Running my hands up her legs, I forced them open, and her eyes widened with realisation.

My smile grew. "Yeah, that's why."

"Kai," she breathed, chest heaving.

Fuck, seeing her turned on was almost enough to make me blow. I sat on my knees, kissed her hip bone, and grazed my teeth along it. She swore loudly, and her fingers tangled in my hair.

God, I wanted her so bad, but I wanted to make her scream first. I wanted to get her so hot and worked up that she'd beg me to take her. I had barely touched her, and she was already panting and trying to shove my head down to where she wanted it.

"You're doing this on purpose, aren't you?"

I nodded against the inside of her thigh. Damn straight, I was.

By the time I kissed the top of her legs, she was as ready as I was.

"Kai, fuck."

"Soon, princess, but right now, I'm going to make you come with my tongue."

She squirmed. "Then, do it."

"Wider," I said, nudging her legs further apart.

I groaned and pulled her closer. I could do this to her forever. I loved the way she reacted, the way she involuntary moved in tune with what I was doing with my mouth.

She could turn a room blue when she was being pleasured, and I would have a hard time staying in control when a string of swearwords mixed with my name left her mouth.

I felt her body stiffen as she came. She cried out something incoherent and pulled my hair until it stung my scalp. Her legs gave way, and I let go of her weight, causing her to crash down on my lap.

Her head flopped against my shoulder.

"I love it when you come like that," I said, rubbing my aching cock against her stomach.

She laughed. "Me, too. You've made me love sex."

She didn't love it before?

I knew why she'd slept around, but I'd assumed she at least enjoyed the physical act.

I didn't know what to say, so I kissed her neck. "Turn around. I'm going to fuck you now."

Sitting up, alarmed, she said, "I'm too sensitive for you to touch me yet."

"I know."

"Kai…"

"Trust me, Tegan. Turn around."

I reached over to grab a rubber from my drawer while she spun around on my lap. We couldn't keep forgetting to use protection.

I could still feel her nervousness. "I won't do anything you don't like," I whispered in her ear as I grabbed my erection and lined it up right where I was dying to be.

She sat down on me and gasped. "I know you won't."

I needed her trust because she'd just come, and this was going to be intense. She sank down as far as she could go, and I moaned into the skin of her neck.

"Fucking hell," I hissed.

She was made for me, fit me perfectly, squeezing me with every movement.

I reluctantly let go of one of her firm breasts and ran my hand down her stomach.

"Kai!" she said, grabbing my hand, as I moved below her belly button.

"Trust me," I repeated.

It took her a second to let go, but when she did, I felt something shift inside me. Her trust meant more than it probably should at this point.

When I touched her, she cried out and tried to squirm away from me. "Kai, I can't. It feels like it's burning."

"Shh, I know." *Come on, just give me a little bit longer.*

I would've stopped, but she didn't stop raising her hips and letting them drop or gripping my thighs so hard that I'd have half-moons cut into the skin. She felt almost too good. I fought to stop my eyes from rolling back in my head.

I pressed a little firmer, and she moaned my name, still clearly overwhelmed as she held back.

"Let go, Tegan."

"I can't," she said through gritted teeth.

She clawed my legs, thrashing on top of me, as I increased the pressure again, rubbing her at the same speed as she fucked me. I wasn't going to last long, so I fucking hoped she was as close as she felt.

"Ahh!" she shouted. "Shit, Kai, shit."

Her walls tightened to the point where I could barely move inside her. Then, they clenched down over and over as she came around me. I followed a second later, biting down on her neck.

"Jesus," she said, flopping back against my chest.

"Glad you trusted me?"

"Oh, yeah."

I laughed and kissed below her ear.

"Want to join me in the shower?" she asked.

"You don't need a reply, right?"

Shaking her head, she giggled and lifted off me. I'd not heard her laugh like that before, so relaxed and free. *What the hell is she doing to me?*

"Give me a minute," she said, smiling over her shoulder.

I watched her walk from my room, staring at her naked form. She was beautiful, so much that I felt a stir downstairs already.

I liked her, but I wasn't stupid. I knew what I was to her. The problem I had was, she was quickly becoming something a lot more to me. I'd gone through five years of hell and fought for the next one to get myself and my life back together. The last thing I needed was something to mess everything up again, and Tegan had the power to do that. She was addictive and maddening, and I knew, if I let myself, I could fall right back into my old ways and have the fucking time of my life with her.

But neither of us needed that.

We did need each other though. Something about her had chosen me. Not in any conscious or deep and meaningful way, but out of the guys she'd had casual one-night stands with, she'd stopped with me. I knew it meant more than just her enjoying me making her come like a train.

I didn't expect it to be easy, and I knew I'd have to watch her struggle, but whatever we had or could have was worth hanging around to find out.

Tegan

ME, MUM AND AVA pulled up outside *their* house thirty minutes after leaving, and I froze. It all looked perfectly normal, a new-looking yellow brick house with a perfectly manicured garden. It might as well have a white picket fence surrounding it instead of the short green hedge.

I so don't want to be here.

The front door opened before we even got out of the car. They must've been watching out for us. At least they were as eager to see us as Mum and Ava were to see them. Taking a deep breath, I shoved every emotion threatening to surface back down as far as it would go, and I got out of the car.

Emily greeted us with a warm smile. "Hi. Welcome," she said, hugging Mum and then Ava.

I stood back and dropped my gaze to the ground.

Please, don't.

Emily seemed to respect that I wasn't in a hugging mood and invited us in. "Carl's in the living room at the minute. He wanted to get up to greet you, but…"

"Oh," Mum said, waving her hand, "don't worry about that. We understand. How is he today?"

I stopped listening and looked around. I was glad the guy was okay. I wouldn't wish death upon anyone, but it was hard to hear how well my father's heart was doing inside someone else.

The ivory walls were lined with wooden picture frames, full of their family history. I recognised one of Lucas with his brother, Jake, and Grace as children. They had the same big, cheeky smiles and were buried in the sand down to their waists.

"Hi."

Startled, I spun around. Lucas smiled and leant against the wall. We were alone in the hallway, but I could hear my mum's voice in the next room.

"How are you doing?" he asked.

I shrugged. "Fine. You?"

"I'm doing good." He had every reason to be doing well; his dad was still here. "You coming through?" he asked, nodding his head toward what I assumed was the living room, the room where Carl was.

Lock it all away.

"Yes," I replied. I followed him through to a large lounge.

Carl was lying back slightly on the reclining chair, covered by a red and white checkered blanket. I hadn't ever seen him before. He smiled as he spoke to Mum and Ava, but he looked pale and tired. Grace and Jake sat on the sofa next to him, like they were guarding him.

He looked up, and his eyes locked on me. I felt the air leave my lungs, as if someone had just jumped on my chest. It took me a minute to regain control, but I did. I smiled—at least I thought I did.

"Hello, Tegan," Carl said.

"Hi," I mumbled under my breath.

I looked to Mum for help. It was too much. My heart felt like it was being ripped apart, and I felt seconds from bursting into tears.

I don't want to cry!

"Come help me with drinks," Lucas said, nodding to the door, seeming to know I was about to lose it.

I smiled gratefully and followed him out of the room. A heavy weight lifted from my shoulders as I walked into the kitchen.

"I know this is a little weird and awkward, but I'm glad you guys came," he said, filling the kettle. "Hot or cold drink?"

"Cold, please."

"Coke?" he asked, holding a can out.

"Thanks," I said, taking it from his outstretched hand.

It was more than a little weird and awkward. It was messed up, and I wanted nothing to do with it.

Emily was doing her best to make us all feel welcome—fussing around, showing us the rooms where we'd be staying, and asking if we wanted anything. I didn't want to stay but my mum and sister want to be close to them. Grace took Ava up to her room to drop her stuff off, and Emily told Lucas to show me up to the room where I'd be staying.

I'd be happier sleeping in the car, but I thanked Emily and followed Lucas to the third floor.

The room was nice, painted in light fawn with a few paintings hanging on the walls. It had a double bed, chest of drawers, and a vanity table. You couldn't really fit anything else in there, but it was big enough for one.

"Thanks for showing me up here and for carrying my bag. You didn't have to do that," I said.

He grinned.

Lucas was gorgeous—tall, muscular, light-brown hair and light-green eyes. It annoyed me. I didn't want to find him attractive.

"No problem," he said, taking a step closer to me. "Hey, are you really okay?"

"I'm fine."

His eyebrows pulled together, like he thought I was lying. I was. Chewing on my lip, I broke our eye contact and stared at the floor.

"Right. I'll be in my room if you need me. It's the one next to this one," he said, handing me my hoodie.

I reached for it, and our fingers brushed. It was only for a second, but I felt something flutter deep inside me.

No, screw that. I didn't want to feel.

His eyes immediately snapped to mine, as if he'd felt it, too. I was stunned and absolutely terrified. This could not be happening. It was just a little glitch. He was good-looking, and that was it.

I took a step back, stiffening my back and clenching my jaw. *I will not feel.* Being numb was easier.

He looked at me, confused and pained, not knowing what I was doing or thinking. My heart beat faster, and it made me feel sick. He needed to go, or I did.

I had to get away from him. "I'm gonna go find my mum." Darting around him, I took the stairs two at a time to get away from him.

This is not happening.

For the first time since Dad had died, I wanted to go home.

Tegan

THE SECOND I OPENED my eyes, my head started pounding lightly, just enough to royally piss me off. The small bottle of vodka I'd brought with me was half-empty and lying on the floor. The hangover wasn't actually that bad. At least it gave me something to focus on.

Every second I spent in *their* house made me sink further into the water. It hadn't even been twenty-four hours yet.

"Tegan?" Ava called through the door.

Sitting straight up, I snatched the bottle from the floor and shoved it under the pillow.

"Are you okay?" She opened the door and leant against the frame.

No.

"Yeah. Tired. You?"

"I'm good. Listen, we're all going to Emily's art gallery. Jake's staying with Carl, so you can stay, too, but it might be nice if you came with us."

If I weren't so torn, I would've laughed. *Go to an art gallery with half of Carl's family or stay here with him?*

"I don't really want to go out. I just want to sleep." At least if I stayed up here, I could curl up under the covers and pretend I was anywhere else.

"I thought you might say that. Emily said to help yourself, but Jake's here, so ask him, okay?"

Yes, Mum! Jesus, I still know not to help myself to things in a virtual stranger's house.

"Okay."

She walked into the room and kissed the top of my head before leaving. I got a glimpse of our old relationship. It was nice, but it could never be the way it had been before, so there was no point in getting cut up over the loss of my relationship with her, too.

As soon as I heard them all leave, I got up, ready to take a shower before my day of hiding in the bed commenced, but a knock on the door made me jump.

Jake?

"Yeah?" I said slowly.

Lucas walked in and smiled.

Shit, why did he stay back?

His eyes immediately fell on mine, and my heart skipped a beat. His gaze was so intense that it made my mouth run dry. I wished that he'd had no effect on me at all.

Clenching my jaw, I pushed away my stupid feelings.

"Art's not really my thing either," he explained. "Do you wanna do something?"

"Something?" I frowned. "Like what?"

"Whatever you want," he replied. "You want to go out somewhere?"

Oh God, have they put him up to this? Is Lucas my bloody babysitter for the day?

"There must be something you wanna do, Tegan."

Hide away. That's the plan.

I stared at him in horror. "Not really," I replied, wishing the ground would swallow me up.

save me

"Come on. We can go anywhere. You must want to do something."

Oh, for fuck's sake! "The zoo," I snapped.

His mouth broke into a breathtaking grin. "You want to go to the zoo?"

Right, dude doesn't get sarcasm. I frowned defensively. "You asked. A lot."

"Okay then, be ready in half an hour." He turned and walked out the door.

Well, that backfired.

I stared after him. *Are we seriously going to the zoo?* I didn't want to go anywhere, especially not with him and his annoying making-me-feel-something ways.

It would be okay though. *What's the worst that could happen?* He wasn't a psycho killer, and my attraction was purely physical. He had a nice face, and that was it. I'd go, and he'd end up annoying me even more, so I wouldn't want anything to do with him by the end of the day. It was perfect.

After a quick shower, I got dressed and decided that makeup wasn't needed for the zoo. And it would help put Lucas off. I needed him to not like me, which shouldn't be too hard. Even I knew I'd changed beyond recognition and not for the better.

Lucas was waiting for me by the front door. He leant against the wall, looking up the stairs. I took him in as I walked down. His squarish jaw and striking eyes made him look like a bloody male model. He was dressed casually in jeans and a grey T-shirt.

Why can't he just be unattractive? I wished he'd had boils all over his face and rotting brown teeth.

He watched me as I walked downstairs. My heart was racing.

Finally, when I reached the bottom, he said, "You ready then?"

"Are we really going to the zoo?" I asked.

It couldn't seriously be somewhere that he'd want to go. I didn't want to go, but I couldn't back down now.

"That's what you wanted. Your wish is my command."

He did a little bow as he opened the door. I couldn't help smiling.

"We're leaving now, Dad, Jake."

I lowered my eyes, grateful he hadn't made us go into the living room to say bye.

Jake shouted back, "Have fun!"

Getting out of the house couldn't have come quick enough. I practically ran to his car. He said nothing but gave me a look that told me he knew I wasn't comfortable with being around his dad. I wasn't really comfortable with being around any of them.

Lucas started the car and pulled out of the drive.

It took just over an hour to get to the zoo. If I had known that before, I wouldn't have suggested going. I'd assumed there was one close by—not that I'd consciously suggested going in the first place.

Besides a little small talk, we stayed mostly silent. I half-wanted to ask about Carl and the surgery, but I wasn't sure I could do it without breaking down. Lucas, although he acted carefree, clearly wasn't. He worried about his dad. I didn't know a lot about heart transplant recipients, but I knew enough to understand that the operation wasn't the end of it, and he would need treatment for the rest of his life. It must be difficult for them all, but at least they still had him around.

"Could you have parked any farther away?" I teased, raising my eyebrow at him.

We were right at the end of the car park.

He looked out of the side window and pointed to a space in the corner. "Yep, there's a free space over there."

"So funny," I muttered under my breath.

I got out of the car. The sun shone down, and the place was fairly packed, but I was hopeful that the day wasn't going to be boring and awkward.

We walked side by side toward the entrance, Lucas making some not-so-inconspicuous smiley looks at me. That was not a good sign. We couldn't happen, so it was best if he just thought I was a massive bitch, like Ava did.

"Good morning. Two adults?" the barely past puberty guy behind the counter asked.

"Please," Lucas responded as he pulled his wallet out of his jeans pocket.

"That'll be thirty-five ninety, please."

Jesus. Not only did neither of us really want to be here, but it was also costing almost forty pounds just to get in. It was my fault for suggesting it.

"Lucas, I'll pay."

He shook his head and handed over his card.

"Come on, I want to."

He shot me a sideways smile. "So do I."

"Fine." God, he was frustrating. *Just let me hate you!*

I softened. "Thank you."

"You're welcome." He grabbed a map and handed it to me.

Once he'd paid for our tickets, we headed into the park.

"Where to first?" he asked.

I shrugged. I really couldn't have cared less, but since I'd made us come and he'd just paid, I had to try to enjoy it.

"Elephants."

He nodded once and repeated, "Elephants."

In a large enclosure were the elephants. Bonus, there was a baby elephant. I started to enjoy the zoo for real, and Lucas was smiling more. As much as I didn't like to admit I needed something—unless it was peace and freedom to forget—I did need to do something normal, something fun that didn't involve stumbling or puking at the end of it.

But, as much fun as I was having, I was left with the heavy drag of guilt. *Why should I get to have fun when my dad is lying in a box?*

I managed to stem the guilt enough to enjoy the day for Lucas and myself, but it was hard. Whatever I did, I felt horrible.

We slowly made our way around the zoo, and I felt like I could breathe a little easier. Although Lucas wasn't the best at playing it cool, he hadn't even tried to touch me, respecting my boundaries.

Suddenly, he stopped walking and said, "Let's go in there."

I looked to where he was pointing and read the sign above the door. "Bat cave? No way. Not happening," I replied, feeling creeped out already.

"Are you scared?" he asked, grinning like a Cheshire Cat.

"No, I'm *not* scared."

"Well, that's good. We can go in then," he said with a cocky smirk that I just wanted to punch off his face.

Gritting my teeth, I seethed behind a tight smile. "Sure."

I followed him into the building and turned my nose up at the musty scent. It smelt dirty, and it was dark. I wanted to leave already. A tall, skinny man stood before our small group, ready to give us the tour.

I wrapped my arms around myself, praying bats wouldn't fly at me. If that happened, I would be fucking out of here. Fighting the urge to cling to Lucas, I followed Tall-and-Skinny behind the group of six others. Lucas walked closely behind me—too closely actually. Even though he didn't touch me, I could feel him. The loss of sight made me hyperaware of his presence.

Dimly lit lights marked the path. The six other people—all middle-aged—looked up with curiosity. Lucas half-looked, alternating between glancing up and looking at me.

He bent down and whispered in my ear, "You scared yet?"

I couldn't answer. A shiver ran down my entire spine.

Keep calm, and get it together. You do not like him.

"Tegan, you okay?"

No, I'm not.

"Yeah, I'm fine," I muttered, pretending something had caught my attention in the dark corner of the room.

I could just about see, so Lucas must have known I was ignoring him, but he looked toward the group. Tall-and-Skinny started spouting more information on bats, and this time, I looked over. Bats were creepy, so the less information I knew about them, the happier I'd be, but it was a hell of a lot better than focusing on what Lucas was doing to me.

"Okay, everybody," Tall-and-Skinny said to the group, clapping his hands together, "this next part is a very small room, so you will need to go in twos. While the rest of us wait, we can have a look up into this tree where you will see bats sleeping."

The first two went in, and after a few minutes, it was Lucas's and my turn.

I tugged on my sleeve, biting my lip. *Don't look at him.*

The confined dark space forced us together. I could feel the electricity. My lungs felt like they were made of lead. I needed fresh air. My skin was alive. *My bloody* skin!

The air thickened. His arm brushed mine so lightly that I barely felt the physical contact, but my traitorous heart felt it. Blood pumped around my body so fast that I felt faint. I wanted to believe it was completely down to being a little claustrophobic, but I couldn't quite make myself.

His breathing came quicker, heavier, and I knew he felt the charge, too.

I need to get outta here.

Spinning around, I took off in the direction we had come.

"Tegan?" Lucas called.

Then, I heard his footsteps thudding behind me. I sprinted.

I blinked rapidly, desperately trying to stop my tears from spilling over. *I don't cry.* I sprinted out of the bat cave. My eyes stung as the brightness from outside pierced through.

Pushing myself harder, I ran and ran, my thighs screaming in protest.

People looked at me like I was crazy as I whizzed past them, but I didn't have time to worry. I pushed myself faster, randomly turning corners without any planned direction. When my legs finally felt like they were made of jelly, I stopped next to a building and slid down the brick wall.

What's wrong with me?

Lucas

WHOEVER SAID WOMEN WERE complicated was understating—seriously understating. A whole new fucking word was needed to describe Tegan. She'd run from me like she was running from a serial killer.

She was damn fast, and between being momentarily stunned and having to dodge a big crowd, I lost her.

I was relatively sure the attraction I felt toward her was reciprocated, but she was having a harder time dealing with it. Sure, it was a little complicated, but life was a bitch, and you rarely got an easy ride for long.

I jogged in the direction where I'd last seen her take off and hoped I'd find her soon. *Fuck, I'm an idiot.* I'd had to keep pushing that little bit more to keep getting closer. The girl had a whole heap of issues, and here I was, trying to hit on her like the dickhead I was.

After looking for what seemed like hours and just before I headed back to the car to see if she'd gone there, I spotted her behind the bird enclosure. She was sitting on the ground with her arms wrapped around her legs and her head resting on her knees. I'd never seen anyone look so down and defeated.

She stared into the distance, empty. I felt like a prick for not being more understanding. My heart went out to her. I liked her too much already. *Shit, I'm in serious trouble.*

Walking slowly, I made my way over and sat down. "Tegan?" I whispered.

She closed her eyes and lowered her head.

"Tegan?"

She finally opened her eyes and looked over at me. "Sorry," she whispered.

"You don't have anything to be sorry for. I shouldn't have—"

She held her hand up and said, "No, it's not your fault. I overreacted."

Overreacted to what exactly?

"Let's just forget it and move on, yeah?" I said.

"That would be good. I feel pretty embarrassed."

"Don't. It's done."

"Thank you. I could really do with a friend right now."

"Friend," I said. "Right. I can do friend." *For now.* "What do you want to do?"

She took a deep breath. "I'm ready to go, if you are?"

I smiled weakly. Of course she wanted to go. I'd rather stay, but I'd pushed it a bit too much for one day. "Yeah, come on."

I wanted to get to know her more, but that would have to wait. Patience—a lot of it, I thought—was needed here.

We stopped off in the gift shop first, so she could buy some of the overpriced zoo crap.

"How cute is this?" she said with that beautiful half-smile, holding up a soft meerkat toy.

I smiled and took it off her, holding it along with the zoo mug, pink snake, penguin key ring, monkey pen, animal sweets, and a hoodie with an elephant on it.

"Aw, Luke, we're definitely getting some of these."

save me

She just called me Luke. Only my mates called me that, and she hadn't met any of them yet. I liked it way too much.

I reluctantly looked away from her to see what she'd added to the pile. Hats. Two of them. If she thought I was wearing a hat with an animal on it, she had another thing coming.

"Tegan, I am *not* wearing this."

"Of course, you will. It's cute."

"Yeah, cute's not really the look I'm going for."

After picking up eight sticks of rock, she was *finally* ready to go. I didn't like any kind of shopping unless it was for cars or car parts, so I had been bored out of my fucking mind in the gift shop. When she walked over to the tills, I could've kissed her and the woman serving.

Tegan rummaged in her bag, looking for her purse. I handed over my card.

"Lucas, no. You can't pay for all this."

"Too late," I replied, smirking at her, as I started to punch my pin number into the machine.

"But you paid the entrance fee. It's fine, really."

"I know it is." I took my card back and grabbed the bags.

Tegan's eyes didn't leave me as we left the shop and headed to the car park.

"You shouldn't have paid for all my stuff," she said, frowning.

"I wanted to. I brought you here."

"I know, but…" Sighing, she replied, "Thank you."

"You're welcome. I had a good time." *Despite being at a zoo while over the age of eight.*

"I enjoyed it, too, actually."

Actually? She didn't expect to enjoy it?

She pulled the hats out of the bag, putting one on herself and holding the other out.

"Oh no, I'm not wearing that."

"Yes, you are. Lighten up, and stop being a baby."

Ironic—her telling me to lighten up when she looked like she was fighting for every damn breath.

63

She reached up and put the cap on my head. *Perfect.* I kept it on because I had been rewarded with a rare smile. I could handle looking like a dick if it meant she wouldn't look so sad for a while.

"See? You look good," she said, laughing at me.

I looked like an idiot.

"Just get in the car!"

We got home an hour and a half later. She had put the hoodie on and had the snake around her neck. I knew she was only seventeen, but for the first time, she looked it, too. This was how you were supposed to be when you were a teenager—carefree and acting stupid.

"They should pay you for all the advertising."

"Oh, whatever. I look great, and you know it."

She did.

I pulled into the drive, and the front door opened. People came pouring out. My heart froze.

Dad?

Leaping out of the car, I prepared myself for the words I never wanted to hear.

"What?" I said.

"Where were you? We were worried," Mum said.

The relief was overwhelming. Dad was okay.

"Sorry. Traffic was bad on the way back."

Alison smiled at Tegan but got nothing back. You didn't have to be a genius to see that their relationship was rocky. Tegan barely looked at her mum—or Ava, for that matter. I didn't know what the deal was, but I wanted to find out.

After a restless night's sleep, trying to think of ways I could help, I finally had an idea. But they were leaving shortly, so I wanted to get Tegan's number and move the plan to texts.

She just needed someone impartial to talk to. I'd imagine her friends and family were too close, but I wasn't. People found it easier to talk to someone they barely knew, and right now, I was definitely someone she barely knew.

"Ava," I said, stopping her outside of Grace's room. I took her bag. "Think I can get Tegan's number?"

She smiled, shoving her hip out and tilting her head. "Did she already say no?"

"No," I replied, trying not to laugh. "Look, I want to try to help her, but I have a feeling she'd just shoot me down if I asked now."

Ava flicked her eyebrows up. "Well, none of us can get through, so you might as well try. Right now, I'd pretty much do anything to have my old sister back. I'm not that fond of the hard bitch she's been."

I felt like I should defend Tegan, but it wasn't really my place, and I could tell from the bitter atmosphere between them that Ava wasn't overreacting. She took my phone and punched in Tegan's number.

"Good luck, Lucas." She took her bag from my hand and walked downstairs.

Her "good luck" didn't fill me with much confidence.

I followed shortly after Ava and headed outside where my family and Tegan's were saying good-bye. Tegan gave me a wide berth, but she had little issue with giving my mum, Jake, and Grace a very short, almost awkward hug good-bye. When I stepped closer, she tensed her body and turned slightly away.

What the fuck is that? I wasn't about to grope her. Rejection stung, and it wasn't just because she didn't want to be anything more than friends. She couldn't even give me what she had given my siblings.

"Tegan," I said once everyone was distracted with walking Alison and Ava to the car.

"Don't," she replied.

What have I done now?

"No. What was that? Why'd you turn away?"

65

She looked at the ground, embarrassed that I'd called her out. Or she was bored. It wasn't always that easy to tell what she was thinking.

"Leave it."

I gritted my teeth. No way was she treating me differently to everyone else after telling me she wanted friendship. That wasn't right.

"I'm not going to leave it just because you said so."

"You make me feel again," she hissed, eyes so dark and wild that she looked like a different girl.

It took me a minute to reply. "Why is that a bad thing?"

She laughed bitterly. "I don't want to. I can't do it, so leave me alone."

"Tegan, come on. We need to leave," Alison called from the car.

I was too stunned to move. She was fucking with my head, and I didn't like it. I didn't do game-playing or complicated, and I wanted nothing more than to be able to leave her alone, like she'd asked. But I knew I couldn't. Whatever was going on, Tegan wasn't an easy person to walk away from.

She didn't find it difficult at all to walk away from me. She confidently strode toward the car without a single look back. My eyes stayed on the car until it disappeared out of sight. She didn't peek back once.

Kai

I OPENED THE FRONT door and groaned, roughly rubbing my face. Elle pushed past me, clearly on a mission. That mission being to annoy the fuck outta me.

Closing the door, I turned around. She had her hands on her hips and eyes narrowed just enough to show that she was pissed about something. I racked my brain, trying to figure out what I'd done this time. I couldn't think of anything off the top of my head—nothing recent anyway.

"And what can I do for you, dear sister?"

"Don't, Kai."

"Don't what?" *Fuck, what has she found out?* My days of drugs and racing were over, but there was plenty of shit I'd done that my family still didn't know about.

"I'm sick of you pretending like everything's fine, that you don't still feel the temptation of drugs and shutting it all out. You stopped talking to us when Isaac died and look why."

Crossing my arms over my chest, I replied, "What the fuck's your point, Elle? Did you just come here to remind me of my screwups? You don't need to, you know. I remember perfectly well."

"Tegan."

Odd explanation.

"What about Tegan?"

"She's messing you up."

"God, I'm getting a headache. And how, oh wise one, is she messing me up?"

"You're secretive, and you've been avoiding me."

"Perhaps because you're borderline psychotic," I muttered.

"Don't make jokes, Kai. I'm so tired of worrying myself sick about you."

"Then, don't. Seriously, I'm not doing drugs again. Search the house if it'll put your mind at ease and get you off my back."

She huffed. "I'm not getting on your back. Excuse me for worrying, but after seeing you throw your life down the toilet for so long, I get concerned when things start to go the same way."

"Nothing is going the same way. Tegan isn't making me want to pop any pills."

"What's going on with her?"

"Nothing."

She narrowed her eyes more and moved further into the house. She was staying. "You're trying to save her when you've got enough going on in your own life," Elle said, sitting down on the sofa.

It was going to take me ages to get rid of her now that she was sitting. Still, I followed and sat at the other end of the sofa, readying myself for a conversation I did not want to have.

"I'm not trying to save her."

"Of course you are. Why else would you be so consumed with this girl?"

That wasn't a bad question. I liked her, I did, but there was more to it than simple attraction to a girl who was out-of-this-

68

world beautiful. I couldn't explain it, and I didn't understand it myself, but I was drawn to her, much like ecstasy really.

"I'm not *consumed*, Elle. She's kind of like I was before I got it together."

Elle's face lost the hard, pissed off expression. "What happened to her?"

"Her dad died. She's not spoken about it, but from what I can see, they were close."

"That's awful. I knew there was something wrong from what I'd heard of her partying, but I didn't know what. So, you're really not trying to fix her?"

"If it were possible to wave a wand and fix someone else's problems, I'd do it. Unfortunately, life doesn't work that way. I know firsthand that the only person who can really change you is yourself."

Other people had helped me. Mum had found me a good bereavement counsellor when she was training to become one, but I was the one who had had to do the hard, painful work.

"You really have grown, Kai."

"Does this mean that you'll back off a bit?"

She pursed her lips. "Um, probably not. You're my little brother, and I love you."

"I love you, too, but I'm twenty-one now. You need to trust that I know what I'm doing—in my life and with Tegan."

"I don't want you to get hurt."

"Not lookin' to get hurt. She and I are friends, Elle. That's all she can do right now anyway."

Fuck trying to have a relationship and thinking about another person when you could barely get up out of bed. Factoring someone else into your life when you were barely living was never a good idea. I could handle it now, but Tegan couldn't.

"So, what are you doing with her?" Elle asked.

Sex. Bike sex. Bed sex. Car sex. Bathroom stall sex. Table sex. Shower sex.

I shrugged. "Just hangin' out."

She arched her eyebrow, completely unconvinced. I grinned.

"Oh, come on, you expect me to believe you're just friends?"

"Elle, I don't expect you to believe anything. I've got to be somewhere in half an hour. Did you want something else?"

"Where do you have to be?"

Nosy bitch.

"Gettin' a new tattoo."

"Another one? You barely have any room left as it is."

I had most of my chest, my right forearm, and legs left untouched. Plenty of room. "Havin' some birds put on Isaac's arm."

My upper right arm was all about the little brother I adored. Things that reminded me of him were right there—clocks with the time he was born and, morbidly, the time he died, dog tags that matched the ones hanging around my neck, and his name hidden in there, all blended together with waves of the ocean and clouds of the sky. The whole thing was black and grey, and I knew he'd have loved it. But it needed birds. There weren't many mornings when I hadn't woken up to a gliding foam bird flying across my room or littered on my floor.

"I hated those bloody things."

So had I. He'd refused the plane ones unless they were Army planes, which they often hadn't been. Birds were cool though apparently.

"Okay, I'll let you get on then," she said, standing up. "If you ever need anything..."

"Yeah, you, too."

Time to add to Isaac's little mural on my arm. I missed him so much that I felt sick, but the tattoos made me feel close to him. I needed that.

Lucas

I DIDN'T KNOW WHAT to do. Tegan was a complete headfuck, and I was losing my mind, trying to figure her out. I made her feel something, but she wanted nothing to do with me.

It made no sense at all.

I thought I'd prefer her not to like me and not to want to be with me.

I stormed off, heading back into the house, in the pissiest mood I'd been in, in a long time, and I went up to my room. *Fuck's sake, what the fuck is going on?* Gritting my teeth, I saw red and slammed my fist into the wall. For the first time, I wished my dad had cut corners when he had the house made seven years ago and put up plasterboard instead of using concrete blocks. My hand throbbed, and blood seeped from the knuckles. *Perfect.*

Shaking it off, I sat on the end of the bed and tried to flex my fingers. Thank God I could. Nothing was broken. I hadn't punched a wall since...actually, I'd never punched a wall before. Good to know she brought out my violent side.

My hand stung, and I watched it swell before my eyes. I really shouldn't have punched the wall.

The door opened, and Mum and Grace walked in. I dropped my hand beside my leg.

"You okay, Lucas?" Mum asked.

"Yeah," I replied, hoping I sounded convincing.

She gasped, looking around me. *Shit.*

"What happened to your hand?" Mum asked.

I turned my hand over, wincing as the fabric of the duvet scraped against the broken skin. "Nothing."

"Er, Mum, why don't you go see if Dad's okay?" Grace said.

Mum hesitated before leaving the room.

"So...spill it. What happened with Tegan?" she said as soon as Mum had shut the door.

"Nothing."

"Oh, come on! You two could barely take your eyes off each other all weekend. I'm not an idiot, Luke. Start talking."

Fucking twin. There was no way I was going to win this.

Blowing out a big breath, I launched into the whole thing. "Okay. The first night she arrived, I took her bag up for her, and our hands touched—one innocent touch that should have been nothing—but she freaked and ran off."

Grace pursed her lips and nodded. Green eyes that mirrored mine shone in amusement. Glad she found the whole thing entertaining.

"When we were at the zoo and...had a moment, she freaked big time and ran away. It took me ages to find her, and then she said she couldn't be anything together. We talked, and she told me she wanted to be friends, which was fine until we got back here. She could hug everyone but not me. I asked her what was going on, and she just said that it was because I made her *feel.* Whatever that means. Oh, then she left abruptly, and I have no idea what's going on."

"Seriously? You don't get it?" she asked, smirking.

"I don't speak girl, Grace."

"Come on, Lucas. Alison and Ava said Tegan completely shut herself off when Simon died. She won't deal with anything. She hasn't cried since his funeral. She goes out, gets drunk, and parties all the time. She won't sing or play the piano anymore. She's pushing everything and everyone away because it's too painful. You make her feel something, which scares her because it means she will have to deal with everything, and she's not ready. That's why she's keeping you at a distance." She broke into a huge smile. "God, I'm good."

"Right," I replied slowly. "Okay, I guess that makes sense. I just have no idea what to do next. Should I call her?"

"You've got it bad, haven't ya?" she sang annoyingly.

"Just shut up, and tell me what to do."

Grace laughed and punched my arm.

I did have it bad though. No girl had ever made me feel like this before. It was stupid and frustrating, but it wasn't something I had any control over.

"I wouldn't call her. She might not appreciate that, and it would put her on the spot. Text her."

"Okay, I'll give that a try. Thanks, Grace."

"Anytime." She smiled and stood up to leave. "Oh, and the hand?"

"Punched the wall."

"Of course you did. I'll be downstairs if you need me."

As soon as she left, I picked up my phone and stared at it, trying to decide on what to write. After pacing the room for a while, I forced myself to send a message.

Hey, are you okay? I really need to talk about before.
Lucas

I pressed Send and instantly regretted it. *That was lame.* Sighing, I ran my hands over my face and waited for her reply. A reply I wasn't at all convinced I'd ever get.

Grace returned to my room a few minutes later with an ice pack for my swollen hand. "She replied yet?" she asked, placing the pack over my knuckles.

"Thanks. No, not yet."

"No probs. And, hey, I'm sure she'll reply soon."

"Yeah, not sure I wanna get it though."

My phone beeped in my hand, making me jump a little. Tegan's name showed up on the screen. Christ, I was nervous to open it, imagining the two words that were probably waiting for me—*Fuck off.*

I'm fine. I'm sorry. I can't.

I stared at the text for a while. That was exactly what I'd expected, but it still made me feel like shit.

"Well, what did she say?"

I handed the phone to Grace without looking up.

"Aw, I'm sorry, Luke. Just give her some time—if she's really what you want?" She put the phone down on the bed and smiled sympathetically.

"She is what I want." I wished she weren't. She wasn't supposed to be. I was just meant to help her, but it'd gone beyond that. "It's fine. I can wait until she's ready."

"Glad to hear it because, under the tough exterior, from what I've heard of the old her, she's a good girl."

Tegan

TODAY WAS AVA'S BIRTHDAY, and I was helping to set up for a small party she was having. Unsurprisingly, she didn't want anything big, just family and a few close friends over. Dad had been big on birthdays, but everything was different now. It felt wrong to celebrate anything at all.

Our living room was decorated with red and white balloons, a large *Happy Birthday* banner, and streamers. Two big plastic bowls of punch sat on the kitchen island—one nonalcoholic and the other swimming with half a bottle of vodka.

Among Ava's guests were Lucas and his family.

The thought of seeing him again made me feel nauseous, nervous, and a little bit excited. The last time we had seen each other didn't end well. Although we'd exchanged a couple of texts, it would probably still be awkward. After all, I had turned him down and run away. I hoped he understood why that was though. I couldn't open the door in case everything I wanted to shut out came pouring in, too.

"Are we all done now?" I asked. "I need to get ready."

"Yes, I think so," Mum replied. "Nan and Grandad will be here soon, so don't take too long."

Does it matter? It wasn't my birthday, so they didn't need to see me right away.

"Sure," I said as I walked out of the kitchen.

I got dressed in my own time. Hearing my grandparents fuss over me because of Dad was about the last thing in the world I fucking wanted. Knowing Mum would freak if I wore anything above the knee—not that I wanted to for a family function—I changed into a full-length sundress and curled my hair. I thought I looked presentable, and I didn't really care if anyone else did.

When I got downstairs, my grandparents, aunt, uncle, and cousin had just arrived and were wishing my sister a happy birthday.

Showtime. I forced a smile.

My uncle looked for me first. He looked so similar to Dad that I wanted to run back upstairs. Uncle Sam opened his arms for a hug. I let him, but my body was too rigid.

"Hey, Tegan," he said, giving me a much briefer hug than usual.

I thought he could feel my resistance.

"Hi," I said.

Nan saved me from the awkwardness by crushing me next. "How have you been, darling?" she asked, playing with one of my curls.

I wasn't even sure of that. *I'm lost, drowning, empty, and angry. Take your pick.*

"I'm fine, Nan. Do you want a drink?" I didn't wait for her answer before going into the kitchen to get her the glass of red wine I knew she would want.

Two minutes in, and I was ready for everyone to leave.

Once our family, Ava's friends, and Sophie and Adam had arrived, I knew, the next time the doorbell rang, it would be

Lucas and his family. Kai had said he'd pop in, but it probably wouldn't be until later.

Ava shouldn't have invited the Daniels. I wanted to see Lucas again, but I also didn't. Everything would be easier if we just stayed away from each other. All I needed was to be able to keep everyone at a safe distance until a miracle happened, and I was suddenly okay again.

I sat at the kitchen island with Sophie and Adam, trying to listen to what they were saying when I was far too on edge to take anything in. I missed being carefree and laughing every five seconds, like they were doing.

My family was mingling in the kitchen and living room, like everything was fine and dandy, and I wanted to scream at the top of my lungs. I felt like I was on the outside, looking in at a life I'd never have anymore. I didn't fit into the family.

"Tegan?" Adam said, waving his hand in front of my face.

His expression said it all. Lucas and his family were here. Now, I really wanted to run. Sophie and Adam only knew of them, but they thought it was strange that Mum and Ava wanted to spend time with them, too.

I took a deep breath and looked up. They were all there, speaking to Ava. Lucas was doing a bad job of pretending he hadn't seen me already.

Why him? Why do I have to like him?

Finally, when he must have felt it was long enough, he looked over, and our eyes met. He gave me an almost sad small smile, and I felt guilty. I hated that. I didn't want to feel anything. I wanted to stay in the zombie state indefinitely.

"I'm gonna go say hi," I said to Adam and Sophie.

They nodded, watching the Daniels with interest.

Lucas and I had agreed to be friends, so I should treat him like one. That involved actually talking to him face-to-face. With that in mind, I poured two glasses of the punch and walked over, handing him a cup.

"Much better than beer," I said, smiling.

He gave me a breathtaking smile, and his pale green eyes warmed. "Yeah? What's in it?" he asked, looking into the cup and frowning.

Okay, so maybe it wasn't the most appealing colour. It had been red when Mum made it, but when I'd added more alcohol and then a bit more still, it'd kinda turned a light orange-pink colour.

"I'll tell you after you've tried it."

He narrowed his eyes at me. "Poison?"

Rolling my eyes, I grabbed the cup out of his hand, took a sip, and gave it back. *My God, there is a lot of alcohol in there.* It burned as it slid down my throat. I managed not to pull a face though. "There. Satisfied?"

"Fine," he said. He brought the cup up to his lips. "Shit, Tegan, what the hell is in it?" he asked, turning his nose up.

"Just a little vodka," I replied.

"A little!"

All right, this is going well. We can do the friend thing.

I introduced Lucas, Grace, and Jake to Adam and Sophie, but before long, Jake had gone off to sit with his dad in the living room, and Grace was integrated into Ava's group of friends. That was fine by me. I got the impression that Lucas's brother and sister weren't my biggest fans.

I felt myself relaxing around Lucas even more. He could be a little intense and wasn't at all subtle, but that wasn't exactly a bad quality. It just wasn't what I needed right now.

Sophie's eyebrow rose when Kai walked into the kitchen. The little cow was definitely loving the tension, so I had a feeling Kai turning up was like Christmas to her.

"Hey," Kai said, wrapping his arm around my shoulders and smiling at me. He so had that cheeky, almost bad-boy image about him.

"Hey back. Want a drink?"

"Boring one, please. I'm driving."

I grabbed Kai a Coke, and he joined us around the kitchen island.

"Lucas, this is Kai. Kai, Lucas."

save me

"Hey," Kai said.

Lucas's, "Hi," was no more than a grunt.

Things had finally settled down, so I really didn't want the evening to get awkward. I felt like I should explain to Kai who Lucas was, but I hadn't told him about my dad yet, and I didn't want to have that conversation right now—or ever actually.

"I like the addition," I said, pointing to the healing birds on Kai's arm.

"Thanks," he replied.

I downed the last of my drink and got a refill. Maybe I should have thought through inviting Kai. He was the one person who didn't know what had happened. He was the only person I had in my life whom I didn't see sympathy from. That was so valuable to me, and if someone said something or if he overheard, that could be gone.

I drank some more.

After the third cold look from Lucas to Kai, I was ready to leave. I was friends with both of them, so there shouldn't be any hostility. Lucas had bloody agreed when we spoke by text that we'd give friendship a try, despite the unusual circumstances. I was not getting involved in any cheesy love triangle.

Grace and Ava came back into the room for more wine and stopped beside me and Kai.

"So, how do you two know each other?" Grace asked, pointing to Kai.

What the hell do I say to that? I met and fucked him in a bar.

"We met at a party."

She nodded and turned her attention to Lucas, making me look at him, too. He was staring at his empty glass, his jaw clenched tight.

Seriously, jealousy? Don't do this to me, Luke.

Kai muttered something about going to the bathroom and left. I wasn't sure if he wanted a couple of minutes away from the hostility, but something told me he wouldn't really give a fuck about that.

"Tegan, how old is Kai?" Mum asked.

Christ, they were popping up everywhere now. Actually, that was a good question. My guess was eighteen or nineteen.

"I don't know exactly," I admitted.

"You don't know?" she spoke slowly, too slowly.

"No, I don't."

"He's clearly a lot older, Tegan. Why are you hanging round with him?" Mum asked.

"We're friends, and I know he's older." I just wasn't sure by how much.

Kai came back into the room, and I gave him a look that screamed, *Run*, but he didn't. Yep, he really didn't give a crap what anyone thought.

"Kai, could I ask you a question, please?" Mum said.

"Mum," I hissed. *Oh God, what the hell is she doing?*

"It's fine, Tegan," Kai said. "You can ask me anything, Mrs Pennells."

Mum nodded once, seemingly pleased that he was cooperating. "How old are you?"

"I'm twenty-one," he replied.

I watched Mum's face harden. She was not happy. I hadn't thought he was that old, but I really didn't care. He made me forget, and it was only four years. According to English law, I was legal, so no one else could say a fucking thing.

Kai had also become a friend.

"Twenty-one. My daughter is *seventeen*!"

Kai's eyes flicked to me for a second. *Well, damn, he guessed my age wrong, too.*

"Mum!" I snapped. *Why can't she just stay out of my goddamn life?*

"No, Tegan. What on earth are you doing?"

What am I doing? What I have to.

"No one can hurt the bitch."

People had stopped talking to watch.

"You need to stop all this right now. No more going out. No more getting drunk with older men. It stops. You have to deal with this properly. You're going to see a counsellor."

Stop, stop, stop, stop, stop.

The air thickened. I found it harder to breathe.

"I'm gonna go," Kai said, apologetically looking at me.

I heard Lucas mumble, "Good," under his breath, which made me roll my eyes.

"I'm so sorry, Kai," I said.

"It's fine. I'll call you later."

I nodded, and he turned and walked out.

Mum turned back to me, tears in her eyes. "I'll make an appointment with a counsellor on Monday."

"I'm not crazy."

"No one thinks you are, Tegan, but you need some help."

I shook my head. I didn't need help. I just needed to forget.

"Leave. Me. Alone," I said, emphasising each word. Then, I stormed off upstairs to my room, slamming the door hard behind me.

Gripping my hair, I tried to focus. *Don't cry. Shove it away.* I sank deeper, desperately trying to push away any feelings. I wanted to feel empty.

Dropping to the bed, I squeezed my eyes closed and concentrated on taking deep breaths. Finally, I started to regain control. *Push it all away.*

Tegan

I LAY ON MY BED, staring at the ceiling, trying to figure out what to do next. I did *not* need to see a counsellor. Even if she made me go, I wouldn't have to talk. This was going to be a *huge* waste of her money.

Someone knocked on my door.

"Go away," I said.

"Can I come in?" Lucas asked through the door.

"I said, go away!"

The door opened, and in he walked anyway.

"I said—"

"Yeah, I heard, Tegan."

I sighed sharply. "What do you want?"

"To make sure you're okay."

Why the hell is he so damn nice to me all the time? It was making everything ten times harder.

"Want to sit?" I sat up, making space for him.

Smiling, he flopped down onto the bed, making me bounce.

"Child," I joked.

He poked his tongue out.

"I refer you to my earlier statement."

He smiled, making my anger melt.

"Was my mum really pissed when I walked off?"

He nodded. "She's upset. She's just being a mum. Kai *is* older; you can't blame her for being protective. She doesn't know what to do to make everything better for you."

How can Lucas say that about Kai being older when he isn't far off twenty?

"He's not that much older, and it's not like we're together or anything. She doesn't need to do anything. I don't need to talk to anyone. *I'm. Fine.*"

"So, you really don't think seeing a counsellor would help?"

Is he just ignoring the fact that I just said I'm fine?

"I don't need to see anyone," I replied.

"I just think, if it's going to help you, then maybe you should give it a go."

"Do *you* think I need to?"

"I think you should do whatever it takes to help you get through it."

"That's what I have been doing," I said, throwing my hands up in the air.

Why can't anyone see that? Not everyone dealt with things in the same way, and just because I wasn't crying and going through Dad's things, like Mum and Ava, it didn't mean I wasn't dealing.

"Really? So, Kai is *helping*, is he?" he asked sarcastically, raising his eyebrows.

"Kai is…a distraction. Yeah, it helps."

His jaw clenched. I didn't know what else to say, so we just sat in silence until I couldn't bear it anymore.

"Luke?"

He looked up.

"You wanna get out of here?"

"Yeah." He smiled. "I know exactly where to go, too. Come on."

We snuck out of my room and down the stairs. Everyone was still in the kitchen, so that made it easier. The front door was about five metres away. I covered my mouth to muffle my giggling at how stupid we must look.

"Come on," Lucas whispered, darting toward the door.

We made it out and into Lucas's car. I started laughing as soon as we were inside his car. We'd make shit ninjas.

"Okay, where are we going?" I asked.

He chuckled and replied, "You'll see. I need to stop off at mine and pick something up first."

"Pick what up?"

"My car."

Huh? Is he aware that we are already in his car? Oh God, is he really drunk? He'd only had one beer after that sip of punch, but I didn't think he was drunk.

"So…we're in the invisible car now?" I asked sarcastically.

"Very funny, Tegan," he replied.

I shook my head. "You have another car?"

"Yep."

"Why are we getting it? Where are we going?"

"I'm taking you somewhere I go a lot, and we need the other car."

"Why do we need the other car?" *What is the point in driving half an hour to his house to get another car when we already have one?*

He smirked. "No more questions. You'll have to wait and see."

"Please?" I asked in my sweetest voice.

"Nope." He looked at me out of the corner of his eye and did another crap job of looking indifferent. He'd make an awful actor.

When we eventually got to his house, he led me to one of the garages at the side of the house and unlocked the garage door. He lifted it to reveal a striking blue Subaru Impreza. I stood there, drooling over it for a bit. I was a bit of a car whore. Dad had loved cars, too, and he'd taken me to a lot of shows and track days.

"You like it?" Lucas asked, following me as I walked round the car.

"Um, yeah!" I said. "It's the STI, too. Nice."

The shocked expression on his face was priceless—mouth open, eyes wide. I wished I'd had a camera.

"You like cars?"

"Yeah, since I was little."

Lucas stared at me like he was trying to figure something out.

Don't figure anything out.

I had no idea what he was thinking, but the way he looked at me gave me butterflies.

I suddenly remembered why we'd come here. "Where are you taking me?" I asked, playfully narrowing my eyes.

"You'll see. Get in." He opened the door and nodded his head for me to do as I'm told.

I sighed dramatically, making him laugh, as I slid into the passenger seat. Guess I was just going to have to trust him.

We drove out of town toward…somewhere. I hated not knowing where we were going, but I did trust him. Still, it would be nice to know where I was being taken, not that it really mattered as long as I was far away from my mother.

He turned down a small track, off-road, and I had absolutely no clue which direction we were going in.

"Luke, can I ask you a question?"

"Yeah," he replied.

"Are you taking me in the woods to have your wicked way before murdering me?"

He laughed and shook his head.

"Actually, I'm serious. Bit creepy that you're taking me down here, to be honest."

"As fun as the first part of that sounds, no, that's not my plan. This is a shortcut."

A shortcut to where?

"We're almost there. Quit whining."

save me

"Better be, and I'm not whining. It's not unreasonable for me to want to know where I'm going."

"Do you trust me?" he asked.

"If I say no, will you tell me where we're headed?"

"No."

I sighed. "Fine."

Lucas didn't respond, but he did grin. *Arsehole.*

We pulled into what looked like an old deserted business park about ten minutes from his house. Two rows of run-down and abandoned warehouses and buildings with no windows or doors lined the ground in front of us.

Why has he brought me here?

"Er, this is it?" I asked. "You don't take girls out often, do you?"

Fighting a smile, he shook his head. "Just get out of the car, Tegan."

The first thing I heard when I got out was loud music, but I couldn't figure which song it was. A few playing at the same time muffled the sounds.

Are we going to an illegal rave?

Tegan

WE TURNED A CORNER, and I realised I was very wrong. Lined up on either side of the road were loads of high-performance cars. Hundreds of people were walking around, drinking, and dancing.

Okay, have I stepped onto the set of The Fast and the Furious*?*

We pulled up against the most gorgeous orange Lamborghini Gallardo.

How is Lucas in this world?

I jumped out of the car and stared at the Lamborghini's beauty. Beside me, Lucas said hello to a few people, but I couldn't take my eyes off the car that I was seriously considering stealing.

"So, Luke, who's the hottie?"

Oh, great.

I looked up and saw three men who all looked similar with dark hair and green eyes. They didn't look like brothers, but I would put money on them being related in some way.

NATASHA PRESTON

"Danny, Zack, and Leon, this is Tegan," he said, pointing to them as he said their names.

Danny, the one who'd called me hottie, took my hand and kissed my knuckles. Like that shit was going to work on me.

"Hello, Tegan," he said, releasing my hand.

I raised my eyebrow and turned to face the love of my life—the Lambo. "Is this yours?" I asked.

"Yep. Do you wanna go for a drive?" he asked, wiggling his eyebrows and dangling the keys in front of me.

What kind of a question is that? "Uh, yeah!"

Lucas eyed me with a blank expression. Not liking the idea of me going off with Danny maybe?

I snatched the keys off Danny and threw them to Luke. He caught them just before they would have slammed against his chest.

"I'm taking your motor, Dan," Lucas said.

"Knock yourself out, dude, but you scratch it and, like always, I'm cutting your balls off."

Lucas rolled his eyes and stuck his finger up at Danny.

I walked round the side and stopped.

"What's up?" he asked, frowning at me.

I looked up at him, getting captured by his light green eyes; they literally took my breath away.

"Tegan?" He waved his hand in front of my face, smirking.

Right, his question. "Um, how do I get in? I mean, the car's really low, and this dress is a little tight…" I trailed off, gesturing to the dress.

He looked down, slightly tilting his head, eye-fucking me.

"Lucas!" I exclaimed, clicking my fingers in front of his face. I was greeted by a schoolboy grin and a deep chuckle.

Bloody pervert.

"Just get in, Tegan. No one's looking."

I raised one eyebrow. There was someone looking—him!

"Right, sorry." He turned his head to the side.

I climbed in the car. There really was no elegant way of getting in it, so I let myself drop in the seat.

90

Luke got in, a lot more elegantly than me, and turned the key in the ignition. The engine roared to life. I stopped myself from stroking the soft leather seat.

"Ready?" he asked.

"Oh, yes."

As he pulled away, I heard Danny shout, "Don't stack it!"

Fuck!

My scalp prickled, and my heart thudded against my rib cage.

Fuck, fuck, fuck.

I gripped the edges of the seat as the air was sucked from the car. Fear gripped me as I pictured the car rolling over, just like Dad's had. I blinked rapidly, trying to stop the images and the tears. Everything was closing in. My vision blurred, and black dots danced in front of my face.

Lucas, sensing something was up, slowed down and called my name. He sounded really far away. I sank under the water, and his voice almost disappeared completely.

I felt the car jolt to a stop, and Lucas touched my hand.

"I-I'm fine," I muttered.

"You're not fine. It's what Danny said, isn't it? About crashing? I would never put you in any danger, Tegan. I won't be driving fast."

"I know. It's just..." I stopped talking, completely unable to finish the sentence.

"Just what happened to your dad."

I looked out the window, clenching my jaw. I didn't want to talk anymore.

"I'm so sorry, Tegan."

Shoving everything away, I met his eyes and smiled. "Can we go for that drive now?"

He blinked twice before replying, "Sure."

You're fine. Just lock it all away.

I couldn't think about what had happened. I couldn't let myself go there. I wasn't strong enough to make it back.

Lucas took me for a ride and after we parked the car back beside his. I was more than ready to get out. Plus, I felt like a dick after my freak-out.

"So, how was it?" Danny asked.

"Awesome," I replied. "I want one."

"When I'm rich, I'll buy you one," Lucas said as he winked.

"Hmm, I'll hold you to that."

Lucas was currently being pursued by two very tall, very bottle-blonde girls. They stood beside him and laughed a little too loudly. I wasn't sure if he knew them or if the other members of Lucas's group had already turned them down, so they were moving on. I got that cool cars were hot, and hot guys with cool cars were double hot, but I was not going to sleep with them to get a ride. But then again, I'd slept with people to be numb, so who was I to judge?

Turning to Danny, I ignored the Barbie sisters playing for Lucas. It wasn't bothering me. We weren't together, and even if we were, I wasn't the overly jealous psycho-girlfriend type.

"So, who bought you the car?" I asked.

He couldn't be more than twenty-one. Unless he'd won the lottery, my money was on daddy.

Cocking his head to the side, he replied, "What you're thinking is exactly how I got it. My parents are so rich that they wipe their arse with fifties. They bought me the car last year. Gotta keep up appearances."

He sounded bitter about his folks, but I had a feeling the Lambo had softened the blow of not having their attention somewhat.

Lucas walked away from his female fans and stood beside me.

"Who's she?" Barbie Number One asked, nodding in my direction.

"This is Tegan. Tegan, this is Sadie," he said.

"Hi, Sadie."

"Seriously, Lucas? How *old* is she? I can't fucking even…" She held her hand up, glaring at Luke, and then stormed off.

"She seems nice," I said sarcastically. "She an ex?"

"Sort of. We went out for about an hour when we were eight, and everyone else was playing relationships at school," he replied.

"I think she still might like you."

Lucas rolled his eyes at me.

"So, what's her deal then?"

"Luke, if you're not gonna get on Sadie, do you mind if I have a go? She's all upset, and I haven't been laid in weeks," Zack asked.

"You're sick, Zack, but go for it."

"Hey, Zack!" I shouted after him.

He turned around and raised a rusty-brown eyebrow at me.

"Be careful; she might go all *Fatal Attraction* on you, too."

He shook his head, chuckling, and walked off. Lucas, Danny, and Leon laughed from behind me.

"I like this one, Luke," Danny said.

"So do I," Lucas replied.

I bit my lip and looked away. *Let's not do this.*

"We need to get the car ready, Danny," Leon said, nodding his head toward what must be his own car.

They bounded off, excited about something.

"Ready for what?"

"Racing." Lucas's eyes widened. "Shit, Tegan, I'm sorry. Jesus, I'm such an idiot to bring you here."

"No," I said, holding my hand up. "I used to go to races and shows all the time. This is good. Granted, the ones I went to were legal, but this is definitely better. Don't feel bad. I'm fine. Is it safe though?"

He nodded confidently. "I know what I'm doing."

My eyes popped. Well, that changed things. "*You're* racing?" I started to panic. My stomach felt like it had been tipped upside down. *Damn it, I care for him.*

"Yeah, I race."

I fought the urge to beg him not to. Deep down, I knew that I had no right to demand he didn't go anywhere, but I wanted to. My dad had died behind the wheel of a car, and he wasn't racing.

"You don't want me to?"

"I don't want you to get hurt," I admitted.

He bent his knees, so he was level with me and smiled. His pale green eyes told me how he felt, and I wasn't at all ready to see it.

"I won't get hurt, I swear."

"You don't know that. Do you race often?"

"Most weeks. If you don't want me to, Tegan, I won't. I understand why you wouldn't want me to," he said.

"I don't know what I want."

Lie. I wanted him to take me home right now, so he wouldn't be tempted to race.

"It's fine, really. I won't do anything stupid."

"Promise?"

"I promise," he said.

We walked through the crowd to Leon and Danny, who were looking over Luke's car. I felt nauseous and a little bit excited. I loved being around cars and watching the races at the car shows my dad had taken me to. Granted, those races were controlled and legal, but I was still looking forward to watching this one. Well, watching other people's races. I was pretty sure I'd be closing my eyes for Luke's.

The first two races taught me street racing was so far away from track racing that it wasn't even funny. They were fucking insane, and I lost count of the amount of times I sucked my breath in and my heart leapt as someone narrowly missed the edge of a building or the crowd. Apparently, it was normal; no one else seemed to be having a mini heart attack every time.

Leon finally hollered for Lucas, so he gave me a smile over his shoulder and walked off, leaving me with Danny. That was fine by me; I liked him—mostly because he wasn't a huge pervert like Zack.

"He'll be fine," Danny said, smiling in amusement at the expression on my face, which was probably utter fear.

I thought I was hiding it well but clearly not.

"Yeah," I replied. "Is he good?"

"He's good. Wins more than he loses. I have a feeling he won't lose tonight."

Because I was here, and he wouldn't want to lose in front of me. I didn't care about male pride. I just wanted him to walk away once the race was over.

Stretching up on the tips of my toes, I managed to see Lucas's car line up next to a souped-up silver Lexus. God, I was not looking forward to this one. Lucas shook the other guy's hand and slapped him on the shoulder. They were friends, so hopefully, there wouldn't be any dirty racing.

Leon shouted something, and a bikini-clad Barbie Number Three raised her arm and dropped it. They really were following the cliché. Tyres screeched as they launched off the start line. Smoke blocked my view for a few seconds. I caught a glimpse of Lucas slightly ahead just before they disappeared around the first corner.

I felt sick and lowered my head. My stomach was in knots, so I wasn't even going to attempt to watch any longer.

"You not watching this?" Danny asked, laughing.

"Can't," I replied, staring at my shoes.

"Lucas will be fine. Look up, Tegan!"

I shook my head. *Not happening.*

There was another deafening screeching of tyres. I jumped in surprise, and my eyes flew open. I gripped ahold of Danny's arm.

"Whoa, Tegan, you're cutting off the circulation."

"What was that noise?" I asked, tightening my grip.

Danny shrugged with the shoulder I wasn't half-pulling down. "Drifting."

"They were drifting?"

That was all well and good in films, but I didn't like losing control that much in real life. Things could so easily go badly when it wasn't controlled by professionals and a whole stunt crew.

"Yeah, there's a pretty awesome corner round the back there, and if you hit it at the right angle, you can drift it."

He sounded so enthusiastic and absolutely thrilled with the idea. I wanted to punch him.

The cars came back into view. I craned my neck, daring a look at the race. Lucas flew over the finish line and slammed on his brakes. Thank God they were both back safely.

Luke made his way over to me with a big grin on his face. It took a second for my legs to start working again, but when they did, I ran over and jumped on him, tightly wrapping my arms round his neck.

He was shocked; that much was obvious from his statuelike state. But then it took him less than a second to respond. His arms snaked around my back, pinning me against his chest. My whole body felt alive again.

No.

Damn it all to hell.

Lucas

SHE WAS HUGGING ME. I stood, stunned, as her arms held me tight for a second before she was gone again.

What the hell was that?

"Um...I'm not sure what I think. It was pretty scary."

My mind was still reeling from the fact that she'd purposefully touched me. That didn't happen; usually, she went out of her way to ensure there was always distance between us.

My heart raced as I looked into her eyes. She smiled as if nothing had happened, and at the same time, my phone started ringing.

"Hi, Dad," I said, reading his name before picking up.

"Lucas? Where are you? Are you with Tegan? We can't find her, and Alison's really concerned."

"Yeah, she's with me. We went for a drive. She needed to get away for a bit. Sorry, I should've told someone."

Dad relayed the message to everyone on his end and then asked, "Are you coming back now?"

I looked over at Tegan, and she stared at the ground, clenching her fists.

"I don't think so. I'll let you know when we're on our way back."

"All right, just look after her."

"I will do. Bye, Dad."

"Bye."

I turned my phone on silent and slid it back in my pocket. *Is she going to freak out now?* I studied her face, trying to figure out what she was thinking. Tegan was pretty unreadable. Most of the time, she just looked bored or annoyed, but there had to be something deeper than that.

She bit her lip and then gave me the most beautiful smile; it literally made my heart miss a beat. "Can we go to the beach?"

"Yeah, sure. I'll just go tell the guys we're leaving," I said, pulling my keys out of my pocket.

We pulled into my driveway to swap the cars back over, and this distance was there again. I was disappointed although not at all surprised. I didn't know how to break down that big brick wall she'd built, but I wasn't about to give up.

"Let's go," I said.

I led her around the back of the house and down the road until we made it to the beach. It was peaceful around here, almost too peaceful. The tourist part of town was half a mile down, so besides a few dog-walkers, you didn't meet many people on the beach.

Tegan had a permanent frown on her face, and I didn't know what was going on with her.

"You okay?" She didn't answer or acknowledge that I'd asked something, so I waved my hand in front of her face. "Earth to Tegan."

She stopped walking and turned to face me. "What?"

"Where were you?"

She looked at me like I was an idiot, and I almost laughed. "What?"

I shook my head. "Never mind. I wanna show you something, but we're going to have to climb that hill over there." I pointed ahead of us. It was quite steep, but I had climbed it so many times now. I'd go up there to think or just get away from everything sometimes.

"Up there?" she asked. "It's steep, and I'll probably fall."

"I won't let you fall."

She thought for a minute. "If I do, I'm holding you personally responsible," she said, raising her eyebrow to show how serious she was.

"Deal," I replied, fighting a smile.

"I mean it, Lucas. If I fall and break or even bruise anything, you'll be my slave until I'm better."

"I promise, you won't fall. But, if you do, I will happily be your slave."

She assessed me for a minute, her incredible green eyes searching for something. I had no idea what, but I was pretty sure I'd give it to her if she'd just ask.

"Okay. Let's go then."

She started walking toward the wrong hill, and I let her walk for a bit.

"Tegan!" I yelled when she was far enough.

She turned around and threw her arms up.

"We're going up *that* hill." I pointed to the bigger one further along.

She came storming back, eyes narrowed, looking like she was about to murder me. "So, you just let me walk all that way up the *wrong* hill?"

"Come on, you would have done the same to me. Your face is so funny," I said, chuckling.

"You are going straight to hell, Lucas."

"Meet you there, Princess." I almost threw up in my mouth when I realised I'd used the nickname Kai had apparently given her. To be fair though, it did suit her sometimes. Still, I wanted to wash my mouth out with bleach.

She growled. "Lead the damn way, or take me home."

"All right, chill. Come on."

She licked her lips, wincing, as we hit the steepest part. "How's your dad doing?"

Wow. She didn't have to ask that.

"He's doing okay. It's still in the early days, but the tests he's had done have all come back normal. Your dad had a strong heart."

"So, is there actually a top to this stupid hill?"

It came as no surprise when she changed the subject the second I'd mentioned Simon. She could, on occasion, talk about my dad but not hers. Never hers.

"Yeah, we're almost there." We weren't even halfway up yet.

She sighed. "No, we're not."

"How do you know?"

"Because I would have said the same thing to you."

"Touché."

She groaned as she realised we had a little ways to go yet. I let her walk in front of me—partly because, if she fell, I wanted to be able to catch her and partly because it gave me a very good view of the back of that dress.

We finally reached the top, and I walked to the side that had the better view of just the ocean. It was a perfect night to bring her here. The sky was clear, and the moon and stars were the only light.

I watched her as she looked out into the ocean.

"Oh, wow, it's incredible up here," she whispered. "I forgot things could be this beautiful."

My heart ached for her. She didn't see much good in the world right now. My dad was ill and had been for a long time, but we had hope. She had a huge hole in her life.

We lay down on the grass, and she opened up about a few minor things, like pranks she and Sophie had pulled at school. I felt like I'd at least smashed one brick from that wall. But, when I attempted to steer the conversation onto the subject of Simon, she cut me off and built another layer.

I felt deflated, like getting close to her was completely impossible and I was fighting a losing battle.

I pulled my phone out of my pocket to check the time when the sky started getting lighter. That wasn't a good sign. *Shit.* It was just after half past three in the morning, and I had eight missed calls.

"Er, Tegan?"

She turned her head, and as soon as our eyes met, my heart started beating faster.

"Yeah?" she whispered.

"It's half past three."

"Really?" She frowned. "Wow, you'd think I would be more tired."

I shook my head, not knowing what to say to that. *Shouldn't she be worried that we have been out all night? Well, she hasn't been for the last fuck knows how long, so why would she now?*

"My parents tried to call, but I turned my phone on silent after speaking to Dad."

"Why are you so worried, Luke?" she asked.

"It's half past three, and I said I would take care of you. Your mum's gonna be pissed." I groaned.

This was just great. Alison was never going to trust me with her daughter again.

"You said you would take care of me, which you have, so where's the problem?"

Really? She isn't getting this?

"It's half past three, Tegan!"

She laughed. "Say it as many times as you'd like, but it's not gonna get any earlier."

"This isn't funny. Come on, we need to go," I said as I jumped up.

"I'm tired now," she moaned, rubbing her eyes as she stood up.

"You can sleep in the car."

"I don't want to sleep in the car."

"Then, sleep when we get back to yours."

"But I'm tired now."

I couldn't help laughing. "You're hard work, you know?"

"Thank you." She smiled as if I had just given her a compliment, and then she started walking down the hill.

Lucas

WE PULLED INTO HER driveway thirty minutes later, and I was scared to get out of the car. Her mum had every right to be pissed off, and I didn't want her not to trust me with her daughter.

"So, are we going in, or do you want to stay out here? I wasn't kidding when I said I couldn't sleep in cars."

I couldn't even crack a smile. "Yeah, I guess."

"Oh God, you're scared, aren't you?" She beamed with amusement.

Glad one of us wasn't panicking.

"I don't want to piss your mum off, Tegan. I want to be…" I realised what I was about to say and quickly shut the hell up.

"You want to be what?"

"Nothing. I just don't want to piss her off. Let's get inside."

I turned to open my door, but she gripped my arm.

"Hold up! That was so a lie. You can't just say that and not finish. Tell me, Luke."

It's not obvious?

"Really, it's not important."

"Well then, there's no reason you can't tell me," she said with a smug grin.

"You don't want to know." I took a deep breath. *Fuck it, here goes.* "I don't want your mum to be pissed at me because…" I paused; my heart was going wild. This could potentially end badly for me.

Raising her eyebrow, she said, "Because…"

"Because I want to be with you, Tegan."

Jesus, how can she not see it? Although she was clearly blocking out a lot right now.

When she didn't respond and her eyes grew more distant, I knew I shouldn't have said anything.

"Please say something."

"I don't know what to say," she whispered.

I could tell what she was thinking, *We agreed to be friends and nothing more.*

"Right. We should go in."

"No, wait. Please, Luke, I don't want things to be weird between us."

"It's fine. It won't be weird, I promise."

It was a crap situation, but I couldn't blame her for not wanting anything to happen between us. I wasn't exactly the king of patience, especially during the wait for Dad's op, but I could appreciate that she needed more time.

I got out of the car after her and followed her up the path. She was as eager to get away from that situation as I was then.

The front door flew open, and I groaned. This wasn't going to go well either. I could feel a headache coming on.

"Where have you two been? I've been going out of my mind," Alison snapped.

"We were just out, Mum," Tegan replied.

She sounded bored, and I wished I'd told her to let me do the talking.

I knew why she acted like that toward everyone, especially those closest to her, but it really wasn't helping.

Alison did nothing but stare.

"Yes, I know *out*, Tegan, but it would have been nice to know exactly where my teenage daughter was."

I stepped slightly in front of Tegan, hoping that she would shut up, so I could defuse the situation. "I'm sorry, Alison. We went to the beach and completely lost track of time."

"Thank you for apologising, Lucas." She looked at Tegan as she said my name.

Tegan rolled her eyes. Sometimes, she played the bitch too well, and I couldn't tell if she genuinely didn't care or if it was all an act to protect herself.

"Well, at least you were with Lucas."

That, I hadn't expected. Nor had I expected the way it made me feel. Knowing her mum trusts her with me is unreal.

"You mean, not with Kai?" Tegan asked.

Where the fuck did that come from?

"It's not okay for you to be out with him. You barely know him, for starters—"

"I've known him a while, longer than Luke. I just didn't ask a whole lot of questions," she said.

"That's not better! How long has it been going on?"

"Seriously, Mum? All the times I said I was staying at Sophie's..." She trailed off.

I wanted to shake her and tell her to stop. And to stop fucking around with Kai.

"You were with him? Are you stupid?" Alison yelled.

Tegan walked off.

"Tegan!" Alison reached out to grab her as she walked past, but Tegan dodged to the side and ran upstairs.

Shit, she was more complicated than I'd first thought.

Alison took a deep breath and wiped the tears from her face. "I'm so sorry you all had to witness that. I just don't know what to do anymore."

All?

Sure enough, everyone but my dad was standing around, watching the showdown. *Perfect.*

Ava hugged her mum as she sobbed harder. I felt so sorry for her. She had to deal with losing her husband as well as a difficult—and that was putting it lightly—daughter. I had no idea what to do either. I thought I could help Tegan, and while I was still determined to do just that, I had a feeling it was going to be a lot more difficult than I imagined.

"Are you okay, Lucas?" Ava asked, pulling back from her mum a little so that she could face me.

I shrugged. "Yeah, I guess."

"She doesn't really like him, you know. We all know why she's doing this."

We all did know why she was doing it, but we couldn't just stand around and let her anymore, no matter how much she wanted to push everything and everyone away.

How the hell have I become so deeply invested in someone else so quickly?

But Tegan wasn't just any girl; both of our fathers had seen to that.

I clenched my jaw. *Screw this.* I was pretty much falling for her already, and I wasn't about to let her push me away, too. "Well, she needs to stop."

No one stopped me as I followed Tegan's path. That wasn't necessarily a good thing. Someone had to try though.

I could hear music coming from her room as I approached. She didn't hear me when I knocked, or she was ignoring me. *Well, if I'm really trying…*

I opened the door and walked in. She was sitting on the bed with a bottle of vodka in her hand. It was only just after four in the morning.

What the hell is she thinking?

I stormed over to her and grabbed the bottle out of her hand. "What do you think you're doing?" I growled.

"I *was* having a drink," she snapped, empty eyes narrowing.

Keep your cool.

Sighing, I sat in front of her. "Why are you doing all this?"

She frowned. "Doing all what?"

"Kai," I spat out his name. "Getting drunk, fighting with your mum, pushing everyone away."

Her face hardened, and she turned away from me.

"Let me help you, Tegan, please. Your dad wouldn't have wanted this."

Her body tensed at the mention of Simon.

She looked at me like she hated me. "Leave."

I shook my head. "I'm not going anywhere."

"I don't want you, Lucas. Why can't you understand that?"

That didn't feel good. It wasn't just her words that kicked the air out of my lungs; it was her tone, too.

"Seriously, just go."

I stood up and walked out of the room, taking the vodka with me. Ava and Grace were talking in Ava's room as I passed. They looked up at me with matching sympathetic smiles.

"Lucas," Grace called as I walked past.

Groaning, I turned around.

"Are you okay? I'm sorry for what she said. She didn't mean it," Ava said.

Since we were having this conversation, I walked all the way in and sat on her computer chair. "Didn't she?"

"No, of course she didn't. You mentioned Dad. That makes her flip out, especially if she's already in a bad mood. She just says the most hurtful thing to get you to stop. She's done it enough times to me and Mum."

"I have no idea what to do," I replied before taking a swig of the vodka.

I was in no better of a position than Alison.

"Neither do we. Ever since Dad's funeral, she's completely changed. I just want my happy, loud, dancing, singing, piano-playing, annoying baby sister back." She blinked back her tears and took a deep breath. "I hate the cold, hateful person she's become."

"I'm sure, in time, she'll be okay," Grace said.

She always was blindly positive. It was actually one of the things I loved most about my twin.

"Yeah, hopefully," I replied, trying to sound like I believed her. "I'm gonna go to bed. See you guys tomorrow." I got up and left, not wanting to talk anymore.

I was staying on the sofa bed in the study, which was, thankfully, upstairs. I didn't want to see anyone else. After removing my jeans and T-shirt, I got in bed for some much-needed sleep. I'd not slept in about twenty hours, so I should've been tired, but my mind was buzzing with thoughts of Tegan.

Tegan

I HATED BEING SUCH a bitch to Lucas and seeing the hurt in his eyes. I felt awful for saying those things, but he just wouldn't stop talking. I should have told him I wanted to be with him, too, because I did. Or I thought I did. *How bad can it be really?*

I knew he would be there for me, but the thought of having to go through what Mum and Ava were going through, all that crying and the pain, scared the hell out of me. I wasn't going to willingly put myself through all that.

If being a bitch meant not feeling the pain I felt the day Dad had died, then it was worth it, no question. If people got hurt or pissed off in the cross fire, then so be it.

I walked down the corridor and stood outside the study door for ages, debating on whether I should go in. Lucas probably wouldn't even want to see me after what I'd said to him. *Why would he?* I reached for the door handle, but something stopped me. *What if he tries talking about my dad again?* Lucas was dangerous, always on the edge of asking questions.

Turning swiftly, I ran downstairs and straight out the door. My breathing came out in heavy pants, and I blinked back tears.

Don't cry. Push it away.

There was one person who could make all the confusion go away. I dialled his number.

"Kai, can you pick me up, please?" I asked the second he answered.

"Huh? It's four thirty in the morning. Is everything okay?"

No.

"Fine. I just need you to get me. Can you come?"

"Yeah, of course. I'm just leaving James's now. You missed a good night. I'm on my way."

It didn't take Kai long to find me at all.

"Hey," he said as he stopped in front of me and wound the window down.

I took a deep breath and opened the door, forcing a smile onto my face. "Hey, Kai."

"Where do you wanna go?"

I shrugged. "Yours."

He nodded and drove off.

The questions never came. He didn't ask why I was running away. I loved that he never asked the difficult questions, almost as if he knew why. Everyone else tried to get me to open up. Kai respected that I couldn't.

Shit, he knows. Of course he did, he probably heard from my friends, but he never mentioned it. I liked him even more.

"So…you're not eighteen," he said.

"Nope. And you're not nineteen."

"Nope."

"Does it bother you?"

He shook his head.

"Has your weekend sucked then?" he asked.

Well, that is that.

Majorly. "It was all right. I'm so not ready to be home now though."

Well, that wasn't exactly true. I was never ready to be at home. Not now.

Sinking back into the seat, I allowed everything to fall away. There was no other shit going on. There was just me and Kai.

He really was pretty fucking gorgeous, and I watched his tattoo-covered arms move and flex as he drove the car. The smell of his aftershave filled my lungs, making me relax further. I was back to being whatever version of me I was now, the one who could just be without having to constantly bat conversations away from heading toward Dad's accident.

I smiled and put my hand on top of Kai's thigh.

I sat on Kai's bed, drinking directly from a bottle of white wine. It was disgusting and had been open for a while; apparently, it was what his sister had bought when his family visited him. He didn't say how long ago that'd been, but from the vinegary taste, I could tell it'd been a bloody long time. Didn't stop me though.

Kai was so easy to be around. Our friendship, although not based on anything particularly deep, was as real as any other I had right now. I could be myself around him and let my guard down a bit more than I could with anyone else. I knew he wasn't going to try and sneak a hard question in at any moment. I needed his friendship so much.

He grimaced as he swallowed the wine and handed me the bottle back. "That is disgusting. I don't know why I bothered trying it. I'm not drinking any more of that shit."

I laughed and shook my head. It was pretty gross, but it wasn't about taste or enjoying a drink. I just wanted to be at that stage where I was as close to being carefree as possible.

"It is gross," I agreed.

Kai took the bottle from me and put it on the bedside table.

"Hey." I playfully narrowed my eyes.

"You don't even like it."

"So?"

He grinned and pushed me backward on the bed. I looked up at him as he hovered over me.

His dark eyes were alight with mischief and lust. "I can think of a few other ways to pass the time…"

I smirked and ran my hands under his T-shirt and across his soft yet hard defined chest. My fingers glided along the bumpy contours, and I bit my lip. "Hmm, a *few* other ways?"

He nodded and very slowly lowered his face. His lips parted about an inch away from mine. *What is taking him so long?* I raised my head, but he moved back.

"Kai," I warned.

His weight pressed me into the bed in the most perfect way, and the hunger in his eyes drove me wild. There was no time for playing games.

"You want me to kiss you?"

I shot him a dark look. "What do you think?"

With a breathtaking smile that made his dark eyes light up, he kissed me hard.

Kai

TEGAN PULLED AWAY WHEN my hand touched her thigh. She lowered her head and looked away.

"What?" I asked.

"I can't do this."

"Okay," I said, backing away a fraction. "What's wrong?"

She ran her hands through the long lengths of her blonde hair. "I don't know. I just...I don't know."

"You don't want sex right now or at all?" Man, I was getting some pretty mixed signals from her.

"At all," she whispered.

On the one hand, I was glad. If she wasn't using sex as a distraction, then maybe she would face what was going on, but on the other, I wouldn't be getting any sex.

"We don't have to sleep together, Tegan. There's no unwritten rule that says you need to open your legs to me."

"I know that, but..."

I nodded and closed my eyes. "But that's what we do."

"Yeah, we have blow-your-mind hot sex, and I...well, I'm a bit of a mess right now."

"It's okay."

"What does that mean here?" She pointed between us and bit her lip. Her cheeks reddened.

"It means, we're not going to go at it like rabbits anymore."

She rolled her eyes and cracked a smile. "Yeah, I got that part. Look, for a while now, the people in my life haven't really been in my life. It's my fault. I made it that way, but it's kind of lonely, and you're the only person who I don't feel like I have to pretend around or put on much of a show."

"You're saying, you want us to be friends, but you're worried that I only want to be around you while I am getting laid?"

Turning her nose up, she replied, "Nice. Yeah though."

"I get it, Tegan, but that's not why I want to spend time with you. I've told you this, and I mean it."

She frowned, genuinely curious as to why I wanted to be around her. It sent me right back there—to a few years ago when I'd thought so little of myself that I didn't understand why my own parents still called me son.

"Now that we're definitely keeping our clothes on, I will say I'll miss the sex."

That made her laugh, and she finally relaxed. "Yeah, me, too. I don't have a whole load of people wanting to spend time with me right now."

That was probably because she didn't want to spend time with them. Back when I had been like her, I would've preferred to chew my own arm off than spend time with friends. When I had come out of it, I was lucky that my friends, James and Holly, were still around, or I would've had no one. Back then, the only people I'd wanted to be around were the ones who didn't really give a shit about me. We'd hung out with each other for convenience and for selfish purposes, and nothing was even remotely real.

save me

Tegan should be cutting me off and telling me she never wanted to see me again. But she wasn't, and I wasn't sure if that was because we had something deep down that might stand a chance when things for her were better or if it was because she hadn't fully committed to turning her life around. I wanted option A, but I couldn't be sure.

"I doubt that's true," I said, "but I know what you mean. Do you want me to take you home, or do you want to chill here for a bit?"

"I think I should go home and see my mum." She was lying. She didn't want to go home, but she didn't want to stay either. "Think maybe we can hang out in the week? If you're not busy."

"I'm sure I can fit you in. Want to go on the bike? I feel like a long ride when I drop you off."

She blushed.

I loved the bike even more after I'd had her across it.

"Good, and yeah, the bike sounds great."

"Sounded better with you moaning over it."

Ignoring me completely, she got up. "Let's go."

I took her home, dropping her off two houses down so that I wouldn't get chased out of town by her mum and crazy-eyed sister. Ava was like one of those creepy-arse dolls that watched you wherever you went.

I rode, mostly without thinking about where I was going, and I ended up back in one of my dark-place haunts. It looked the same—run-down, going nowhere, and lifeless. There was no ambition here other than getting so off your face that you wouldn't think about what a dead-end life you were leading.

Most of the windows in the houses along the long stretch of the high street were boarded up. Graffiti was the only colour around; everything else was grey and dull. Police rarely bothered coming here anymore unless there was a murder.

I left my bike in a mate's garage and went to have a look around. A year ago, this had pretty much been home, and I hadn't even cared how shitty the place was. It had given me everything I needed to not really exist for a few years.

115

"Kai!"

I turned around and immediately tensed for a fight. That was how it was around here. Most people were off their tits on whatever shit they could find to shove in their system, so you never knew who was going to turn on you. Plus, I'd not been back since the day I left.

"Fuck me, man! It is you!" Declan said, slapping my shoulder.

"Hey, Dec. How's it going? I borrowed your garage, by the way."

He nodded. "Yeah, not bad. Take what ya want."

He was only saying that because, the day I'd left, I had given him my last two hundred for drugs.

"What are you doing back here?"

That was a good question. "Just visiting."

"Ain't no one just visit here."

"How's your mum?"

Deirdre was the sweetest woman. She never let the fact that her ex-husband had left her at eight months pregnant and with no money or a place to live bother her. Nor did she let it get her down that she had to work three jobs to support her two kids or that, every time she got anything nice, it would get stolen.

"She's good, man. You stopping long enough to see her?"

"Not sure yet. If I don't, tell her I said hi."

"I'm on my way to The Grind. You comin'?"

The Grind was what everyone called the nameless club in the shittier part of town. I had no idea why. It sounded as deadbeat as it was, so I never questioned it. I'd been high as a kite many times in that fuckin' club. It was where we'd spent almost every night when we weren't out doing over shops or mugging some rich bastard. I was like Robin Hood—had he kept everything he'd taken.

"Nah, can't stop long."

"You just come back to take a look?"

"Somethin' like that," I replied.

"You shouldn't come back here, Kai."

I tensed again. His pupils were dilated, but then I didn't remember them ever being normal.

"Why's that?"

"You did the thing we all wanna do. You got out. No one thinks you're a wanker for leavin', ya know?"

"Oh, good."

I hadn't thought they would've. Then again, I hadn't really thought about them much at all after I left. They were just there, same as me. Besides Dec and Kellen, no one had had my back, and I was sure they only had because I had a bit of money, could run fast when we needed to get away on foot, drive fast when we needed a driver, sell ice to an Eskimo, and throw a decent punch.

"Seriously, man, you don't need to be back here. You know there ain't nothin' good in this place. Go, Kai. You're better than this. Same as Kel." Turning around, he walked away without looking back.

Kellen had left before I had, but he'd shown his face a few times. I hoped Kellen finally got out for good.

Dec was right, but most people were better than this—him, his mum, and sister included. When I'd left four years ago, I'd told myself I would come back at some point. Now, I knew I never would.

I'd seen all I needed to, and I knew that, no matter what happened to me in the future, I'd never call this place home again.

I left without looking back.

Tegan

As soon as I couldn't hear his bike anymore, I turned around and headed in the direction of the bus stop. Going home wasn't an option, not while they were still over. The bus I wanted was fifteen minutes away.

Sitting down on the bench, I pulled my purse out to make sure I had enough for the fare. Walking wasn't happening.

My phone showed far too many missed calls, texts, and voice mail messages for my liking. Wow, they weren't giving up easily. I just wanted to be left alone for a while. I slipped my phone in my bag and closed my eyes. It was getting harder. Things were supposed to be getting easier with time, but it wasn't. I just wanted things to go back to how they were, so I wouldn't feel like a stranger, and I could breathe again.

The journey on the bus took twenty minutes longer than it did in a car, but with every mile I put between myself and home, I relaxed more. If Mum said she wanted to move, I'd be collecting house brochures in a flash. Everything at home was filled with Dad, and I couldn't stand it.

The bus was filled mostly with old people and young mums. I felt like I didn't even belong on a shitty old bus. Looking out at the passing landscape, I wondered what the hell I was going to do—now and in the long term.

Before Dad had died, I'd had a plan—go to sixth form and study music, get good grades so that I could go to university, and then work toward my dream job. I wasn't sure what that dream job was yet, but I'd known it'd involve the piano.

Dad had dreamed of opening up a music shop, said it was so that he could supply me with instruments whenever I'd need to jet off around the world and play. I hadn't been so far up my own arse that I thought I'd be able to travel the world and play music in some form, but I was certainly going to do my best to be able to do that. Now, the idea just made me feel sick.

I needed a new plan, but my future looked blank. Right now, I had no idea what I was doing or even what I was thinking half of the time. I could look at decisions I now made and think, *Tegan would never have done that.* Well, Tegan was elsewhere right now, so fuck it all.

As the bus reached my stop, I made my way to the door. "Thanks," I mumbled to the driver as I got off.

It was around nine thirty at night, and the sun was still holding out, just barely. Well, at least I wouldn't get cold.

Without thinking too much about where I was going—or more importantly, why I was going there—I trudged up Lucas's hill, pushing on my thighs to help myself get up. He would come here to think things through and clear his head. I wasn't expecting miracles, but I hoped it'd do the same for me.

It was so pretty up here with the waves gently crashing against the shore. I sat close to the edge and played with the blades of grass.

New plan, Tegan, come on. Sixth form?

Facing my friends—the ones whose messages and calls I'd ignored for months—was the last thing I wanted.

save me

I sighed in frustration and lay down on my back with my arm slung over my eyes. It was useless. I was just going to be a disappointing fuckup, and to be honest, I didn't even care all that much.

"Tegan?"

Lucas's voice made my heart leap.

I sat up and looked around. *Should've known he'd figure out where I was.* "What do you want?"

He stepped closer, standing over me. "What the *hell* are you doing?" His voice was too calm and too controlled.

"What does it look like I'm doing?" I said sarcastically, standing up to face him. I dug my nails into my palms. I didn't want to fight with him, but I didn't want to want him more.

"We had no idea where you were after Kai dropped you off. Anything could have happened, Tegan," he snapped.

"I don't care what happens to me," I replied. It was one of the most genuine things I'd said to him. I really couldn't care less. Part of me wished I were in the car with Dad when it crashed.

Lucas's face paled. Grabbing my wrist, he whispered, "Don't say that. Maybe you don't care, Tegan, but the rest of us do."

I ripped my arm from his grip. "Don't touch me."

He let me step away, like I had known he would. "You need to stop this. You *have* to deal with what happened."

No, I really don't.

His words were like a sledgehammer to my chest. Anger boiled over, and I wanted to punch something. Punch him. Punch the whole fucked up world.

Spinning around, I headed back down the hill.

"Tegan," he called after me.

"Just leave me alone, Lucas!" I screamed.

I was breathing heavily, and my hands were shaking violently. I fought harder than I'd ever had to stay in control. Over and over, I chanted to myself, *Let it go, and block it out*, as I sped down toward the bottom, all the time ignoring his footsteps behind me.

121

Stopping at the bus stop I had gotten off at, I busied myself with looking at the timetable. He was still there, still hovering around, slightly glaring at me.

"Tegan, let me drive you."

I ran my finger down the column of times to find mine.

"Fuck's sake, Tegan, just come and get in my car!"

I'd never seen him so pissed off before. *Whatever.*

"No," I replied.

He sighed and stepped in front of me. "Please. I can't just leave you here."

"Why not?"

"Because I care about you. Everyone does. You can hate me and ignore me the whole way back, but I need to make sure you get home safe."

My fucking bus wasn't due for another hour.

"Fine, I will ignore you the whole way. Where did you park?"

"At my house."

As soon as he told me, I took off in the direction of his place, leaving him trailing behind.

"Are you still pissed off with me?"

"Yes," I bit out.

"I'm sorry, Tegan, but it's true. We all just want you to get better."

I stopped abruptly and spun around. "I'm not sick, Lucas. Just shut up, and take me home."

He didn't try talking to me anymore, and the whole car ride home was silent and awkward. I watched out of the corner of my eye as he effortlessly changed gears and swept around the corners. His grip on the steering wheel was just that little bit too tight though, giving away how angry he was.

As we approached my road, he slowed down. "Look, I'm sorry for what I said and how I said it. Can you talk to me now? I hate it when you're pissed at me."

I forced a smile. "We're fine. I just want to forget about it."

save me

He nodded and pressed his mouth into a thin line, clearly wanting to say something else. Arguing with him sucked, but I was done. Done with everything and everyone. I just wanted to sleep.

I walked into the house and went straight upstairs.

Before I could think too hard and run to the safety of my room, I turned around and went back down. They were talking about me, of course. All of them were in the kitchen, and Mum was quizzing Lucas on where I'd been.

Listening to them discuss everything that was wrong with me wasn't high up on my list of things I wanted to do. As I went to go back upstairs, I saw the music room door was open. I stood outside and stared in.

The large grand piano sat in the middle of the room. It had lost so much of its beauty. I didn't really want to play it, but at the same time, it was calling me.

Time stood still as I gingerly took steps closer to it. For the second time today, I felt my hands shake.

Taking an uneven breath, I found the courage to reach out and glide my hand over the top. It even felt different. It was just a piano. *Why is it so hard?*

I sat down on the bench and raised my trembling fingers over the keys. The scent of Dad's aftershave was definitely still in here. I tried to ignore it. Even though I knew he was gone, it gave me false hope that he'd walk through the door at any minute.

Without any thinking or planning, I started playing his favourite song. The music flowed through my mind, my voice changing to his in my head. I imagined him sitting at the piano, gracefully touching the keys and singing happily.

When I finished the last note, I opened my eyes, half-expecting him to be there. He wasn't though, of course.

Something dropped onto my lap. A tear. Raising my hand to my cheek, I felt the dampness.

A strong hand touched my shoulder, and I knew it was Lucas. I squeezed my eyes shut and lost the battle for the first time since Dad's funeral. I couldn't stop it. A tidal wave of ugly, raw emotion hit me, and a deep sob erupted from my stomach.

I missed him so much. I wanted him back. It was too soon for him to leave me.

Bending over, I let it out and gripped my hair as I tried not to let the grief swallow me whole.

Soon after I'd started crying, Lucas sat beside me, picked my limp body up, and curled me on his lap. It took me an hour to calm down. I couldn't take a breath without sobbing, and I was exhausted.

His shirt was soaked where I'd cried solidly for sixty minutes.

"Sorry," I mumbled, pulling back and wincing at the state of his T-shirt.

"Don't apologise," Lucas replied. "Are you okay now?"

"No," I finally admitted aloud. "I'm really not okay."

He nodded somberly. "What can I do?"

"Nothing. I'm not your problem. You don't need to do anything. Thank you for staying with me though." I shuffled back, so I was no longer on his lap or in his arms. That was harder than it should have been. I wanted to snuggle back and have him hold me until it all stopped hurting.

"Don't shut me out," he said. "I can help you."

"How?"

He didn't have an answer for that because there wasn't one. I would just have to deal with it on my own. Or not. I felt worse than I had in a long time, and every single part of me ached in the most painful way.

I shouldn't have allowed myself to do that. I wanted those huge iron gates to be back up and for my emotions to be locked safely away.

"I should go find my mum," I told him.

"Sure." He frowned, sighing so quietly that I almost didn't hear him.

Everything with Lucas was different. We were barely friends, but we seemed like so much more.

"Mum?" I called, walking through to the living room.

She was on her feet by the time I got to the room.

"Honey, are you all right?" She sniffed and pulled me into her arms.

No. Fuck, I didn't want her to hug me. I closed my eyes, pushing everything away as hard as I could. *Don't feel. Don't care.*

I pulled back and did my best to smile. "I've got a headache, so I'm gonna go to bed."

"Of course. Do you want me to get you some painkillers?"

Shaking my head, I took a few steps back. "I'll get some, but thanks."

Lucas watched silently as I walked past him. I felt weak, and I fucking hated it.

Never again will I let anyone make me feel like that.

Lucas

"LUCAS?"

I looked up to see Alison and Ava in front of me.

"She's in her room. Give her a minute to sort herself out."

When Tegan and I had gotten back, she'd ignored everyone and shut herself in the music room.

She was more upset than she'd ever tell anyone, even herself. I hated leaving her like that, but she needed time.

After thirty minutes, after Tegan moved up to her room, her mum and sister had had enough worrying and had gone to check on her.

I was a little surprised. "She wants to see me?"

"Yeah. She said—and I quote—'Don't let him come up for five minutes because I look like crap.' And then she ran to the bathroom." Ava tried to impersonate her voice. She failed miserably, but it made us all laugh and lightened the mood.

"So, she's good? Was she crying again?"

Alison shook her head, her eyes darkening. "No, I don't think so. She's so…controlled now. I don't know how she does it."

"Have you thought any more about counselling for her?" Mum asked.

"I have, but getting her to agree is impossible. She's seventeen, so I can't force her, as much as I want to. I just wish she'd wake up and see what she's doing to herself and the rest of us."

"You think Kai helps?" I asked. "She told me he does, but I can't see how."

She shrugged. "Oh, I don't know. I can't imagine he is helping either, but if Tegan believes it, I'm not sure if I should try to take that away."

I knew she should. Tegan needed someone to tell her what to do and to mean it. If it were up to me, I'd ban her from ever seeing him again. Hell, I'd ban her from even thinking about him. It wasn't just the jealousy talking either. She needed a clean break from all the bad to focus on healing and moving forward.

Five minutes later, I knocked on her door.

"Come in," she called out.

That made a nice change from her telling me where to go.

She was sitting on her bed, watching *Family Guy*, and she looked fucking gorgeous. She definitely hadn't been crying again, but she did look sad. Her smile hid nothing.

"Hey."

"Hi," she said weakly as she patted the bed.

I sat down, crossing my legs at the ankles, and looked over at her. "You okay?"

"Yeah." She laid her head on my shoulder, and it was ridiculous how much that small contact made my heart race. "I'm sorry about before, Luke."

"It's okay," I replied.

"It's not okay. I just needed you to stop talking, but you need to know that I didn't mean any of it. I really am sorry."

"You're forgiven," I said.

She leant around and hugged me, burying her head in the crook of my neck.

I stroked her long hair. "So, does that mean you want to be with me?"

"Luke..." She hesitated, and I felt my heart drop. "I just..."

Fuck, why did I go there? I turned my head away, not wanting to look her in the eye when we had the same conversation about how she, in fact, didn't want to be with me.

"No, Lucas." She was pulling my arm, so I faced her again. "Look, it's not that I don't want to be. Believe me, I do. I just need to take this slow. Really, really slow."

"So, you do want to be together?"

"Yes. I just don't want to rush anything."

Smiling, I put my arm around her. "Okay, I can do slow. Can I take you on a date? Nothing heavy or serious, just a casual date."

"Yep," she replied. "Just don't expect—"

I held the hand up that wasn't trapped behind her back. "No expectations, I swear. Where do you want to go?"

Laughing, she replied, "The zoo."

"Is that the only place you can think of?"

"Apparently. Anyway, you shouldn't ask me. If you were a real gentleman, you would surprise me."

"You hate surprises."

She shrugged.

"All right then," I said.

"All right what?"

"I'll surprise you."

She shook her head. "No, I was kidding."

"You can't have it both ways, Tegan."

"Yes, I can. I have breasts."

I laughed and tilted my head, getting lost in eyes that held so much hurt. "Thank you."

"For?"

"Giving me a chance."

"I'm giving *us* a chance. Just be patient with me."

I had a feeling this was going to take all the patience I had, but I was willing to give it a go. I had to make things better for her and see what these feelings I had for her were all about.

Tegan

LUCAS TRACED THE BACK of my hand with his thumb.

I didn't know why I'd insisted on taking it slow. Going slow was stupid. I had nothing to lose. So what if it went horribly wrong and he realised I wasn't worth it in a few months'—or weeks'—time? At least we would be having some fun.

I looked up at him. "Lucas?"

Glancing down but still half-watching the TV, he replied, "Yeah?"

"I changed my mind."

I had his full focus then.

"What?"

Christ, he's slow.

I hooked my leg over his and sat up, so I was straddling him. *Yeah, this is definitely a good idea.* His eyebrows shot up, but it took only a second for his hands to grip my waist.

"Are you actually going to kiss me, Luke?"

Laughing once, he pulled me closer, and his lips lightly touched mine. He was a tease, but I liked the way his breath tickled my skin and gave me goose bumps. As he groaned, his hand slid up my side. I wasn't sure how long I could sit on his lap, a centimetre from his face, and not kiss him. My skin was on fire. Everything was on fire, and he was doing nothing but looking at me and copping a feel of the side boob as he went up before settling his hand into my hair.

Whatever self-control he'd had vanished quickly, and then he kissed me hard, desperate, and so deep that it made my toes curl and my body arch into him.

He slightly pulled away and whispered against my mouth, "Are you sure you want to do this?"

I wasn't sure of anything anymore, but he made me feel…something.

"I'm sure," I replied.

He kissed me again until we were both panting, and things were starting to get a little bit more heated.

I could feel how aroused he was, and I was reaching the point where I just thought, *Fuck it*, and I wanted to strip him. Something was shouting, screaming, that it wasn't a good idea, and this time, I couldn't ignore it.

"You okay?" he asked when I removed myself from his lips and his lap.

His hand had just started traveling up my top, and I wasn't convinced that I wanted it there. I wasn't completely convinced that I didn't either.

"I'm fine," I said. "This is just a little soon for me."

I was aware of how ridiculous that sounded, coming from me, but if we wanted this to be anything more than a shag, we were going to have to not get naked.

"Okay. I can wait, you know? I don't expect sex, Tegan. Hell, I didn't even expect you to tell me you wanted to give this a try."

I nodded, biting my lip. Having a sex conversation with a guy was weird. Usually, there would be no questioning or asking. We'd just do it, and then I'd go on my merry way, pretending like everything was still fine.

While watching TV, we fell asleep, and when I woke again, it was getting close to midday. Lucas smiled like he'd won the lottery. Clearly, he saw something in me that wasn't there.

"You want to go get some lunch?" I asked, stretching my muscles out.

"Definitely. I'm starving."

I was so glad he hadn't pushed talking about my dad or asked more questions because I was already sick of people asking me to explain every single thing I did or felt.

Lucas followed me off the bed and downstairs. I gave him a chaste kiss before going into the kitchen.

"You can do that whenever you want, you know, Shorty?"

Oh no. Spinning around, I put my hands on my hips and raised my eyebrow. A little dramatic, but the situation called for it. "I am not short."

He laughed, throwing his head back. "You had to stand on your toes to kiss me."

"Whatever." I turned and walked off.

I was average size, maybe a little shorter. Anyway, he was giant tall. Or maybe just six foot.

We joined my family and his for sandwiches and cake. No one mentioned last night or the fact that Lucas had slept in my room. It did mean that they'd guessed we were together. Mum looked happy, like she thought this was the answer to all my problems. I hoped it was.

"So, are we watching football while the girls are shopping?" Carl asked.

I had to look away. That was something my dad would have done. He had asked my uncle that when he, my aunt, and cousin all came to visit.

According to Mum and Ava, I should feel a sense of closeness to Carl. After all, he shared something with the guy we all loved like crazy. I didn't feel close to him. I felt like I wanted to run every time I saw him.

"Yeah, after, we're all meeting at the pub for dinner," Jake replied, handing his dad a glass of water that Ava had passed to him.

I tried to ignore Carl swallowing a bunch of pills. I didn't know exactly what they all did because I was too scared to ask, but I knew they were basically keeping him alive.

And then I registered what the plans for the day were. Shopping with Mum, Ava, Emily, and Grace. *No.* Not only were Mum and Ava like bloody besties, but also they'd each formed pretty strong friendships with Emily and Grace. I wasn't sure who I wanted to spend the day with less.

"Are you looking forward to it, Tegan?" Grace asked.

No. "Sure," I replied.

Lucas's siblings tolerated me. I could tell that they had major reservations about Lucas being anywhere near me. Not that I blamed them. Still made it a bit awkward though.

"Actually, I might go with the guys and watch football," I said.

Gender stereotypes could fuck off. I'd rather sit in a bar and watch men run around in shorts than go shopping with four women who would undoubtedly have a better time if I weren't there.

Ava frowned and sat down, grabbing a sandwich. "You can't invade their man time, Tegan."

"I don't mind," Lucas said as he put his arm round me.

Well, that confirmed *us* then.

She rolled her eyes. "Yeah, I bet you don't. But what about Jake and Carl?"

Jake shrugged. He minded.

Carl said, "I don't mind at all."

I was pretty sure that Carl only liked me because he felt like he had to.

"See?" I said.

"Okay, fine. I'm sure we'll find some time to talk later," Ava said.

"I'm sure we will," I said sarcastically.

Like she wanted to talk. Recently, all of our conversations had looked a lot like lectures. Miss Perfect didn't like how I had been handling things. Well, I didn't like how she'd handled my handling of things, so we were both shit out of luck there.

After lunch, I went to get ready but ended up in the music room, staring at the piano. I missed Dad so much.

When the hell will the part where it gets better happen?

I felt like I was barely holding on the whole time. Not letting it wash over me was constant and exhausting. So many times, I'd given myself permission to let it in and go through what Mum and Ava had gone through—were going through. But I was too scared of feeling how I'd felt the night he died. I would do *anything* to avoid hurting that much again.

I felt Lucas's arms come round my waist, and he pulled me against his chest. Focusing on him, I turned round and slipped my hands in his.

"You know I've never been to his grave. Do you think he'd be upset?"

Lucas looked shocked that I'd volunteered that piece of information. As a rule, I didn't talk about Dad, but hell, I was trying.

"I didn't know him, but from what I've heard, he was a pretty great guy, so I'm sure he'd understand."

"I think I want to go tomorrow. Will you come with me?"

"Of course I will," he said, flashing that gorgeous smile at me.

I stretched up and kissed him, making him smirk.

"Thanks. Ready to go to the pub?"

"Yeah, come on."

The pub we were going to was my favourite. Inside were the original red brick walls with a huge open fireplace. Tables and chairs were dotted around. There was an area with a large TV on the wall and three big brown leather sofas. The bar was carved out of light oak. There were two other rooms; one was the dining room, and the other one had two pool tables. It was cute and relaxing.

"Tegan!" Gino yelled in his sexy Italian accent. "*Vieni qui, bella.*" Translated, that meant, *Come here, beautiful.*

Gino and his husband, Robbie, owned the pub.

Rounding the bar, he opened his arms and locked me in a bear hug. "I haven't seen you in ages. *Mi sei mancato.*"

"I missed you, too, Gino. Where's Robbie?"

I'd picked up a little Italian from a couple of holidays we'd been on there, and Gino had pretty much forced me to learn.

"Getting changed. His last outfit was awful apparently."

Robbie was perfectly groomed at all times, good looking and so white-blonde that he made me look dark. Gino was the exact opposite with his olive skin, dark brown eyes, and equally dark brown hair.

"Right. Okay then," I said.

He laughed. "So, who are these beautiful men, bella?"

"Gino, this is Jake and Carl." I pointed to them, and he shook their hands. "And this is Lucas." I put my hand on Luke's chest.

He wrapped one hand round my waist and shook Gino's hand with the other.

"Hey," Lucas said.

"Where are Sophie Kai, his friend, Holly, and his other friend, the one who gets uncomfortable when I look at his arse?"

Ah, that would be James.

Yes, he would get uncomfortable when Gino stared, but it was funny. Adam would also get uncomfortable, but I'd seen less and less of him recently. He was constantly busy.

"Kai was going out on his bike and then playing poker with James. I'm not sure what Holly and Sophie are doing."

Robbie appeared at the bar, wearing dark blue denim jeans, a black belt, a crisp black-and-white shirt, and black shoes. "Hey, Tegan," he said, giving me a crushing hug, too. "What can I get you since it looks like Gino hasn't bothered asking?"

Rolling his eyes, Gino walked off to serve another customer.

save me

We ordered drinks and sat down at a table with a good view of the TV. I chose the table closest to the window, so Luke and I could sit on the bench but still have a good view of the screen.

"So, you're on hugging terms with the owners?" Lucas asked.

"I go out a lot."

Before he could say anything, I kissed him, not particularly wanting to get into what I had been like not so long ago. I knew Luke had let it go when his tongue swept my bottom lip. It was also the time that Carl and Jake cleared their throats.

I pulled back, face flushed, and sipped on the drink that'd appeared in front of me while I was kissing Lucas. Not one to get embarrassed easily, Luke glared at his dad and brother.

After about ten minutes, I decided that I didn't like men when they were moody because their team was losing, so I went to sit with Gino. He leant across the bar and poured two shots of Limoncello.

Lucas went outside to get his phone out of his car and came back five minutes later, looking ready to kill. I'd never seen him so angry.

Hopping off the stool, I made my way to him. "Everything okay?"

"No," he said through gritted teeth. "I just met your *amazing* friend. Kai's a real dick, Tegan."

"Where is he? What happened?"

"Was here. Outside with another guy."

James?

My heart was beating a little too fast and not in a good way. "What happened?"

"Apparently, you'll be back in his bed before long."

I frowned. "What? Kai said that?"

"Yeah, and then his mate shoved him back in the car."

What is he doing here? And what the hell is that?

Lucas took a deep breath and brushed my hair behind my ear. "Let's just forget the arsehole, okay?"

I didn't want to forget Kai. Something was going on. He had never shown any jealousy before. We were friends and had agreed on that. I felt a sinking cold feeling in my chest. I needed him as a friend, but I couldn't have that if he wanted more.

"Was he drunk?"

Lucas snorted. "Sure looked it. Nice catch, by the way."

"Hey!" I snapped.

"Sorry. Seriously, let's forget him."

Nodding, I followed Luke back to the table. Something wasn't quite right with what he'd just told me. Kai didn't know I was with Lucas yet, and I didn't believe he would've just said something like that unprovoked. I was going to find out though.

Tegan

I WOKE UP, STILL feeling absolutely exhausted. I'd not slept all that much in the past few days, and it was taking its toll.

Lucas would be leaving tomorrow, and I wanted to ask him to stay a bit longer. But he had to work.

I found myself back in the music room at five in the morning, staring at the piano. Dad's aftershave scent still filled the room, or I was imagining it did. It was comforting and painful at the same time. When it finally faded away, that would be it forever.

The room felt smaller. The walls crept in inch by inch until I felt like I was in a prison cell. My heart raced, and I braced myself against the piano.

Shit, I can't breathe properly.

Someone touched me, and I guessed it was Lucas because the arms curled around my waist. His chest was pressed to my back. I concentrated on staying in reality and not letting my mind pull me under.

"Hey," he said, "you all right?"

He didn't sound all that concerned, so he'd obviously missed my near meltdown. I wasn't all right. I felt like I was going to collapse in a ball and cry for hours, but instead, I nodded.

Calm down. Push it away.

I forced Dad out of my head and heightened the wall around my heart. *Fuck feelings.*

"What are you doing up so early?" I asked. *I have got to get out of here soon.*

"I went to sneak into your room, but you weren't there."

"Oh. Well, give me a minute, and I'll go back up." Walking out of his arms, I gave him a flirty smile over my shoulder and went back to my bedroom.

No less than ten seconds after I'd gotten back in bed, Lucas came through the door, quietly shutting it behind him.

I gasped. "How dare you sneak into my room and break the house rules."

He rolled his eyes, smiling, and climbed onto the bed. I waited for a smart-arse reply, but it was clear that wasn't his next move when he kissed me, laying me down on the mattress. I preferred his plan.

His tongue slipped in my mouth, and the kiss became a little more urgent. He pressed half of his weight down on me, and I wrapped my legs around his waist. Being with him like this felt more than it had with anyone else, probably because all I'd experienced was meaningless, but I still felt like something was missing. That something was probably me though.

"Lucas, I'm ready," I whispered against his lips.

He pulled back and rested on his arms. His green eyes were filled with lust and uncertainty. "I don't think you are, Tegan. You might want it right now, but I think you'll regret it after. I'm not taking that risk. I can wait."

"You're so sweet, you know."

I was ready for sex, how could I not be with my track record, but perhaps he was right. I didn't want to rush yet another thing with him.

save me

I ran my finger along the edge of his jaw and bit my lip. "Just because we're not gonna have sex doesn't mean we can't fool around a little."

His eyes darkened. "Really?"

I nodded and pulled his head down, so I could kiss him. He was back into it in an instant, tongue wrestling with mine and hands wandering down, caressing my sides, as he headed for the ultimate goal.

My body was on fire. I was so definitely ready for fooling around.

Lucas's hand reached my pyjama shorts, and I gasped as he lightly brushed his knuckles between my legs. I arched my hips, needing more friction, and moaned his name into his mouth. When his hand dipped under my shorts, I thought my heart was going to stop altogether. I was so turned on, so needy, that all I wanted was for him to get me off, like right now.

He kissed me harder and slipped his finger inside. His tongue moved quicker against mine as he swirled his finger around inside me. I pushed up, meeting him thrust for thrust. My fingernails clawed the fabric covering his back as he took me higher and higher.

He added a second finger, and I bit down on his lip as I fell apart, clamping around him as I climaxed.

"Shit," he murmured against my mouth once the aftershocks of my orgasm had worn off. "I've wanted to do that for a while."

I'd wanted him to do that for a while.

My chest heaved, and I groaned at the loss of him as he pulled out and sat up.

"You can do that anytime you like," I said.

Smirking, Lucas got off the bed and rearranged his erection so that it was less obvious.

"What are you doing?" I asked.

Shouldn't he be taking his jeans off?

"Going back to my room before we get caught."

"What? But I haven't even played with you yet."

141

He laughed and shook his head. "Plenty of time for that, shorty. You can owe me one."

Smug bastard wasn't getting anything from me. I narrowed my eyes as he laughed again and left.

Lucas was sitting in the lounge, drinking coffee with everyone else, when I walked in after my shower. I sat next to him, making sure he saw me glare at least once.

"You still want me to come with you today?" he asked, trying not to smile.

No.

I didn't want to go to Dad's grave at all, not ever, but I had to do it.

I swallowed what felt like sand or broken glass. "Yeah, if you don't mind."

He leant down and kissed the side of my head. "Of course not, babe."

How am I going to visit Dad's grave when I almost fell apart in the fucking music room this morning?

But, apparently, I was never going to get better if I didn't try. Personally, I didn't think there was anything wrong with continuing how I had been. I didn't hurt nearly as much as Mum and Ava did.

I stared down at my dad's headstone and held on to Lucas's hand as tightly as I could. It was warm, but I felt icy cold, and I was trembling. He watched me, and although I couldn't focus on anything but a lump of stone with Dad's name carved into it, I knew Lucas was contemplating picking me up and taking me home.

I felt nothing real. There was just a cold numbness that I was growing used to.

"Tegan?" Lucas said. He sounded far away.

I looked up. "Please take me home now, Luke."

save me

Frowning, he nodded. I could see the questions in his eyes. He wanted to know why I was an emotionless robot.

"All right, come on."

We drove back to my house in silence, but it wasn't awkward. I could feel his mind working, trying to figure out what was going on with me and how he could fix it. I appreciated it, but there wasn't a magical fix. If there were, I would've taken it long ago.

On the way back, my phone beeped with a text from Kai, and I was glad to have a distraction.

Party at mine tomorrow. You in?

I wasn't sure if I wanted to go. Well, I did want to, but I probably shouldn't, not after what he'd said to Lucas. But I had a feeling there was more to it than what Lucas had told me. Kai wasn't a bad person.

I tapped back a reply.

Count me in.

After I put my phone away, Lucas reached over and took my hand in his. "You okay?"

"Yeah, I'm fine," I replied.

We got back to mine, and Mum immediately started quizzing me on how it had gone. I told her it was fine, and she pushed harder, not believing that I was okay.

"Mum, I'm all right, but I don't wanna talk about it."

Taking a step back, as if I'd burned her, she looked away. She seemed to flip the switch on me so quickly.

Fuck's sake! Gritting my teeth, I walked off. I repeated in my head, *She's only trying to help,* but it did little to stop my mood from plummeting.

Lucas followed me upstairs but wisely said nothing. We watched a couple of films until Mum called us down for dinner. Walking ahead to talk to his dad and brother, Lucas entered the kitchen before me. I took a detour and opened the music room door.

143

My insides twisted up as I remembered the last time we'd played the piano together. It was the day he'd died, and he had been helping me practice for my exam. I walked deeper into the room, and the closer I got to the piano, the thinner the air became.

I felt myself sink to the floor, sink deeper into the water, and when I hit the ground, I curled my arms around my legs.

I felt the first sob right down in my gut. I missed him so much that I felt like I couldn't breathe. A fog of black smoke engulfed me, and all I could focus on was the gaping void where Dad used to be and the pain of knowing I had to do it all without him now.

"Why did you leave me?" I whispered angrily. I gave in to the grief, sobbing until my throat was raw.

Tegan

MY HEAD WAS BANGING, and it wasn't even from alcohol. Crying for most of the night until I had fallen asleep really made me feel like shit and not just physically.

It was only bloody six in the morning. *Why the hell is that the time my body decides to wake?*

Lucas was asleep beside me. After he'd found me crying my heart out on the music room floor, he'd carried me up to bed. I guessed Mum had relaxed on the no-boyfriends-in-your-room-overnight rule this time.

I carefully got out of bed, not wanting to wake him and have to convince him that I was okay just yet. I went downstairs and curled up on the sofa. Me and Dad always got up early—not six early, granted—and would either watch rubbish morning TV or quietly play the piano.

I took a few deep breaths. *Keep it together.*

There was no way I wanted to feel the way I had last night. I didn't know how Mum and Ava allowed themselves to go through that every single day. I was done.

Grabbing my phone, I sent Kai a text. I still needed to talk to him about Lucas, and hanging out with him would take my mind off everything.

> *What time tonight?*

His reply took a couple of minutes.

> *8. What the fuck time are you texting me at?*

Oops. It was early.

> *Sorry. Couldn't sleep.*

> *You're on drink duty for that. Lucas coming?*

No, he's going home today.

> *Cool. I'll pick you up at 7.*

It started at eight—unless he was really serious about me being on drink duty and I'd be helping with setting everything up. Also, Lucas leaving wasn't *cool.*

I felt slightly better that I would be doing something, getting out of the house tonight. I felt like I'd been run over. I was emotionally drained and needed to not think. Vodka would also help.

But how will I tell Lucas? He wouldn't be happy about it. Not that he had a right to tell me what to do. I didn't feel like I should have to obey him, but I didn't want to piss him off or make him feel insecure.

"Morning, honey," Mum said as she sat beside me.

I tried so hard to smile, but I just didn't have the energy. "Morning."

"How are you feeling today?"

"I'm all right."

Lie, lie, lie.

"Do you want coffee? I know I could do with one."

"Please, Mum."

It was another hour before anyone else got up, and Mum started making bacon sandwiches for breakfast. Lucas and I spent the rest of the time in my room—not fooling around—until he had to leave.

"What are you doing on Saturday?" he asked as he finished packing his bag.

"Nothing. Why?"

"I'm racing again. You want to come watch?"

I smiled halfheartedly. "Yeah, I'll come, but I can't guarantee I'll be watching."

He chuckled and winked. "I'm not going to get hurt."

"You'd better not. I kinda like you."

"You only kinda like me?"

"Yes, only a bit."

"Thanks," he replied sarcastically.

I giggled, fell forward into his arms, and kissed him. He slipped his tongue in my mouth, making my body heat up. I was so ready for a repeat of yesterday.

His head wasn't in the gutter with mine as he pulled back and picked up his bag. "I'm gonna miss you, babe."

"Me, too," I replied.

I followed behind him, feeling deflated that he was leaving. At least I had tonight to look forward to.

Jake bundled their bags into the boot, and Grace helped her dad into the car even though he was fully capable of doing it himself. I got that they needed to make sure he was okay though.

I flopped my head forward on Lucas's chest, and he kissed my hair.

"I'll be back on Friday night to take you out, and I'll see you again on Saturday," he said.

"Where are we going on Friday?"

"Don't start that again."

I pouted.

"Hey, I…" Taking a deep breath, he said, "I know this has all been fast, and we're probably one of the most unlikely couples, but…I…I love you, Tegan."

I blinked in surprise. *He what?* My first thought was, *Why? What is there about me that he could possibly love?*

I didn't want to love again, but there was something about him that made me feel like I was worthy. But it also made me question his sanity at the same time.

If Lucas could love me, then surely I wasn't that evil, or there was something redeemable in me. He made my heart ache in a good way for the first time since my dad had died.

If Lucas was willing to put everything into us, then so was I. "I love you, too."

Grinning from ear to ear, he kissed me.

"God, I am so glad you said it back. That was pretty terrifying."

"Of course I did," I replied.

"Lucas, come on!" Jake yelled from Luke's car.

Sighing, he gave me another kiss and walked away, mouthing, *I love you.*

"You okay, Tegan?" Ava asked as she slung her arm over my shoulder while they drove off, out of sight.

"Yeah, I'm good." At least I thought I was. That moment with Lucas was so surreal, and I wasn't completely sure I believed him. "I need to get ready for tonight."

Mum and Ava worriedly looked at each other and then turned back to me.

"You're going out tonight?" Mum asked quietly.

I rolled my eyes. "Yeah, but don't worry; it's not like before. I just want to have fun with my friends. The past couple of days have been kinda hard," I replied while looking at the ground, willing myself to keep it together. I was tired of crying so much, and I'd only done it for a day.

"Okay," Mum replied. There was not one part of her that was okay with it, but she still didn't say a word.

save me

At half past six, Sophie came over, so we could do our makeup together and have some pre-party drinks.

She frowned into the mirror, her eyebrows knitting together. "It's too revealing, isn't it?" she asked, turning her body from side to side and staring at her chest.

"No, Soph, you look good."

There was definite cleavage, but it didn't look bad.

She turned around and wolf-whistled. "Very hot, Tegan! You on the pull tonight?"

I slapped her arm. "No, I have a boyfriend, remember?"

"He doesn't have to know."

"Stop being a ho. I'm not going to cheat on him."

She rolled her grey eyes. "Monogamy is overrated."

It was only overrated because her ex-boyfriend had cheated on her. She was thirteen at the time, and he'd kissed the new kid. Since then, Sophie had had a love-hate relationship with guys—one that saw to her screwing whomever she wanted and telling them to do one after. Now, she had a bit of a name for herself, but she wasn't the whore people thought she was. People were rarely as bad as others judged them to be.

Kai called at seven to say he was just down the road. Understandably, he didn't want to come knock on the door, for fear of my mother going psycho again. I took one last shot of vodka, winced as it burned its way down, and headed out to Kai's car.

"Evening," Kai said with a cheeky grin on his face.

"Good evening, gorgeous," Sophie purred.

Well, she's waited three seconds. New record, ladies and gentlemen.

Kai grinned at her, but I could feel his resistance. He'd mentioned in passing that he wasn't into easy women anymore. Fuck knew why he had gone for me then. I hadn't exactly made it difficult when we met. Whatever his reasons—slow

149

couple of months maybe—I was glad. I liked having his friendship.

I sat back against the passenger seat and felt relaxed, properly relaxed, for the first time in days. There were no expectations with Kai, and he didn't try to dig deep to find out what was wrong and fix me. I appreciated that more than I could ever express.

Kai pulled into his drive, and we went inside.

"What do you need us to do?" I asked.

Sophie frowned. "Us?"

"Yes, you're helping, too!"

"Sophie, you can move the end table into the corner to make room for the speaker. Freddie will be here in a minute, so watch out for him."

"Is Freddie hot?"

Kai blinked, his dark lashes fanned out over his eyes. "Well, I don't think so."

"Yes, he is," I said even though I had no idea who he was.

We'd be here forever if I didn't just tell her what she wanted to hear.

"Perfect." She clapped her hands and put her bag down, ready to get to work.

"You can help me with drinks," Kai said, leading us through to the kitchen.

"Can I talk to you about something?" I asked once Sophie was distracted, watching out the window for her *hot* man.

He looked over his shoulder as he pulled bottles and bottles of alcohol out of the cupboard. "Sure."

"It's about what you said to Lucas at the pub."

He stilled. "Yeah...look, I'm sorry."

"Why did you say it?"

He ran his hand through his jet-black hair. "I don't know. He was being cocky, and then I was a dick. Men do that shit, right?"

Being cocky meant, Lucas had told Kai that we were together and possibly told him to back off. I wanted to ask what Lucas had done, but I didn't want to drag it out and make it into a big thing. As long as it was done and I was okay with both of them, I was happy.

"That's all it was? Nothing else to it?"

"I know the score between us, if that's what you're asking. He mouthed off, and so did I. Don't worry; it's done."

"Good, because I really want you in my life."

"Back atcha, princess. Now, want a shot before the party wankers drink my house dry?"

Laughing, I threw my bag to the side and nodded.

About an hour later, the party was in full swing, and I received a text from Lucas.

I'm bored as hell! What are you doing? I miss you.

He didn't know I was here. I'd chickened out earlier and not mentioned anything. But I couldn't lie to him now, so I replied.

I'm at Kai's party with Sophie. Miss you, too.

The *with Sophie* part was incredibly important. Not that it should be. He hung out with friends of the opposite sex. As far as I knew, he'd never slept with any of them, but that didn't matter. The physical part of my relationship with Kai was over.

Okay, I'll leave you to it. Have fun, and I'll call you later.

I wasn't entirely sure how to take that, so I decided to take it at face value and believe that he was okay and genuinely wanted me to have fun. He'd said he trusted me, and I'd not given him a reason not to. I wasn't going to either.

"You okay?" Kai asked as he sat down and handed me a beer.

"Thanks. Yeah, I'm good."

"Sophie's looking for you."

I groaned. "Any idea what she wants?"

His big schoolboy grin told me he did, but he shook his head anyway. Groaning again, I went to find her. It didn't take long. She was on the sofa, pouting.

"What's up?" I asked, flopping down next to her.

"What do you think of him?" she asked, pointing to a guy talking to a girl by the window.

"He's nice." *But he's already talking to a girl.*

She scrunched her nose up and proceeded to quiz me on the hotness of every other male in the room. "Yeah, he's nice but nowhere near as hot as Lucas or Kai."

"Hey, hands off," I warned, laughing.

She'd just said it to wind me up anyway. I shouldn't have taken the bait.

She raised her eyebrows. "Which one?"

"Lucas," I replied, rolling my eyes.

"Seriously? Kai is unbelievably gorgeous. If I were you, I *so* would."

"You're not me, and I already have. I'm happy with Lucas, thank you."

"Well, if you're happy with Lucas, then I'll go see Kai."

I gestured my hand in Kai's direction, and she squealed, kissed me on the cheek, and ran off.

Good luck, Kai.

I sort of wanted to go and help him, but he hadn't warned me that I'd be helping Sophie with choosing tonight's lay, so he could fucking fend for himself.

I ended up doing a line of vodka shots with Holly in the kitchen. After the sixth one, I was stumbling around, and my head was swimming. It wasn't doing much for the persistent headache, but I didn't care.

save me

Kai stopped beside me and threw his arm around my shoulder. Lucky for me because I had been seconds away from falling on my arse.

"How many of them have you had?" Looking at all the empty shot glasses, he laughed.

"I think six," I slurred.

Kai chuckled, poured three more, and handed one to me and Holly, keeping one for himself.

"Last one, okay?" he said, clinking the glass against mine.

I nodded, and my head hurt more. "Yeah, okay." I downed the shot, not even feeling the burn anymore as the alcohol slid down my throat.

By three in the morning, everyone had left, and I was lying on the sofa, watching the ceiling spin. Sophie had gone upstairs with some guy, and Kai was having a real hard time with it—because they were in *his* bedroom.

"They're in my bed, Tegan," he said for the four thousandth time.

"Yes, Kai, I know."

"I'll never get my bed clean. God, I'm gonna have to buy another one tomorrow."

"You could just change the sheets," I said, giggling. "I'm sure they won't make too much of a mess."

"Glad you find this funny."

"Well, if you had been nicer to her, it could've been you up there."

"No, thanks," he replied, turning his nose up. He suddenly laughed. "Hey, if you wanna go home, you have to go up there and get her," he said.

That wiped the smile off my face. I loved Sophie, but there was no way I wanted to see her naked and filled with cock. "I'm so not going up there. I need a blanket."

153

"Sorry, I'm not eighty."

I glared, and he pulled his hoodie over his head.

All right…

"Have this," he said, laying the oversized hoodie over my body.

I smiled and tried to make sense of all the moving ink on his arms. As I was drunk, the waves looked like they were actually crashing against the shore.

I yawned and curled up tighter. "Wake me up when they're done," I said.

Then, I fell asleep almost immediately.

I woke up to the light blinding me. My head throbbed, and my throat was dry. Groaning, I looked over my shoulder and saw Kai beside me, right on the edge of the sofa. I'd snuggled against the back of it, and he must've gotten on behind me.

That wasn't the best position to wake up in even though he was barely touching me and we were both fully clothed. I slowly sat up and pushed myself up onto my feet, so I was crouching. I had a headache from hell, the room was spinning, and I had to pull a fucking ninja move just to get off the sofa, unnoticed.

Standing up fully, I used the back of the sofa to steady myself, and I crept forward, so I could get off at the end.

I almost made it when I heard a deep chuckle.

"The walk of shame has changed," Kai said.

I winced and turned around. He was lying on his back now with both hands behind his head. His eyes had never looked so light and as amused as they did right now.

Prick.

"I didn't want to wake you."

"We didn't do anything, Tegan. Holly and James had the spare room, and there was no way I was going in mine."

"I know. It's fine."

"I was a perfect gentleman."

Glaring, I asked, "What do you mean?"

"Well, you kept begging me for sex, but I had to turn you down because you were far too drunk."

I laughed and rolled my eyes. "Of course I did. Now, I really need to pee, so I'm gonna go." I hopped down from the sofa, proud that I hadn't fallen over, and went to the bathroom.

Sophie and the others came down shortly after I'd woken up, and Kai cooked us bacon, sausages, eggs, beans, and toast. It was much appreciated and helped to soak up the alcohol still sloshing around in my system. Sophie's special friend for the night didn't join us; he'd kissed her and left.

Kai dropped us off at Soph's and went back to go ride his bike for a while.

"So, you're really telling Lucas about last night?" she asked again.

I'd told her about waking up with Kai beside me, and she thought I was crazy to tell Lucas. Even though nothing had happened, I had a feeling he'd want to know something like that.

"Yeah, I have to."

"No, you don't. How would he ever find out? It will only piss him off, and nothing even happened."

"I know, but if it were me, I'd want to know."

"And what if he breaks up with you?"

I gulped.

"Exactly, Tegan. You'd be an idiot to tell him."

"But it would be worse if he found out later."

"Well, I'm not gonna tell him, and Kai..." She stopped and smiled. "Yeah, Kai might. They really don't get along, do they?"

"They don't, but Kai wouldn't do that." *Ugh, morals suck.*

I walked home after our talk and saw a note on the counter from Mum, saying they'd left to go to the village fair for the day and to meet up with them when I was ready. There was something I had to do before I went out.

Flopping down on my bed, I resigned myself to the inevitable. I was going to tell Lucas.

"Hey," he answered on the first ring.

"Hi," I said quietly. My stomach was all tied up in knots. *Please don't take this badly.*

"You okay, babe?"

"Yeah, but I need to tell you something about last night."

He hesitated and then said, "Go on."

I took a deep breath. "Last night, I stayed at Kai's with Sophie. We weren't going to, but she met someone and spent all night in Kai's room with him. I fell asleep on the sofa." I paused a second to breathe. "I woke up, and Kai was sleeping beside me. Nothing happened, I promise."

Silence.

"Luke, I'm sorry. Please say something."

"I'll call you later."

"No, Luke—"

"Tegan, you know I don't like the guy, so please, give me some time. I'll call you later." He ended the call.

Fuck's sake! Sighing in frustration, I buried my head in the pillow and groaned.

Tegan

LESS THAN AN HOUR later, there was a knock on the door, and Lucas stood smiling sheepishly behind it. He winced at the pissed off look on my face. "Hey, babe."

"*Hey, babe?* That's all you have to say to me?"

"Can I come in?"

I stepped out of the way to let him through even though I felt like slamming the door in his overreacting face.

"Calmed down?" I asked.

"I'm sorry. I know I didn't handle that well."

"No, you really didn't." I tilted my head back and tied my hair into a loose ponytail. "Nothing happened."

"I know. I believe you. I guess it just freaked me out because of your past with him."

"Hey, key word in there, Luke, is *past.*"

"Yeah. I'm sorry. On the way over here, I was thinking about how badly I'd reacted, and I realised that you didn't have to tell me because I never would've found out, but I love that you did. I trust you."

Sophie was so wrong. I was glad I'd told him the truth. I wasn't that honest and open with anyone else in my life, but I was really trying with him.

"So, are we cool?" he asked.

"We're cool," I replied, stepping into his embrace. "Thank you for coming all this way, so we could sort it out."

"Of course. Do you want me to stick around?"

"I thought you had a lot to do?"

"I do, but I want to make sure you're all right."

"I am now." I kissed him. "And I don't want to keep you. I know I've been doing that a lot, and I'm meeting up with my mum and Ava at the fair"

"I'll drop you off then."

I was happy now that we'd sorted things out, and after a quick change of clothes, I was ready to go to the crappy fair.

"Are you sure you don't want me to stay longer?" he asked as he pulled into a parking space.

"No, it's fine, really." I smiled. "I'll see you on Friday."

He kissed me again.

I reluctantly pried my hands off him, got out of the car, and waved as he drove away. I headed off to try to find Mum and Ava, but the steady stream of floats driving through town was making it hard.

Someone grabbed me from behind, making me jump. I spun around to fucking punch them but stopped when I saw who it was.

"Damn it, Kai!"

I punched him on the arm anyway, and he laughed.

"Your face just then," he said, trying and failing to get a grip on his laughing.

"Whatever," I mumbled, folding my arms over my chest.

"I'm sorry, princess."

He wasn't.

"Buy me an ice cream, and I'll forgive you."

He smiled. "You're easy. Come on."

"What are you doing here anyway? Didn't think this was the sort of thing you'd be into."

He shrugged. "Got bored."

We ordered ice cream and headed deeper into the parade.

"So, Sophie and Mark never showed their faces again?"

"Nope, but at least they're in his bed."

We turned the corner, and I finally saw Mum and Ava looking at a jewellery stall. Kai stopped walking as he saw them.

"Are you scared of my mum?" I asked, giggling at the expression on his face.

He quickly composed himself. "No, I'm not scared."

"Come on then." I smiled.

He reluctantly walked with me. I knew it was awkward, but Lucas, Mum, and Ava needed to get over it. Kai was my friend, and there wasn't anything anyone could say to change that.

"Hey," I said to their backs as we approached.

Mum and Ava spun around.

"Oh, hi, honey." Mum's eyes fell on Kai, and he smiled a little too much. "Kai."

"Hello, Mrs Pennells," he replied.

I laughed but covered it up with a cough. Kai nudged my arm.

"So, what are you two doing?" Mum asked, eyeing both of us.

Oh, just off to shag on a float!

I hated that they were so suspicious of me and Kai. *I wouldn't bloody cheat!*

"Not much." I licked the cone as my ice cream dribbled down the side.

"Oh. We're going to get a drink now if you two would like to join us?" Mum asked, looking at Kai.

Kai smiled uncomfortably again. "Er, sure, that would be great. Thanks."

"Good, well, let's go."

This is going to be a barrel of laughs.

Mum and Ava led the way to the local pub, and Kai and I trailed behind, neither of us really wanting to have a drink with them.

He couldn't have just said no?

"Why don't you find a table, and I'll bring the drinks over?" Mum said.

"I'll get them," Kai replied.

Mum shook her head. "Please, I want to. What would you like?"

"Okay, thank you. Foster's, please."

I couldn't help admiring how cute Kai was when he was nervous. He didn't seem to care that much at Ava's party, so I wasn't all that sure what had happened to change him from not giving a single fuck to nervous and super polite.

"You girls want your usual?" Mum asked.

We nodded, but I was pretty sure that Mum didn't know my real usual, and I'd end up with a bloody Coke.

Kai, Ava, and I found a table near the window and sat down. The silence was weird. Ava didn't like Kai and made no attempt to just be nice anyway. I tapped my fingers on the wooden table while we waited for Mum to come back. Six seconds into my "It's Raining Men" finger-drum solo, Kai slammed his hand down over mine.

"That's getting annoying fast," he said, removing his hand and pointedly staring at me.

Well, the silence is getting awkward.

Ava cleared her throat.

Right, apologies. I forgot the touch of a hand is a promise now.

Mum walked over to the table with a tray holding two glasses of wine, a beer, and my damn Coke. I would need something a lot stronger if I was going to get through this.

Why did Kai agree to it again?

"Thank you, Mrs Pennells," Kai said.

"You're welcome, Kai."

I wanted to bash my head on the table. *How much sickly politeness can they fit into one small exchange?*

As much as he didn't want to care, Kai cared a lot about what my mum thought of him. I didn't. She could hate him if she wanted; it wasn't going to change my mind. I didn't give a single fuck what people thought about me.

We all made it through the first drink. Yes, Kai and I practically downed ours. Having drinks with someone who thought you were committing sin with the person on your left was plain uncomfortable. I wasn't sure why all the judgment since both Mum and Ava had friends of the opposite sex that they managed not to screw every time they set their eyes on them. *Double standards.*

"We're going to check out more of the fair," I said, standing up.

When Kai leapt out of his seat at the first syllable, I realised just how bad it'd been for him. I thought it was pretty sweet of him to suffer through that for me. It couldn't be that great to sit with people who had a clear dislike of you.

"Okay, we'll see you at home later then," Mum said.

"Thank you for the drink, Alison," Kai said, following behind me, just as eager to get away.

Once we were outside, he turned to me. "Well, I think it's safe to say, I'm still on their shit list."

"I'm sorry about them."

He shrugged. "Don't worry 'bout it. I kinda understand why they're not my biggest fans."

So could I, but they could have at least been polite to the guy. He'd actually done nothing wrong at all.

"So, how come Lucas isn't here?"

"He's street racing."

Stopping dead in his tracks, he faced me. "Racing?"

"Yep. What's with the face? I find it hard to believe you've never raced a car before."

"No, I have…when I was seventeen."

"Oh, and what do you do for fun now since you're so beyond racing? Play chess?" I teased.

Kai's eyebrow rose suggestively, and he smirked. "I think you know what I do for fun now."

I didn't blush often, but the way he looked at me, like he was replaying one of the times we'd had *fun* in his head, heated my cheeks.

I slapped his arm. "Stop thinking about it."

There was an uneasy feeling as I remembered some of those times. I shouldn't be thinking about it now. I was with Lucas.

Shaking his head, he batted my hand away. "Can't. Sorry. Once you've been above, beneath, behind, or beside someone, you reserve the right to fuck or re-fuck them in your mind whenever you want."

I wasn't too sure what to say to that, so after an extended blank stare, I moved on and pointed to a Knock the Coconut Down game. "Come on, you can win me one of those giant Smurfs."

"Good morning. Are you having a go for the little lady?" the balding man behind the table asked.

I wanted to punch his peanut-shaped head in for the *little lady* comment. *Arsehole.*

Kai nodded, and I couldn't miss the fucking smirk as he watched me shoot daggers at the sweaty mess in front of us.

"Three balls, three chances, to knock the coconut off. You get one down, and you get a stuffed toy."

It wasn't bloody rocket science.

He handed Kai the three wooden balls, and Kai threw the first one. Shit, he had a good throw. It smashed into the coconut, knocking it sideways, but it didn't fall.

"Good shot, son," Sweaty Mess said, chuckling obnoxiously loud.

He was on my bloody list since his comment, so now, everything he did was grating on me.

Wanker.

The look of determination on Kai's face melted my heart a little. It was only a cheap stuffed toy, but because I wanted it, he was going all out to get it. The next ball was swung harder and launched through the air with purpose. The coconut dropped to the floor with a light thud.

Sweaty Mess burst into laughter again, holding his potbelly. "Nice. Which one ya want, little lady?"

I wanted to tell him to shove it, but Kai had won it and probably pulled a muscle in his arm from throwing that hard, so I forced myself to smile as I pointed to a Smurf above my head.

"I thought you'd want the girl," he said, laughing again and reaching up to take it down.

I wanted to back up, take a good run, and slam my body into his stomach. I was small and didn't weigh a whole lot, but I was confident I could knock the air out of him.

"Thank you," I said to Sweaty Mess. Then, I repeated the same to Kai, my smile turning genuine for my friend.

"You're welcome. Couldn't have you *not* getting what you wanted now, could we, princess?"

Little prick. I glared, which only made him laugh.

"I'm calling him Kai," I said, holding up the Smurf.

"You're naming a teddy after me?" He raised his dark eyebrow and turned his nose up in disgust.

I nodded.

His distaste quickly morphed into something that looked a lot like it would get him in trouble. "You going to cuddle up to it while you're naked and in bed?"

And there it is.

"Oh, yeah, every night," I replied sarcastically.

"You know you could have the real thing." He threw his arm over my shoulder as we walked toward the horse carousel.

"Well, thanks for the offer, but this Kai is way cuter." I held up the Smurf for emphasis.

Shaking his head, amused, he helped me get on a horse and stepped back.

"You're not coming on?"

"If you think I'm getting on a fucking pink pony and going round and round in circles for—"

"Okay, okay. I'll see you in a minute."

"You'll see me about twenty times in that minute."

The horse lifted as the ride started to move.

163

"Lucky me," I replied dryly, earning myself a wink and a half-smile.

Tegan

"PRINCESS, I FEEL LIKE a five-year-old," Kai said, looking over at the small children in the teacup next to ours.

"That's because you're acting like one. Smurf Kai is maturer."

"Stop calling the damn Smurf Kai!" He chuckled, shaking his head.

When the ride stopped, we jumped off. We were having some good old-fashioned immature fun.

"Where to now?" Kai asked.

"Um..." I stumbled slightly but managed to correct it.

"All right, you need water." He dragged me through the crowd to the food stalls and sat me down on a free table. "Stay," he said, pointing at me and trying not to smile.

Saluting, I leant back on the chair as he walked off to one of the stalls. I watched him buy three bottles of water—*two of those have better be for him*—and then he walked back over to me.

Kai made me drink a whole bottle, saying I needed to sober up. I wasn't exactly drunk. We'd only snuck a couple of beers in between rides, but I did as he'd said. He stretched his arms, his T-shirt pulling up to reveal some of that mouth-watering six-pack. I quickly looked away, and when I looked back, he was smirking like an idiot.

"How come you're still here? Earlier, you said you were leaving," I asked before he could say anything.

He clutched his heart. "Do you want me to go?"

"No. I'm glad you're here. The fair is so bloody boring."

"Why did you come?"

I looked down at the ground. I came for Dad. Just before he'd died, he'd promised Mum he would go this year.

"Hey?" He lightly pulled my arm, getting me to look at him.

"Um, I came for…" I took a deep breath. "For my dad."

Kai leant over, wrapping his arm around my back. Resting my head against his shoulder I sighed.

Do not cry. Get it the fuck together.

I hadn't spoken to Kai about my dad, even after the incident at Ava's party. He knew, of course, but he never mentioned it, and nothing had changed.

"Are you okay?" he whispered.

I nodded, unable to speak yet.

"He would be so proud of you."

I pushed my face into him, clenching my jaw. "No, he really wouldn't. He'd be disappointed."

I knew I had been acting like a bitch. Somewhere, deep down, I was still there, but I didn't even know how to find that girl anymore. I had no idea how to go through the grief my mum and sister had gone through and make it back out again. I couldn't do it. I was weaker than them and found it easier to shut everything out.

"Shh, it's okay." He rested his head on mine and held me tight. "You could never be a disappointment, Tegan. I see you, what's underneath the pain, and I know you're not a bad person. You're incredible and beautiful."

"You forgot, intelligent and funny," I joked, blinking back more tears.

I couldn't even comment on his "I see you, what's underneath the pain" comment.

He laughed and replied, "Yeah, and modest, sarcastic, hard working, and—"

"Okay, I get it," I cut him off, slapping his chest and laughing. Wow, I had gone from meltdown to laughing in seconds. "Thank you, Kai."

"Anytime, *princess*. You want me to walk you home?" he asked.

"Can we go to yours?" I didn't want to go home to the lecture about Kai that I knew would be waiting for me.

"Sure, but I've not got my car or bike here."

"Wait. Walk?"

He smirked. "No car."

I laughed and shook my head. "Fine, let's go." Grabbing his hand, I stood and pulled him up too.

Kai and I spent the rest of the afternoon at his watching films and having a small water throwing fight, which I lost. I changed into one of his T-shirts, as mine was completely soaked, and we settled down on the sofa to order something to eat.

"So, who are you avoiding at home then?" he asked after ordering the pizza.

I stared at him for a minute. *How the hell does he know that?*

He smiled. "I do pay attention to you."

I flopped back on the sofa. "Mum. Ava, too, probably. They're gonna give me a hard time over you."

"Right, because you're in love with me even though you have a boyfriend." He said *boyfriend* as if it were a dirty word.

167

"Yeah, that's it," I replied sarcastically, rolling my eyes, making him laugh.

I really didn't care what anyone said. Kai and I hadn't crossed any lines, and I really wanted him in my life. No one was going to stop me from being his friend. Ava could judge all she wanted.

We ate pizza and played the Xbox. Well, he played. I was rubbish at it.

It was starting to get dark, and I already had three missed calls and four texts from Mum.

Kai drove me home and stopped just down the road. "You want me to stay here?" he asked.

"Nah, the lecture's gonna happen anyway."

He nodded and we pulled up outside my house. The front door opened before I had even got out. Not a good sign.

"Just be honest. No one can blame you for loving me." He laughed.

I slapped his arm hard. It hurt my hand, but he didn't flinch.

"Er, Tegan?" He nodded toward my house.

Lucas, Jake, and Grace were standing outside with Mum and Ava, and none of them looked particularly happy.

"Oh, crap."

"So, this is gonna be awkward, huh?"

Understatement.

We both got out of the car, and he walked to the boot to get the Smurf. Kai wouldn't let me have it in the car because people might see.

I smiled at Lucas, which he returned with a fake one.

"Hello, Kai," Lucas practically growled.

"Lucas." Kai nodded once and turned to me. "Here, don't forget Smurf Kai." He handed it to me.

"Oh, now, it's Kai, is it?" I whispered.

"Hey, you're the one who named it."

I glared at him for a second.

He laughed and walked round to the driver's side. "See you tomorrow, princess."

"Hey, Luke. How come you're back?" I smiled and hugged him.

He loosely put his arms around me, not his usual greeting. "I came back to see you."

No, he came back because Mum had called him, asking if I was with him when I hadn't gone home, and he'd guessed I was with Kai. He was here to check up on me.

He sounded pissed off. His eyes were dark and tense. I ran my hand over his cheek and jaw. His face softened as he looked into my eyes. He slowly leant down and kissed me. I pulled him closer, deepening the kiss.

He pulled away too soon, resting his forehead against mine. "Tegan, why are you wearing his shirt?"

"We had a water fight. I lost."

He nodded, smiling weakly.

"How long are you back for?" I asked.

"Two days. We got some more time off work."

I smiled and pulled him into another kiss.

"What's happening tomorrow?"

"Party at Holly's. Her parents will be back soon, so this is the last one. You wanna come?"

"No, it's fine. You have a good time. Is Kai going to bring you home, too?"

I laughed at that. "No, he'll be drunk. We were going to stay at Holly's, but I can get a lift home from someone."

"Stay at Holly's. I'll pick you up in the morning."

"What are you going to do?"

"Pub with Jake, Grace, and Ava." He kissed me hard, ending the conversation.

I dug my fingers in his back, pulling him closer.

Lucas, Ava, Grace, Jake, and I sat in the lounge, watching *Dirty Dancing*—Ava's choice. I cuddled up to Lucas's side. My eyes were getting heavy, and I kept drifting in and out of light sleep.

"Tegan, your phone."

I opened my eyes, looking at Lucas.

"What?" I rubbed my eyes, trying to wake myself up.

He handed me my phone.

Without looking at who it was, I sleepily answered the call, "Hello?"

"Hey."

"I'm sleeping, Kai."

Out of the corner of my eye, I could see everyone glaring at me. Jake was looking at Lucas.

Back. Off.

Kai chuckled. "You're talking."

"This'd better be good."

"It is. I just wanted to see if you were okay and to tell you to keep my T-shirt. It looks better on you."

"I know, and I was planning to."

He laughed down the phone.

"You can keep mine, too. Pink will suit you," I said.

"Is that your subtle way of telling me that I look gay?"

"You don't have to be gay to wear pink."

"I know. I was kiddin'. So, you cuddled up with the Smurf?" he asked, changing the subject.

"I thought you said this was gonna be good?"

"That hurts, princess."

"Okay, I'm going. You're being boring."

"All right, but before you go, I need to tell you something. Holly's pregnant."

"What?" I sat straight up. "Why the hell wasn't that the first thing you said? All that T-shirt crap you were going on about."

He laughed again.

"How? When?"

"So, I'll leave you to it. You're tired."

I could practically see him smirking.

"No, don't go! How pregnant is she?"

"I don't think there are different levels, Tegan. You're either pregnant, or you're not."

"You're killing me," I replied sarcastically.

"She's four months."

"Really? Shouldn't she be fat by now?"

save me

I heard another low chuckle.

"I don't know. I wouldn't mention that to her though."

"I won't. Did they only just find out?"

"Yeah, apparently, she still had periods. I could have lived without knowing that."

The blood drained from my face. I jumped up and walked quickly to the kitchen.

"Tegan, you there?"

I looked at the calendar. *Shit, shit, shit.* I was two days late.

"Tegan?"

"Yeah?" I whispered. My head felt light. All of me felt light. *Shit!*

"You all right?"

"Yeah. Sorry, I spaced out a bit. I'm gonna go. I need my beauty sleep."

"No, you don't. I'll pick you up tomorrow."

"Okay. Night, Kai."

"Night, princess."

I held the phone to my head for a while after he'd hung up. My limbs refused to work and lower the phone.

I couldn't be pregnant. There were only a few nights when Kai and I hadn't been as safe as we should have been. I hadn't even thought about it at the time.

Oh God, I was gonna be sick. My eyes stung. I took deep breaths to force the tears back.

"Tegan?"

I spun around, plastering my I'm-fine face on.

"Everything okay?" Lucas asked.

I nodded and grabbed him, holding him tight and breathing in his scent. "Everything's fine," I lied.

He kissed the top of my head and stroked my hair.

Women were late all the time. I'd been a few days late before. I was just a little late. It didn't mean I was pregnant.

171

Kai

"HELLO?" TEGAN SAID DOWN the phone.

"Hey, princess. You ready?"

"Yeah, I'm ready whenever you are."

"All right, I'll leave now. See you in ten."

"Cool. See you soon."

I hung up, trying to control the fucking annoying thudding of my heart.

I looked forward to seeing Tegan a lot more than I should. She was important to me—that much, I could admit—but I didn't want to have any real feelings for her yet. I wanted her to get better, and then I'd see if anything could happen. Now, she was with that prick. I was feeling jealousy for the first time since Isaac had died, and I saw two brothers kicking a ball together in the street. After that, I'd been locking everything away for so long.

After texting Holly back, telling her I was on my way, I got in the car and drove to Tegan's. I wasn't to wait down the road anymore, which I half-liked. It was great that she didn't want to hide me away, but at the same time, there was some serious tension when I was around.

Taking a deep breath, I rang the doorbell, and Tegan's mum answered.

"Hi. Is Tegan ready?"

"I think so. Come in."

I stepped into the house.

Alison turned to the stairs, shouting, "Tegan, Kai's here!"

Chewing the inside of my mouth, I looked around to have something else to do. Alison might have let me in, but it was clear she wasn't thrilled that I was still hanging out with her daughter. I understood why. Tegan was younger. If I'd known exactly how much younger when we met, I probably would have walked in the opposite direction. It was too late now.

Tegan walked downstairs, followed by Lucas. I tried to stop turning my nose up, but it didn't really matter. They were so transparent. I could see that he was trying to fix her, and she was looking in all the wrong places to be fixed.

She grinned. "Hey."

The stone-cold stare from Lucas just proved my point. Too overprotective, too intense, and too determined to be her white knight. She was the one who needed to be strong, and when she finally was, she'd see how wrong he was for her. I just hoped she'd see that I was right.

"Bye," Tegan snapped. She was gritting her teeth at the less than warm reception I was getting from Lucas and his brother, who'd poked his head around the door. Grabbing my wrist, she tugged me out of the house.

I'd noticed at Ava's party that they were fine with Adam. It was obviously just me. They probably knew that I wanted...something with Tegan even though I wouldn't mention it unless I was making a *joke*.

"Tegan?" Lucas called after us.

"Just keep walking, Kai. I've had enough," she said.

We reached the car seconds later, and we both got in.

"Drive. I don't want to talk to any of them."

"Sure? You don't want to sort out whatever the hell is going on?"

"No, I don't. I'm sorry for how Lucas and Jake acted back there."

I shrugged and pulled off, driving away. "Don't worry about it. I get why they don't like me much."

"They're stupid."

"Stop stressing about it. It's fine. We know we're not off shagging at every opportunity, and so should Lucas. You're allowed to have friends of the opposite sex, so forget about their reaction or what they say."

"Yeah, you're right."

I fake gasped. "I'm what? Say that again."

"Oh, ha-ha."

"No, go on, and say it again."

"Shut up, Kai."

Laughing, I pulled into Holly's drive. "Try not to get too paralytic tonight, okay?"

She rolled her eyes. "Yes, sir."

I unclicked my seat belt, but Tegan sat dead still. She paled.

"Hey, you okay?"

With a little shake of her head, she replied, "Yeah, sorry. Was in another world. Let's go in."

I led her through Holly's house and headed to the kitchen to get us a drink. "Okay, what do you want?" I asked, gesturing to the bottles of alcohol in front of us.

Biting her lip, she grabbed a can of Coke. "I'll just have this."

What?

"You're not drinking?"

She shook her head, avoiding looking at me.

I smirked. "Wow. You're not pregnant, are you?"

The colour drained from her face for the second time in as many minutes.

Shit.

"Tegan?" I said, my blood running cold.

She opened and closed her mouth twice before shrugging.
Shit!

I gulped. *Fuck, I'm not ready for a kid.*

Tegan looked as terrified as I felt. I was gonna throw up or pass out.

Man up.

Clearing my throat, I said, "We need to do a test."

She looked even more terrified. I took her hand and started to walk, but she tugged, making me stop.

"Wait, Kai."

"What?" I stepped closer, put my hands on her shoulders, and bent my head to her height. "We have to know."

"We? You don't."

I frowned. *What the fuck is that?* "This is my…problem—if that's the right word—too. If you think I'd let you go through this alone, then you clearly don't know me at all."

"No, I don't think you'd do that. I don't…I don't know what to think right now. I'm *seventeen*. I can't have a baby. I'm screwing everything up, and I don't know how to stop it. I'm so scared, Kai." She was on the verge of tears.

I'd watched her struggle with her emotions plenty of times, but it'd never hurt me to see it before. This was half my fault. I'd ruined my parents' lives for a while, and here I was, doing the same thing to a fucking teenage girl.

I wrapped my arms around her, holding her close, showing how sorry I was. "It'll be all right. We just need to find out one way or the other first, okay?"

"Okay," she whispered against my chest.

I felt as low as I had the first day I decided to change my life and had to acknowledge the shit I'd done.

We left Holly's house, lucky that no one had really paid any attention to us and that Sophie hadn't shown up yet. The closer we got to the supermarket, the more withdrawn Tegan became. She stared out the window, expressionless. Her body was sitting beside me, but her mind was somewhere else.

"It's going to be okay," I said. *I promise.*

"How?" She took an uneven deep breath. "What if I am?"

save me

"Hey, don't worry. If you are, then we'll do whatever you want."

She sniffed and wiped her cheeks. "What do you mean?"

I pulled into a parking space and turned to face her. She searched my eyes. Hers were distant. I remembered that; the loneliness of feeling like you were so far away from everyone, even the people you were supposed to be close to, was suffocating.

"If you want an abortion, I'll take you to the clinic and hold your hand. If you want the baby, I'll come to scans and let you scream at me when you're giving birth. I'll get up in the middle of the night to change dirty nappies and make bottles. Please don't worry, and *please* stop crying. I promise you, everything will be okay."

Her eyes glossed over again, and I knew she believed me. I'd do it. I wasn't the person I used to be. I wouldn't leave her to deal with something I'd had a hand in. If I were nine months from becoming a dad, I would step up and pretend I wasn't shit scared.

"Thank you," she said.

"It's okay," I said, reaching over and stroking the soft skin over her jaw. "You wait right here, and I'll go get the test."

She didn't say anything. She just looked at me.

Figure it out, Princess. You're supposed to be with me.

I got out of the car and tried to walk confidently. If there were anyone inside whom I knew, I was not going to be happy. Elle would have a field day with this. I knew where the pregnancy tests were—ironically, near the condoms—so I headed straight there, looking over my shoulder.

A few people were dotted around, pushing trolleys and grabbing items from the shelves. No one paid much attention to me besides two teenage girls. I didn't give a shit what they thought, so I picked up a test and headed to the self-serve checkout.

The girls followed a little ways behind me. I was used to that, and I kind of hated it. People saw a face and didn't care what was beneath. I used to love it, having no one look further than skin-deep. Now, it just reminded me of what I never wanted to be again.

I scanned the test and prayed to everything out there that there wouldn't be a problem with it. Sighing in relief when the self-service actually worked, I paid and got the hell out of there as soon as I could.

Tegan was chewing her lip when I got back. She could hide her emotions semi-well, but right now, she was all open.

"Hi," she said between chewing.

"All right?"

She shook her head. Neither was I.

A baby. My *baby.*

My heart sank to my stomach. I couldn't be responsible for keeping a small human alive.

I smiled, despite my inner panic.

"Thank you," she said.

"What for?"

"For not freaking out. For not running away. For going in there and getting a test, and for what you said before."

Oh, I'm freaking out all right.

I looked deep into her green eyes. "I meant it, Tegan. Everything will be fine." It had to be. I wouldn't let it *not* be, no matter how afraid I was.

She nodded, smiling weakly. "Can we go back to yours to do this?"

I started the car. "Of course."

We drove back to my house in silence, each trying to act cool for the other. She fake smiled a lot more than usual. I wanted to reassure her again, but I wasn't sure how many times I could say it would be okay before she saw through the facade. It might not be all right. Sure, whatever happened, we could make it work, but it would be far from fucking easy. Apparently, babies required a lot of care, care I knew sod all about.

We got to mine, and I barely remembered any of the drive. Letting us into my house, I followed Tegan into the living room.

"Do you want a drink or…" I asked.

The corner of her mouth tried a smile. "A bottle of vodka sounds good right about now."

I laughed, scratching the back of my neck. "Yeah, but if you're cooking little Kai Junior, you can't drink."

Yeah, make a baby-related joke. That'll make everything easier.

She laughed, too, despite the seriousness of the situation. "Kai Junior? Wow, I can't believe you can make me laugh right now."

"Are you worried about Lucas?" I asked.

Her face fell.

Well, she hadn't been before.

"He's not gonna want me if I am. Who would?"

Oh, fuck that.

I cupped her chin between my thumb and finger. "Don't. If that's all it takes to scare him off, he doesn't deserve you."

"Thank you," she replied.

I could see in her eyes that she didn't believe what I'd said, but she wouldn't right now. She had a rock-bottom opinion of herself.

"Okay, I'm going to do it." Taking a deep breath, she pried the bag out of my hand.

I was a little tense, no surprise. I stepped with her.

"Um, Kai, this is the solo part."

"Right, yeah. I'll wait here then." *Idiot.*

I waited downstairs for far too long. It took what? Like five seconds to piss on a stick and then a couple of minutes for the result? I was certain that she'd been upstairs for hours. Logically, I knew otherwise, but time was an evil bitch.

When my stomach was in knots and I felt like I was going to hurl, I went upstairs and knocked on the bathroom door. "Tegan, you okay?"

"Just waiting," she replied. "It's open. Come in."

Am I ready to go in? Well, that didn't matter. I'd possibly knocked up a seventeen-year-old girl. I had to be ready.

I opened the door and felt like I'd been punched in the gut. Tegan was sitting against the bath, arms around her legs, staring at the test. Her eyes were full of fear, pure fear that made me feel like even more of a prick.

Wrap it up! Always wrap the fucker up!

I sat beside her. "Is it ready yet?"

She had the test facing down.

"Should be," she muttered.

"Okay. Want me to look?"

"Seriously, why aren't you freaking out? You say everything so casually, like this is a regular occurrence."

She frowned, and I knew what she was thinking.

"No, this is the first time I've had this happen. Whatever that thing says, we'll get through it."

"Are you trying to convince me or you?"

"Both," I replied honestly.

"Ready to find out if it's Kai Junior or not?" she said.

"For the official record, if you are, you just agreed to that name."

She rolled her eyes.

"You want me to look?" I asked.

"No, it's okay. You went and got it, so I'll look." She turned it over.

I swore, the world stopped moving, and nothing existed but me, Tegan, and a little stick that had the potential to change our entire lives from here on out.

"Well?" I asked.

"It's negative, Kai."

Relief—that was all I felt. I could breathe easy again. "Thank fuck for that."

As she laughed, her shoulders sagged, and colour returned to her face. "Yeah."

"All right, I don't mean to brag, but I told you, it would be fine."

She raised her blonde eyebrow. "You so did not know. Christ, you named it!"

Grinning from ear to ear, I wrapped her in a tight hug and seriously considered framing the negative test. Tegan got up and chucked it into the bin the second I let her go.

save me

Turning to face me, she held her hand out. "Take me back to Holly's. I definitely need a drink now."

"So do I," I replied, taking her hand.

I towered over her petite frame as I stood. She hugged me again, and it was so unexpected that it took me a second to respond. Even though the top of her head barely reached my shoulders, she still fit against my body in the most annoyingly perfect way.

This bloody girl—someone else's girl—was exactly what I wanted. Sometimes, it really did suck to be me.

Tegan

KAI AND I ARRIVED back at Holly's an hour later, and the only person who noticed we'd even been missing was Sophie. She raised her eyebrow and smirked. She could think what she liked though. I wasn't pregnant, so that kind of trumped everything right now. Sophie assuming we'd been off having sex wasn't going to bother me. Although the cow should know I wouldn't do that.

"Drink, Tegan?" Kai asked, weaving us through a small crowd in the narrow hallway.

"I *really* need a vodka and lemonade."

Smirking at me over his shoulder, he replied, "You need *one*, huh?"

I felt like I needed about ten of 'em. Pregnancy *scare* was not a strong enough word. I was scared about having kids in the future, but right now was downright petrifying. I knew the basics—change nappy and feed—but beyond that, I was clueless. Christ, I even sucked at looking after myself.

Kai poured me a small vodka, but before he could move the bottle, I tipped it, adding more in.

"You're gonna be paralytic. I can see me spending the evening holding your hair back."

"Don't pretend like you don't love it," I joked.

"Yeah, but usually, I'm getting sex out of it." He shrugged.

My mouth hung open. "Are you serious?" I squealed.

Now, I knew our...relationship hadn't been based on anything deep when we were sleeping together, but I assumed he cared on a more basic level and wasn't just looking out for me to get sex.

His dark eyes gleamed. He was joking...possibly.

"Oh, chill. You know I'm kiddin'," he said. He finally allowed himself to laugh. "Your face just then..."

"Payback is going to be a bitch, Kai," I said, glaring.

He ran his hands through his bed-head black hair. It never looked like he'd bothered, but it always looked pretty much sexy as hell.

"I'm terrified," he replied sarcastically.

"And I'm going to ignore you."

"Right—until you tell Holly to come find me because you feel ill."

He had a point there.

I'd lost count of the times he had looked after me when I was beyond drunk. After I'd first told Lucas we couldn't be together, when we were at Luke's house, I'd been drinking more and more, and Kai always took care of me. I never really thought about it before, but if it wasn't for him, I could have gotten myself into some really dangerous situations. I was never in any fit state to protect myself, say no, or do anything really. I owed him a lot.

I threw my arms around his neck. He was still for about two seconds, and then his strong arms had me pinned against him.

"Thank you," I whispered into his shoulder.

"For?"

"For not letting me get raped or murdered."

"Okay…" he replied slowly. "You're welcome."

I let go, and he dropped his arms.

"I mean it. I don't know what I would've done without you."

"It's okay. We all need a little help sometimes, right?"

I needed more than a little help.

"Yeah, I guess."

He shrugged. "You know, if you're feeling really grateful, I can think of a couple of ways you can say thank you."

Rolling my eyes, I replied, "I'm sure you can."

"Hey," he said, holding his hands up, "if that's how you want to pay me back, it's fine."

"You have such a dirty mind."

He laughed in disbelief. "Hello, Pot…"

Turning on my heel, I walked off with my drink, smiling to myself.

Halfway through the night, I slipped off to Holly's room to reapply some makeup. It was hot in the house, and I was sure I'd look like a panda by the end of the evening if I didn't sort it out.

I was about to apologise to someone sitting on Holly's bed when I realised it was Kai. He looked up and half-smiled.

"What's up?" I asked.

He shook his head. "Nothin'. Just needed to get away for a bit. It's boiling down there."

I couldn't tell if he was being honest or not, but I decided to believe him because, if something were up and he wanted me to know, he'd tell me.

"I know. My face is melting," I said, turning to look in the mirror. The damage wasn't as bad as I'd thought. I ran my fingers under my eyes.

"What are you doing?" he asked.

"Trying to improve this," I replied, pointing to my face. "It's not going well, but I can't expect miracles."

He frowned deeply in the mirror, and his dark eyes looked almost black. I wasn't sure how much he'd had to drink, but he was definitely on the edge of drunk.

"You have no idea, do you?"

"Sorry?"

"You're like that song."

Oh, much clearer.

"'Just the Way You Are.' It was playing at work the other day, and all I could think about was you. Stop trying to change, and stop beating yourself up because you're not perfect. I *know*. I know what it's like. I know how hard you're struggling, but you're still getting up and doing it. You're amazing, and you certainly don't need crap on your face to make yourself look pretty."

I gulped. For a moment, I was stunned. Kai was a sweetheart with a bit of a dirty mouth, but I never imagined him to say that or to think it.

Moving across the room, I sat beside him. "You're too sweet, you know."

He lifted and dropped one shoulder. "I just say it how it is."

"Also, I never knew you were a Bruno Mars fan."

Leaning forward, he rested his elbows on his knees and twisted his head to look up at me. "Well, I like that one."

I liked it, too. Liked the lyrics and loved that someone could think that about someone else. I just never thought anyone would think much of me anymore. The fact that Kai thought I didn't need to change made me feel a little better about myself, and I skipped reapplying anything in favour of getting Kai to do a couple of shots with me.

After the rest of my idiot friends joined the shot bandwagon, it didn't take too long for me to get drunk.

I was roasting hot. Wiping my forehead, I squinted my eyes to try to pick Kai out from the crowd.

God, does Holly have the heater on?

I felt faint, and I only just made it to the front door as my head started to get really clouded.

Breathing in, I leant back against the wall and closed my eyes. The cool air cleared the light-headed feeling, and I was sure I wouldn't pass out now. The next thing I felt was a warm palm pressing against my head. My eyes fluttered open, and what looked like two pools of melted dark chocolate stared back at me.

Kai. Thank God.

"Shit, Tegan, come on," he said, scooping me up in his arms. "Do you feel sick?"

I nodded against his shoulder. I was definitely feeling sick, especially after he'd lifted me. He took me upstairs and set me on the floor of the bathroom, locking the door behind us.

"It's okay, princess."

No, it wasn't. My stomach did all sorts of somersaults, and I felt the all-too familiar feeling creeping up my throat. Flopping forward, I hugged the toilet. Kai was just in time to pull my hair back and tie it up before I threw up about a bottle of vodka.

"I'm sorry," I slurred.

"It's okay," he said, rubbing my back.

With unwelcome tears stinging my eyes, I was sick a bit more.

"Are you okay? You finished now?"

I nodded and stood up with a little help from Kai, and then I rinsed my mouth out with mouthwash and water.

"Ugh, I feel like crap," I said.

"Follow me. I'm taking you to the spare room, so you can sleep it off."

I wasn't going to argue with that. I needed to curl up in bed and let sleep work its magic.

Kai pointed to the double bed. "Sit there, but don't lie down."

No, I wanted sleep. "I'm not gonna choke to death on my own tongue if I lie down, Kai."

His jaw clenched. "Just humour me. Please."

Throwing my hands up, I got on the bed and replied, "Fine."

Holly's parents' spare room looked like they'd plucked it right out of one of those modern-home magazines or a posh hotel. Everything was brilliant white and super clean. The bed was comfortable, and that was pretty much all I cared about right now.

In minutes, Kai was back with two glasses of water and handed one to me.

"Drink it all. I know, I know," I said, smirking at him.

He was literally seconds from saying it.

Narrowing his eyes, he sat down and put the other glass on the bedside table. "Do you need to get changed before you crash?"

"Yeah, but I have nothing to change into right now." There was no way I could sleep in jeans and a tight top, and I didn't know where my overnight bag was. "Take your top off."

"Tegan!" He fake gasped. "You need to stop making these advances toward me."

"Kai, I'm drunk and tired, and I can't sleep in my clothes."

Gripping the bottom of his T-shirt, he pulled it off his head and threw it at my face. I laughed as the material hit my head, just managing to hold the water away before it spilt everywhere.

"Are you going to make me turn around while you undress?"

"No, please get a good look."

He either hadn't noted my sarcasm or just didn't care because he didn't look away.

"Kai!"

Raising his arms, he turned to face the wall, and I managed to get changed in semi-privacy. I got into bed, and without asking if I was decent, he came back over and got in beside me.

We're sharing a bed?

I wasn't sure if that was a good idea—not because I was worried something might happen, but because...well, I probably shouldn't share a bed with another man when I had a boyfriend.

I was going to say something, but Kai was here because I'd gotten drunk, and he wanted to make sure I was okay. I didn't really have a right to kick him out of bed and make him sleep on the floor.

"Lie on your side, princess," he said, shoving me over.

I laughed and battered his arm away. "You're going a little over the top."

He laughed and sat up against the headboard.

"What are you doing?" I mumbled, half-asleep already.

"Sleeping."

"Sitting up?"

"There's no sofa in here, and the floor's hard."

Now, I felt bad. "Lie down. I promise not to jump you."

"You don't have to promise that," he said.

With a deep chuckle, he scooted down and lay beside me. I watched with heavy eyes as his chest rose and fell. The sound of his breathing was comforting, soothing, and I quickly fell asleep.

I was woken up in the morning by my so-called friend shaking my arm. As I drifted back into consciousness, I heard my phone ring and then Kai's voice.

It took me all of *no* seconds to fully wake up when he said Lucas's name. My head felt fuzzy as I sat up too fast, but I still managed to slap Kai's arm with my blurry sight.

"Hold on," Kai said, laughing, "she's right here."

I took the phone and held it to my ear. "Hey, Luke."

"Hi. Are you ready to be picked up?"

Fuck, he sounds angry.

"Um, I need to get ready first. Can you give me half an hour?"

"Okay."

"Thanks," I replied. Then, I gave him Holly's address.

I ended the call and turned to glare at Kai.

"Hey, you wouldn't wake up," he said, holding his hands up. "Was he mad?"

Oh, he was loving this. There was a definite smug arrogance in the way he'd asked that.

"He was fine." I got off the bed, and my overnight bag was on the floor.

Kai had to have found that because it definitely hadn't been here last night.

Was it?

"How did this happen?" I asked, pointing to my bag.

He kicked one leg over the other at the ankle. "Got it this morning."

"So, when I was making you take your top off..."

"No. For once, I wasn't working on an agenda to see you half-naked and in my shirt. I was a bit preoccupied with worrying about you."

I bit my lip. Okay, I felt horrible. "Sorry."

He shrugged. "Understand why you thought it. If you weren't off your pretty little face, I would've tried it."

Suddenly, I didn't feel so bad anymore.

"Prick," I muttered, snagging my bag and going to the bathroom. I could still hear laughing through the wall as I turned the shower on.

Lucas turned up exactly half an hour after we'd spoken.

"Hey," I said, giving him a kiss after Holly had let him in.

His arms held me tight, almost too tight, and he touched his forehead to mine. "Hey."

"Come through. I've just got to say bye to everyone and grab Soph."

I led him through to the lounge, so we could get Sophie and drop her home.

Lucas laughed as he saw her face. "What happened?"

Oh, yeah...

Sophie had still been in a deep sleep when I came downstairs, so of course, that meant we'd had to draw on her face.

"Kai and James," I replied. "And maybe Holly and me, too."

save me

The boys were still at it, doing some big drawing down her arm. Sophie was a heavy sleeper anyway, but when she'd been drinking, it was almost impossible to wake her before she was ready to get up.

"Okay, I think that's enough now," I said, trying to grab the eyeliner off them.

Kai snapped his hand away before I could get it. "Not yet, princess. I have one last thing to do."

I rolled my eyes and pulled Lucas down on the sofa. I leant over to see exactly what they were doing.

I gasped for two reasons. One, they'd drawn a massive cock on her arm. Two, they'd used *my* eyeliner to do it.

"Hey, what the hell? That's mine!"

"Remember what I told you last night," Kai said, smirking.

I remembered even though I had been wasted. Apparently, I didn't need makeup. I wasn't completely convinced, so I would still wear it.

Sophie groaned and stretched. "Tegan?" she slurred, holding her head. "I'm dyin'."

"You're just hungover, hon. Or possibly still drunk."

She groaned again and said, "I'm thinking about having sex with Kai."

Kai looked at me in sheer horror.

"Okay, want me to tell him to meet you upstairs?" I asked.

"Yeah," she said.

"Kai, will you meet—"

"No," he snapped. "Sophie, sober up already."

She laughed and cracked her eye open to wink at him.

Now, I wasn't shy when it came to guys, but there was no way I could come out and admit I wanted sex right in front of them. Christ, if they'd overheard me saying something like that, I'd move towns.

"Okay, you want to say bye, Tegan, so I'll carry the pisshead to the car," Lucas said, standing up and cradling a still very intoxicated Soph in his arms.

I gave everyone a hug good-bye and stopped by the front door to glance at how awful I looked in the mirror. Messy bed hair was awesome on Kai but did nothing for me.

Kai grabbed my wrist and turned me around. "Just the way you are."

I felt the air leave my lungs, as if he'd just punched me. He gave me that little bit more strength to believe that I was capable of more than what I was doing and didn't have to hide away quite so much.

"Thank you," I said.

I gave him a quick kiss on the cheek. He nodded and took a step back.

We dropped Sophie off at her house and dropped Lucas's car at mine, so we could go for a walk. I needed the fresh air to clear my head. He took my hand as we walked along the path. It was a gorgeous, warm morning, and for the first time in ages, I was looking forward to the day.

"So, how was it last night?"

"It was really good."

"Did you get drunk?"

I winced. "Yeah, a bit. I was nowhere near as bad as Sophie though."

"Did Kai look after you?"

I nodded. *Where is this going?*

"You two are pretty close, aren't you?"

"Yeah, he's a good friend."

I closely watched him. His face was emotionless, green eyes flat. I had no idea what he was thinking.

"I'm glad he was there for you," he said, smiling. It was a genuine smile, too.

We turned the corner, and I froze, realising where we were.

Lucas looked up and then back to me. "Are you okay? Do you want to go?" His voice sounded so far away.

Everything inside me hurt. I could barely breathe; it was so painful. I could feel the water rising, lapping around my face, threatening to take me under.

save me

Why did I come here?

Those six words crushed me every time. *In loving memory of Simon Pennells.*

Lucas

TEGAN STOOD SO STILL and stared at her father's grave. I wish I had known where we were walking.

"Tegan, baby, come on." I pulled her to me, wrapping my arms securely around her. "Do you want to go home?"

I felt her nodding weakly against my chest. I took her face in my hands and kissed her forehead. She didn't look upset. She looked empty. I wasn't sure which one I preferred.

The walk back to her house was silent. I had so many questions, but I wasn't sure where to start.

"Do you think you should see a counsellor?" I asked.

Her grip on my hand loosened a fraction. "No."

I do. "They might be able to help."

"Will talking to someone bring my dad back?"

"Well, no, of course not. It—"

"Then, it won't help."

"They can help you deal with it, babe."

"I *am* dealing with it, so please drop it."

"Tegan, I think—"

She shook her head. "No. Drop it. I don't want to talk, not to anyone. So, can we just forget it, go back to mine, and watch a film?"

Sighing, I caved in. "Yeah, we can do that."

I couldn't help taking her not wanting to open up personally. She was my girlfriend. She should want to let me in and let me help her. But I wasn't going to give up. I cared about her too much to let her do this on her own.

Not knowing how to handle her right now, I followed her lead. We watched a film, and when it finished, I sat up, and she untangled herself from me.

"Let's go out. You're not here for much longer, and I want us to have fun."

"Where do you want to go?" I said, kissing her cheek. "And please don't say, to the zoo."

She laughed and looked up at me. "What if I wanted to go to the zoo?"

"Then, I'd take you, I guess. But how about dinner and a movie?"

"Sounds perfect to me. I don't know what's on though."

I shrugged. "Doesn't matter."

We weren't going to pay a whole lot of attention to it anyway.

"Do you want to eat there?" I said, pointing toward a little restaurant off the main street.

"No!" she snapped as she pulled me in a different direction.

What was that all about?

There must be something or someone in there that she was avoiding, and it bothered the shit out of me.

"Let's go here." She pointed to a Pizza Hut just up the road.

It wasn't quite what I'd had in mind, but at least it wasn't somewhere with tiny portions that would leave me hungry ten minutes later.

We were immediately seated in a small red booth.

I reached over and held her hand. *Time for more difficult questions.* "Why didn't you want to go to the other restaurant? What's wrong with it?"

She gulped, and her eyes emptied of what little emotion had been left. "We went there for my sixteenth. Dad made a big speech and gave me this." She held up the heart charm on her necklace.

I had looked at it before. Engraved on the back in small letters were the words, *A daughter is a gift of love.*

I nodded and squeezed her hand. Shit, now, I felt like an arsehole for asking. "Do you want to talk about your dad?"

"I...I think so." Her voice was barely a whisper, and her eyes looked so sad. She took a deep breath and let go of my hand. "I don't really know what to say, Luke."

I shuffled round and pulled her into my arms. "You miss him, and that's okay. That's normal. You don't have to shut yourself off. You're allowed to feel however it is you feel."

"I wish I could have had just one more minute with him. Just sixty seconds, so I could tell him I loved him." Her voice broke.

I watched her focus hard on staying in control. She took a long deep breath and clamped her mouth together. She was good at keeping her emotions in check; I'd give her that.

That was sort of the problem though. *How long will it be before she loses that control, and it all pours out?* I was fairly certain that it wasn't going to be pretty when it happened, which was why I was trying to get her to do it gradually now. I felt like I was trying to run underwater though.

"You all right?" I asked, willing her to just let it out and shed a tear, to do something.

197

Leaning up, she kissed me. "Yeah, I'm fine. Are you having a starter?"

I'd lost the chance again.

I moved back to my seat, and through dinner, Tegan acted like everything was normal. There was no trace of the girl who had just been sad over her dad's death. I didn't know how she was able to do it. I didn't think I would be strong enough to lock something like that away. But perhaps it wasn't about strength; perhaps it was more about desperation.

"Have you thought any more about sixth form?" I asked.

She picked up a slice of pizza. "Not really," she said, looking at the table, avoiding eye contact.

"You've not missed that much. You could catch up pretty quickly, if that's what you're worried about? I can help you."

"It's not that. Everyone knows what happened, and I can't stand people feeling sorry for me."

"Tegan, it's something you want to do. You can't let other people stop you. They're your friends, so of course, they're sympathetic. It's not a bad thing."

Her eyebrow kicked up, telling me that, to her, it was a bad thing.

She thought for a minute, and just when I assumed she was about to tell me to drop that, too, she nodded. "Will you come with me to talk to the head of sixth form tomorrow?"

I almost fell on the floor. I had been prepared for her to shut me down, but her agreeing with me, I had not been.

"Yeah, of course I'll go with you," I replied, unable to keep the smile off my face. It was a step in the right direction.

After dinner, we went back to hers because she didn't feel like going to the cinema anymore. I was relieved because, after today, I was pretty beat.

"So, what do you want to do instead of the cinema?" I asked, lying back on her bed. God, it felt good to be lying down.

She had a mischievous smile as she got on the bed.

What's she up to?

Her leg swung over me, and then she was straddling me.

"Hmm," I said, gripping her thighs, "I like this plan."

Leaning over, she kissed me, staying just within reach. I wanted to kiss her hard and deep and make us both forget our fucking names, but she was playing.

"Stop teasing," I said as she lightly brushed her lips over mine again.

I could just grab her and flip her over, but I was very interested to find out what she was up to.

She sat up and yanked her top over her head. "No more going slow," she said, reaching for the zip on my jeans.

Tegan

LUCAS LAID ME BACK on the bed, kissing me the whole time. His lips left mine for about two seconds when I removed his shirt, and that was it. He'd kissed me a lot before, but this was different.

Lucas kissed down my neck, and at the same time, he ran his hand over my stomach and hips. It was like he wanted to touch every single part of me, not that I had any complaints.

He sat up, breathing hard and ripped a condom packet open. *Okay, we're done with the foreplay.*

"Luke," I whispered when he entered me so slowly I thought I was going to pass out from the feeling.

Lucas made me feel safe again. I wrapped my arms and legs around him and tangled my fingers in his hair.

He groaned against my collarbone and then kissed me, dipping his tongue into my mouth. It felt so good. I bit down on his lip as he moved faster, and that made him go harder.

"God, Tegan," he murmured into my mouth, curling his arms under my back and holding me tight against him.

He was all around me, literally, and in that moment, I was completely with him.

He was softer, gentler, with me than anyone else had been, and even though I didn't want to claw at him, it was perfect and intimate and just how I needed it to be.

I came apart, clutching his body and kissing him until long after we were spent.

I woke up, alone again. I really needed to talk to Mum about that. I didn't want Luke and I to sleep in separate rooms. Logically, at seventeen, I knew that Mum was well within her right to say no, but I also knew it wouldn't be that hard to get her to agree.

Right now, I had something else to worry about—school. I knew there would be questions and looks. I didn't want anyone to talk to me about the accident. That was inevitable though, so I had to find a way to deal with it or ignore it.

I'd called the school and spoken to the head of sixth form, Mrs Baker. She was also my old English teacher, who had been promoted over the summer holiday and was now in charge of helping a bunch of sixteen- and seventeen-year-olds prepare for university. Mrs Baker was also the one who had been phoning regularly and spoken to Mum about getting me to go back.

I got dressed and put on some makeup, trying to calm the churning in my stomach. I didn't do much to my face because I never used to, and I didn't want to stand out any more than I already would.

Once I was ready, I went downstairs to eat something. Mum, Ava, and Lucas hung over me as I ate and then shoved my phone in my bag. It made me more nervous that they were nervous. Missing so much time had put me behind, and apparently, if I waited just another couple of weeks, I'd have to defer until next year. That, I didn't want to do. Being a year behind all my friends—if they were still talking to me after I'd stopped talking to them—would suck.

"Good luck. Have a good day," Mum said again as I was about to walk out the door.

I needed that luck. I just hoped that my friends would take the hint and appreciate that I didn't want to talk.

"Thanks. I will," I replied, brushing past her, as I felt her about to hug me. I couldn't let her hug me.

Lucas was taking me because I couldn't possibly make the five-minute walk alone, so I got in his car and waited for him to follow. Honestly though, I kind of loved that he wanted to be there for me.

"In a rush?" he asked as he got in the driver's side and started the engine.

"Just want to get it over with."

He smiled tightly.

What now?

The ride to school was done in silence. I could practically see about a million questions flying through his mind. It was only a matter of time before he started pushing harder for answers that I wasn't even sure I had. He made things easier, but at the same time, he made it ten times harder.

"You ready to go in?" he asked as we stopped outside school on the road.

"Yeah," I said even though I was shaking my head.

Laughing quietly, he replied, "It'll be fine. I'll wait here until you get out."

"Thank you," I said, opening the door. "You can come wait inside though."

I took a deep breath and got out of the car, and Lucas followed. He grabbed my hand as we walked to the building.

"Tegan," Josie and Laura called, running over to me from across the courtyard.

"Hey," I managed to get out as they attacked me in a huge bone-crushing hug.

"You're coming back?" Josie asked.

I nodded, and that brought on another round of hugging. Guessed they didn't hate me for cutting them off when Dad had died then.

Laura nodded to Luke. He was standing just behind me with his hands shoved in his pockets.

"This is my boyfriend. Lucas, these are my friends, Josie and Laura."

They exchanged a quick hello, and then I had to get to my appointment.

I led Lucas into the sixth form building and headed to Mrs Baker's office. There were seats outside, so Luke sat down and grinned up at me. He looked proud, and although I liked that, it felt loaded. If he was proud of me, I could let him down, and I didn't need that responsibility.

"Tegan, welcome back," Mrs Baker said, opening the door.

She stepped aside and let me in. I didn't look back at Lucas because I couldn't handle it right now. I already felt the weight of disappointing him—something that would probably happen eventually—crushing me.

She sat at her scratched-to-hell desk, and I sat on the faded red chair, opposite her.

"How have you been?" she asked, tilting her head.

Seriously, if I had a pound for every time I've heard that...

"I'm doing okay," I replied. "I'd like to start back as soon as possible. Do you think my teachers would give me the work I missed?" I asked.

She smiled, pushing her bleached blonde hair behind her ears. "We're getting straight to it, I see."

Yeah, I didn't want sympathetic small talk.

"Of course we can arrange to get you the missed work. Catching up isn't going to be easy. I've compiled a list of what you'll need to do, and it's a lot. We're all behind you though, and I have no doubt that you can do it. Now, because you've missed so much, I suggest you drop one subject and stick with the three you want to take through to A-level. That's Music, English Literature, and Sociology, yes?"

I nodded. I still wasn't sure on Music. A few months ago, that was the only one I had been one hundred percent sure of. Something was forcing me to stick with it though, and I liked to think it was Dad.

"All right. Well, it's half-term break next week, so why don't I get you some work posted to your house to complete over the break, and you can come back the Monday after with whatever you've completed."

This was getting real.

I licked my lips. "Okay."

"Now, your first period is free, so if you come straight here on Monday morning, we'll use that hour to go through everything that you might still need to do."

"Thank you."

"You're very welcome, Tegan. I can't tell you how pleased we all are that you've decided to come back. You're a bright young girl, and it'd be a shame to see that potential go to waste."

I didn't feel bright, capable, or full of potential, not anymore.

"Thanks," I repeated, not really knowing what else to say.

She nodded and clapped her hands together. "Well, we'll see you on Monday then."

I stood up. "You will."

"Have a good weekend, Tegan."

"You, too."

I left as quickly as I could, so I wouldn't change my mind. Lucas was on his feet the second I opened the door.

"That was quick," he said.

"Yep. Going back the Monday after half-term break."

"That's great," he said, like it was the answer to all my problems.

If he thought returning to school would suddenly make everything all right again, he was going to be hugely disappointed. I already felt like I'd let him down.

"You guys ready?" Jake asked, tapping his foot on the floor.

"Yes!" I replied, squirming, as Lucas kissed my neck.

Lucas, Jake, Grace, Ava, and I were going to go to Robbie and Gino's pub. Kai, Holly, and James were going to be there, too, so it was guaranteed to be a good night.

"*Bella!*" Gino shouted as I walked through the door.

God, I loved that man.

"Hey, Gino."

I hugged James and Holly while Lucas, Jake, Grace, and Ava sat at a table, ordering drinks. Jake and Grace liked me about as much as Ava did. They put up with me, but I could see in their eyes that they wanted Lucas to run. He probably should.

"Where's Kai?" I asked.

"Pissing," James replied.

I turned my nose up. "Lovely. Thanks."

James shrugged and walked off to the pool table.

"Want to play doubles?" Holly asked, nodding to the table.

"Um, in a minute, I will." *Probably shouldn't leave everyone five seconds after walking through the door.*

"Okay," she said before walking over to James.

I turned around just as Kai came out of the bathroom. He smiled and winked when he saw me. I felt like I could breathe again. There was at least one person who wasn't actively trying to change me.

Kai

I WALKED OUT OF the bathroom, and my eyes instantly fell on Tegan, like fucking always. She looked stunning, like fucking always. I couldn't believe she was self-conscious about how she looked. But I knew what it was like to be so broken that you didn't feel there was anything good about yourself anymore.

She looked up and smiled.

Yeah, just friends isn't enough.

I walked over and pulled her into my arms, giving her a friendly hug, just as I'd done with Holly. When Tegan's petite body pressed against mine, I wanted to groan. I didn't get to touch her nearly as much as I wanted to—or where I really wanted to.

Lucas looked less than pleased that I'd given her a hug. It'd lasted a second, and he was the one who got to take her to bed, so he could sit the fuck down.

Great, we're all sitting together.

He had no idea how bloody lucky he was. Although I knew she liked him and she thought she loved him, he wasn't good for her. He didn't understand how lost and angry she was right now. Hell, Tegan barely understood it.

I'd wanted to properly ask her out about two seconds after meeting her, but I knew straightaway how broken she was. I could see it in her empty freaky green eyes, feel it in the way she'd force a smile on her face.

I'd been there, and I knew distractions were the only way you could cope, and no one could fix you but yourself. If I'd steamed in there like him and tried to make everything better, I'd have doomed us from the start.

She clearly wasn't ready to deal with her dad's death yet, and Lucas trying to help her do it was only going to screw him over in the long run. He had her now, but I'd rather have her forever.

Ava and Jake had sat down on either side of Lucas on the bench. I wasn't sure if they were picking sides, but if they were, they'd just made a big mistake. The only place for Tegan was now next to me.

"I'm starting sixth form on the Monday after the break," she said.

"Yeah? That's great."

Step one: Do normal shit you used to.

"Thanks."

I leant closer and whispered in her ear, "So, do you have to wear a uniform?"

"You pervert!" she whisper-yelled.

I laughed. "I'm joking." *Not really.* "What are you studying then?"

"English Lit, Sociology and Music," she replied, lowering her voice when she said *Music.*

"You want to do something in music? Gonna join a rock band?"

She looked up, and the stress evaporated from around her eyes. "I think so, not the rock-band thing. I used to want to spend my whole life playing the piano, but I'm not sure now."

"You suck now?"

I could feel Tegan's followers glaring at the side of my head, but I didn't give them the satisfaction of looking up.

"Yep, I'm awful. Forgot all the keys and everything."

"Hey, you could always be a backup dancer."

"And, if that fails, there's always stripping, right?"

I shrugged one shoulder. "It's a wonderful art."

"Tegan plays the piano beautifully," Ava said. "I don't see any sort of dancing in her future."

"Bit judgy, Ava," Tegan said.

Thankfully, she'd responded before I could say something similar but a lot less diplomatically. My aunt used to be a dancer before she broke her leg badly, so now, she taught it. I did not like people talking or thinking shit of my family. Or sort of anyway, Ava didn't know my aunt.

"Oh, I'm not saying it's beneath you, Tegan, so calm down. You just don't need a backup plan."

Tegan had already moved to Plan B. She had done that the second her dad died. It was up to her if she wanted to scrap that and go for what she really wanted again.

Tegan gave her sister a tight smile and turned her attention back to me. "I'm not sure what I'll do yet, but I have plenty of time to figure it out."

"Yeah, you're not that old yet," I said.

She wasn't that old at all, and that was still a little bit of an issue for me. I wished she were eighteen even though she was perfectly legal when we had been shagging like bunnies. I'd just feel better about it if she had officially been an adult.

After an hour, it was clear that Tegan was serious about cutting down on the alcohol. Instead of downing her drinks, she would have one or two alcoholic ones and water or Coke between.

We stayed in the same place at the table, talking most of the time. I didn't care that Lucas barely took his eyes off her or that Ava gave me the occasional dirty look. I wasn't exactly sure what they thought could happen if they didn't watch us like hawks while we were at the same table as them, but it was fairly amusing.

I grabbed Tegan's phone and scrolled to the Settings.

"What are you doing?" she asked, leaning over and trying to see.

"Setting a ringtone for me."

Her eyebrows pulled together in confusion.

"Bruno Mars," I said, smiling.

I was more of a rock guy—I needed drums, bass, and guitar and for the band to have sat down to write the material and music themselves—but I didn't mind Bruno Mars. I might as well have written "Just the Way You Are" myself. No matter how messed up and confused Tegan was, no matter what mistakes she'd made, to me, she was perfect. I saw past it all.

She smirked. "Shouldn't that be your ringtone for me?"

"Nope. I already have one for you."

"Do I want to know?" she asked cautiously.

"Probably not." I laughed. "It's Kings of Leon's 'Sex on Fire.'"

Her mouth hung open. With a wink, I got up to get a round.

Before my back was completely turned, I saw Tegan move to sit on Lucas's lap. Quickly looking away, I swallowed acid and tried to ignore the ache in my chest.

Fuck, that hurt.

Tegan

Lucas, Jake, and Ava climbed in the car, waiting for me to finish saying good-bye to everyone. I was sober, which I was quite proud of. I knew I drank too much, and I wanted to stop doing it. At least, I mostly wanted to stop.

Kai, however, was very drunk. He stumbled as he tried to prove to us that he could still walk in a straight line. Apparently, his straight line had rounded corners. James put his arm around him, practically carrying him to the car.

"Princess," Kai slurred, throwing his other arm around my neck.

I giggled. "You're so wasted, Kai."

"No. No, no, I'm not." He stopped abruptly, making me and James stop, too.

"Okay, get in," I said, shoving him toward the car.

"You coming with me?" he asked, wiggling his eyebrows.

I shook my head, laughing at how pissed he was, and I gave him another shove. He grabbed me as he fell backward, and we both ended up halfway in the back of the car.

"Man, you're a bad drunk," I said, shaking my head and taking James's hand as he helped me up.

Kai was lying on the backseat with his butt and legs hanging out. "I think I might be drunk."

"Oh, really?" I rolled my eyes as James grabbed Kai's legs and pushed him in the car.

"Don't sleep on your back," I called before I slammed the door shut. "Good luck," I said, smiling at James.

He chuckled and hugged me. "I'll need that luck."

Yeah, he really would.

I waved good-bye to Holly and James before jumping in the back of Jake's car.

"I'm tired, Luke." I yawned.

He wrapped his arm around me and kissed the top of my head. "Sleep then. I'll carry you to bed."

I liked the sound of that even though I wouldn't be able to sleep in a car. Maybe I could pretend, so I could get him in my room and then convince him to stay.

Mum had gone to bed by the time we all got home. I waited for Ava and Jake to go before dragging Lucas up to my room.

"Clothes off, Luke."

His face lit up, and he was naked in seconds. I giggled and pushed him down on my bed. Sober me didn't really take charge all that much, but I wanted to this time. I smiled and climbed on top of him, kissing him hard and dragging my fingers across his chest.

Lucas was gone when I woke up again. It drove me crazy. I threw on some clean underwear, jeans, and a T-shirt, and I went down to find him. I called Kai on the way to see how he was feeling. With a bit of luck, I'd wake him up.

Groaning down the phone, he muttered, "What?"

"Good morning," I sang loudly.

He groaned deeper. "Shh. Fuck, Tegan, it's too early for this."

I walked into the kitchen where everyone was sitting, watching me. I smiled at Luke.

"It's almost eleven. How's the head?" I asked Kai.

"I hate it. I hate my head."

Laughing, I said, "You know, you're quite funny when you're hungover."

"Well, I'm glad my slow and painful death is so amusing."

"Self-inflicted, Kai."

"Come make me some bacon sandwiches," he said.

I could almost see him pouting and widening those big chocolate eyes.

"Yeah, I think you should sleep more. I'll come over later and make sure you're okay."

"All right. Wake me up with bacon."

"Okay. Don't sleep on your back," I said, grinning.

"Fuck off," he replied before hanging up.

That went better than I'd thought. It wasn't often or at all really that he was the drunk one of us two.

I walked over to the table and sat down next to Lucas. It'd been a while since I'd been out and not gotten wasted, and it felt nice not to have a fuzzy head.

Mum had made bagels, eggs, and bacon for breakfast. My mouth watered.

I wasn't sure if it was just a fluke or because I hadn't been drunk last night, but I felt more positive today. Luke was going to take me out somewhere, and things were just looking up.

"I'm ready," I said as I reached the bottom of the stairs after putting a little makeup on.

"Hey, you look beautiful." He leant down and kissed me, making my heart race. "Let's go."

He grabbed my hand and led me to Jake's car. I looked over at him and fluttered my eyelashes.

"I'm not telling you, shorty."

Damn it.

We drove for about thirty minutes, and after what must've been about thirty guesses, I gave up. I'd probably said it already, and he'd just told me no anyway. Finally, he pulled up next to a perfectly manicured huge park.

It was absolutely stunning. Tall trees and a stone pathway surrounded the perimeter. In the middle was a large pond and seating area. At the side was a wooden play area. I was too busy looking around that I didn't notice Lucas had opened my door.

I got out and said, "It's beautiful, Luke."

"It's okay. You're beautiful."

I rolled my eyes. "Where did you get that one from?"

"Come on, that's one of my best lines," he joked. He kissed my forehead. "Is it working though?"

He didn't need lines or romance. I wasn't the most romantic person, and honestly, I would just prefer for him to tell me I'd be getting lucky tonight, but I loved that he wanted to be sweet and do nice things for me.

"It all works, Luke," I said, standing on my toes to kiss him.

We walked along the side of the park a little awkwardly as I held on around his waist. I almost felt like a different person, but I didn't want to get too happy about it because I wasn't sure what I was doing to change. I wasn't naive enough to believe that all was going to be great from here.

Lucas seemed to know exactly where he was going. He led us through a rosebush archway, and I stood still. There was a gorgeous, tall white horse with a grey stripe down its head. Behind it was a wooden carriage.

"Seriously?" I said. *Okay, perhaps I like a bit of romance.*

"Do you want to go for a ride?"

"Of course I do! This is amazing!"

He smiled widely, melting my heart. I thought I fell in love with him a bit more.

We climbed in the carriage, and Lucas put his arm around me.

"How did you find out about this place?"

"We used to come here as kids. The horse and carriage would visit some weekends. This is one of those weekends."

"Thank you," I whispered.

Then, I attacked his lips. I didn't care that a man was sitting about a metre away or that children were probably around. Lucas didn't seem to mind either. He nipped my bottom lip, and I felt like I was going to combust. I wanted him.

He pulled back, having considerably more self-control than me. He took a deep breath and stroked my cheek. "I'm supposed to do all this shit. What are you thanking me for?"

I wasn't sure if he'd lost or gained points for calling romantic stuff "all this shit."

"I mean, for everything, Luke. If it wasn't for you, I would still be going out and getting drunk every night and arguing with Mum and Ava." That was half true.

I would still drink. It was a *lot* less, but I would get drunk, and I was still fighting with Mum and Ava. Lucas couldn't fix everything though, and I didn't expect him to. I was trying to figure out how to do that for myself with his support.

"I'll always be here for you," he murmured against my lips before kissing me again.

I didn't believe that. At the end of the day, everyone was alone. No one was going to be with you forever. You just had to enjoy the time while you had it.

"We need to get back soon. I have to leave at four," Lucas said after we'd eaten by the pond and had a long walk around the park.

"I hate the part when you leave."

"Yeah, me, too. I'll be back over on Friday though."

We got back to mine, and Lucas had to pack his things to leave. I sat on the sofa bed, pouting. We were still sort of in that hands-all-over-each-other phase—when family wasn't around—so saying good-bye, especially for a week, was hard.

He smirked. "I love that you don't want me to go."

"But you have to. I'm not going to go downstairs to say bye."

Nodding, he zipped up his bag and scooped me into his arms. "I love you."

I kissed him. "I love you, too."

He shuffled, and I let him go.

"I'll see you Friday." Bending down, he kissed my forehead.

I watched him leave, and then I waited to hear them drive off before going downstairs.

"Ava," I said when I heard Mum's en-suite shower, "can you give me a lift to Kai's?"

"Now?" she asked, frowning.

"Please?"

"Okay."

I ignored her disapproving gaze and got in her car.

"Is this a good idea?" she asked, pulling out of the drive.

Fucking hell. "Why wouldn't it be?"

"Lucas *just* left."

"Okay, what do you think I'm doing with Kai?"

She shrugged the arm that was holding the gearstick. "I have no idea. Do you?"

"Yeah, actually. What's your problem with him?"

"I have no problem with him, but I think you're playing a dangerous game. Even worse, you don't seem to be able to see it."

"I'm aware of how it might look, but the people who know me know that I wouldn't cheat, and I don't ditch friends for a boyfriend."

She said nothing more, but she didn't need to. Her dark green eyes watched me, judging the entire time.

"Thanks, Ava," I said as we pulled up outside his house.

"No problem," she replied with a fake smile.

I got out as soon as I could, and I didn't look back.

I knocked on the door and waited. "Kai!" I shouted, knocking harder.

If he is still asleep...

The door opened slowly.

"Princess," he mumbled, squinting his eyes.

Wow, he looked rough. His black hair was beyond sexy bed hair, and his eyes were glazed over and tired.

"Ooh, you don't look good," I said, laughing, as I walked past him.

"Thanks," he replied sarcastically.

I watched with amusement as he flopped down on the sofa and closed his eyes.

"Have you eaten anything?"

He mumbled something I couldn't understand and shook his head.

"I'll make you bacon sandwiches then." Looking after him was weird. At least I got to pay back a small amount of what he'd done for me.

Groaning and rubbing his temples, he replied, "You're the best."

I made him drink a whole glass of water and take some painkillers before he ate. Six bacon sandwiches and a cup of strong coffee should sort him out.

Kai inhaled his food. "Thanks for coming over."

"No problem. You've done it enough times for me."

"Yes, I have, pisshead."

"Don't get too cocky, or I'll start talking louder." My voice got progressively louder toward the end of the sentence, and I laughed when he winced. "Why did you get so drunk then?"

He shrugged. "I honestly don't know now."

There was a reason he'd gone overboard, but he didn't want to share. I knew how that felt, so I didn't push him for a real answer.

He leant to the side, resting his head on top of mine. "Wake me in a week," he said.

"Christ, am I as difficult as you?"

Barking a laugh, he replied, "Princess, you're in a whole different league."

Tegan

KAI STRETCHED IN HIS sleep and rolled on me a little more. Half of his body was now draped over mine, pinning me to the sofa. He had been asleep all afternoon. He'd called his dad this morning and told him he was too sick to come into work. I doubted his dad believed him.

I was bored of watching TV, and I'd made the mistake of throwing the remote to the other side of Kai, so I couldn't reach it. I wasn't about to be stuck with the news though.

"Kai," I whispered, nudging him, "I'm bored. Come on, get up."

He groaned and cracked his eyes open. "I'm tired."

"You've been asleep all day. I wanna do something."

He smiled and wiggled his eyebrows.

"That's not what I meant," I said, trying not to laugh at his expression.

"Just a matter of time, princess," he said.

Ignoring him, I slipped out from under half of his weight.

"Where are you going?"

"To kick your arse at Fifa." Grabbing the controllers, I threw one at him.

He laughed. "You think you're gonna win?"

Not at all, but I'm beyond bored, so why not try?

We played Xbox for a while, and I was actually getting better. I'd learnt the buttons, so I didn't have to press them all really fast and just hope. Still, I couldn't beat Kai though. The closest I came to winning was when he scored thirteen goals, and I got two, and I thought he'd let me get those two.

Kai ordered a pizza for dinner, and we continued playing for a while. At ten o'clock, Mum called, saying Ava was coming to pick me up. Kai offered to take me, but he might still be over the limit, and there was no way I was going to risk him getting hurt.

"She still out there?" Kai asked, laughing at me from the sofa. He'd kicked his legs up, and he was leaning back with his hands under his head.

"Yep." I moved away from the window and sat on the recliner, opposite him.

Ava was in her car, waiting outside Kai's house. She wouldn't come to the door, and it was pissing me off. She didn't like him because she thought he was a bad influence and that I couldn't control myself. I didn't need anyone's influence to fuck my life up. I was doing a great job of that all by myself.

So, out of principle, I was waiting until she took the stick out from her arse and knocked on the door. I'd thought that, after she'd spent some time in the pub with him, she would be okay but obviously not.

"How long are you gonna make her wait?"

"Oh, I'm sorry, did you want me to leave?"

Smirking, he replied, "Well, I didn't want to come right out and say it."

"Piss off."

He laughed until we heard the doorbell ring.

"Finally." I walked to the front door with Kai trailing behind. "Hey, Aves," I said as I opened the door.

She looked like she was sucking on a lemon. "Are you ready?"

I nodded even though I wasn't, and I slipped my shoes on.

"See you later, Kai," I said, shoving his shoulder.

"Later," he said, leaning down so that I could kiss his cheek.

Ava and I got in her car, and she started the engine but then stared at me with the dirtiest look.

"What?" I asked.

"What are you doing?"

"Sitting in your car."

"You can't have them both," she snapped.

I knew what she was getting at, but I still replied, "Why not?"

"Are you serious, Tegan? You really expect Lucas to be okay with you being with Kai, too?"

I laughed. *Christ.*

"This isn't funny," she said.

"No, it really is. I don't *have* Kai, Ava. We're friends," I said. "Seriously, you have friends who are guys. Why can't I?"

"You kissed him."

"On the cheek. The same as I do with Adam, James, Holly, and Sophie."

She raised her eyebrows at me, as if she wasn't convinced that Kai and I were just friends. "And what would Lucas think of you kissing Kai on the cheek?"

"It's nothing he hasn't seen before. Lucas isn't that insecure. He knows I would never cheat on him. So, can you drop this grudge now, please?"

"Fine, it's your life," she said, sighing. Her face softened, and she got that look like she was about to bring up something I didn't want to hear. "We're going to Dad's grave tomorrow morning. Do you want to come, too?"

My chest grew tight to the point where I could barely take a breath. I wanted to be able to go there and be close to him, but I wasn't sure if I'd physically be able to. Shutting my feelings off when I was there was ten times harder, and it exhausted me.

"Um…"

"Mum and I'll be there, too."

I couldn't believe it when I heard myself say, "Yeah, I'll come."

Ava was shocked and did little to hide it. "Okay. Good."

We got home, and I went straight to bed, but I decided to call Lucas before I fell asleep.

He answered straightaway, "Hey, shorty."

"Hey. What are you doing?"

"Lying on my bed, talking to my beautiful girlfriend."

I rolled my eyes. "Yeah? What's she like?"

"She's all right."

"Only all right?"

He laughed.

"Hate you."

"Hey," he said, faking hurt. "Anyway, how was your evening?"

"Good. I almost beat Kai at Fifa."

"Almost? What was the score?"

"Thirteen, two," I said, smiling proudly.

He laughed but quickly covered it up. "So, it was a close one then?" he joked, chuckling.

"You can go off people, you know."

"Sorry," he said, smirking because he knows I'm not really going off him.

"I can't wait till Friday."

"Neither can I. I miss you."

"I miss you, too," I said, yawning. "I'm going to go to sleep before I collapse on the phone."

"Okay, speak to you tomorrow."

"Yeah. Night." I hung up the phone, and that was when I heard Mum crying. I felt horrible.

I crept out of my room and along the hall. Ava's hushed voice travelled through the door.

save me

Mum sobbed, and I felt every single one of them squeezing my heart. I didn't want to cry. I blinked rapidly and gulped.

Everything inside me screamed to go to her. I wanted my mum, needed her, but I didn't feel like I could. We weren't close right now, and we'd never been as close as she and Ava. Mum didn't need me. Every time she looked at me, I could see in her eyes how much of a disappointment I was.

I gripped my hair and took a shaky breath. Turning around, I sprinted back into my room and ducked under my covers. I couldn't go in her room.

Just hours later, I woke up, gripping the sheets and gasping for breath. I'd dreamed about Dad. Oh God, I was going to throw up. My body shook, and I curled up in a ball, buried my head in my pillow, and cried until my throat hurt.

I could see it still—his car rolling, his face as he realised he was about to die. In the dream, the car had set on fire, and I'd seen his face burn, turning black and peeling. That hadn't happened, but my fucked up mind had made it worse.

When my tears had dried and I'd managed to calm down somewhat, I sat up and took a sip of water. When I was little and had had a bad dream, I would always go to Dad, and he would sing to me until I fell asleep again. I didn't feel like I could go to Mum or Ava, so I curled back up with the quilt wrapped tightly all the way around me, and I tried not to focus on the big gaping hole he'd left in my heart.

I missed him now more than ever.

"Tegan." Mum lightly shook my arm.

I groaned and looked up at her.

"Morning, honey. We're visiting Dad in an hour. Do you still want to come?"

No. After my dream last night, I didn't want to do anything at all. I didn't even want to exist for a while. My eyes stung from crying and not getting a lot of sleep, and I felt like shit.

"Yeah," I replied, forcing myself to sit up. As much as I didn't want to go, I didn't want to sit at home alone where his memory was everywhere.

She smiled and kissed my forehead before leaving me to get ready.

I got up, had a quick boiling hot shower, and dressed in jeans and a tank top.

To say that I was nervous was an understatement. I was terrified. I wasn't sure why Ava was able to deal with things in a healthy way, and I wasn't. We had the same parents, shared genes, had the same upbringing, but we were so different. She had *super together* built into her, and I had *extreme fuckup* built into me. I wanted to trade.

Mum and Ava walked slightly ahead, stopping every few steps so that I could catch up. They looked forward to visiting him, so they could tell him what was going on while I was doing everything I could just to move closer.

With every step I took, my heart grew heavier until I was sure it'd fall into my stomach at any second. Loneliness gripped ahold of me, weaving itself through my body and into my soul. I just wanted him back. I would give up anything just to have him back.

They sat down in front of his grave and started talking to him, smiling, with tears in their eyes. I stood beside them, staring at his name on the stone, as my dead heart broke even more.

"Do you want to say something, honey?" Mum asked in her soft voice as she reached up and took my hand.

Why did you leave me, Dad?

I shook my head, not looking at her.

"Okay, you don't have to." She let go to focus on Dad again.

I wrapped my arms around my waist, holding myself together. Nothing hurt so much as missing him and trying to find my way without him. I didn't know how to do it. We'd talk about everything and talk everything through. I was so completely lost without him here to guide me.

I needed a drink to block it all out before I sank any deeper than I already was.

Kai

I HUNG UP THE phone with Alison, feeling sick. It was three in the afternoon on a Sunday, and Tegan was wasted. She was wasted and asking for me. Part of me loved that because I wanted her to need me, but I didn't want her to keep doing this shit.

The moment when she realised what she was doing and started to turn it around couldn't come soon enough. But there were no guarantees that'd happen anytime soon. It could be years. She could be one of those people who ended up forty and bitter.

I was waiting for something that might never happen and as much as I knew I should probably walk away—because I'd worked too hard to let someone else pull me under—I couldn't help this feeling that I was supposed to be in her life. I was probably just being a big twat, and meeting her meant nothing more than a handful of one-night stands.

I could imagine what state she was in, and I hated that she had done it to herself. It was frustrating, watching someone with so much potential not give a shit and continually flush their life down the toilet. Now, I knew how my family had felt while watching me go off the rails, and I felt even guiltier for putting them through it.

I arrived at Tegan's house ten minutes later, and Alison let me in.

"She's in her room," she said, closing the front door behind me. "I'm not too proud to admit that I don't know what to do with my daughter anymore. I'm scared for her, Kai."

I could see the worry and stress in her eyes.

"There isn't much any of us can do besides be there when she finally asks for help. Don't be too hard on yourself. This is up to her." Giving her a small smile of what I hoped looked like encouragement, strength, and support, I made my way upstairs and into Tegan's room.

My heart ached as I saw her curled up on her bed. She looked younger than she usually did. She also looked lost and in so much pain.

"Princess," I whispered in her ear as I picked her up.

She mumbled something that I couldn't make out, but she was pale, and I knew what she needed. I grabbed a hairband from the top of her bedside table and went into the bathroom, sitting her in front of the toilet and quickly tying her hair up.

Alison and Ava stood at the entrance of the bathroom and watched. Their concern-filled eyes never left her.

"I feel sick, Kai," Tegan said, slurring her words.

"I know you do. It's okay," I said, rubbing her back.

She leant down, groaning, but she wasn't sick yet.

"You know what to do?" Alison asked.

"I've looked after her a few times before," I replied. Fuck, I wish I hadn't needed to though. "Can you get her two glasses of water, please?"

Tegan coughed and finally emptied her stomach of vodka.

save me

"You okay? You done?" I whispered when she raised her head again.

She nodded and slumped against my chest.

After a few minutes, I picked her up, stood her at the sink, and gave her, her toothbrush to freshen up. Her eyes were now bloodshot, and her skin was blotchy. I wished feeling like shit would discourage her, but I knew she'd be this drunk again.

When she finished brushing her teeth, I helped her get back into bed. Alison had put the two glasses of water on the bedside table.

"Here," I said, handing Tegan the first glass of water.

Not losing her sense of humour, she laughed quietly and took it off me. Usually, I'd get a snide comment but not today. She must really be feeling ill.

She finished the water and smiled up at me. "There. Happy?"

"Ecstatic." I chuckled, and she rolled her eyes, lying back against the wall.

"I'm sorry, Kai," she said, tugging her bottom lip between her teeth.

"Hey, you don't ever have to be sorry with me. It's okay."

"How often does she get like this?" Alison asked, wiping tears from her face.

"She doesn't get *this* drunk all that much anymore."

Tegan looked up at us with a frown. Well, if she wasn't going to talk to her mum, Alison was obviously going to ask someone else.

"You need to stop this," I said to Tegan, tucking her hair behind her ear.

"I know," she replied. She might know that, but it didn't mean she was ready to change it. Or even that she knew how to change it. "I'm tired, Kai. I need to sleep."

I stood up and pulled the covers right up to her chin.

"Night," she whispered.

"Night, princess."

Once she fell asleep, I followed Alison and Ava downstairs.

"Is there anything we can do?" Alison asked.

Maybe. I was going to have to try something. I couldn't watch Tegan do that to herself over and over. But I was terrified that I'd push her away. "I'm going to take her to my mum."

Alison's eyebrows knitted together. "Why?"

"She's a bereavement counsellor. She trained shortly after my brother died."

Why did I just tell them that? I only really spoke about Isaac to my family.

Alison's head cocked to the side, and she got *that* look on her face. "I'm very sorry to hear about your brother."

"Thank you. It was a long time ago. It's how I know what to do when Tegan gets like that, how I know that there's little we can actually do until she's ready. I was exactly the same as her when Isaac died. Worse, actually."

"That's awful. Do you mind if I ask what happened?"

"He had leukaemia. He'd just turned six when we found out. There wasn't a match." *I wasn't a match.*

I was supposed to fix it.

Alison's eyes filled with tears. "He was just six."

"It was awful. Everything happened so fast. We expected to be told he had a virus and he'd be given antibiotics, but barely two months from being diagnosed, he died." I brushed my fingers over the dog tags hanging under my T-shirt. "We thought he was going to be okay. God, he went downhill fast, lost weight, wanted to sleep a lot, and got bad headaches. When he died, I lost it. I was fifteen and so angry with everyone and everything that I did whatever it took to block out the guilt and the pain.

"Tegan's no different. Nothing she does is because she's a bitch or whatever she calls herself. She's just trying whatever she can to stop herself from hurting."

Ava wiped her eyes. "How long did it take you to heal?"

She wanted me to say a few months or a year, tops. It had taken me almost four years to admit my life was in the shit and that I needed to change, and then it'd been a few months more to fully leave my old life behind. Then, it was almost another year until I resembled anything I used to be, only now in grown-up form.

"I went off the deep end at fifteen, and I was twenty by the time I could say I'd fully sorted myself out."

Ava winced. *Definitely not the answer either of them want.*

"I don't know if I can watch my daughter do this to herself for the next four years," Alison said.

"It's different for everyone."

"Simon would have known what to do with her. They were so close, always playing music together or going to car shows. Most things I learnt about my daughter, I learnt through Simon telling me. I worry that she doesn't feel like she can talk to me."

"I don't think she feels like she can talk to anyone right now. I'm hoping my mum will be able to change that. She's had a lot of experience with grieving children and teenagers."

"Thank you, Kai," Alison said.

I nodded once. "I understand that I'm probably not your first choice for a friend for her, but I do care."

"I can see that, and I'm sorry for how we've both behaved in the past."

"It's forgotten."

We stayed talking until late, and Alison asked me to sleep over in case Tegan woke up. I slept on the sofa and woke up with a crick in my neck.

Tegan stood in front of me, smiling sheepishly.

"Hey, you okay?" I asked.

She nodded. "Are you?"

Stretching my neck out, I replied, "I'm fine."

"I'm sorry about last night."

"No apologies. You must have a wicked headache."

She groaned. "I've already taken some paracetamol, but it does feel like I'm being sledgehammered from the inside."

I wanted to make a self-inflicted joke, but really, who the fuck was I to say anything?

Alison and Ava stopped behind Tegan. They seemed to be joined at the hip.

"How's your head now, honey?" Alison asked her daughter.

Tegan smirked and repeated my words, "I hate it."

I gave her a dark look. "Very funny, princess."

"It was actually."

"You should get some more sleep. You look tired still, and I'm taking you to see my mum today."

She frowned and pursed her lips. Confusion suited her. "Don't you think it's a little too soon for that?"

"No, I think we're ready for it."

She laughed again.

"My mum's a bereavement counsellor," I said, waiting for her reaction.

Her face paled, and after a minute, she nodded slowly. "Okay."

Alison gasped, not hiding her shock at all.

Tegan ignored it and asked, "How long has she been doing it?"

"She's fully qualified, if that's what you're worried about."

She rolled her eyes. "Funny. That's not what I meant."

Okay, I guess it's time to tell her.

Alison and Ava left the room, giving us privacy for this conversation.

"She qualified after my brother died."

I watched her face slowly drop.

She was sitting beside me in seconds. "Your brother?"

I nodded. "Isaac had acute myeloid leukaemia. We found out when he was six. He needed stem cell and bone marrow transplants, but Elle, Carly, and I weren't a match, and the hospital couldn't find one in time. He died within months of being diagnosed. I was fifteen and a wreck after."

"I'm so sorry."

"It's okay. I can think about him and talk about him and not have it tear my insides apart now."

save me

Her eyes darkened, and I knew she understood just what I meant. "Will you tell me about him?"

"What do you want to know?"

"What was he like?"

"He was my shadow. I couldn't go anywhere or do anything without him wanting to follow me. As annoying as he could be, we were close, and I would've done anything for him. I was his hero, apparently. He was obsessed with the Army." I gulped, gripping the dog tags around my neck. Remembering still fucking hurt.

Tegan squeezed my hand.

"I lost count of the amount of times I stood on one of those little plastic soldiers. He wanted dog tags, and I didn't have the heart to tell him that the British Army didn't wear them. I bought him these ones," I said, releasing them from my grip. "I found some nice ones—men's ones, as the kid ones were just toys. He deserved the best. They cost a fortune, pretty much all the money I'd saved from my paper route, but it was worth it to see how happy he was. In the end, when he knew there was nothing that could..." I closed my eyes. "When my little brother knew he was going to die, he gave them back to me and said he didn't want them to be buried underground. He wanted me to wear them. I've not taken them off since."

Tears rolled freely down her cheeks. "I'm sorry, Kai," she said as she buried her head in the crook of my neck.

"Shh, it's okay. Everything's going to be all right," I whispered in her ear as I rubbed her back.

After she calmed down, I decided it was time to test the water. "How are you doing now? It's okay to admit you're struggling."

She closed her eyes, and the pain etched on her face kicked me in the gut and took me right back to when Isaac had first died.

"I can't..." she whispered. "I just want to talk to him, even just for a second. He can't just be...gone."

I squeezed her trembling hand. "You can still talk to him whenever you want to."

"It's not the same. I can't have a conversation with him. I can't hear his voice," she replied so quietly that I barely heard her.

It wasn't the same, not at all, but it was all we got when someone died.

"You can't hear him, but you knew your dad, so you know what he'd say in reply."

She looked at me like I was crazy.

"Okay, say you went to him and asked for advice because you'd fallen hopelessly in love with your best friend," I said, pointing to myself, making her roll those pretty, unusual green eyes, "what would he say?"

"He'd tell me I need to get help for my delusional friend."

She giggled. It was probably my favourite sound in the world.

Fuck, I have it bad. When is she going to ditch the overbearing prick?

Tegan diverted the conversation well away from her dad. I knew I couldn't push too much, so I followed her lead, which was getting breakfast to hopefully help her hangover.

After we ate, I made a call to my mum, and she, of course, told me to bring Tegan over ASAP. I imagined half of her wanted to help Tegan, and the other half wanted to check out the girl who had me all caught up and acting like a huge pussy.

When I walked through the front door of my parents' house, my mum, dad and sisters were waiting in the entrance hall. Carly and Elle had converted the double garage into their cupcake business base, so they were often around. Mum worked from home. Dad was hanging back because we had stocktake at work, and like me, he didn't want to be anywhere near it. Even though us kids had moved out, everyone was always home, and my mum loved it.

They stood there and stared at Tegan with idiotic smiles. Subtle, they were not. Glaring at each one of them, I introduced everyone, and Mum took Tegan into her office just off the side of the house.

"So," Carly said as we sat in the lounge and waited, "that's Tegan, hey?"

Here we fucking go.

"She's very pretty."

Pretty didn't even begin to cover it.

"She is," Elle agreed. "Though you usually go for *tall* blondes."

I didn't want to tell her that, for five years, I just used to go for *breathing*, so I shrugged. "Don't really have a type, Elle."

Dad laughed completely out of the blue. The what-the-fuck expression was plastered across each of his kid's faces.

"What?" Carly asked.

Dad looked at me with the smuggest smile I'd ever seen. "You've gone and fallen in love with her."

I hate how easily he can read me. And fuck's sake. I have.

Tegan

AFTER SPENDING A LOT of time locked away while completing schoolwork, I went to my counselling session.

Kai's mum, Melanie, was so nice. She didn't push me to talk about something if I found one of her questions too hard, which I mostly did. The session was more of us chatting than her questioning me, but I had a feeling she got a lot more information out of me than I realised.

She led me out of her office, and I almost bumped into Carly and Elle. They were grinning a little too much.

"So, you wanna see some embarrassing things from Kai's childhood?" Elle asked.

Like she needs to ask.

"Absolutely," I replied.

I followed them down the hallway to what I guessed was Kai's old room. Melanie came along, too, shaking her head at her daughters.

His room was dark blue and black and pretty plain, probably because he didn't live here anymore and had taken most of his stuff with him. It didn't look like his house now though. His house was light and inviting. This was so an angry teen's room.

I sat down on the bed with Carly and Elle while Melanie went to get some photo albums. I wondered what he had been like when he was a teen. It would've been interesting to know him then.

"His room sucks, right?" Carly said. "Mum won't redecorate it."

"Why not?"

"Keeps him grounded."

I frowned but had no time to ask why as Melanie came back.

How can a dark room keep you grounded? It made no sense.

"Ooh, show her the space phase ones first," Elle said.

Yeah, I definitely want to see those.

Apparently, when he was five and six, he had been obsessed with space—to the point where he'd covered objects in his room in foil and made himself a helmet. I could imagine a smaller version of him pretending like he was flying a shuttle. It was adorable.

After many more stories, a lot of them involving space and astronauts, we went downstairs. Kai and his dad, Rob, were in the lounge.

"Hey, spaceman," I said as I sat down next to Kai.

He shot a dark look to his mum and sisters, who didn't even try to hold back on concealing their amusement.

"I can't believe you told her!" he said, sounding annoyed but not at all surprised.

"Oh, they didn't just tell me. I saw pictures."

His mouth hung open.

"You looked so cute with that foil hat."

"Right, we're leaving," he said, standing up and pulling me along by my wrist.

save me

Laughing as I was being hauled toward the front door, I caught a glance at a picture of him on the wall. He was really young, maybe five or six, and had a big toothless grin.

"Hey," he snapped.

Okay, I really loved it when he was embarrassed.

I was almost thrown into his car, and for the whole way home, he ignored me. Partly because I made space and astronaut jokes the entire time, but he was still being a little bitch.

I spent the next day hanging out at home and the evening with Sophie. Friday rolled around, and it was time for my date with Lucas. I spent ages getting ready, or it just took ages because I was getting ready around Netflixing another episode of *Orange Is the New Black*.

"Tegan!" Ava shouted up the stairs. "Lucas' car just pulled up."

About time.

He wasn't even late, but I was impatient.

"Be right down," I called, ruffling my hands through the roots of my hair and then grabbing my phone.

He hadn't even gotten out of his car by the time I was downstairs.

"Don't wait up," I said to Mum before walking out of the house.

"Hey, shorty," he said, walking up the path and holding his arms out for me.

I walked straight into him and curled my arms around his waist. "Hey, yourself. So," I said, pulling back, "where are we going?"

"I'm not telling you."

Not cool.

"Why?"

"Because it's a surprise."

I smiled. "And what if it wasn't a surprise?"

"Then, I could tell you, but this is so…"

Dropping my arms, I pouted. He really did need to understand that I did not enjoy surprises.

"Fine. Let's go somewhere then," I said.

He was pretty amused as he watched me stomp to his car like a child.

"What are you doing?" he asked, shutting his door and grinning at me.

"You know, when you think about it, you're basically kidnapping me right now," I said, ignoring his question. *Why can't he just bloody tell me where I'm going?*

His mouth kicked up at the side, and he started the car. He just looked sarcastic. "Right. Damn that consensual kidnapping."

"Have I told you recently that I hate you?"

"Yes, I think that was during the last surprise."

"So, when are you going to catch on?"

Seriously, you know someone doesn't like surprises, don't surprise them!

When he parked near the bottom of a hill, I glared. "Lucas?"

"It's not steep. There's a gradual climbing footpath to the top."

I could see the sandy path curling around the green hill. At least I wouldn't discover new muscles with this one.

Groaning, I got out of the car and he followed. *We can't just go to the cinema?*

We walked slowly, hand in hand, looking out at everything getting that little bit smaller, the higher we got. The hill was probably only four or five stories tall, but it gave a great view of the cliffs and sea in the distance. Everything was pretty flat where I lived, so I loved visiting Lucas.

We reached the top, and I gasped. He had a small picnic basket sitting on a blue blanket and little silver lanterns lining the edge of the material.

save me

"Luke, this is amazing," I whispered. "When did you do this? How has it not been stolen?"

He laughed. "I texted Grace when we were on our way. My idea but my sister's hard work."

Wow, I didn't think Grace liked me enough to help Lucas do something like this.

"If we don't see her before I go home, thank her for me," I said before giving him a kiss.

"I'm glad you like it, and I will. Come on, I'm starving."

Of course.

He kissed the top of my head and tugged me to the picnic. "You hungry, too?"

I wasn't really, but there was no way I wouldn't stuff my face since he had gone through all the effort of organising this for us.

"Yes, feed me," I said, sitting down between his legs and opening the hamper.

He had chicken salad sandwiches, cocktail sausages, salt and vinegar crisps, a huge bar of Cadbury chocolate, marshmallows, jelly beans, and Oreos. Not exactly healthy, but it was all some of my favourites.

"You're the best, Luke."

"Remember that for later."

Like I wouldn't want sex with him. I rolled my eyes and tucked into a sandwich.

"So, how badly are Grace and Jake teasing you for being romantic?"

"Grace, not at all. My brother and dad, however…"

"Didn't you say your dad proposed to your mum in rose petals?"

He'd briefly told me that when we were first talking and trying the friends-only thing.

"Yeah, but he's a fucking hypocrite."

I laughed and leant back against his chest. "How is your dad?"

I knew that, although he was doing okay, he had been finding it hard to relax. That was understandable. His body could reject my dad's heart at any moment.

"He's all right. His blood pressure is slightly high because of the medication he's on, but the doctor is monitoring it."

I wasn't sure what upset me the most—that my dad didn't have his heart anymore or that it could fail, be cut out, and be thrown away like trash.

I wasn't sure what to say, so I just said, "I hope it settles down soon." I honestly did hope that Carl's blood pressure improved because I wanted him to live a long life, just like my dad should have.

We ate until we were feeling ill and talked for well over two hours. I felt lighter than I had in a long time, but I also couldn't kid myself and think that it was because I didn't have so many things safely locked away. I wasn't sure if I was getting better at dealing with everything or getting better at ignoring it.

"Tegan…"

"Go on," I said, looking up over my shoulder.

"You'll call me if you ever need anything, won't you? I don't care where I am or what I'm doing. You're more important to me than work."

Okay, that was sweet and totally unexpected. "Yeah, of course."

He pressed his lips to the top of my head. "Good. Now, can I talk to you about something without you getting mad at me?"

I guess we'll find out in a minute.

"Yeah."

I felt his chest expand as he took a deep breath.

"When you were drunk, why did you ask for Kai?"

I turned on my side to face him. His eyes were tense.

"I didn't really think about it, but Kai knows what to do when I'm like that. He always has, so I ask for him. I don't want to. I hate that I do it and that I ruin his night all the time. I want to not be like this, Luke, but I don't know how to stop."

"Kai's mum has helped?"

save me

I nodded, and he smiled.

"Well, I'm proud of you for getting help."

I didn't get help, not really. It was kind of thrust upon me, not that I wasn't grateful or didn't understand that I needed something.

"Next time you are drunk, maybe you should call me instead though?"

"Yeah," I agreed even though I wasn't sure I could.

When I was out of it, I didn't consciously decide who I wanted. I'd just call the person I knew who could help the most.

Lucas opened his mouth to say something else but quickly closed it again.

"What?"

"Nothing." He bent his head and kissed me.

"Tell me. Please."

He sighed and took my hand, playing with my fingers. "About Kai." He paused for a second to study my face.

I nodded for him to continue even though I was getting bored of Kai talk from everyone who had an opinion on my friendship with him.

"I know you're friends, but it bothers me, how close you two are." He winced. "Look, I know I have no right to, and I would never ask you to change your relationship with him, but I just want to be honest and say that I don't like it."

His not liking it wasn't a surprise, but I'd made myself clear that I was friends with Kai and nothing more, and no one was going to tell me what I could or couldn't do.

"Luke…" I stopped talking when I realised I actually had no idea how to handle this. "Okay, Kai and I are friends. He means a lot to me, and he's been there for me so many times. He understands because he lost his brother and handled Isaac's death as well as I'm handling my dad's. I want to be with *you,* but I won't change my relationship with him. Maybe that's really selfish, I don't know, but other people have a boyfriend as well as other male friends, so I don't see why it should be different for me. What happened with him is in the past, and I would never cheat on you."

He nodded slowly, frowning, as he thought about what I'd said. "Okay. I can accept that. I do trust you, Tegan. I guess I just needed a little reassurance."

"I don't mind reassuring you if it's what you need to hear and to help you keep on trusting me. Kai's really been there for me."

"I know, and I'm glad he has been."

"Are you cool now? Can we get back to our date?"

He didn't reply. Instead, he laid me down and kissed me until I felt dizzy.

Just after midnight, the temperature had dropped, and we were both getting tired, so Lucas took me back to mine. He gave me a long, deep kiss before leaving me to go back home.

Tegan

After Friday night, I spent most of Saturday with Lucas, too, and it was the perfect weekend. He was so sweet, like going-to-give-me-a-cavity sweet, but it was nice to just be able to relax without drama. I could feel things getting scary-serious fast, but he made me feel something close to happy, so I didn't want to put the brakes on.

Lucas squeezed my hand as we stopped in front of Dad's grave. All I felt was a cold emptiness that reflected my life right now.

"Hey, you okay?" he said, running his thumb over my lip.

It was only then that I felt the sting as I'd been biting it.

I released my lip and smiled up at him. "I'm okay."

"Do you want to say anything?" he asked.

No, I definitely didn't. Well, I wanted to be able to. That was the normal thing to do, right? But the thought of talking to a lump of rock above my dad's cold body made my stomach turn, and I didn't want to open the emotions gate and let it all flood through.

"No, I can't."

Kai had said I would know what he'd say back to me, but I still wasn't ready for silence after I finished speaking.

"Do you want me to?"

Frowning, I said, "Okay."

He didn't know my dad, so what could he have to say to him?

"Hi, Simon. You've probably been watching pretty closely, so I just want to start by assuring you that I won't hurt Tegan. I know the situation isn't exactly the norm, but that doesn't mean we can't make it work."

He was answering questions he thought other people would have for us or be saying about us.

"I bet you've been worried about her, but I promise you, we're all here for her, Alison, and Ava. Nothing will happen to any of them while we're around. I can't thank you enough for what you did for my dad."

Fuck. My blood ran cold.

"Things were bad, really bad. He was just healthy enough to have surgery. Any more time, and he would've been too weak to even take the anaesthetic."

I'd known it'd been bad, but I hadn't known Carl had been *that* ill.

"The day we got the call, we were overwhelmed with relief and worry. It wasn't until I met Tegan at the hospital that I realised what my dad's second chance at life cost another family."

I wanted him to stop, but I couldn't move.

"I wish it could've been another way. I wish I could have met you and had you interrogate me face-to-face. I wish the girl I loved weren't so lost. But she's getting better, going to school."

"I'm so proud of her, and I know you are, too. I won't let her down, Simon, I swear. You gave my dad, my whole family, a chance to be happy and a reason to carry on. I'll do the same for your daughter."

save me

Is that what this is? Is Lucas with me out of guilt?

I took a step back and pulled my hand from his.

"What?" he said, turning around. "Hey, no, that came out wrong. I'm not here because I feel I owe it to Simon. There is nothing I could ever do that would set us straight. I'll do whatever I have to do to make you happy again because I love you, Tegan. That's all there is to it."

I wasn't sure if I believed him or not.

"Okay," I said. "Can we go now? Kai will be picking me up soon."

I'd never needed to get away from Lucas so much. I wasn't going to go out but right now I need to. My head was spinning. I wanted to believe him. He had no reason to lie, not really. But my level of self-respect and self-worth was at an all-time low, and I knew I wasn't the best person in the world, so I couldn't understand why he'd want me.

He hesitated but then replied, "Sure."

Back home, Lucas watched me like he was trying to figure out some hard math problem. Or he was trying to figure me out, which could quite possibly be more fucking frustrating. I hoped he figured me out soon because I would love to know, too.

I never usually wished my time with Lucas away, but I was doing so now, and when Bruno Mars blasted through my phone, I couldn't answer it quickly enough. "Hey, Kai."

"Hey, where are you?"

I gasped. "Are you early?"

He laughed humourlessly. "Where are you?"

"You sounded like such a stalker then," I said, laughing.

"Maybe I am. Look out your window."

I rolled my eyes but sneaked a look out of the corner of my eye. Of course he wasn't outside my window; he couldn't bloody levitate.

"Anyway, are you at mine?"

"Yeah."

"Outside?"

"Yeah."

"My mum and Ava out there?"

"Uh-huh."

I laughed. "Awkward?"

"Maybe," he replied.

"Want me to hurry up?"

"That would be great."

They were better with Kai after he'd looked after me when I was wasted, but it was still a little uncomfortable. Ava thought it was inappropriate that I was still friends with him, and I thought she was a twat.

"Cool. I'll be there in a bit. Have fun."

"Thanks, princess," he replied sarcastically.

"Why does he call you princess?" Lucas asked.

Oh, good, he was listening in.

"Apparently, I act like a diva."

"Oh," he replied.

I wasn't sure if he assumed Kai called me princess because he thought I was one—in the good sense. That could add to Lucas's dislike of Kai. It really wasn't in the good sense though. Kai thought I was a brat. I probably was.

We walked downstairs, and I saw them standing in the front garden.

"Does he not get on with Alison and Ava?" Lucas asked.

"They get on okay, but they're not entirely happy because he's older, which is just stupid."

He nodded tightly. There wasn't that much he could say because he was only a year younger than Kai, still a few years older than me.

"Hey," Kai said, smiling in relief as I stepped outside. "Lucas," he added.

"Kai," Luke said with no enthusiasm whatsoever.

Oh, this is fun.

I was just going to ignore it. There was no way I was picking sides.

"Hey, spaceman—"

Kai held his hand up and warningly raised one pitch-black brow.

save me

"Ready to go?" he asked.

I nodded.

"Have a nice time, sweetheart, and be safe," Mum said.

Kai waited in the car while I said good-bye to Lucas. He kissed me longer than usual and then got in his car to drive back home.

Kai was smirking at me when I got in his car.

"So, you gonna let me drive?" I asked.

"Yeah, sure."

I stared at him for a second. *Did he just say yes?*

"Just show me your driving licence, and we'll switch places," he said. "See? You're still a baby."

I laughed with no humour. "I hope that makes you feel like a dirty old man."

His eyes narrowed, and I sat back in the seat, smiling to myself and feeling very smug.

"I'm not that old, thank you, and as I remember, I met you in a club. You have to be eighteen to get into a club, so technically, jailbait, I should be pissed off with you." He tried to keep a straight face, but I could see him struggling with it.

I knew, in about five minutes' time, I'd have the perfect comeback, but right now, I had nothing. "You know you suck, right?"

He threw his head back and laughed. "Tegan, out of the both of us, I'm definitely not the one who *sucks*."

That wasn't exactly true, but I didn't want to get into a conversation about all the times he'd had his mouth on me, so I kept my mouth shut and slapped his arm.

Driving to the house Holly and James were viewing, Kai would snicker now and then, still very pleased with himself. I got out of the car and ignored him.

Joan, Holly's aunt, was an estate agent, so she let them have the keys for a few hours, as the house was empty. The house was at the end of a row of four and looked pretty cute with a little wooden fence and colourful flower beds.

Holly and James were waiting outside for us, and I could feel Holly's excitement. Still ignoring Kai, I followed them inside after saying a quick hello.

"Are you not talking to me?" Kai asked, failing again not to laugh.

I looked away from him and just knew he was shaking his head at me. We walked into every clean, bright room, and for a new house, it actually didn't look that boring and samey as they usually did. It still needed personalizing, but it was plenty big enough.

"I love it, I love it, I love it," Holly chanted as we walked into the back garden.

She'd said that about every room, so I was pretty sure James would be getting his chequebook out real soon.

"Come on, talk to me," Kai said, groaning and trying to step in front of me.

"You shouldn't have been a dick to her then," Holly said, poking him in the chest.

"You don't even know what I've done," he replied. Technically he hadn't done anything with his little jailbait remark but this was amusing.

"But I know you've done something."

I rolled my eyes. "Fine, I forgive you for being a prick."

"Thanks," he replied sarcastically.

James grabbed Holly's hand and said, "Let's go see upstairs again. I want to make sure we can get all your clothes in the room."

"There are three bedrooms, James."

"Yeah, I know!"

I heard her nagging at him as they walked back inside. I was left with Kai.

Narrowing my eyes, I crossed my arms over my chest. "Are you ready to be nice to me now?"

He opened his arms. "You only ever need to ask, and I'll be as nice as you want, whenever you want."

I slapped his chest. "Ha-ha."

Dropping his hands to block my blow, he asked, "So, where's your crazy friend?"

I knew he meant Sophie. "Why is she crazy?"

"She keeps texting me."

"Yeah, you're right. She must be crazy if she likes you."

He glared. "I know you don't mean that. You've been under and over me enough times."

I really had brought it on myself. "She's with Will."

"Ah, Will's this week's conquest then."

I slapped him again in Sophie's defence.

"He's not a conquest. She just likes to try before she buys."

He laughed. "Right. Hey, I'm all for doing what the fuck you want, but a reputation as a slut is hard to shake and makes it difficult to get the person you want to trust you to actually trust you."

"Hey, I was like her before," I said.

His words made me feel ashamed, not that I hadn't been already. Losing my virginity in the backseat of a car was a particularly low point.

He ran his fingers over my forehead, flattening my frown. "You were nothing like her."

"You didn't know me right after my dad died, Kai."

"So, tell me."

I looked at him like he'd grown another head, and then I started to consider it.

"Tell me." He snorted. "It can't be that bad."

Oh, it was.

"Okay. I was innocent before he died, like nun innocent. A few days after his funeral, on a drunken night, I lost my virginity to Adam's older brother in the back of his car. Then, I started sleeping with random guys at clubs and parties, and I didn't care what happened to me. Before I met you, there was a different guy almost every time I went out, and I hate myself for it."

"I'm sorry, princess. Your first time shouldn't have been like that," he said as he wrapped me in his strong arms.

"It's fine. Not every girl gets flowers, candles, and expensive hotel rooms, Kai."

"You should have," he replied.

I smiled and kissed his cheek. "Thank you."

"My pleasure. Hold on, I was one of your passing random guys?"

"You were, but I just can't seem to get rid of you," I teased.

Completely unexpectedly, he bent down and bit my neck, making me squeal.

"Boundaries!" I yelled.

Laughing, he pulled back and winked. I was still in his arms, and I was pretty sure I couldn't overpower him to get out.

"Whoa!"

I looked up to see James and Holly at the back door.

James pouted. "Hey, we want to be the first ones to christen the garden, so knock it off."

"Very funny," I replied dryly, shoving Kai off and slapping his chest for the third time in as many minutes.

He did nothing but flash that cocky smile.

Kai

I WOULD DAMN WELL love to christen the garden or any room with her. She drove me crazy and could literally get me hard with just one look. I wished I'd met her right after her dad died. Maybe then she wouldn't have lost her virginity on the backseat of a car. I wasn't an angel, but I wouldn't have let that be a girl's first time. Well, not anymore anyway.

Back at mine, Tegan and I sat on the sofa, waiting for Sophie and Mark to get here. She'd spent the day with someone called Will, but she had moved on already. I didn't even know as many people as she'd slept with.

"Don't leave me alone with Sophie tonight, Tegan," I said as Holly let them in.

She giggled and grabbed my hand. I felt her touch down south.

"I got your back. Don't worry…Astro."

"Astro?" I asked, raising my eyebrows.

"Spaceman's just too long."

Fuck my family.

"No," I said. "No space-related nicknames, or I'll have a chat with your mum. There must be something I can use against you." Of course I wouldn't really have a conversation with her mum since I was pretty much the Antichrist.

We decided to keep things low-key, eating greasy Chinese and watching something funny on TV.

I positioned myself on the edge of the sofa beside Tegan. That way, wandering-hands Sophie couldn't cop a feel. I didn't mind an assertive woman, but I wasn't keen on sex pests. Thankfully, Sophie seemed to be a one-man woman tonight, but I wasn't taking any chances.

"I'm so full," Tegan said, handing James her half-eaten chow mein.

He'd polish that off and everyone else's leftovers, too.

Pig.

Tomorrow, Tegan would be starting back at sixth form, and although I wanted to keep her here for as long as possible and drive her home in the early hours, I knew I couldn't. I didn't want her to feel like shit on her first day back, so we were doing a late afternoon thing. Selfishly, I did want to keep her longer. I wanted to do a lot of things with and to her actually.

By the time the vultures had downed all my beer and stuffed their faces full, it was getting later and time for them all to do one.

I bundled a very reluctant Tegan in my car and waved the others off. I was almost certain that Sophie was giving Mark a blowjob as he drove off. She wasn't that short.

"I feel like a child," Tegan whined as I drove towards her place. "It's still early."

"Well, at least you're handling it maturely. You have to get up early in the morning, and if I don't take you home now so that you can get a good night's sleep, I know you'll be chewing my ear off tomorrow."

She folded her arms over her chest and pouted as I pulled up outside her house. I knew she didn't like being home much, but this was ridiculous and a bit amusing.

"Hey, now, you look like a child, too."

She gave me a dark look and tried not to laugh.

"Wanna come in and watch a movie? I'll even let you choose," she said.

"Can you not entertain yourself for one night?"

She saw straight through me though. I was sure *hell yeah* was written all over my face.

"Great. So, what do you wanna watch?"

"*One* film, Tegan, and not a long one."

"Aw, Kai, don't beat yourself up too much, you're not that small."

I should've expected that as soon as I'd said "long one." Rolling my eyes, I got out of the car and ignored her laughing behind me.

She let us inside and we went up to her room. Her mum and sister were either out or asleep because we didn't see them, not that Tegan tried to find where they were.

We sat on her bed and watched *Letters to Juliet*. Turned out, it wasn't my choice after all. Didn't really matter though. Tegan got ready for bed, and I had an awesome view of her legs in tiny shorts.

Ava popped her head around the open door. "You two want a drink?"

That was the second time in less than half an hour that she'd asked. It was obvious what she was doing, but it was really unnecessary. I wasn't about to jump Tegan's bones when she had a boyfriend and her family was just downstairs—unless she asked nicely.

Tegan, reaching her limit, snapped, "We're not having sex, Ava!"

Oh, dear God, what do I say now?

I smiled, trying to make it look natural, when all I wanted to do was laugh. Ava was being fucking annoying, but Tegan had successfully shut her up.

Turning on her heel, Ava stalked off, shaking her head.

Just when everything was going to shit on screen—though it'd be fine in ten minutes time, no doubt—Tegan fell asleep.

I crept off the bed and brushed her blonde hair out of her face. *Fuck, she is beautiful.* Her long eyelashes cast shadows on her face, and her pink lips pursed, ready to be devoured. Okay, I needed to leave before I did something I would not at all regret.

Her phone rang, and Lucas's name flashed on the screen.

"Princess." I nudged her shoulder, but she didn't even flinch.

Shit. I pressed the Answer button. "Hello, Lucas."

"Kai? Where's Tegan?"

I nudged her again, and she groaned.

"Go away, Kai," she mumbled sleepily.

Chuckling, I replied to Lucas, "Er, she's asleep."

"Yeah, I heard," he said, sounding amused. "So, how was the house?" he asked, forcing small talk.

"It was good. I think they're gonna buy it."

"Cool. So, she's at home now?"

"Yeah, she was bored and wanted to watch a film. I think she might be nervous for tomorrow, too."

"Right. Yeah, makes sense. Can you tell her to call me when she wakes up?"

"Sure." *I won't be here…*

"Thanks."

We hung up at the same time, neither of us wanting to drag out the conversation any longer.

I put the phone down and got back on the bed. Willpower was never my strong point. "You awake?"

She didn't say anything, so I kissed the top of her head.

I love you.

"She sleeping?" Alison asked as she came into Tegan's room twenty minutes later.

"I'm not sleeping," Tegan mumbled into her pillow, throwing her arm over my stomach.

save me

Perfect. I was gonna get a hard-on when her mum was standing right there.

"Sure you weren't," I said.

Alison came in and sat on the bed with us. It was getting awkward pretty fast, and I was trying desperately to control my hormones.

"Whatever, Astro. What's the time?" Tegan groaned and sat up.

"Astro?" Alison asked.

Tegan laughed, suddenly waking up. "Kai had a big space phase when he was younger."

"Okay, *princess*, it was a long time ago, and I really don't think we need to bring it up."

"Aw, but you looked so cute with your little foil helmet."

I turned to Alison. "What dirt have you got on her?"

She laughed and stood up. "Lots. I'll go get the photo albums."

Tegan grinned. "You know she doesn't have anything on me. I'm perfect."

"Of course you are."

Her playful facade faltered for a second. She didn't believe that at all.

Who fucking is?

"Here." Alison came back in and handed me an album.

"Seriously, Mum?"

I flicked open the first page and ignored Tegan shooting daggers into the side of my head. She was a cute kid—all big green eyes, unruly blonde hair, and cheesy smiles.

Alison leant over. "This is Tegan when she was three. It was the first Christmas when she was excited about Father Christmas. She dressed up as an angel and wanted to be the one on the tree. When we said she couldn't actually sit up there, she threw a huge tantrum."

"Yeah, I can believe that," I said.

Tegan mumbled something about hating us both, but I couldn't care less. This show-and-tell was golden.

"So, have you got any really embarrassing pictures?" I asked.

I flicked through the albums while Alison told me stories. Both Alison and I were laughing. The little princess was not.

"Are you guys finished?" Tegan asked, frowning adorably.

I closed the last album. "For now, yes."

"I hope you know I'm going to be seeing your mum again on Wednesday, and I'll be asking her for stories, too."

Damn, I didn't think of that.

I put on a poker face and smiled. "Knock yourself out."

"I will."

Ava came in next—she really couldn't help herself—and she sat beside Alison. She looked between me and Tegan and raised her eyebrows. She clearly had a problem with us.

My side was touching Tegan's. *Ooh…*

"What are we talking about?" Ava asked.

"Embarrassing moments from Tegan's childhood," I replied.

"And we've finished. You suck, Kai!"

Laughing, I nudged her. When Ava and her judgmental eyes weren't around, things were actually pretty normal. Alison was cool with me now, and I felt more and more comfortable around her.

"You ready for sixth form, honey?" Alison asked.

Tegan groaned. "Yeah."

Alison tilted her head. "I thought you were looking forward to it?"

"I am, but it means getting up early again."

"You don't have to get up that early," I said.

She pointed, lifting an eyebrow. "It's before ten."

"Well, yeah…"

"So, Kai, do you have a girlfriend?" Ava asked.

It wasn't a question that surprised me. The timing did though.

I clenched my jaw. She knew the fucking answer to that.

"No," I replied.

save me

If Alison wasn't here, I'd have said something a little more colourful.

"Let's go, Ava," Alison said as she got up.

She looked embarrassed that her daughter had asked me that. It didn't bother me, not really. I was fine with people not liking me.

"Tegan, don't be up too late, okay?"

Tegan nodded at her mum before she closed the door.

"I'm sorry about my idiot sister."

"Hey, it's fine." I'd had worse.

Tegan

I COULD HAVE KILLED Ava for asking Kai that. It wasn't even a general getting-to-know-someone question either. It was loaded, and everyone had known exactly *why* she was asking. And she called me a bitch.

There wasn't really anything I could say to Kai without getting into a conversation I didn't want to have. He knew the deal—everyone knew the fucking deal—so there was no point in going over it. I had to believe that, if Kai had started to feel something for me, he could either deal with it or tell me we needed not to spend as much time together.

"You should sleep soon, princess. It's getting late. Oh, and Lucas called while you were sleeping. He wants you to call him back," he said.

"I will soon, but I'm gonna get a drink. You want one, too?"

Smirking, he replied, "Please."

I got up and left, needing a little bit of space to call Lucas and hopefully run into Ava and tell her to back the fuck off. I didn't interfere in her life, so she needed to stay out of mine.

I dialled Luke's number.

He picked up almost immediately. "Hey."

"Hey, Luke. Sorry I missed your call. I was sleeping."

"Yeah, Kai said. So, what are you doing now?"

Translation: Is Kai still there?

"Just getting us some drinks. We're watching movies to take my mind off school tomorrow."

"You'll be fine. I'll come over tomorrow after work and take you out to dinner."

"You don't have to do that."

We didn't live that far apart really, but it was a little too far to be doing short, frequent visits.

"I want to see you. In case you've forgotten, I'm completely in love with you."

"Yeah, well, I might love you, too."

"Thanks," he said sarcastically.

"So, where are we going to eat tomorrow?"

"Wherever you want, babe."

"Hmm, I'll think of something." It would have to be somewhere that served large portions, or he'd be hungry five minutes later. "I'm gonna go. I'll text you in the morning, okay?"

"All right, speak to you tomorrow. Have a good day at sixth form. I love you."

"Thanks. Night," I said. I hung up, made our drinks and carried them up to my room.

"Thanks," Kai said as I handed him his drink. "You going back to sleep anytime soon?"

I shook my head. "Can't. I'm nervous as hell, so I know I won't be able to sleep yet. Want to watch another film until I'm tired?"

"Sure," he replied, more than happy to chill at my house until the early hours.

save me

We were so comfortable around each other that we could sit for hours and not even speak. I'd known Sophie and Adam a lot longer, but there was no denying that I was closer to Kai.

We finished watching another film, and it was almost midnight. I *really* needed to sleep, but I didn't feel at all tired.

"I should go and let you sleep, Tegan, or you're going to feel like shit tomorrow." Kai sat up.

I pouted. "I'm not tired. Can you just knock me out?"

Chuckling, he shook his head and swung his legs off my bed. "I don't think I'll be doing that."

"Ugh, you're a sucky friend. At least sing me to sleep."

He sighed loudly, pretending to be annoyed. "Fine, I'll sing to you, and then you can stop your whining, *princess*, and get some bloody sleep."

I could argue with him for calling me princess this time, but I didn't even really care as long as I got some rest before sixth form.

"Lie down."

I did as he'd said, and he laid against the wall beside my bed. My face was by his arm, and I stared at Isaac's tribute on his skin. It really was beautiful and showed just how much Kai loved his little brother and wanted a constant reminder of him.

I wasn't at all surprised when he started singing "Just the Way You Are." Maybe it was the only song he knew. Kai was more into rock music, so it was probably the only soothing one he knew.

His voice was gorgeous—low, deep, and sexy. He could sing professionally, but I knew there was no way he'd ever want to do that.

By the time he started the chorus for the second time, I was out of it, falling asleep with a smile on my face.

In the morning, I woke up late. My first day back, and I was going to miss the bell. Rushing around, I was so nervous that I couldn't eat, for fear of seeing my breakfast again.

School was only a two-minute walk, so the second I was ready, I headed out. It was the beginning of June, a lovely, hot day. I'd only have about seven weeks to catch up before the summer holiday, but I was determined.

My phone rang on the way, Bruno Mars telling me it was Kai calling.

"Hey," I said into the speaker.

"Morning," he said.

"So, what time did you leave last night?"

"Just after you fell asleep. I just wanted to call and wish you luck for today, not that you'll need it."

"Thank you. I need to go now though. I'm just coming up to the gates."

"Okay, and the offer's still there—you know, if you need a ride, just call me."

"Thanks, but I'll be okay. I'll call you later."

"Bye, princess."

"Bye."

I stopped dead as I spotted Lucas's car parked between two others.

What the...

He got out as I approached, and he leant against the door. "Hey, babe."

"What are you doing here? Not that I'm not happy to see you." I walked straight into his arms and held on tight. All my worrying evaporated as he held me.

"I wanted to come and wish you good luck in person. I knew you'd be freaking out."

"Thank you."

His lips sealed over mine, and he softly kissed me for a long time. It was completely inappropriate, and I hoped no one was watching, but I didn't really care that much. He was here, and that was all that mattered.

save me

I pulled away when he tried deepening the kiss. I actually needed to go into school—like, five minutes ago. "I'm running late. I have to go."

"I know. Have a good day."

"Thanks. God, I can't believe you came all this way just to wish me luck."

"Call me when you can, and I'll see you tonight."

He released me, and I waved over my shoulder, walking toward my group of friends, who were waiting by the door to the sixth form building. They looked very interested in what they'd just witnessed.

I took a deep breath. *Well, at least Lucas will be a good icebreaker.*

Seeing me with my boyfriend wore off quickly, and we were back to having nothing to say. Josie, Laura, Lance, and Billy stared at me. These people were supposed to be my friends, but it was awkward as hell. I wanted lessons to start already, but we still had ten minutes, and I was counting down the seconds.

I entered the classroom and took a seat before I could change my mind and run.

"How are you doing?" Valarie asked, dropping down in the seat next to me.

Valarie was in everyone's business all the time. Her follower, Alsa, sat on the other side.

"Fine," I replied tightly.

"We're so sorry about your dad."

My throat closed.

"We all are," Laura added. "I don't know what I'd do if I lost my dad. You're so strong."

I wasn't, and I felt myself dip under the water.

Josie, a girl I thought who would help me, said, "If there's anything we can do…"

"Have you thought about planting a tree? We did that for my grandad," Valarie said.

I wanted to run. The room felt tiny. I felt tiny. Everyone looked at me, waiting to see if they'd eased my pain any. They meant well, but it wasn't going to work. I didn't want to talk about it.

"Um, I'll think about it," I replied, wrapping my arms around my stomach, holding myself together.

"Tell us if there's anything, hon. I know what you're going through," Alsa said.

Closing my eyes, I tried to block them out. It was painful. Their words felt like burns on my skin. Everything they said was a reminder of how much I'd lost, and it hurt so much that it took my breath away.

"Tegan, you okay?" Josie asked. "Shall I get someone?"

I wanted to ask for my dad.

Opening my eyes, I stood up and replied, "No, I'm fine. Just need the bathroom."

I rushed to the ladies' and closed myself in the closest stall. No one was in here, thankfully. Leaning back against the graffitied wall, I slumped to the floor.

I'm okay, I chanted over and over, trying to convince myself.

My heart ached.

Why did my dad have to die? He'd never done anything bad in his life. He had been a good person, but now, he was gone, and I was drowning.

The day had started well, but I just wanted to run now. I wasn't sure if I could do this.

Lucas

I SAT IN THE lounge, watching football with Dad and Jake. My life had recently revolved around Tegan and worrying about her. I felt like I'd turned into a shit son. Dad was still a priority, and I spent a lot of time stressing over how he was doing and what could happen, but I felt like I hadn't been around for him as much as I should.

I hated that she'd had a shit week at sixth form. We'd all come straight to theirs for a weekend to support them all. Alison, Ava, and Tegan were so important to us, so there was no question about packing up and coming here.

Alison was upset that Tegan had been having a hard time settling back in. Apparently, she would come home every day in a worse mood than usual. I'd noticed a difference, too. Her phone calls had been shorter, and she was distant.

Watching the game with Dad and Jake used to be something I'd look forward to, but all I wanted was to be upstairs with Tegan. But I wouldn't go up. She needed space, and I needed space. Plus, I wanted to show Dad that I was there for him. Of course, whenever I apologised to him, he would tell me to shut up. He just wanted things to go back to normal, like when we did our own thing. Things couldn't be normal though.

"Luke, focus," Jake said, nudging me in my ribs with his elbow.

I turned my attention back to the television and tried to watch the game. "Fuck off, Jake."

"Easy," Dad said. "You wanted to relax, Lucas, so do it. If you'd rather be with Tegan, then go up there. Neither of us is going to hold it against you."

Jake grinned. "We'll take the piss, you loved up twat, but we won't be arseholes about it."

"Oh, good," I replied sarcastically. "I'll check on her at halftime."

Mum, Grace, Alison, and Ava sat in the conservatory, occasionally looking in our direction through the window, so we knew what they were talking about.

I wondered if Grace had shared her reservations about me and Tegan with anyone else. She didn't really want us to be together until Tegan got herself straight. The more Grace said it to me, the more I worried that she was right. I didn't want to be the reason Tegan wasn't moving forward. We'd gotten together quickly, and things were serious straightaway, but I thought I could help her. I wasn't convinced I was helping anymore.

The game stopped for halftime, and I went upstairs to find Tegan and see how she was doing. No matter how much she pretended she was okay, everyone knew the truth. Tegan was struggling, much more than we probably assumed. At this point, I had no idea what would be for the best.

She wasn't in her bedroom, but the covers looked like she'd been in bed.

"Tegan?" I called out.

But I got no reply.

We'd have seen her if she'd come downstairs.

save me

I left her room and headed to the bathroom. The door was ajar.

I saw the blood first, and as I pushed the door open, I saw my girlfriend lying on the floor. Every muscle in my body locked up.

Her eyes were closed but red and puffy around the edges. Her face was stained with tears. The small pool of blood was coming from a gash on her wrist, the razor blade discarded next to her lifeless pale body.

"Tegan!" I shouted, snapping back to life.

Fuck, no.

I dropped beside her, and with shaking hands, I shook her shoulders. "Tegan, wake up. Talk to me. Baby, no. Come on, get up."

She was clammy and cold.

"Help!" I bellowed in the direction of the door.

Pressing my forehead to hers, I pleaded, "Wake up. Please, don't do this to me."

I fought the urge to chuck up. The smell of her blood burned the back of my throat.

I felt the same level of fear as I had when Dad went in for the transplant, and I wasn't sure if I'd see him alive again. It took me right back there to a place of pure terror and the feeling of having absolutely no control.

Alison screamed her daughter's name and dropped on the other side of her. Someone, I wasn't sure whom, was already on the phone, snapping that they needed the ambulance service.

I hadn't cried since Dad's diagnosis, but I couldn't hold off now. "Wake up, please. Tegan, please. I love you. Wake up."

A small bottle of pills was also beside her. I picked it up and launched them against the wall.

What the fuck was she thinking?

"You're okay, you're okay, you're okay," Alison chanted, lifting Tegan's head and placing it on her lap. She started stroking her hair. "Everything's fine. You're okay."

Ava hugged her mum from behind, sobbing into her back.

"It's all right, Ava. She's fine. I can't lose her, too. She's okay. My baby will be okay."

Only she wasn't fine. Her chest rose and fell, but it looked weak.

Please.

Time stood still as we waited for someone to come and help her. I didn't know what to do. Jake had a towel to her wrist, but beyond that, we were clueless. I was too stunned to even think straight.

Then, we heard sirens and all sat up. I'd never been so happy to see anyone as I was when Grace showed two paramedics into the room. We were told to step out of the room and give them space to work. Alison stayed beneath Tegan, telling the paramedics that she would be okay, and Jake took over, giving them helpful information.

And I...well, I stood by the door, watching in horror, as the girl I loved lay limp on the floor. Mum and Grace both hugged me and whispered comforting words. I didn't feel anything other than panic and despair. I wanted to believe Alison, but I knew she was just saying what she needed to believe.

Tegan was picked up and whisked out to the ambulance, and Alison got in the back of it.

I followed and watched them drive away. It didn't feel real. All I wanted to do was wake up.

"Lucas," Jake said, slapping my back. He frowned at me like I'd lost it. "Come on, we gotta go. I'll drive you."

I had no idea how we'd gotten to the hospital or the waiting room, but we were sitting around in a cheery blue room, waiting for news. Alison was still convinced that Tegan would be okay. Watching her pain over her daughter was unbearable. But then so was what I was feeling.

When we'd got to hospital, Tegan was being worked on, and I couldn't see her. I just wanted to know what was going on, but the nurse didn't have minute updates.

Sitting on a chair since I'd arrived, I'd been staring off into space. I couldn't lose her. She was only seventeen fucking years old. Tegan had to be okay because there were so many people in her life who needed her to be. She had to get better— physically and mentally—and live the long, happy life she deserved.

I should've done more.

Blowing out a painful deep breath, I ran my hands through my hair.

"Lucas?" Jake shook my arm. "Hey, come on, Luke. She'll be fine."

"Jake, if she dies, I can't..."

"Can't what?" he asked cautiously.

"I don't know."

I wouldn't do what she had, not ever, but I knew that, if she died, a piece of me would, too. She'd lost so much when Simon was killed. I was supposed to make it better. I needed her to get through this, so I could do that.

"Mrs Pennells?" a doctor said as he walked into the room.

I was on my feet along with everyone else.

"We've pumped Tegan's stomach, and we're now giving her some oxygen. She's awake but drowsy. We thought she'd need stitches on her wrist, but fortunately, the bleeding stopped, so we should get away with just bandaging it. However, if the cut opens and bleeds again, she might need to have them. I'll ask that only immediate family come through to see her now."

That was all I needed to hear. My tense muscles relaxed a little.

Alison burst into tears. "She's okay. Oh, thank God."

The doctor nodded. "We're referring her for counselling, and she'll need to stay in for a day or two. We'll see how she is tomorrow."

"When will she start counselling?" Ava asked.

"We'll arrange for her to see someone here. Her name's Judy Cross, and she's incredible. Judy will assess Tegan and then arrange for her to see someone local to you. The key is finding someone you're completely comfortable with, whose expertise fit your needs."

"She's been seeing someone once a week now," Alison said.

He nodded. "Okay, well, perhaps she needs more frequent sessions, but you can discuss that with Judy."

"Yeah, okay," Alison said. "Can I see her now?"

"Of course, Mrs Pennells."

"Can I come? Please," I asked. I'd get down on my knees and beg if I had to.

Ava looked like she was about to object even though I'd not been allowed yet.

"Please?" Alison added, backing me up. "I know you said immediate family but Tegan would want him there."

"Okay, but you can't stay long."

"I just need to see that she's all right."

We walked down the corridor past a few private and shared rooms. Ava said nothing but the tightness in her eyes showed she wasn't thrilled that I was coming along.

"Right, this is her room. I'll be back in a while to check on her," he said as he gestured down the hall.

Tegan was lying on the bed, staring at the ceiling. Fresh tears stained her face.

She'd never looked so lost or so down before. I wanted to run away as much as I wanted to stay. Being with her was hard, but at this point, I couldn't imagine not being with her. It hadn't been long, but I felt so connected to her.

I walked over and stroked her cheek. "Hey, shorty," I said.

My heart squeezed as I saw her lying on that bed. She blinked heavily and looked a little dazed. The oxygen mask was lying around her neck, and there was a bandage on her wrist.

"Hey," she said weakly, not looking away from the same spot on the ceiling. She was so pale that she looked ill, like she had the flu. But she was here.

"Honey, what…" Alison asked, trailing off.

I didn't think she could finish the sentence.

A tear rolled down Tegan's cheek. I gently brushed it away with my thumb and kissed her forehead.

"I'm sorry," Tegan whispered. She rolled onto her side, curled up as small as she could, buried her head in the pillow, and cried.

I knew time was a healer, but I didn't feel like we had much time. She probably needed months, years, but she was hanging on by a thread.

"It's okay now," I said, stroking her hair. "I love you. You're going to be all right. I promise, Tegan, you'll be fine."

She cried until she choked. That made her calm herself down. The whole time, she ignored that we were there, and when she was done, she stayed in her protective ball and stared into space.

We had so many questions for her, but neither I nor Alison and Ava had a clue as to how to handle this Tegan. Not that we'd had a clue how to handle her before either.

"Honey, I need you to talk to me," Alison said. "I have to hear you tell me that you'll never do anything like that again."

Squeezing her eyes closed, she replied, "I won't. I'm tired. Please let me sleep."

Alison and Ava frowned at each other, but I got understood why we were being shut off. Tegan couldn't look at us, couldn't talk to us. She was ashamed and regretful, and that made me finally feel like she had a chance at coming back from whatever dark place she was in. Thank fuck for that.

"Sleep then, baby," I said before kissing the top of her head.

She'd be fine. But I wasn't sure if our relationship would be.

41

Kai

Tegan didn't answer, so I slipped my phone back into my pocket and concentrated on the conversation my parents, sisters, and grandparents were having.

Nan had fallen over again last week and sprained her ankle. I'd lost count of how many times we'd told the stubborn woman to stop using the bloody stepladder.

She was taking a while to heal, and if there was one thing Nan hated, it was feeling useless. We were over her house to try to take her mind off of it, and it was at my expense since Tegan had just been mentioned for the ten millionth time in three short hours.

"So, tell me more about this girl," Nan said.

I glared at Mum, and she looked away quickly. She wasn't supposed to tell the nosy old woman anything about Tegan because I had known this would happen, but she just couldn't help it.

I sighed. "She's just a friend." I had to force the last word out.

That was all Tegan wanted from me though, so it was tough luck, Kai.

"Really, honey? Your mum said you were in love with her."

"I'm going to make some tea," Mum said, jumping up and making a quick exit.

Why the fuck would she have told Nan something like that? And how fucking obvious is it?

"You love her?" Nan asked.

"Yeah, it's so painfully obvious," Elle said.

Oh, good, that obvious.

Groaning, I shoved my hands through my hair.

Elle laughed. "Don't worry; she clearly still thinks you're cool with being friends. See, Nan, Tegan has a boyfriend, but it's complicated. Kai's in love with her, and they're so great together. She just hasn't realised how she feels about him yet."

I didn't even need to be here.

Nan raised her eyebrows at me. "You should just kiss her."

I laughed. *Yeah, that'd go down well.*

"Thanks for the advice, Nan, but I think I'll wait."

"Just what every girl wants—a guy who waits," she said sarcastically. "Whatever happened to fighting for what you want? That's what you should do, honey—go and tell her how you feel."

My phone rang. *Alison? Why is she calling me?*

"Hello?" I said.

"Kai."

My heart stopped beating when I heard her sobbing.

Tegan. Fuck.

"What?" I whispered, trying to stop the churning in the pit of my stomach.

"She's in the hospital," she said. It sounded like she was shaking.

I froze. *How bad is it?*

"She swallowed some tab-tablets."

I felt like the floor had been whipped away. *She tried to kill herself?*

"Kai? Are you there?"

"I'm on my way." I hung up the phone and pulled my keys out of my pocket. I ran out of the house without pausing to explain what'd happened. Nothing else mattered but getting to Tegan.

"Kai! Kai!" Dad grabbed my arm just as I was about to get in the car. "Stop for a second. What's going on?"

"Tegan. I have to go, Dad," I said, pushing his hand away. "She's in the hospital. I gotta go."

I suddenly felt like throwing my guts up. *She fucking tried to end her own life. How the hell didn't I notice her sinking that low? I've been there, for fuck's sake.*

"I'm driving," Dad said, snatching the keys from my clenched fist.

I nodded and ran around to the other side of the car.

I stared out the window as Dad drove as fast as he could toward the hospital. Nan's place wasn't closer so it would be a couple of hours before I got to her. Anything could happen in that time. I didn't know how bad the situation was, and I was too scared to call. If it were the worst, then at the very least, I'd have another two hours of thinking she was still breathing.

For the first time since I'd found out Isaac had leukaemia, I prayed. I wasn't sure what I was praying to. Anything or anyone that could do something.

"What happened, Kai?" Dad asked after twenty-five minutes of listening to me tap my fingers on the leather seat.

"She tried to..." *Fuck.* "Kill herself." *God, that isn't easy to say out loud.*

I squeezed my eyes shut and clenched my jaw. Dad said nothing.

"I don't know how she is," I said.

Jesus, I needed to know. It couldn't wait. Fuck ignorance or whatever, I found the number for the hospital and dialled.

I was put through to two different people before someone could help.

"Tegan Pennells," I said. "She was brought in a little while ago. I need to know how she is."

I was put through to a ward and felt myself lose patience every time I had to wait to know if the girl who had stolen my heart had crushed it completely. When a nurse picked up, I relayed the same message.

"Are you family?" she asked.

"No, I'm her friend, but please, can you just tell me if she's okay?"

"I can't give out any information without the patient's or guardian's permission. I'm sorry."

"Well, can you ask her mum to give her permission?" I asked through clenched teeth.

She sighed. Fucking sighed. "What's your name?"

"Kai Chambers."

"Hold a minute."

Like I can do anything else.

She was gone for what felt like an eternity.

"Hello?" she said.

"I'm here. Is she okay?"

"She's had her stomach pumped, and she is quite drowsy but doing well, considering…"

"So, she's going to be okay?"

"She's doing fine."

That wasn't exactly what I'd asked, but I'd take it right now. Leaning back against the headrest, I let out a deep breath. "Okay, thanks."

She hung up without another word.

Dad looked at me out of the corner of his eye. "Is she okay?"

"At the minute, yeah."

We drove the rest of the way in silence. Dad made a couple of phone calls to Mum, and I was under strict instructions to tell Tegan that Mum had upped her sessions to two a week, more if Mum felt Tegan needed it.

Finally, we arrived at the hospital. I jumped out at the entrance, and Dad went to park.

save me

I walked through the doors and immediately wanted to turn around again. Isaac had died in here. I felt physically ill as I tried to force out the images of his final days.

Thankfully, I didn't have to go anywhere near the children's ward as Tegan had been put with the adults and had her own room.

"I'm here to see Tegan Pennells. Where is she?" I said, leaning on the reception desk of her ward.

"Are you family?" she asked. The nurse, an aging woman with deep wrinkles and grey hair, was obviously a different woman than before. She was polite.

I was fucking fed up with people asking me that. "No, I'm her friend, but—"

"I'm very sorry, but only family can visit right now."

Like hell. I bet Lucas is in there.

"Please, I'm a friend, and I just need to see her. I won't get in the way. Come on, five minutes, please."

God, if she were young, I would've flirted, but that wouldn't get me anywhere with her.

"You're not family, sir, so I'm sorry, but I can't allow you to go in."

"I don't care," I snapped.

"Sir, I understand—"

"In here, Kai!" Tegan shouted from a room next to reception.

Her voice, although weak and groggy, was all I needed. My heart started beating again.

The nurse sighed. "Five minutes."

"Thank you," I said, shoving off from the desk.

I stopped walking when I saw Tegan. I thought I'd also stopped breathing. Everything faded away, and there was only her. She was curled up on the bed, exhausted but perfect.

"We'll give you some time," Lucas said. He kissed her on the cheek and walked out with Alison and Ava.

I hated the prick, but that was pretty decent of him.

I didn't take my eyes off of Tegan once as I walked over to the bed. My heart felt like it was trying to rip out of my chest.

She's okay.

I sat down and pulled her into my arms. I wanted to speak, but I couldn't. She cried when I dug my fingertips into her back, but I knew it wasn't because I was hurting her.

"Shh," I whispered. *Fuck, she is okay.*

She sobbed into my neck for a little longer while I tried to figure out why I still felt far too many emotions to count.

"Sorry," she said, pulling away and wiping the remainder of her tears. She was pale, much more than usual.

She was feeling pretty sick about now, I'd imagine.

"Promise me, you'll never do anything like that again. You're my best friend, and I can't lose you."

Looking up, she smiled with her eyes and replied, "I promise. You're not getting rid of me that easily."

"Good, 'cause I kinda like having you around." Let's face it; I loved having her around. "When can you go home?"

I wanted her out. People died in this building, and she had no place being here.

"I'm hoping tomorrow. I have to see some counsellor in the morning and convince her that I don't want to die. Hopefully, she'll believe me, and I can get the hell outta here."

I took a deep breath. "You don't want to die, do you?"

She shook her head and pleaded with her eyes for me to believe her. "What I did was stupid, but it made me realise that I want to live. Really live."

I believed her and sighed in relief. "Good," I whispered. I kissed the top of her head. "My mum said you have to have two sessions a week with her. If you need more, let her know."

"Thank you," she said. "Oh, how are your grandparents?"

She is seriously asking me that after everything that's just happened?

I did not want to have this conversation, but I also couldn't talk about death and suicide anymore either. "They're good. They want to meet you."

"Really? Talk about me much, do you?" she asked.

Shit.

"A little."

She tilted her head and continued to stare at me.

save me

"So, tomorrow, you're busting out," I said, trying to stop her intense little gaze from pulling my true feelings out of me.

"I'll be bugging them to let me go from the second I wake up."

"If they won't let you, I'll get you out."

She laughed and winced. "I'll hold you to that."

"You all right?"

"Yeah, but I've never felt so sick before in my life. I just need to stay still, and I'll be fine."

I pulled the thick blanket over her. "Sleep it off, princess."

"I will if you sing to me," she whispered, already settling down and closing her eyes.

I quietly sang "Just the Way You Are" in her ear until she fell asleep.

Kai

I SAT AT MY DESK at seven in the fucking morning, trying to focus on the computer screen. I'd never been in so early before, especially on the weekend. In fact, this was only the second weekend of the year I'd worked.

I was going crazy at home. Work was supposed to take my mind off Tegan and what she'd tried to do. It wasn't. I felt sick and angry and as terrified as the day when we'd found out Isaac had leukaemia.

Visiting time for me—a non-family member and non-boyfriend—wasn't until one o'clock. Lucas shouldn't even be allowed to go in the morning, but Tegan's mum had swung it somehow. I fucking hated him.

"You all right?" Dad said, walking into my office and closing the door behind him.

I shrugged. "Sure."

"Tegan doing okay?"

"She's doing all right, yeah."

Dad sat down, and I knew I was about to have a deep and meaningful conversation with him.

"That's good. She's a great girl."

I was glad he could see that, too. Under the I-don't-give-a-shit-anymore exterior, she was an awesome person.

"How are things?"

"Things?" I asked, pretending like I didn't know what he was talking about.

"You. How are you?"

"I'm fine, Dad."

"You finally get your life together, and you meet a girl you really like, but she meets someone else."

"Thank you. Anytime you want to bring that up…" I said.

He held his hands up. "I'm sorry. I just worry about you. Don't want to see you hurt."

Then, I definitely wasn't going to tell him that being in love with someone who was with someone else fucking killed.

"I'll be all right. She's got a lot of stuff to go through, and as much as I want to be with her, I wouldn't want to do that until she was okay."

"You think she'll want you?"

"Why do you say it like that? No qualifications and working for my dad, I'm a fuckin' catch!" I couldn't keep the sarcasm from my voice. Now, I knew I wasn't going to be many people's first choice, but I would do whatever it took to make Tegan happy.

He rolled his eyes. "You know I didn't mean anything by it. If you two are meant to be, you'll find each other. I just worry about you putting everything into this when she's with this Lucas, and you don't know if she'll be single anytime soon."

I wanted to either ban Lucas's name or get everyone around me to refer to him as Pukas. He made me feel sick. But I should probably exercise a little more maturity than that.

"Maybe they'll work out, and if he truly makes her happy, I'll be happy for her. But I remember what it's like—when you don't know how you feel or who you really are anymore. I wouldn't wanna be the guy coming into a relationship with someone who felt that way. What you want when you find yourself again isn't always what you thought you wanted when you were…elsewhere."

Dad sighed. "I'm sorry, Kai."

"What for?"

"You're very much in love with her."

"You're sorry for that because?"

"Because it might not work out the way you want it to."

"Life has a habit of doing that. Whatever happens, I'll be all right."

I'd never make the first move, so she'd either realise Lucas wasn't for her and I was, or I'd stay the friend. As long as I could be one of those to her, I'd be fine.

"I hope so, and you know, I don't think there's just one person out there for you anyway."

I raised my eyebrow. "Never let Mum hear you say that."

He cracked a smile and then added, "I'm serious. Millions of people move on or lose someone they love and find another. You've probably got *the one* in every county."

"*Definitely* don't tell her that."

"Son, I've not made it this far without having an in-front-of-Mum filter."

"You went back to Mum after your post-uni breakup. How can you believe your one-in-every-county theory?"

He shrugged. "I've only lived in this one."

"Touché. I get what you mean though. I'm young and ridiculously good-looking, so plenty of fish in the sea."

"Hmm. You know you're playing this too cool and casual?"

"Whaddya want from me?"

"The truth," he said.

"Fine. I won't be perfectly all right. It'd suck, and I'd hate every second of watching her be with him ten times more than I already do, but there's nothing I can do but wait it out and hope she'll realise *we* should be together. Happy?"

"Happy you're being honest, yes."

Sighing, I leant back in the seat and closed my eyes. "I want to be the one with her right now, holding her and telling her that, if she ever did anything so fucking stupid again, I'd kick her arse."

I was angry, fucking angry. Isaac had lost his life, and Tegan had almost thrown hers away by choice, but I understood what it was like to be in such a dark and desperate place that you didn't know if there was even a way out.

"I want to be the one who makes it better, and I know, right now, Lucas isn't even doing that. I think he's masking it, and it's bound to blow up eventually—again. I want to be with her so fucking bad, but I want it to work in the end." I sat up. "What happened to me?"

Dad laughed.

"No, seriously? God, I'm annoying myself. I'm such a sappy twat. How have you not punched me by now?"

"You're in love."

"So? If I start sounding like Romeo, kick me."

He shook his head, sighing. "Suck it up, son. Even the most macho of men turn a little soft for the one they love."

"Not saying I'm macho, just not like a little girl."

"You've never considered telling her how you feel? Maybe if she knew…"

"No," I replied. "She doesn't need that. I won't be the one who screws things up even more, and I won't risk her telling me to do one. If we happen, I want to know it's because she wants it and not because I've messed with her head and made her question everything."

"But you want her to think you should be together."

"No, I want her to *know* we should." There was a massive difference. "I want her to know we're meant to be together when she's thinking clearly. I don't want any confusion in her mind when and if she makes a choice."

"What if she's too lost to see it? Some people need a nudge."

I shook my head. "She'll be lost until she deals with her dad's death and allows herself to grieve. After that, I'll just see what happens. I won't screw anything up with her."

"And what if she goes ahead thinking all you want is friendship, and things with Lucas go well?"

My chest ached.

What would I do if they stayed together? Watch them get engaged, move in together, get married, have kids?

I roughly rubbed the ache. "I'll deal with that. I like to think I know her pretty well, and if I think she's got feelings for me, even if she doesn't realise it, then I'll do the bastard thing and kiss the crap outta her. But, unless I see that she feels something for me, it's all on her terms."

"Kids nowadays." He tutted. "Well, when everything blows up, I'll be here."

"How reassuring, Dad. Thank you."

Raising his hands over his head, he stood up. "If you play games…"

"It's not game-playing; it's called patience. But, if patience doesn't work, I'll just—"

"'Kiss the crap outta her.' Yeah, I got it. Good luck, Kai." He left the room, laughing under his breath and shaking his head.

Tegan's ringtone blasted through my phone.

I had it answered and up to my ear in an instant. "Hey."

"Hey, Kai," she said.

"You okay?"

"I'm…good, I guess. Are you back at your nan's now?"

"Er, no, I'm at the office now we're home. I'll be at the hospital to see you later."

"What? Kai, you and your dad should go back to your nan's and spend the weekend with your family. I'm fine, really. I think I'm getting out later anyway."

There was no way I was going anywhere. I couldn't. Dad had refused to leave, too. He was worried that, if the worst happened, I'd need someone.

"I don't want to go back," I said.

"I'm so sorry. I feel awful that I ruined your weekend."

"You haven't ruined my weekend."

She'd nearly given me a heart attack, but she hadn't ruined my weekend.

"Tegan, don't feel guilty."

"You're mad?" she whispered.

Yes. "Don't you ever do anything like that again."

"I won't. I was so…" She gulped and took a deep breath. "I don't know how to explain it. There was just darkness and pain, and I couldn't breathe. There was no way out that wouldn't hurt more than ending it. But, now, I know I don't want to die. I want to live, and I want to do something that'd have made my dad proud of me."

I closed my eyes and ran my hand through my hair. "I get it."

In the four years I had been lost, there were many occasions when I'd considered ending it all. Difference was, I'd never tried it. When it had come down to it, I couldn't put my parents through the pain of burying another child.

"What time are you visiting?"

"I can't come until one."

"What? My mum will be here in a bit, so just come now."

It didn't take a lot to convince me to go see her. "I'll see you soon," I replied.

"Bye."

I hung up, feeling a little more relieved and a little less angry.

There was no one around when I got to the hospital. Well, there was, but I avoided the doctors and nurses and slipped through the ward door when the nurse's back was turned.

Alison and Ava were already in Tegan's room, and I could tell why she wanted me there. They were, understandably, watching her like a hawk, exchanging looks that screamed, *Don't let her out of your sight.* I'd be the same, but, fuck, Tegan must feel suffocated.

Lucas was sitting in the corner of the room, drinking coffee. It was clear from his icy stare that he didn't want me around. I couldn't give a shit what he wanted though.

"Hello, Kai," Alison said at the same time as when Tegan looked up and beamed.

That was why I was here. That petite girl who tied me up in knots and made everything seem that much better.

Even though I'd made my peace with my past, I'd still struggle with the darkness, struggle to keep it from sucking me back in, but Tegan brought this light with her, not that she could see it. I had worried that she'd suck me back into the darkness, but the opposite had happened. She made me want to achieve more.

"Hey," I said, giving her family a quick nod and making my way to the bed. "Know when you're getting out yet?"

She turned her nose up. "They're doing the paperwork. Apparently, I should be out soon. Sorry, they told me just a minute ago, or I wouldn't have asked you to come."

"Don't worry; it's fine. Hey, I spoke to my mum last night, and she added Mondays to your sessions. That day good?"

"Perfect. Thank you." She looked over to her mum. "Please? I don't want to talk to some stranger."

Alison nodded. "Whomever you're comfortable with, sweetheart. Remember what Judy said; you have to be comfortable. I'll speak with her, and perhaps she can contact Melanie, too."

"Thanks, Mum." Tegan turned to me. "Tell Melanie I'm in then," she said, grinning up at me.

"Will do," I replied, trying not to get lost in her big, bright green eyes while standing right in front of her family and Pukas.

Dad was right. I was completely in love with her.

Tegan

"DO YOU WANT SOMETHING to eat or drink?" Mum asked, rearranging the blanket so that it was fully covering my legs.

"I'm fine, Mum, thanks." My stomach still felt dodgy, and I didn't want to eat much beyond toast.

She smiled weakly and sat down beside me. I laid my head on Lucas's shoulder, and he put his hand on my knee. He'd not left my side since I came home, and neither had Mum or Ava. I was being watched twenty-four/seven. It was exhausting to pretend like I was okay when I wasn't.

The atmosphere was tense. No one could relax, and it made me feel worse. I could see the panic in Mum's eyes every time I would go to the bathroom. I wasn't going to do it again—it was stupid, so stupid—but I had no idea how to convince everyone else that I wouldn't.

Time was the key. I knew time healed a lot, but it moved too slowly for me. When you were desperately willing for months to pass so that you wouldn't feel so bad, months seemed to take years. Time sucked.

I kept my eyes on the TV, trying to ignore Lucas and Mum having a silent conversation about me. I shuffled, trying to show them that I was still in the room. I'd prefer if they just came out and said whatever was on their minds.

With the tenth *discreet* look between them, I'd finally had enough.

Standing up, I said, "I'm going up to have a nap."

"I'll come with you." Lucas stood, too.

I was about to argue, but I could see that he'd made up his mind. He was coming with me.

"Okay," I replied. I smiled even though all I wanted to do was scream and plead with them to give me half an hour where I could have some space.

We walked up to my room in silence and lay down on my bed.

"You okay?" he asked.

I pressed my lips to his, not wanting to answer that question again. His kiss was softer than usual and almost too gentle. The passion was gone completely. Even when we just had a quick kiss, there would always be something between us. This time, I didn't want to deepen it, didn't want to run my hands through his hair or wrap my legs around his waist. He wasn't into it, and neither was I.

I eventually gave up and pulled away. Sighing, I curled up into his side until I fell asleep.

I woke up an hour later, feeling only slightly better. Lucas was staring down at me, and I really hoped he hadn't been awake and watching me the whole time. *How much trouble can I get into while I'm asleep?*

"Hey," I said.

"Hey, shorty. You feeling okay?"

"Yeah." The sick feeling in my stomach was almost gone. My wrist was another matter though. It still stung like a bitch, and if I knocked it against something, I'd want to punch someone. It wasn't even a huge cut, so it shouldn't hurt as much as it did.

"Honey," Mum said, knocking on the open door.

I sat up and waved my hand for her to come in.

"I just spoke to Melanie, and your session is at five thirty tomorrow. Is that okay?"

I nodded, playing with my fingers so that I wouldn't have to look into her eyes.

"Do you want to come down for dinner? I think you should try eating."

"Sure," I said, biting my lip. But I knew I'd just end up eating something plain and dry rather than a proper dinner.

As I walked into the kitchen, Lucas's family turned to look at me. It seemed like they were always here now, and I knew that it was because they were desperate to pay us back. Their support was nice, and I knew Mum loved having someone she could rely on, but it was hard to see Carl so much.

I avoided him completely as I sat down. He was okay now—or as okay as he could be since his life expectancy was lowered. He made me feel horrible and selfish. I probably had every reason to feel that way, but I hadn't taken those pills to hurt anyone.

Laid out on the table were about six different dishes—salads, pasta, steak, chicken, and chips. I took a plate and put a little pasta on it. There was no way I was even going to attempt to eat any kind of meat. The sick feeling might have subsided, but I still felt delicate, and I couldn't handle anything heavy.

"So, what are you two planning on doing for the next two weeks?" Emily asked me and her son.

Lucas shrugged his shoulders. "I don't know. What do you want to do, Tegan?"

"Don't mind what we do," I replied.

No doubt, it wouldn't be what I wanted to do. I missed the intimacy. He didn't look at me in that way anymore. I appreciated it was a bit too soon for things to heat up, but I was scared that he didn't want me anymore and was waiting to break up with me until I was emotionally stronger.

All I wanted was for him to show me that we'd be okay.

Carl popped a pill in his mouth and took a swig of water. He was so much stronger now, compared to when I'd first met him. I was glad that he was doing well, and deep down, although I was still mad at my dad, I was proud of him for giving other people a chance at life.

"You okay, Tegan?" Ava asked.

Smiling, I nodded and attempted to eat another mouthful of pasta.

Eating when Mum, Ava, Lucas, Emily, Carl, Jake, and Grace were *discreetly* watching you was horrible. All eyes on me all the time was suffocating, but it was completely my fault.

I ate quickly, finishing just after Lucas, and then I excused myself to my room. Of course, I wasn't alone though, as Lucas followed me. We watched TV but didn't really watch it, and then we fell asleep early.

I woke up just before seven, starving and thirsty. A decent night's sleep had done wonders for me, and I felt almost human again. I needed food. Creeping out of my room so that I wouldn't wake Lucas, I went down to the kitchen to make some toast.

"Hi," Ava said as I almost bumped into her. She flicked the kettle on and held a mug out, asking if I wanted one.

"No, thanks. I'll just have water."

"You hungry?"

"Starving. I'm making toast. Want some?"

For the first time since Dad had died, we were having a normal conversation where I wasn't giving her a load of attitude, and she wasn't looking at me like an alien had taken over my body.

"I've just had cereal, thanks. How come you're awake so early on a Sunday?"

Shrugging one shoulder, I popped a slice of bread in the toaster. "Eleven hours of sleep probably."

"Lucas still up there?"

"Yeah. He'll probably be out of it for another couple of hours at least."

"How are you feeling, really? No more sickness? What about your arm?"

"Sickness has gone, and arm is okay." It was better since I'd redressed the bandage and taken painkillers. I pulled on the sleeve of my top even though it more than covered my wrist.

I stayed in the kitchen with Ava for a little while, and although she watched me like a hawk, it was the longest we'd spent together in a while that we weren't arguing.

An hour later, some of the others started getting up. Mum was immediately fussing over me, asking if I was comfortable, felt sick, felt unhappy, was hungry, was thirsty, or wanted to talk. I wanted an hour where we could be relatively normal, and no one was watching for pills in my hands.

"Mum, I'm fine, honestly. I am feeling hungry again though. Are you still cooking breakfast?" I wasn't hungry at all, but we both needed her to focus on something else for a while.

Lastly, Lucas and Jake finally came downstairs, just in time to drink their first round of coffee before the food would be ready.

Lucas pulled his chair closer to mine and sat down. "Hey," he said.

Tapping the tips of my fingers on my mug, I replied, "Hey."

"How long have you been up?"

"A couple of hours."

"You should've woken me."

I shouldn't be pissed off, but I was. He'd never asked me to wake him before.

"Why would I have done that? I often wake up first." Even I knew I sounded a little more defensive than was necessary.

His mouth thinned, and he busied himself with making his drink. Though he didn't reply, he knew exactly what I was getting at and that I was right.

I ate a small second breakfast, trying to bat back questions and take the heat away from me. I was getting better at it.

Once I finished eating, I attempted to have a shower, but Lucas followed me upstairs.

"Luke, I won't be long. You don't have to wait in my room for me."

He smiled. "I know, but I want to."

Want was the wrong word. He felt like he had to in case I tried something stupid again.

"I won't do it again."

"I know."

"Then, please go downstairs with everyone else, like you usually do, and I'll be down in ten minutes."

He sat on my bed, considering it, while I collected a change of clothes.

Sighing, he replied, "Fine, I'll be downstairs."

He left my room in a strop, but I really didn't have the energy to worry about it right now. He needed to be away from me for longer than five seconds.

Carrying my clothes and a towel into the bathroom, I locked the door and closed my eyes. I finally felt relief because I would be alone for a little while.

The stress and shame washed down the drain with the water, and I felt ten times better. There was an undertone of lemon in the bathroom, as I imagined Mum had scrubbed it pretty hard all week after my wrist had bled on the floor.

I'd just turned the water off and wrapped my body in a towel when someone knocked on the door.

"Tegan, are you okay?" Lucas asked.

"I'm fine, Luke." I'd not even had ten minutes yet.

"Can I come in?"

"I'm just getting ready." I scrubbed the towel over my body, being careful to avoid my wrist. The hot water and steamy air made the cut sting. Through the door, I heard my phone ringing. "Can you get my phone, please, Luke? I'll be out in a second," I said, quickly pulling on my clothes.

He didn't respond, but I heard him talking on the phone to someone. I opened the door, and he walked over to me, holding the phone out.

"Guess who?" he whispered sarcastically before turning around.

I looked at the screen and said, "Hey, Kai."

Lucas sat on my bed, staring at the floor.

"Well, hello, Princess."

"Why are you so cheerful?" I asked, sitting down on the bed but not getting too close to Lucas.

"Because we're going to the beach in three weeks."

"We're what?" I asked.

"Holly's rented a beach house for a weekend—Friday after work until Sunday—and she's making everyone go. You up for it?"

He hasn't asked something like, *Are you going to go off on the deep end again?*

"Seriously? I'm definitely in. Who else is going?"

Lucas finally turned to look at me, but I didn't look at him. We'd have that argument when I hung up.

"Me, you, Holly, James, Sophie, Mark, and Adam and his girlfriend. I forget her name."

"Adam's coming, too? Wow."

"Yeah. Sophie convinced him. I don't know how, and I don't want to know."

I laughed and rolled my eyes.

"Awesome. I can't wait," I said.

God, more than anything, I needed to get away for a few days. I would have three weeks to convince Mum to let me go.

"Good. I gotta go. I'm meeting my dad. I'll call you later," he said, chuckling.

"Okay, bye." I hung up the phone and took a deep breath.

"So, where's he taking you?" Lucas asked tightly.

"He isn't *taking* me. Holly's booked a beach house, so we can all chill before she has the baby."

"Right," he said, staring forward still. Not once had he looked at me since I took the call. Supposedly, he was okay with Kai, but he'd not done much to prove that.

"Would you be like this if Adam had asked me?"

He was silent, so we both knew the answer.

"It's different," he said.

I looked at him, waiting for an explanation.

"You didn't spend months having sex with Adam."

"No, we just went out for five months a couple of years ago," I mumbled.

Lucas had known that, and he'd also known Adam and I were only fourteen then, and it was no big deal.

I sighed and moved around, so I was facing him, and he finally looked at me. "Lucas, do you trust me?"

"I trust *you*, Tegan."

"What do you think Kai's gonna do? He's a *friend*, and I love you."

His face softened. He put his arm around me and rested his forehead on mine. "I love you, too, and I'm sorry. I know you wouldn't do anything. I just get a little jealous."

A little jealous?

"We've talked about this before. I'll always be friends with Kai."

He sighed. "I know, shorty."

I thought he wanted to say more, but he kissed me instead, which I definitely preferred.

"So, where are you going?" he asked.

I smiled and kissed him again. "To a beach. I didn't ask which one, but they're all pretty much the same, right?"

"You didn't ask where?"

I shook my head and shrugged. "It's in England."

He laughed and gently pulled me onto his lap. "I'll miss you."

"I'll miss you, too, but it's only for three days, and you can catch up with your friends. I've been stealing you so much lately."

He smiled. "Wanna go see them together now? There's a race this afternoon."

God, I really wanted to get out of this house and get some fresh air. "Heck yeah. I'll grab my hoodie."

Lucas never took his eyes off me as I taped a small bandage over my wrist and slipped my hoodie on. I hated the cut and hated even more that I'd have a scar, but at least I had something to show me where I never wanted to go again. The angry red gash kept me just above water.

While I put a little makeup on and got my phone, Lucas left me and went to clear our outing with my mum. She'd say yes to him, and we both knew we'd have a better chance if I wasn't there. I couldn't control my mouth when she questioned what I wanted to do. I felt like everything was an attack or a judgment.

I relaxed further when we were in Lucas's car and on our way.

"So, how are you gonna get your mum to agree to let you go to the beach?" he asked.

"I have no idea. Right now, she won't let me go in the garden alone."

"Do they all know about what happened?"

"No, just Kai." I'd thought about telling Sophie, but I wasn't sure how she'd react, and I couldn't handle her looking at me like I was made of glass or had gone insane. "I don't want anyone else to know."

"Of course," he replied.

"You know they'll all be too drunk to realise if they've left you at the beach, right?" he said. "Well, except for Holly. She'll look out for you, won't she?"

I nodded, and he seemed happier about me going, not that he shouldn't be. If he were going away with friends, I'd tell him to have a good time and have a drink for me.

I didn't need looking after, but I wasn't in the best position to argue that. "I'll be fine, but Holly will definitely be looking out for everyone. She's firmly in mum mode now."

We finally pulled up next to Danny's car, and Lucas ran round to open the door for me. I stretched up and kissed him, making him smile. Lucas and Danny slapped hands. Some girl was here with him, too, but she looked nothing like Barbie. She was pretty, taller than me—but that wasn't hard—and she had hair that I couldn't decide if it was dark blonde or light brown.

Lucas turned around. "Annie, hey." He hugged her, and they kissed each other on the cheek.

I was pissed off but only by the double standards.

Lucas grabbed my hand and pulled me forward. "Tegan, this is Annie."

"Hi," I said.

She nodded and replied, "Hey, Tegan."

"All right, race time," Danny said, bouncing up and down like a child.

Lucas went with Danny to get his car ready, leaving me alone with Annie. *Great.*

I smiled up at Annie. "You staying to watch?"

She nodded. "Yeah, let's make our way over to the wall."

Last time, I hadn't sat on one of the falling down walls for two reasons. It had been full of half-naked women at the time, and I could barely move through fear.

We hopped up and waited for the race.

"So, how long have you known Lucas?" I asked her.

"We went to school together, so a while."

"I can't imagine Luke at school."

"He was the naughty kid, always getting sent out of class for doing or saying something wrong," she said. "He turned into a bit of a ladies' man in his teenage years. Well, until we got together." She smiled shyly, and her cheeks turned pink.

"How long were you together for?"

"On and off for about a year. I don't think we were together for longer than about two or three months at a time though."

"Hey, shorty." Lucas stood in between my legs and kissed me.

save me

"I was just talking to Annie, and I was about to get her to dish the dirt on you."

He looked horrified and widened his eyes at her. Laughing, she winked at me.

Wow, out of all the women here, the only one I liked was the one who had probably slept with my boyfriend.

She jumped off the wall and said over her shoulder, "Back in a minute. Just going to wish Danny luck."

When she was out of earshot, I wrapped my arms around his neck and said, "So, you didn't mention she was an ex."

He groaned, looking uncomfortable.

"It's fine, Luke. You had a life before me, and I'm really not that jealous or insecure."

He nodded and kissed me. "All right, I'll talk to your mum for you and get her to agree to you going away. I do think it'll be good for you to have some fun with your friends. You deserve fun."

"I love you," I said.

"Love you, too," he said before properly kissing me and making my toes curl.

He's back. We're back. Finally.

Tegan

I WOKE UP TO Lucas, Mum, and Ava in my room, looking at me. It was creepy, and starting the day with a mini heart attack sucked. Mum's eyes snapped to my wrist, and I looked away, shoving my arm under the covers. It didn't hurt now, and the redness was subsiding, but it might as well be neon red and glowing. Everyone would spot it, and I was feeling really self-conscious.

It'd been almost two weeks since I got home, and no one had left me alone for more than five minutes. And I was counting. Showers were super quick because, if I was in there for longer than a couple of minutes, someone would knock on the door until I was done.

Having so many people care enough to watch over me, standing over me all the time, was pretty overwhelming. It was like they were just waiting for me to fuck up again, and I was working on making sure I wouldn't.

Since I'd gotten back, Mum had also put me on lockdown from school. I was ready to go back and get my life on track again, but she didn't think so. I was giving her one more week, and then I would go with or without her blessing. I'd worked hard to catch up once, and I still had some work to do. I didn't want to do it again.

"Morning, honey. Do you want breakfast in bed or downstairs?"

I looked at her for a minute. *Is that really my mother?*

"Tegan?" she prompted.

"I'll come down," I said, shaking my head.

We weren't usually allowed to eat upstairs, and it bothered me, for the first time ever, that it was an option now. For someone who'd claimed she wanted everything back to *normal*, she wasn't doing a good job of actually *doing* it.

The only relief I'd get was when Kai picked me up to take me to his parents', so I could have my twice-weekly sessions with Melanie. The second I got in his car and shut the door, I'd feel human again rather than like a pet project. I was so thankful that I had a session today.

When Mum and Ava walked out, I turned to Lucas. "How long have they been in here?"

"Not long."

Liar.

Sighing, I got out of bed. "Let's go eat."

I didn't need to look around to know that he'd be behind me in a second; he didn't give me an inch of space.

I slipped a hoodie on before I went downstairs, so I wouldn't have to see Mum get that pained look in her eyes whenever she saw my wrist. Kai texted as I reached the kitchen, asking if I wanted to go to Holly's for pizza night with the guys tonight. I wanted to. I really badly needed some time where I could relax, but I wasn't sure if that'd be allowed.

Taking mugs out of the cupboard for tea and coffee, I swallowed my nerves and turned to Mum. "Can I go to Holly's tonight, please?"

"I don't think tonight's a good idea, Tegan."

"Please? Just for a couple of hours."

Her lips pressed into a firm line. "I really don't think you need to be going to any parties."

"It's not a party. It's me, Kai, Holly, James, and probably Sophie, too, watching a film. No party, I promise. Please, Mum."

"No, Tegan."

I felt like screaming. She was well within her rights to tell me no after everything I'd done, but I was suffocated, and I'd never needed anything more than I needed to leave this house for a while.

"Okay. Just going to the bathroom," I said. I had to get away from her for a second and chill out.

"Where are you going?" Lucas asked, following me out of the kitchen.

I turned around. Luke was in front of me, and Mum and Ava were watching from the door.

Oh, for fuck sake!

"I'm going to have a shower now since breakfast won't be ready for a while," I said as calmly as I could.

I turned around and shot a text back to Kai, telling him what was going on. Lucas was shadowing me, but I didn't acknowledge him.

I reached my room by the time Kai replied.

> *Sucks. She'd better let you come next weekend, or I'll have to bust you out!*

Why can't he bust me out now?

Luke followed as I opened my wardrobe to pick out something to wear.

He sat on my bed, watching my every move. "You okay?" he asked, breaking the silence.

I smiled. I tried hard not to take my frustrations out on him, but sometimes, it was difficult when he wouldn't even let me shower in peace.

"Fine," I said, grabbing some clothes and heading to the bathroom.

I managed to shower and get dry in peace, but just as I was getting dressed, I heard a knock on the door.

"Tegan?" Lucas called.

I took a deep breath. "Almost done."

Well, he gave me nine minutes. That's a new record.

I finally walked back into my room, and he was sitting on the end of my bed, looking pretty stressed.

"What time is Kai picking you up?"

"In an hour."

Luke followed me downstairs, and we ate breakfast together. I tried to make myself smaller, so I wouldn't get much attention.

Kai pulled up outside my house, and I almost ran out of my room. All Lucas and I had done after breakfast was watch TV, but it was exhausting. I felt like I had to be extra cheery to convince him that I was okay. I wanted to be perfect for my mum, my sister, and Lucas but I wasn't, and I struggled with getting my head around what was expected and what I could actually live up to.

Right now, I was still a mess. I didn't quite know how to get things straight, and I was fed up with feeling like I had taken a step forward and then nine back.

"Tegan, Kai's outside," Mum said as I came downstairs with Luke.

"Yeah, I just saw his car."

As I went to walk past, she stepped in my way. "Sweetheart, I'm sorry about earlier, but I really don't think you should be in that environment yet."

"I appreciate that, and I don't want to be in that environment right now. But it *isn't* a party."

"Okay." She paused and then added, "After what happened, you need to earn my trust back."

save me

"I know I do. Believe me, I do know that, but how can I when you won't give me a chance to? I understand why it's hard for you, but you have to give me the freedom to prove that I won't do it again and that I am trying. I've barely left this house, and someone is watching me the whole time. I can't breathe, Mum, and I certainly can't show you that I'll never do anything so stupid again when this is how we're living."

"You're right," she said.

I'm what? I knew I was right, but I never expected her to say it.

"You can go for two hours. That's it."

"Seriously?" Two hours felt like two weeks. "Thank you, thank you, thank you!"

"Two hours, Tegan," she repeated. "Either Lucas or I will take you and pick you up, okay?"

I nodded and squealed. Those terms were perfectly okay with me.

The doorbell rang. I kissed Lucas and almost sprinted from the house.

"Hey, Kai," I said as I tugged the front door shut behind me.

I grabbed his wrist and pulled him back toward his car.

He laughed at me as I threw myself in his car.

Resting his arm on the top of my open door, he said, "You drunk?"

"Nope, but I'm coming tonight. I get two hours."

"Yeah? That's great. Your mum's trying, too. Need me to take you?"

"Mum or Luke has to."

Kai would have to drive past my house to get to Holly's, but there was no way I was going to question Mum in case she changed her mind.

307

Melanie ushered me into her study when I got there, and Kai went off to find his dad.

"How are you?" she asked as we settled down on her big sink-right-into-it armchairs.

Every time she asked that, I'd fight the urge to just tell her I was okay. This was a place I was supposed to be honest.

"I'm better than I was last week, but everyone is still crowding me."

She tilted her head.

"I know, I know. That's totally all my fault, but it's not helping me to move on."

"Have you considered, it might be helping them?"

"Briefly. I can't see how it would though. Sure, right now, it might help, but by watching me twenty-four/seven, they're not moving forward."

"Perhaps it's a little too soon for your mum to be thinking about moving forward."

I hadn't thought of that. I'd just assumed we all wanted to move past it right away.

"Maybe. But then where does that leave us?"

"Time, patience, and honesty are what's going to heal this, Tegan."

I didn't think very highly of any of those things at the minute.

"She's letting me go to Holly's tonight."

"Well, that's a big step, and it can't be easy for her."

"No, I guess not. I want her to trust me."

"You're scared you'll do something that will break that?"

"Yeah. It's already pretty nonexistent. I worry that I'll snap under the pressure of having Big Brother watching all the time, and that'll be it."

She leant forward. "How do you mean?"

Oh God, not her, too. I felt like getting a tattoo of, *I will never OD or hurt myself again*, on my forehead.

"Not like that. I don't want to hurt myself or worse. I just mean, I'll say something or run out."

"You can control that."

"See, there's the thing. I don't feel like I can control a lot anymore."

"You're more in control of your emotions than you give yourself credit for."

All right, sure, I was good or used to be good at pushing everything and everyone away, but I'd explode sometimes. I'd ignore and ignore and ignore, and then everything I was shoving away would boil over suddenly. I would be left wondering what the hell was going on.

"I don't know. I'm sick of feeling like I'm on a never-ending roller coaster."

"Life is a lot like that. When something happens that's out of your control, it's not about getting off the roller coaster, but about learning how to ride it and see it through."

"Only to have it stop and be launched onto a new one? Life sucks."

She laughed and leant back. "Often, it does, yes. But you don't have to allow it to *suck* forever."

I nodded. "Learn to ride the roller coaster. What if I don't know how to do that?"

"Some things can't be learnt in a day."

I was worried that it'd take years.

After my session, Kai took me straight home. He was so strict about that. I wanted to hang out for a while, but my sessions would last an hour each time, and Mum would question me if I came back late.

"How was it?" Lucas asked as I flopped down on my bed next to him. He was lying on my bed, watching a show about really big lorries driving on ice.

"Good."

He rolled onto his side and traced patterns on my hip. I tried not to let it affect me because he'd been very hands-off recently, but I couldn't help that my blood was pumping that little bit faster.

"You okay?"

"Yeah," I replied breathlessly as his hand dipped a bit lower. "I love you, Lucas."

Groaning, he rolled on top of me, and his hands and lips were everywhere. For the next hour, we made up for all those nights he'd lain beside me and not touched me.

And, when he dropped me off at Holly's that evening, I was feeling a hundred times more positive about the future.

Holly opened the door and gave me a tight hug. I hadn't seen her in two weeks.

"Come in," she said as she pulled me into the house.

I checked out her bump. It was so cute.

In the living room, Sophie and Mark were kissing on one of the chairs. They didn't even notice I had walked into the room, and no way was I going to interrupt that face-eating-fest to say hi.

James shouted, "Hey," as he whisked past me to go into the kitchen.

"I've got him on drink duty," Holly said, following him into the kitchen.

Kai looked up at me from the recliner he was sitting on and gave me a lopsided smile. "Hey," he said, shifting over and patting the seat.

I didn't need to be asked twice. I sat down and lay back in the chair. "Hi."

"I'm tired and hungry."

Rolling my eyes, I replied, "Poor you."

"Kai, order the pizza!" Holly shouted from the kitchen.

Handing him his phone from the side table, I kicked my eyebrow up. "Don't forget a Hawaiian."

save me

Sophie let Mark up for air when the pizza arrived. I'd not seen her much either, pretending to have a virus so that she wouldn't come over. Swallowing a bunch of pills, cutting myself, and almost dying was something I deeply regretted and didn't want everyone to know.

"Okay, everyone, write a celebrity's name on the Post-it and stick it on the person's head to your left, but don't let them see it," Sophie said once she'd demanded we all sit on the floor around the pizza boxes.

I felt about eight years old, but it was all good fun, and I needed fun. Kai did, too. He'd been just as worried about me as my family and Lucas, but now, Kai and I were here and relaxed. I could feel him loosening up.

I looked between each of my friends and was so grateful that they accepted me for who I was. Only Sophie had known the pre-screwup Tegan, so it always surprised me that Kai, Holly, and James wanted to be anywhere near the person I was now.

Kai was on my right, so he was choosing for me. God knew who I was going to be. I had to pick one for Sophie. Jordan, before she switched back to being Katie Price—it was an easy decision. I looked at Kai and laughed. James had given him Hugh Hefner.

"What? How bad is it?" Kai asked, nudging my shoulder.

Laughing, I shook my head, and he rolled his eyes.

"James, what've you done?"

James winked and started the game off, asking if he was male. He was Lady Gaga, and there were those stupid rumours.

Fifteen minutes in, and we'd all guessed ours, besides Kai. I was Kim Cattrall from *Sex and the City*. It could've been worse, but Kai still got a slap.

He sighed, rubbing his face. "Okay, so I'm male, old, and American, and I have been married more than once?"

"Yes," Holly, Soph, and I said at the same time.

"I'll give you a clue. You've had *a lot* of sex," James said after another five minutes of watching Kai guess.

"I'm Sophie?" Kai joked, making everyone laugh.

Sophie throw a wadded up Post-it ball at him.

"All right, do I live with anyone?" Kai asked.

"Lots of people," Mark replied.

Kai frowned, going off somewhere in his mind to think about that one.

"Have I slept with Kim Cattrall?" he asked, chuckling.

Oh, there is so a double meaning there.

"You wish," I said.

"Yes, I do," he said, laughing.

I laughed and shook my head.

Thirty-five minutes—that was how long he'd been guessing for. We'd all played a few more different games, but Kai was still trying to get his first.

The front doorbell rang, and I knew it'd be Lucas. My two hours were up.

"I'll get it," Holly said.

"Come on, Kai!" I snapped. It was just getting ridiculous now.

Lucas chuckled as he walked into the room and saw us sitting in a circle with pizza boxes and Post-it notes everywhere.

"Am I Anthony Hopkins?" Kai asked.

I deadpanned. "Are you doing this on purpose?"

He groaned and shook his head.

I got up and hugged everyone good-bye.

On my way out, I bent over and whispered in Kai's ear, "You're Hugh Hefner!"

His mouth dropped open. "I should've gotten that."

"I know," I said, waving to the best idiot friends in the world.

Tegan

I WOKE UP TO the sound of Mum crying again. Usually, I would leave it to Ava, but I didn't want to tonight. Mum and I had just started getting closer, and I wanted to be there for her. Nerves rattled in my stomach even though this was my bloody mum and I should feel confident, going to her.

I crept into her room, and my heart fell a little. She was sitting up in Ava's arms. Of course she was already here. I went to turn around because Mum didn't need me, but I caught their attention, and they both looked up.

"Sorry, I didn't know you were in here already," I said, backing up.

"No, come in, honey," Mum said, wiping her tears with a tissue.

Biting on my lip, I considered an excuse to leave. Not that I really wanted to, but I felt like I was intruding. Mum held her hand out, so I walked over to the bed and sat on the other side of her. I felt weird, being with both of them, like I was in the way or just here because Mum didn't want to hurt my feelings. Deep down, I knew different, but my insecurities were strong.

"Are you okay?" I asked.

"I am now. I have my girls," Mum replied. "Why don't you both sleep here tonight?"

I blinked in surprise. Ava had a lot recently, but I hadn't slept in my mum's bed since I was a baby.

"Okay," I said, still completely unsure of how I felt about it.

I lay down, and then Mum and Ava sank down. We lay in silence for a few minutes.

"So, Lucas called me," Mum said.

I turned to look at her. "Oh?"

"He mentioned a trip."

"Right," I said, fiddling with the duvet.

"You can go."

"I can what?"

Mum smiled. "You can go. I've seen you trying, and you've been getting more involved. I'm trying, too. So, you can go, but there are going to be conditions. Probably a lot of them."

"Thank you," I whispered, feeling choked up. "I'll stick to whatever conditions you have."

"I know you will. Because you'll want to leave the house again before you're thirty."

I would because I didn't want her to spend her days worrying that her daughter was going to do something stupid again.

Mum turned her head toward the ceiling and closed her eyes, smiling.

Dad's pillow was under my head. I was hoping it would still smell like him but it didn't. My pulse started to race, and I felt short of breath. I closed my eyes and focused on the calming exercises Melanie had taught me. I forced my breaths out evenly and tried to think of something good rather than the heart-tearing loss. Finally, I managed to calm myself down enough to fall asleep.

save me

"Hey!" I said, opening the front door to Kai and bouncing on the spot.

Today was the day we were going away. Mum finally trusted me enough to let me go. We were working on trust, and so far, I had followed every single rule perfectly, so I could build our relationship. The sun was shining, and I was going away with friends.

"Excited much, princess?" he asked, laughing.

I rolled my eyes and followed him as he walked through the hallway, apparently staying for a bit. He stopped by the music room. I'd opened the doors this morning and taken a peek inside. After staying with Mum and Ava last night, I felt a little less lonely, a little less afraid.

"Nice piano."

"You play?" I asked.

"No, but how hard could it be?"

I raised my eyebrows and pushed him into the room. Mum and Ava were watching us from the kitchen and got up to follow us.

Little bitch is going to see how hard it can be!

He sat down on the stool and cracked his knuckles. Then, he stared at the keys.

"In your own time, Kai."

He smirked up at me and started to play "Just the Way You Are." Well, I use the term *play* very loosely. He hit the keys—the wrong ones—in time to the song. I cringed. It was bad, very bad, but the look of pride on his face made me, my mum, and sister laugh.

Finally, the noise stopped, and I bit my lip. "That was…great," I muttered.

"All right, let's see you play it."

I did. I let my fingers elegantly glide over the keys as I played the same song he'd just murdered. There weren't many

315

things I could do well, but I could play the piano. I felt heavyhearted when I finished the song. I enjoyed playing, but I didn't want to when Dad wasn't around to enjoy it with me.

When will the guilt over every little pissing thing end?

"Wow," Kai said, dragging me back from getting sucked in by guilt. He looked down at me, his dark chocolate eyes alight in awe. "That was...yeah..."

I smiled and stood up. "Thanks. Are you ready to go now?"

He nodded, still looking at me like I'd just cured every disease in the world. *I just played the damn piano!*

I got up to grab my stuff and say my good-byes. Kai trailed behind me, Mum and Ava as we left my house. He was carrying my bag and took it to the boot of his car.

"Are you sure you have enough stuff?" he asked sarcastically.

I gave him a dirty look.

"Remember, honey..." Mum said.

Like I can forget.

I grabbed Kai's arm as he walked back around to the front of the car. "I shall not leave his side, I swear."

"I'll look after her—making sure she eats, gets her naps in, builds a sand castle, and all that," Kai said, smirking.

Mum laughed. "Thank you. Now, you be a good girl for Kai."

Oh, good, she's playing along. Bunch of bloody comedians today...

"You all suck." I got in the car, shutting the door on their laughing at my expense.

I waved to my mum and sister as Kai pulled out of the driveway. The further away we got the more I relaxed. I'd not realised just how much I needed to escape for a little while.

"So, I guess you can play the piano," Kai said after we'd been driving for a few minutes. "You should do it professionally."

"I thought about it once, but I really wanna be a forensic scientist."

His head snapped round, mouth open and eyes wide.

"I don't really, but that was so worth it."

"Ha-ha."

We pulled into the café car park and met up with Holly, James, Sophie, Mark, and Adam and his girlfriend, Megan, for breakfast before we headed out. I hadn't seen Adam for a while, so our hello hug was a squeezing one. I'd missed him.

Three hours later, we finally made it to the beach house. I was quickly informed that I would be sharing the twin room with Kai, as everyone else was all coupled up and wanted the doubles.

I'd shared a bed with him before. Hell, I'd shared bodily fluids with him before, so it shouldn't be weird, especially since we had separate beds, but it was. I was fairly confident that I'd be fine with Lucas sharing a room with another woman— sleeping didn't mean shagging—but I wasn't at all confident that he'd be fine with me sharing a room with Kai.

"You okay with this?" Kai asked as we lugged our bags through the bright white house to our room. "I can sleep on the sofa if you want."

All right, that's sweet of him.

"No, it's fine. I don't mind sharing," I said, throwing a pillow at him.

He laughed and threw it back on my bed. Our beds were against opposite walls—white walls, of course—so we weren't even that close.

"Okay. Hey, what do you want to do first?"

"Um…walk on the beach and get fresh doughnuts."

He smiled. "Sounds like a plan. Then, we're cracking open a couple of the many bottles of booze James brought."

"I like this weekend already." His smile faltered slightly, so I added, "I won't get shitfaced, but I'm so having a few and relaxing. I'll even let you cut me off if you think I've had too much."

"Deal," he said. He'd bloody enjoy that. "Now, lead the way to the doughnuts. I'm fuckin' starving."

Kai

I WATCHED TEGAN OUT of the corner of my eye as she got into bed, wearing some very short shorts and a tiny little top that clung to her figure. This was going to be torture. My balls were going to fucking explode.

"Night, Kai," she whispered.

"Night." I sighed.

I wanted to hop over to her bed and peel those pyjamas off her body. I missed the soft touch of her smooth, milky skin. I missed her taste and how her nails would cut into my skin when she really lost control.

Sighing yet again as Tegan's breathing turned heavier, I looked up to the ceiling in the darkness. I was as hard as I'd ever been in my life, and I wanted nothing more than to reach below the covers and take care of business, but I didn't want her to wake up. I also didn't want to leave the room with a raging fucking hard-on and have anyone see.

It took me almost an hour to fall asleep, but when I did, it was a pissing restless sleep that had me waking up every hour. I was horny as fuck and wound so tight that I felt like snapping at everything.

At five in the morning, I couldn't lie awake anymore, so I got up, made a coffee, and took it outside. The shower was loud, and I didn't want to wake anyone, so the freezing morning air would have to be my substitute cold shower.

I sat at the metal table to the side of the front door, freezing my arse off. My eyes stung like a bitch. Loving Tegan was getting harder to handle, that was for sure, and there wasn't a thing I could do.

I groaned and slammed my head down on the table.

"You okay?"

I jumped and looked up. Tegan was standing by the door with a blanket wrapped around her body.

"Hey. Yeah, I'm okay."

"Why are you outside, in the cold, at half past five in the morning?" she asked, rubbing her hands up and down her arms under the blanket to try to keep warm. She sat down on the chair beside me.

"I, er, couldn't sleep. Why are you outside, in the cold, at half past five in the morning?"

She cringed. "Sophie woke me up, and I realised you were gone, so I came to make sure you hadn't been kidnapped," she said before taking the mug from my hand and taking a long sip.

I laughed and rolled my eyes. "How did Sophie wake you up?"

She raised her eyebrows.

"Oh, right."

Someone should be getting off. Lucky them.

"Well, I'll stay out here for a bit then." No way do I wanna hear that right now.

She smiled, and her green eyes lit up. "Me, too." Handing me my coffee back, she asked, "Are you all right?"

"Fine. Why?"

"You've been…I don't know…different, I guess."

"Different how?"

She shrugged. "I'm not sure. Maybe I'm imagining it. You're okay though?"

"I'm fine, princess."

"Is it Isaac? You can talk about him to me, you know?"

My hand instinctively curled around the dog tags. "I know I can. It's not him. Honestly, I'm fine. What about you?"

"I'm okay."

"You don't sound so sure."

Giving me a sideways glance, she replied, "I hate that you can read what I don't say."

I'd practically been her; although my story was far less pretty. I made Tegan look like the picture of together.

"Bacon sandwiches?"

She nodded. "Sounds good."

After breakfast, we all went to the beach for the day. The girls were wearing bikinis, determined to make the most of the temperamental English summer. I stayed in the boy camp, which was about two feet from the girls. They were lying out on towels, drinking in the sunshine before venturing into the sea. We sat on the sand, drinking beers and not talking about hot male celebrities.

I felt relaxed, lying around on the beach, eating junk, and occasionally perving on the girl I was—let's face it—fucking in love with.

Tegan had left her mobile phone with me to go paddle in the sea, and I'd already taken two calls from Alison in under an hour. Lucas had texted a few times, but of course, I hadn't read them. Not only were they private, but I also knew they'd just turn my stomach. He was the soft, whipped type, so I knew they'd be sappy messages.

Not that I could judge much. I'd tell her I loved her as often as I could, if I were in his position. *Bastard.*

Tegan

"OKAY, GUYS, SO WE'RE playing Truth or Dare, and if you don't answer honestly or complete the dare, then you have to run down the road, naked. You also have to drink every time you pussy out and pick Truth. Those are the rules. Now, who's going first?" James said, winking at Holly.

I'd like to see him try and make her run around, naked. She'd rip his head off.

"Don't look so worried. You have an awesome body," Kai said, smirking at me.

I rolled my eyes and nudged him in the side with my elbow. My body—minus my face—was about the only thing I was happy with, but I wasn't happy with what I'd done to it.

The game started pretty slow, mainly because everyone was wisely picking Truth. But, with each empty glass, more and more Dares started to creep in. Sophie ate a red chilli, James put on a lot of makeup, and Kai currently had hot-pink fingernails.

I bit my lip as I took another peek at his nails.

He glared. "I am man enough for this not to bother me. You've been under and over me, you know."

Oh, good, we are getting into the history of our shared sexual past.

"I never said anything. I think you look very pretty, and, hey, the pink is a nice contrast to all that black and grey on your arms."

"Just wait until it's your turn."

"Like I'd ever be dumb enough to choose a Dare from you."

He glared one last time and then got back to the game. I was having a really good time and not just because of all the funny shit that had happened tonight. I was with people who didn't know about what I'd done, and the one who did know never treated me any differently. Those were definitely things to smile about.

"Tegan," Adam said.

"Dare!"

He grinned. "I dare you to dye your hair brown."

"No. No, no, no."

"Excellent. A naked Tegan, it is," he replied, giving Kai a high five.

Pricks.

"Adam, come on, anything else."

"You know the rules. Clothes off, princess," Kai said, grinning from ear to ear.

I groaned and put my head in my hands. "*Not* a permanent dye. I'm serious. I want it to wash out quickly." *Why, why, why am I doing this?*

"I'll run to the supermarket and get it."

"Get a black one!" Kai shouted to Adam. "Hey, a drastic change isn't always a bad thing."

Does that have a heavier meaning to it? Does he think I need to change?

"Do not get black!" I screamed to Adam, and then turned back to Kai to continue our conversation. "Yeah? What was your change?" I asked.

save me

He tapped the Isaac half-sleeve on his arm.

"It's not the same."

"Kind of is. Doesn't matter what change it is. Sometimes, you just need to be broken from the cage you're trapped in. It can happen in so many different ways, not always what you'd expect."

"What broke you?"

He smiled sadly. "That's a story for another day."

I was determined not to be a pushy person, but, man, I wanted to know what he'd been through. He didn't share that much about what he had been like before he'd sorted himself out. Not that I could blame him. I didn't particularly like visiting that part of my life either, and I hadn't come through it yet.

I had no idea what would break me.

Kai's semi-admission had my mind spinning, and I only remembered that I was about to dye my hair for the first time ever. I was also dying it brown.

You don't want to run naked, you don't want to run naked, you don't want to run naked. Perhaps if I chanted it enough times, I would believe it.

Right now, I'd rather strip off. I'd always been blonde. From the moment my hair had lightened at the age of seven weeks, I'd been a blondie. Going brown and for a fucking dare was drastic. But then maybe Kai was right; maybe I needed drastic.

Adam walked back in, kind of strutting as he clearly was enjoying this, and held the dye out.

Grabbing the box out of his hand, I checked that it wasn't permanent. It'd last for twenty-four washes. I could easily do that in a day.

"I can't do this to myself, so someone is going to have to help me," I said.

Sophie jumped up. "I volunteer."

Glaring, I replied, "I have no best friend."

"You'd so be first in line if this were the other way around. That," she said, pointing at me, "is friendship. Now, sit down, and stay still. I am going to *really* enjoy this."

Sophie applied the, thankfully, light-ash brown hair dye, and I closed my eyes through the whole thing.

I pictured myself and thought about the fact that I didn't really know who that person was anymore. *How much difference can hair dye make? I want to believe that it will be the answer, but how can it be?* Hair colour didn't have that much power and certainly not magical ones.

After twenty minutes, Sophie and I went upstairs to wash the dye out.

"I'm going to look stupid," I said.

"You'll rock brunette."

She rocked brunette. I was going to look stupid.

"It's not me."

"What is you, Tegan?"

My stomach turned to ice. That was the first reference she'd ever made about the fuckup I'd become.

"I don't know."

"Then, keep an open mind, and bend right over the bath. I don't want to get this everywhere."

I did what she'd said.

What is me? That was a very good question.

I had the opportunity to reinvent myself, but the only person I wanted to be was the one I had been before Dad had died, and since I didn't know how to go back there, I was pretty much screwed.

Sophie washed my hair and went back downstairs, so she could wait with the others to see it. I stayed in my room and kept it wrapped up in a towel.

Jesus, I'm an idiot. It was just hair. Plenty of people changed the colour of their hair every day, and I was stressing about it so much that I felt sick.

"Tegan, come on!" Kai said, coming into the room and laughing at me. "Are you gonna take the towel off anytime soon?"

I shrugged. "Not sure if I want to see."

"Well, I'm sure, and I want to see. Let me look."

I scowled at him and pulled the towel off my head. My hair fell in a half-dried tangled mess around my back.

He just stood there, staring at me.

"It's hideous, isn't it?"

"No," he said, shaking his head.

"Really?"

"Really. Fuck, you look so different but so you at the same time."

Helpful.

"In a good way?"

"Yeah, in a good way. Look, I'll leave you to dry it, but if you're still hiding out here in fifteen minutes, I'm dragging you back downstairs." He handed me my phone. "And Lucas called." He turned around and walked back out.

I dialled Lucas's number.

"Hey, shorty, how's it going?"

"You're tall, and Sophie dyed my hair brown." That about summed it up.

"Whoa. Why? I didn't know you wanted to dye your hair."

"I didn't, but I wanted to run around naked even less."

"Okay," he said slowly. "So, you've just done this?"

"Yeah, I've not even looked at it yet."

"Right…"

I frowned. "What? Don't like brunettes?"

"That's not it."

"Then, what is it?"

"I don't know. Sometimes, I feel like I'm the last to know everything about you."

If he were here, I would've hit him.

"What? Lucas, I didn't plan it. Dying my hair was a dare."

Wow, I'm definitely not telling him I'm sharing a room with Kai!

"That's not all I'm talking about."

"Well then, would you care to enlighten me?"

He sighed. "I don't want to fight."

"Me neither, but we'll see how this goes. What do you mean?"

"I mean, with dealing with your dad's death, with everything else in your life. I'm trying to help you, but I don't know how to do that when you won't talk to me."

"All this came from me dying my hair?"

"No, of course not, but you're away, and…God, I don't know. I just miss you, and…shit, I feel like I should've helped by now."

"You're being a dick, and I'm not talking to you like this."

"Tegan—"

"No, don't. Jesus, you have no idea what I was like before you—"

"Because you barely tell me anything."

"How are we having this conversation right now?" *Did I step into another dimension?* "I have to go, Luke. I'll speak to you later."

"Yeah," he said, sighing. "I'm sorry, okay? Enjoy the rest of your time away, and we'll speak when you get back. And send me a picture of your hair."

"Okay. Bye."

"I love you," he said before hanging up.

I had no idea what had just happened. Lucas, although he'd asked questions, had never been that full-on or crazy before. He was right that I hadn't volunteered that much information about my past, but it wasn't something I wanted to talk about, and he'd never said that was a deal-breaker.

With anger toward Lucas outweighing my nerves over my hair, I brushed it through, dried it, and then looked in the mirror. I didn't feel any different—just pissed off—but I sure as hell looked different. Brunette matured me, physically anyway. I didn't particularly like it, possibly because it was such a big change, but I didn't exactly dislike it either.

I waited for the big revelation, the thing that would click into place, so I knew exactly what I would have to do to get the old me back, but it never came, of course.

save me

Showing my new colour off didn't seem like a big deal compared to my fight with Lucas and disappointment that I hadn't changed at all, so I walked downstairs and stopped in front of my idiot friends, who were drinking from the same whiskey bottle with really long neon green straws.

Things didn't seem so bad again. I could forget who I was, forget what had happened with Lucas, and enjoy the time I had with the people who never bitched at me for not being more open or more adaptable or not more like Ava.

Sophie and Holly were the first to see me.

"Tegan, it looks amazing," Sophie gushed.

"Brunette suits you!" Holly added.

Maybe it did.

"Thanks," I said. "Now, gimme a straw. I need to get fucked."

Kai raised his arm. "I can help with that."

"Of course you can," I replied sarcastically. Then, I took the spare straw.

Screw everything. I'm getting drunk.

I woke up in the morning and went to go to the bathroom. On my way out, I jumped at my own reflection. *Fucking brown hair.*

Kai laughed from his bed, throwing his head back and clutching his stomach.

Perfect.

"I hate you."

He laughed harder. "You should've seen your face."

"You're an arsehole, and I want to be blonde again."

I left the room but not before I heard him say, "Well, you should have gotten naked then."

329

We spent the day at the beach again, built a massive sand castle, buried each other, and ate fish and chips. I didn't want to go home to reality ever again. I could quite happily live here forever.

In the evening, we went to a local club, and Holly found a table, so she could rest her tiny baby bump.

"Okay, shots, everyone?" Adam asked, getting up to go to the bar. He left before we had a chance to reply, but he knew everyone's answers.

Two shots later, and we were scattered all over the club, occasionally crossing paths at the bar or dance floor.

"So, which girl have you got your eye on then?" I asked Kai, trying to follow where he was looking.

"What?"

"You're staring at who?"

"Oh, I was looking at that guy."

Huh? "Wow, was I so bad that I turned you?"

He rolled his eyes. "He looks like what I imagine Isaac would now. Do you ever get that?"

"See people who remind me of my dad?"

He nodded.

"Sometimes, I'll hear someone laugh who sounds like he did, or I'll smell his aftershave."

He looked back at me. "You have changed."

I have? "What?"

"A few weeks ago, you would've changed the subject."

I felt cold. *Not sure I really want to talk about my dad right now.*

"So, now, I'm fixed?" I said, forcing myself to laugh.

"No, things rarely get fixed before they break that little bit more." He took my hand. "You'll be okay."

I wasn't so sure.

Rubbing my head with my free hand, I tried to make sense of everything flying through my head. *How can other people know what's going on with me when I don't?* Kai was the only one I trusted to know or even have the closest guess. He'd been me—a worse version, apparently.

He let go of my hand and tapped the table. "Stop stressing so much. It looks like you're trying to make sense of a foreign language you've never heard before."

"Oh, good."

"It's not hopeless, Tegan, but until you're ready and willing to let the grief in all in, there's no point in letting it get to you."

"Right. This is hurting my head; can we talk about something else? Better still, can we just go?"

It was only ten thirty, but I was beyond done with being around people for one night.

He stood up. "Yeah, come on."

Holly and James had left a while ago. Adam, Megan, Sophie, and Mark were all drunk and dancing somewhere.

"It's Isaac's birthday in two weeks," Kai said. "Me, my parents and sisters all go camping for the weekend every year. It was his favourite thing to do. Around this time, I see more of him in everyone and everything I come across."

Hence, the older Isaac-looking guy in the club.

Kai's pain was spread all over his face, and it made my heart ache. I hated it.

"It's okay. You don't have to say anything, Tegan."

"When you camp, do you have to pee in a bush?"

He laughed. "That's probably the best thing you could've said. No, there are proper toilets and showers. So, how are you doing?"

"I'm good—apart from the hair," I replied, swirling a lock around my finger.

"Really?"

"Yep, because I'm not thinking about any of the other stuff right now."

"Solid plan."

I shrugged. "I thought so. Want to get a hot dog from a stand? I'm starving."

"Sounds good," he replied, slinging his arm over my shoulder.

Kai dropped me off at my house, and Mum was waiting at the end of the drive. She hugged me tight when I got out of the car. It still felt weird. I felt like I was hugging just Ava's mum and not mine, too, but I was trying.

"Did you have a nice time?" Mum asked, stroking my significantly darker hair.

"Yeah, it was really good. I needed to get away for a while."

Mum nodded. "I know you did. I like the colour."

"It's growing on me."

"Well, come on in."

I spent two hours drinking tea with Mum and Ava and telling them stories of the weekend. And then, like usual, they left. Of course they'd asked if I wanted to join them at the nail salon, but it wasn't my thing. Not at all. Besides, Lucas had texted, saying he was coming over.

I was nervous as hell when I opened the door.

He smiled awkwardly. "Hi."

Stepping back to open the door wider, I replied, "Hi."

He looked different. Distant.

"What's up?" When I was met with silence, my heart dropped. I added, "Lucas, what's wrong?"

Lucas

SHIT. HERE GOES. "LOOK, I love you, Tegan, but I don't think us being together right now is what you need."

She watched me, expressionless, as if she hadn't heard me.

"I just think you need time alone to work through everything you've got going on, and I'm stopping you from doing that. You were always looking for distractions, and I know you said I make you feel again—and I love that—but what it boils down to is that I'm a distraction, too."

"You're not a distraction."

"Yes, I am. I might not be an intentional one, and it might be in a different way than Kai, but it's still the same thing."

"Fuck that! You have no idea what's going on inside my head."

"Because you never tell me."

"I'm fine."

"You're not fine, Tegan. It wasn't that long ago when you tried to take your own life."

Her eyes teared up, and I felt like a proper arsehole.

"Fuck you!" she shouted, face turning angry in an instant. "I wouldn't do that ever again, and you know it."

I lifted my hands. "I know. I do. But, Tegan, you have to understand why I'll do anything, try anything, to help you get through this."

"And breaking up with me is the way to do that?"

"If it's what needs to happen, yes."

"Why don't you just tell me you've had enough? I can take it."

"That's not what this is. You think I want to end things?"

"Well, yeah."

I sighed harshly. "I don't, and if you'd stop for a second, you'd see what I'm really trying to do here. You know this is the right thing to do, but you're too stubborn to admit it."

"Okay, fine, we're done. Thanks for doing that for me, by the way. You can leave now."

I hated it. Hated that she looked so hurt and so angry. And I hated that this had to happen in the first place.

"Don't be like that," I said.

"You just broke up with me, and what? You expect me to be cheering and hugging you?"

"God, I knew you'd be like this."

"Wow, Lucas. Seriously, just go."

Raising my hands, I surrendered to the knowledge that this was never going to go well, and there was nothing I could do to convince her that I wasn't just bored of her. She'd never see it herself, and she'd hate me forever. It sucked, but I wasn't in control of anything from this point on. Not that I'd ever felt I had control over anything where she was concerned.

"Whatever you think, I do love you," I said, turning on my heel and walking away.

I had to force myself to walk out of the house and close the door. Thankfully, Alison and Ava were still out when I left. I couldn't handle talking to anyone right now. I was pissed off and felt horrible.

save me

Breaking up with Tegan isn't what I wanted, but what choice did I have? She wasn't moving forward. As much as I hated to admit it, I had been a distraction, just like everything else.

I took my car home and went up to the hill to clear my head. The hill seemed steeper this time. All I wanted to do was go back to her house and tell her I hadn't meant it and that I'd made a mistake.

For her, I hadn't made a mistake though. She needed a clean break, so she could focus on all the shit she had to work through. I wasn't convinced that, if we'd met under normal circumstances, she'd have wanted to be with me at all. We had been drawn to each other, but now, it was time to figure out if it was real.

I lay down on the grass and stared at the sky. No part of me had felt so crappy before. It was different shit compared to when we'd found out how ill Dad was. This was all my doing.

I didn't know how long Alison and Ava were going to be out for, and I hated the thought of Tegan being alone. Walking away from her was the hardest thing I'd ever done. Calling Kai to go to her was the second.

He sounded shocked that she and I were over but agreed straightaway to go over and see her, like I had known he would.

When I couldn't put it off anymore, I dragged myself up and walked home. It was getting dark and cold. All I wanted was to crash.

"Luke, where have you been? I just spoke to Ava. What's going on?" Grace asked, yanking me into the house.

If she'd spoken to Ava, then she knew exactly what was going on.

I shook my head and walked up to my room. I couldn't deal with her questions when I was finding it pretty hard to function beyond walking and sleeping.

There were pictures of Tegan and some of her stuff in my room. She was smiling in every single one, but even I could see that she wasn't happy. I couldn't look at her and see the sadness behind her smile anymore. Something had to change.

"Lucas, can I come in?" Grace called through my door.

Like she's going to go away.

"Yeah."

She was in my room in a flash. "So, what happened? Ava said that you and Tegan broke up. Why?"

"Because it's what she needs," I replied, scrubbing my hands over my face.

"Did you have any idea that she wanted to break up?"

I looked at Grace, shocked. She thought Tegan had broken up with me. Of course she did. Grace had been happy that I was happy, but I could see what she wasn't saying. She'd thought Tegan would hurt me. Well, I was the arsehole in this one.

"I broke up with her, Grace. She didn't want to. I didn't want to either, but I had to."

She sat down, crossing her legs. "Why did you have to?"

"Because of Simon. I've been stopping her from dealing with it. I can see that now. I thought I was helping, but I wasn't. Before she can focus her attention on someone else, she needs to be able to take care of herself."

"But I thought you were helping. I mean, before you got together, she was sleeping around, and—"

"Yeah, okay," I said, cutting her off. I didn't need to hear about that or talk about how shit scared I was that Tegan would go back to it. "She wasn't really dealing with it though, was she? Christ, Grace, she tried to end her own life."

She thought about it for a minute and nodded. "I think you've done the right thing. She didn't though, huh?"

I shook my head and stared up at the ceiling. That was an understatement.

save me

"So, what happens now?"

I looked back at my twin. "I wait and hope she'll still want me when she's dealt with everything."

Grace bit her lip.

"Just say it," I said.

"Okay…what if she doesn't?"

Blowing out a deep breath, I replied, "I don't know. Whatever happens, I'll be all right, so don't worry about me."

Tilting her head to the side, she pursed her lips. "I'll always worry about you."

"So, you thought she'd be the one to break up with me?"

Wincing, she said, "Sorry. I like Tegan, I do, but I don't like how she is. I know that's selfish because it's pretty clear why she's behaving like this, but you're my brother, and you deserve the best. Tegan isn't in the position right now to give you everything you deserve."

"That's pretty much why I ended it. She can't be in a relationship right now, and it was selfish of *me* to try to make her."

"You didn't make her."

"I didn't hold a gun to her head, but I sure as hell wasn't as strong as I should've been. I wanted her, and I didn't even stop to think about what was really best for her."

"Don't make this out to be all your fault."

I smiled. She'd fucking defend me even if I were completely in the wrong.

"I'm not. She's no angel. I'm not blind, and I'm not putting her on a pedestal. What I'm doing is taking responsibility for my part in this, and for the first time since I met her, I'm doing the right thing for us both."

"I'm proud of you, and I hope this works out the way you want it to."

"You don't think it will?"

She shrugged. "All I know is that she's not herself, and we've never met who she really is. We don't know what she'll want when she finds that person again…*if* she finds that person again."

337

"I need sleep, Grace."

"Hint taken," she said, untangling her legs and getting up. "I really am sorry that things got so messy, Luke, but have faith, okay?"

Nodding, I removed my T-shirt and flopped down on the bed, too tired to think about it anymore.

Kai

I TAPPED THE DOG tags with the pads of my fingers and stared at my little brother's grave. "Happy thirteenth birthday, buddy," I said.

Six years had passed, and I still missed him so much. I couldn't help wondering what he'd be like and if he would've discovered girls yet.

Isaac would probably have been planning his Army career if he still wanted to do that. I was pretty confident he'd have wanted to. The Army phase had started at two, and he had still been obsessed at six.

"Mum made the Army tank cake again this year. Bet you're sick of that by now."

I'd hated those cakes right up until I sorted my life out at twenty. That was five years of wanting to throw the cake at the wall. Now, I got it. Isaac was physically gone, but he was still just as much a part of the family as the rest of us. *Why shouldn't we celebrate his birthday, too?*

I wrapped my fingers around the tags and gripped hard. Part of me wished he hadn't given them to me. He'd loved them and never taken them off. But it was up to me to wear them in honour of him now. It was my turn to keep them with me.

"If you were here right now, we'd be go-karting. Remember when you were little and would only go on them with me? Dad tried to get you to go on with him, but you weren't having any of it, so I only got one fast go on my own the whole time we were there. That didn't matter to me though. I know you were a lot younger and got on my nerves, but you were the person I loved the most, Isaac. Right from when you were a little baby, I was obsessed with looking after you. I think it was because you'd finally saved me from being the only boy with two sisters. I love you, bro. Nothing will ever change that. I gotta get going, but I'll come back soon, okay? Enjoy being thirteen from wherever you are now."

I stood up and left. My heart felt like it was made of lead. Isaac was the only person I'd cried over, and I really didn't want to be weak on his birthday.

I got in my car, and that was when my phone rang with Tegan's ringtone. I knew what it was about. I'd taken a call from Lucas just before getting here, but I'd had to see my brother first.

Pressing Answer, I started the car and put her on speaker. "Hey, princess," I said.

"Hi," she replied, deflated.

"What's wrong?" I asked since I wasn't supposed to know.

"Lucas broke up with me," she said.

It was clear from her quiet tone and hushed voice that she'd been crying. I had known that. Lucas had called, and I had planned on going over to hers after visiting Isaac, but I couldn't tell her that.

"I'm sorry, Tegan. You okay?"

"I'm fine, I guess. You doing anything?"

Cake had been eaten, and I'd visited Isaac, so I was free. "No. Want me to come over?"

"Please."

"Right. See you in five."

"You're the best," she said before hanging up.

I pulled into her drive a few minutes later, and Tegan met me by the door. Her eyes were red, and her hair was in tangles.

"Hey," I said, walking up the path.

She tried a smile. "Hey."

Opening my arms as I approached, I braced myself as she flew at me. Her body collided with mine, and I tightly held her petite frame. I wanted to rip Lucas's head off and buy him a beer at the same damn time.

"Let's get in, Tegan," I said, walking her backward.

"I don't want to talk in front of Mum and Ava. Let's go to my room."

She pulled away, and against every instinct in my body, I allowed her to step out of my arms.

I didn't hear her mum or sister as we walked upstairs, but I did hear the TV in the living room.

Do they know what's happened?

"Wanna watch a film?" Tegan asked, throwing herself on her bed after closing the door.

I nodded and walked to her bookcase to find one.

"Nothing with men in it," she said.

Whoa, she's hating all men right now. What does that say for me?

"Right," I replied.

What film has no men in it? Every film has a fucking man in it!

"Just put *The Texas Chain Saw Massacre* on."

There were men in that one, but they got murdered. She was worrying me a little—or maybe I was worried for myself.

I put the film on and sat next to her. She immediately snuggled up to my side, wrapping her arm around my waist. I guessed she didn't hate all men then. I wasn't being yelled at.

"You gonna tell me what happened?" I asked, running my hands through her soft newly brunette hair. All I knew was that he'd ended it, no details though.

"He doesn't want to be with me anymore." She shrugged, as if she didn't care. "He thinks I need to be alone to deal with everything. It's crap though. He just wants to be single."

It wasn't crap. She did need that, and thank fuck Lucas had finally realised that.

Jesus, I can't believe I'm about to say this. "I don't think that's it. I think he genuinely believes it's the best thing for you."

"Yeah, well, he's wrong."

I nodded, not really knowing what else to say that wouldn't completely slam the guy or sound like I was begging to get back in her pants. She'd just been dumped, but here I was, thinking about her naked. Plus, I couldn't lie to her, and I'd just end up defending him. He couldn't have actually wanted to break up with her. No one was that fuckin' stupid.

Tegan didn't mention it again, so I assumed I was here because she wanted me to be and not just because she wanted to be with someone while she cried. That, I could happily live with, so we watched the film in silence with her lying over me and me trying not to get hard.

When the film finished, I stretched. "You wanna go out?" I asked.

She looked back at me, horrified, and pointed to her face.

What's wrong with her face?

"What?"

She rolled her eyes. "I'll cook something or maybe we can persuade my mum to because there is no way I'm leaving this house, looking like a mess."

I nodded and followed her downstairs, not even bothering to reply to her looking-like-a-mess comment.

"Hi, honey," Alison said as we walked into the kitchen where she and Ava were now gossiping and drinking wine. "Hello, Kai."

I smiled. "Hey."

"We're really hungry, Mum," Tegan said, pouting.

I shook my head, discouraged.

"Really?" Alison replied sarcastically, smirking.

Tegan nodded.

save me

"Good thing I ordered far too much Chinese food ten minutes ago then."

She beamed and replied, "You're the best."

"So, do you want to talk about it?" Ava asked.

They did know then. Tegan had more than likely banned them from saying anything. Her relationship with them was rocky, and that kind of made me resent them a little. It was fucking obvious that she was going off the rails, but they were doing nothing really to pull her back in. And I also knew that blaming them was wrong because, if someone didn't want help, there wasn't a lot you could do about it.

"Not now," she replied as she hugged my arm. "I just want to eat and chill with Kai."

Ava raised her eyebrow, but I couldn't give a flying fuck about what she thought about that innocent action because Tegan's breast was pressed against my arm.

Tegan

THE LAST WEEK HAD been horrible. I missed Lucas like crazy and just wanted him to come back and tell me he'd made a huge mistake. I'd called him twice, but each time had just ended up in an argument, so I didn't try again.

I was able to kid myself for a while that it'd work out, but I'd woken up twelve hours ago with a firm understanding that we were done, and he wasn't interested. It sucked, but I knew it was what I needed to move on—or try to move on.

Another thing that'd changed dramatically was my relationship with Mum and Ava. I wasn't as close to them as they were to each other, and I didn't ever expect that, but things were improving. Once a week, we would have a girls' night, get takeaway, wine—Coke for me—put on questionable coloured face packs, and paint our nails. I wasn't that girlie, but actually, it was nice.

I felt stronger now—physically, mentally, and emotionally. Seeing Melanie twice a week was really helping, and she made me see things in a different way. I'd still have bad days, but they were less frequent.

I sat on the sofa, eating ice cream and watching *Scream* on a Sunday night. I was a total loser, but I couldn't be bothered to do anything.

"You sure you're going to be okay on your own?" Mum asked, leaning against the wall.

"Yeah, fine, Mum. You guys have a good night."

Mum and Ava were going to a candle party. Yeah, a *candle* party.

"Okay. Kai's going to stop over in a minute," she said.

Kai stopping over meant that she'd called and asked him to come and babysit me. *Perfect.*

"Come on, Mum, we'll be late," Ava said.

"Yeah, don't want to miss a second of the fun."

"Don't be so sarcastic, Tegan," Mum said, nudging my arm, smiling. She stood up and grabbed her handbag.

They'd not gotten out the door when I heard Kai's voice. She didn't even want me to be alone for two seconds.

"Hey, princess," Kai said, walking into the room.

When he saw me, his face fell a little.

What? I smoothed down my hair. *Do I look a total mess?*

"Hell no, Tegan. Get up."

"What?"

"This is way too depressing and cliché." He gestured to the ice cream. "You need to go out."

I groaned. "I don't want to go out."

He raised his eyebrows and sat down next to me.

"Please, can we just stay here?" I asked, pouting and giving him my puppy-dog eyes.

Rolling his eyes, he kicked his feet up on the footstool and lay back. "Fine, but you need to stop eating the ice cream."

My mouth popped open. "Are you calling me fat?"

"No, of course not. You're not fat. I didn't mean that. It's just…" Sighing harshly and glaring, he added, "You did that on purpose."

I laughed, nodding. "So, what do you want to do?"

"Hmm, let me think…what can we do while we're alone?"

Oh, of course. "I walked right into that one, didn't I?"

"You did. Want to watch something? Nothing depressing. It's got to have fast cars, a bit of nudity, and blood."

"Going all out on the stereotype, huh? Sounds good to me though." I handed him the remote and lifted the blanket up, so he could get under it.

"Are you going to let me feel you up under there?"

I arched my eyebrow. "No."

"Then, I'm not boiling under a blanket."

"You're lovely," I said, dropping my arm.

Laughing, he flicked through the channels and found an action movie. "So, how are you doing? And don't just tell me that you're fine."

I shrugged and scooted closer, laying my head on his shoulder. "I'm doing okay now. It's over, and there's nothing I can do but move on."

"You're sure it's over?"

"Really sure. The last time we spoke was awful. I accused him of never really caring, and he told me to grow up. I don't understand how he could have cared if he walked away, you know? You can't tell someone you love them and expect them to believe you when you leave."

"I don't know. Sometimes, loving someone means making hard decisions. If someone you loved would benefit from you not being near them, you'd go, right?"

I glared. "You're supposed to be on my side, Kai."

"Hey," he said, holding his free hand up, "I am on your side. I do, however, think there's more to it than what you think."

"Maybe. No point in obsessing over it now. He's made his decision. Are you all ready for camping this weekend?"

I felt his body tense beside mine.

Kai had come to terms with losing Isaac, but Isaac's birthday camping trip was coming up, and Kai was fooling no one when he tried to show it wasn't hurting him. I knew what that felt like. I didn't want to tell Mum how much I still struggled after everything I'd put them through. I wanted them to believe everything was getting better and would be okay.

"I guess," he said, not looking away from the TV. Gulping and gripping my hand, he added, "Will you come with me?"

My heart ached. Kai, usually always smiling and a bit cocky, was sullen and withdrawn.

"Yeah, of course I will."

Cracking a smile, he squeezed my hand. "Thanks. You gonna hate it?"

I shook my head even though the idea of sleeping out in the cold wasn't on the top of my list, especially at the end of October. "It'll be fine. I'm not peeing outside or eating anything you caught though."

"We take food, and there's a toilet and shower block a minute's walk from where we camp."

"What? You don't actually camp at the proper site?"

"No, we camp a bit farther into the forest, near a stream. Isaac loved it there. We used to tie a rope to a tree and swing across the water," he said, smiling at the memory. "The amount of times I had to push him across that fucking thing..."

"My dad tried to get me to go camping once."

"You didn't do it?"

I shook my head against his shoulder. "Nah, attempted it, but I got bitten within an hour and made him take me home. There was no way I would lie awake in the freezing cold all night while mosquitoes feasted on my blood."

Kai's body rocked beneath mine as he laughed quietly. "I promise, the only thing that'll bite you next weekend is me."

"Don't think I won't spray you with insect repellent because I'd gladly do it."

"Please, you'd love it. Hey, so when you went to car shows and races together, did you make your dad book a hotel?"

"Hell yeah, I did. The ones that were over a couple of hours away anyway."

I'd loved the ones that were far enough for us to stay over. Dad would book a family room, and we'd eat a ton of junk food in the living room area before starfishing in double beds across the hall. There was no better dad than him, and I still found it hard to accept that he was really gone.

Kai, almost as if he sensed that my mind was pulling me into the dark void, kissed the top of my head and muttered, "Can I at least cop a feel over the top?"

It was enough to bring me back, make me laugh, and thump him on the arm.

My phone alarm went off at stupid o'clock for sixth form. I only had three days left before summer though, so I made myself get up and have a shower. I felt like I'd had no sleep at all. Last night, I'd dreamed about the accident again. I couldn't remember it all, just small parts, like the crunching of metal and the heat from flames that'd never been there.

During the day, I could successfully block everything painful out, but at night, I had no way of locking it up. I didn't want to go to school and be around people. I wanted to hide away and pretend that I couldn't smell rubber from the tires and hear Dad pleading for help.

Mum and Ava kept away, sensing that I really just wanted to be a hermit for a while.

After I snapped, "I'm fine," they backed right off.

When I left for sixth form, I did it without saying good-bye. They had the photo albums on the arm of the chair again, and I couldn't even deal with that on a good day.

I got halfway there when my stomach started churning up. The thought of spending the whole day smiling, laughing, and pretending like I was fine when I'd watched my dad die in my dreams last night made me feel sick. I turned around and headed to the one place I knew where I'd be safe from endless questions and those can-you-see-how-fragile-poor-Tegan-is looks.

Arriving at Kai's office, I stopped at the front desk.

"Hello," the receptionist said, brushing her perfect platinum hair out of her eyes. "Can I help you?"

"Hi. Yeah, is Kai here?"

"I'll just see if Mr Chambers is free. Can I take your name?"

Mr Chambers. I couldn't imagine him in a work environment, being high enough up the chain that he was called Mr Chambers.

"Tegan Pennells."

She smiled and picked up her phone. "Hello, I have Miss Pennells in reception for you. Okay, thank you." She hung up and smiled again, grabbing a folder. "He said to go through. I'll show you to his office."

"He has his own office?" I asked as we walked down a hallway of glass walls. Walls with some sort of magical blind system inside the glass. How the hell you closed the blinds in there, I had no idea.

"Yes, it's just here on the left." She knocked on the door and waited for him to answer. "Here's Miss Pennells and the folder you wanted," she said, walking to his desk and putting it down.

"Thanks, Jade," he replied, frowning at me as I turned a laugh into a cough. "Yes, I have to work, *princess.*"

Smiling, Jade made her way out and closed the door.

I walked over and sat on his desk. "Do you though? You're in this office all by yourself. No one would know what you were doing. I bet you're playing Solitaire right now," I said teasingly, looking over at his screen.

I was a little disappointed to see he hadn't been playing games.

He smirked. "See? Working. What are you doing here anyway?"

"Couldn't face going in today. I had a bad dream."

He looked at me for a second longer than necessary. "Right, you can be my PA for the day then. First job, coffee. I'll show you to the kitchen."

And that was exactly why he was the only person I wanted to be around when I was feeling like shit. I followed him to the kitchen and leant against the worktop. The blinds were closed in here.

"What's the deal with the walls?" I asked.

"They separate the rooms."

"Oh, so funny," I said sarcastically.

Chuckling, he playfully nudged me. "Turn that little knob on the frame, and it'll open and close the blinds."

Okay, that's cool. "Wow, all you have to do is twist this, and then you can have private sex in your office."

"If you want to try it out..." he said, flicking the kettle on.

I wasn't at all ashamed to admit that I was considering it. Kai in black trousers and a shirt was just as sexy as T-shirt or hoodie Kai. He had the top button undone and the sleeves rolled back, exposing his neck and forearms.

"Thanks, but I don't think I want your dad to hear me having sex."

"But my coworkers are fine?"

"Well, no, but more fine than your dad."

"Of course," he said, rolling his eyes.

"Hello again, Tegan," Kai's dad said as he came into the kitchen with an empty mug in his hand.

"Hi." *Wow, thank God he didn't come a minute earlier.*

"So, I hear you're coming camping with us. How are you with bears?"

My heart stopped. He had such an honest and straight face that, even though I knew bears in the UK were confined to zoos, I still panicked.

Kai and Jason laughed.

"Tegan, he's joking," Kai said.

"I know."

Jason took over making the drinks, and Kai leant against the worktop, angled toward his dad the same way as I was. He was closer to me now. We'd stood this close before, closer even, but it felt different now. His breath cascaded down my neck when he laughed, and I had a hard time keeping up with the conversation.

Things with Kai had always been hot, and now that I was single, I couldn't help thinking about all those times and all the things he'd done to me. Biting my lip, I leant into him and was pretty sure my face was flushed.

Kai

AFTER WORK, I TOOK Tegan back to mine. We stood in the kitchen, trying to figure out which pizza to order for dinner. One of her arms was curled around my back, and her cheek was pressed against my chest. I should let go, but I couldn't move my arms from around her waist because, frankly, I wanted to feel her up for a bit longer. She was in no hurry to move either.

She had been doing a lot better since Lucas broke up with her. She was back to smiling more, and she could talk about him now. The person she still wouldn't talk about much and the one she needed to was her dad.

"Hawaiian pizza?" she asked, scanning the menu.

"Sounds good. I'll order, and you put *Friends* on."

We were making our way through a bunch of TV shows, starting with *Friends*.

Conveniently, the episode was about a girl who wanted to go to space camp. Tegan never said one word, but she didn't need to. Her smirking was enough to tell me what she was thinking. Ignoring her was hard to do. I was drawn to her. Without meaning to, my eyes always drifted in her direction. Thankfully, stuffing my face gave me something else to concentrate on.

I'd just finished the last slice when she turned to me and grinned.

"Hey, you want me to make you a hat like that? You have foil, right?" she asked, nodding to the foil hat the little girl was wearing.

I sat forward. "You have a five-second head start, princess."

Her eyes widened in alarm, and she leapt off the sofa. I gave her three seconds, and then I was up, too. She was fast, but I would always catch up with her, no matter how fast she was or how far she drifted. I reached her just as she burst into the bathroom.

I scooped her up and pinned her back against my chest.

"Kai," she squealed, laughing and wriggling in my arms. "I'm sorry, okay? I'm sorry!"

"You're only sorry because I caught you. Now, you're going in."

She gasped as she realised what I meant. With one arm keeping her in place, I turned the shower on and laughed in her ear.

"No, come on. Let's talk about this. I made one little joke, and you're throwing me in a shower?"

"Yeah," I replied.

"That's not fair!"

"Never said it was."

She planted her feet on the floor as I tried to push her forward. "No! Kai, don't."

So, I wouldn't get her in there alone. I lifted her off the ground and stepped into the shower.

We were soaked in seconds, clothes sticking to our bodies. Tegan squealed again, batting my arms with her hands. I couldn't stop laughing. The water was warm, but it would turn cold if we were in here for too long. I was about to turn it off and get her out before she got ill, but she twisted herself around, so her pert breasts were squished against my chest.

I hardened instantly. Her hair stuck to the sides of her face, and her T-shirt was plastered to her body. Her glare softened as I stared at her like a moron. In the bright light of the bathroom, her green eyes had never looked so crystal clear.

Fuck it.

I pulled her up, crushing her against my body and smashed my lips down on hers. I wasn't gentle, but neither was she. Her fingers dug into my scalp and tugged painfully at my hair. I moaned as I shoved her against the tiled wall, and she wrapped those legs around my waist.

I almost lost it when she ground herself against me. Her clothes needed to come off.

She reached between us and grabbed the bottom of my T-shirt. I pulled back enough to let her take it off, and then I got her topless. When her wet, naked chest grazed mine, I groaned into her mouth.

"Kai," she muttered, rolling her hips and causing friction that made my eyes roll back into my head.

I dropped her legs and worked on getting her jeans off. At the same time, she shoved mine down. I loved that she was as eager and needy to get down to it as I was.

My skin screamed, and my dick throbbed to feel her. I picked her up and entered her hard. Her back hit the wall with the force, but it just made her gasp and dig her heels into my butt.

I kissed her again, fucking her mouth at the same wild pace I used to slam into her. She was tight; that hadn't changed one bit. I fought to stay in control. I didn't want this to end quickly or at all. She got under my skin in the best way, and nothing had ever felt as good or as right as when I was inside her.

She broke out of the kiss, her head making a thud as it hit the tiles. "Kai," she groaned, meeting me thrust for thrust.

The water sprayed down on her breasts and stomach. I arched backward, delving deeper. Digging my fingers into her hips, I bit out a string of swear words as her walls tightened around me.

Moaning long and loud, she came around me, milking me, until I felt like my knees were about to give out, and I was spent.

Collapsing against her, I planted my mouth over hers and kissed her until the aftershocks wore off. I let her down when her body went limp.

"You okay?" I asked, turning the shower off.

She slumped against the wall, chewing on her lip, and she nodded.

I needed more than that. I needed her to tell me she was fine and mean it. Sex with her was out of this world and more than just sex, but it wasn't worth it if it meant losing her.

"I'm getting cold," she said, wrapping her arms around her body.

I got out and handed her a towel with my heart in my stomach. I couldn't have ruined everything. She was right there, too. She'd wanted it just as much as I had. That had to mean something.

As she wrapped a towel around herself, I dried my body with a smaller one and followed her into my bedroom.

"You know you can wear whatever you want," I said, nodding to my drawers.

"I know," she replied as she dropped the towel.

I knew I was supposed to be a gentleman now, but my eyes immediately dropped to her breasts and the beaded pink nipples, then lower to the delicate curve of her hips, those hip bones, and then that triangle between her legs.

I licked my lips. *How the hell am I supposed to move from this spot, let alone find her something to wear and get dressed myself?*

She tilted her head to the side, stepped forward, and ran her hands over my stomach. "I don't want to get dressed yet."

I blew out a breath. "Okay."

She smiled. "Lie down on the bed."

save me

There was no way I wasn't going to do that. I moved backward and lay down when my knees hit the edge of the bed, never taking my eyes off her.

"Right back on the bed."

I scooted up. "So, now that you have me where you want me, princess, what are you going to do to me?"

The corner of her mouth kicked up, and she climbed on the bed, only she didn't come up face-to-face with me. With a mischievous glint in her eyes, she lowered her head and took me in her mouth. My hips jumped up involuntarily, and I swore under my breath.

I almost came as she wrapped her hand around the base and pumped slowly, teasing me. "Princess..." Now was not a time to play.

She laughed, which I felt vibrate through my entire body. Hissing through my teeth, I grabbed a handful of her thick hair and pumped my hips, unable to hold off any longer.

It felt too good—being in her mouth and feeling her tongue swirl around me, over me.

Swearing again, I pushed her away and flipped her onto her back. She panted as I held her hips and positioned myself at her entrance. She squirmed, trying to get us all lined up.

Fuck, it was hot when she was like that.

I wanted to tease her, but watching her try to get me inside herself drove me crazy. She gripped around the top of my back and pulled me forward. I entered her and shuddered as her walls clenched, pulling me deeper.

Her mouth fell open, and her eyes dilated. Thank fuck because there was no way I could hold off for that long. She moved with me, raising her hips at the same desperate pace as I was going. I wanted it to be slow and to take our time, and even though we'd had sex not long ago, it still felt like ages, and we both needed it just like this.

Lowering myself, I scooped her into my arms, burying my head in her neck, and I slammed into her with such force that we moved up the bed. She gasped, wrapped her legs around me, and bit down on my shoulder.

Her orgasm came fast and hard, and she held onto me so tight that I had a hard time moving. But it was the way she cried out, incoherently saying my name, that had me following suit seconds later.

I rolled over and brought her with me. She hummed, and I felt her breathing grow heavier as soon as she got comfortable lying on my chest.

It took me a minute to realise what we'd done, and I hated myself instantly. We hadn't used a condom. I felt sick at the thought of putting her through another pregnancy test.

"Tegan," I whispered, "we didn't…use anything."

She sighed sleepily. "I went on the injection after the last time."

Oh, thank God for that.

I let her sleep for an hour while I watched her breathe in and out, occasionally sighing in between. She looked so peaceful when she slept. All of the pent-up grief, sadness, and anger evaporated when she drifted off. I wanted that for her all the time, but I knew from firsthand experience that those feelings would never completely leave her.

"Hey, you need to wake up," I whispered in her ear, stroking the bare skin on her back, as she lay almost all the way on top of me.

She groaned. "I'm asleep, Kai."

"Then, you sleep talk."

"Shh," she mumbled against my chest, giving me goose bumps.

I laughed quietly, not wanting to wake her even though I needed to. "We need to go soon."

"Fine," she said, rolling off and opening her eyes enough to glare.

"I'll go see if I can salvage your clothes."

The answer was no.

The bathroom was a watery mess, and our clothes were in soaking piles on the shower floor. She was definitely going to have to wear something of mine. Thankfully, I wasn't the one who would have to explain that to her mum.

save me

When I walked back into the bedroom, Tegan was asleep again. She was on top of the covers and naked. I could've happily let her stay the night while I fought against every urge to touch and taste her.

I stroked my fingers over her breasts and down her stomach. Her eyes flicked open, and she smirked right as I got to her hip.

"I don't want to go home," she said breathlessly.

"I don't want you to either, but you need to pack for tomorrow."

"I know. Fine. Am I going to need to borrow your clothes?"

Grinning like a Cheshire Cat, I nodded.

Tegan

I FOUND MUM AND Ava in the kitchen, whispering to each other. They stopped as soon as they saw me.

Wow, not at all obvious.

"Hi, honey. Did you have a nice time?" Mum asked. She was hiding something. "Another water fight?" Her eyes scanned over my damp hair.

I twirled a damp lock around my finger. "Uh, yeah." *Sort of anyway.* "So, what's going on?"

They exchanged a look, and I could tell they were seconds away from trying to convince me that nothing was happening.

"I'm not an idiot, so please just spit it out."

"Nothing's going on. We spoke to Emily today, and apparently, Lucas isn't doing so well," she said.

Not doing so well? It's his fucking fault!

"He's been out racing a lot, and..." She stopped talking.

"And he misses you."

No way was that it. There was more to it. She wasn't just going to say he missed me. Screwing around with girls was probably more like it. Not that I could say much after tonight though.

"Tegan, are you okay? Do you want to talk about it?" Ava asked.

"No, thanks. I'm gonna go to bed. Night," I said. Then, I walked out of the room.

I missed Lucas, but I wasn't going to mope around. He wouldn't have ended it if he hadn't wanted to, no matter what crap he'd spouted to not make himself look like the bad guy. I'd have preferred him to just tell me he wasn't into us anymore.

The thought of him with another girl—or girls—hurt, but I'd have to deal with that. It wasn't as if I'd pledged my allegiance to the Celibacy Club either. I didn't feel guilty for what had happened with Kai. I was single.

Fuck Lucas Daniels.

I stripped, threw on the closest pyjamas, and got into bed. My phone rang just as I settled down and wrapped the quilt around myself.

I picked it up and held it to my ear.

"Hey, princess. You left your bra here," Kai said.

I laughed and rolled my eyes. "Yeah, I left it for you."

"Kinky. You sound tired. I'll go, and speak to you tomorrow."

Seriously, he called just to say that?

"K. Bye, Kai," I mumbled. I laughed. "That rhymed. Your name rhymes with *bye*. Okay, yeah, I really need sleep. Night." I hung up to the sound of him laughing, and I felt myself drifting as soon as I shut my eyes.

save me

I woke up at eight and rolled over, still expecting Lucas to be there, but of course, he wasn't. I needed to get over him soon because missing him was a bitch.

After showering and shoving the rest of my things in my bag, I left the house. I was on my way to visit Dad before my camping trip with Kai and his family.

School was over for the summer holiday. I'd managed to catch up, but next year would be my final year, so I would have to keep my head down and not miss any time. I was going to use the summer to hopefully get myself straight so that boy drama wouldn't interfere with my A-level. School still wasn't something I enjoyed. I'd done a good job of alienating most people, so I kept to myself a lot, but that was fine by me.

Mum and Ava were still in bed. I was going to meet them for breakfast later and then head to Kai's.

"Hey, Dad," I whispered as I sat down, facing his headstone. I still felt like I was drowning somewhat, but it was getting easier every time I came.

"So, I'm going camping today. I know you're probably laughing right now." I realised I was smiling, not something I did here all that much. "I didn't think I'd ever go either, but Kai needs someone right now, and I know how that feels."

Dad would be in stitches over me sleeping in the great outdoors. If he were going with me, he'd probably make jokes and tell me horror stories.

"I miss you so much, Dad. I hate it at home without you. It's too quiet. I wish I hadn't gone to bed early that night." I took a deep breath, swallowing razor blades. I didn't want to cry here all the time. I needed to change the subject. "I called Lucas again a while ago. It did *not* go well. I'm doing what you would've told me to do, and I'm moving on. Maybe he and I can be friends one day—if we can speak for longer than five minutes without arguing. I kinda miss talking to him, so I hope we can sort things out."

I continued talking to Dad for almost half an hour. It felt nice to be able to talk to him again. It wasn't the same, and it would never fill the void, but I felt close to him again and not just because I was physically close to where his body rested.

"I have to go now. Mum's taking me and Ava for a late breakfast before I go, and you know how much she'll moan if I'm late." I stood up and cautiously put my hand on his headstone. It was cold and sent a chill down my spine. I quickly pulled back and gulped.

Don't think about it.

"Sorry, Dad," I mumbled, embarrassed by my reaction. "I love you, and I'll come back soon...if I make it out of the forest alive," I said.

I laughed to myself, knowing he would've been laughing with me. He might've even thrown in a wolf-attack statistic for good measure, too.

Mum and Ava were waiting in the car when I arrived home. That was never a good sign.

I got in the car and grimaced. "Sorry I'm late." *Sorry I'm late.* Wow, it had been a very long time since I'd apologised for being late.

Mum visibly relaxed. "Everything okay? You talked about everything you needed to?" she asked, looking at me through the mirror.

"Yeah. It was...good." I didn't really know how else to describe it. It hadn't really been good, but it wasn't as heart-wrenchingly painful as it had been when we first buried him.

"That's great, sweetheart."

"I'm proud of ya," Ava said. "I've been seeing more and more of my annoying little sister every day."

"Thanks," I replied sarcastically. Honestly, I had been, too. It was nice to feel more like myself.

She laughed. "I'm kidding. It feels good to be...I don't know...*normal* isn't the right word."

"It's okay. I think I know what you mean."

"Well, you two ready for breakfast then?" Mum asked, already backing the car out of the drive.

She had a tear in her eye, but it wasn't a sad one. She was happy. I was sort of happy, too, I thought. Well, I didn't feel like I was drowning in the deep end and unable to swim anymore, so it was a big improvement.

In the restaurant, Mum cleared her throat and set her tea down. "So, there's something I want to tell you two." She looked nervous.

I felt sick. *Did she have another man?* The hairs on the back of my neck stood up. I was all ready to freak the fuck out at her and defend Dad.

"What?" I asked, pressing my fisted hands into my lap.

"I've decided to open a boutique, just like I've always wanted to do."

Air left my lungs in one big relieved rush.

"Wow, Mum, that's amazing," Ava gushed. "Oh, can I help you pick out the clothes?"

"I know. I can't believe I'm finally going to do it! And, yes, you can definitely help. I'll need you both to help. I want to do something positive with the money your dad left me, and I think this is it."

Dad had left us all a lot of money. The guy had insured himself for a shitload to make sure his family would be okay if anything happened to him.

"So, what do you think, Tegan?" Mum asked, nervously watching me.

It was then I realised I hadn't said anything, and I looked like a terribly unsupportive daughter. I had no desire to be that ever again.

"I think it's great, Mum."

I was happy for her, I really was, but I didn't want to talk about the money Dad had left us. I didn't even know the exact amount I would get when I turned eighteen. I'd refused to go to the reading of his will. All I knew was that it was a lot, but no amount of money could make up for not having him here.

Mum squeezed my hand over the table.

"Have you found a shop yet? What are you going to call it?"

"Not yet, but I'm viewing some potential places next week. I was thinking of calling it Simon."

I blankly stared at her. "You're naming a boutique after Dad?"

"You don't think it's a good idea?" she asked.

I shook my head. "No, I mean, it's a nice idea, but this is Dad we're talking about. He hated shopping, and if you hadn't bought him new clothes, he just wouldn't have gotten any."

She thought about it for a minute and eventually nodded. "You're right; he hated shopping. Maybe we can come up with a name together?" She looked between me and Ava.

"Ohh, what about Bliss?" Ava suggested.

I rolled my eyes and tried not to laugh. Bliss sounded like a hair salon or spa.

Thankfully, I got a text message, and I pretended to be distracted, so I wouldn't have to respond to Ava's suggestion.

> *Princess, found your earring. I love that you're a freak in the shower!!! ;)*

That was the third text from Kai today, referring to the shower. In all fairness, it was a *very* good shower. I reread the text and smiled.

"Hey, what about Chic Freak?" I said.

They both looked at me.

"I love it," Ava said. She looked at Mum.

"Chic Freak. Tegan, that's perfect. You just came up with that?"

I nodded. *Yeah, I'm so taking credit for that one.*

Tegan

AFTER BREAKFAST AND MANY discussions about the shop, we drove to Kai's. His family was already outside, trying to load everything into just two cars. Mum grabbed my bag out of the boot and pulled it along the ground.

This summer is going to be great.

"Honey, you're not going to need all this stuff," she said as she let go of the bag's handle near Kai's car.

Kai cocked his dark eyebrow up. "Er, princess, we're camping for *two* nights. You sure you need this all?"

"Yep," I replied, kissing his cheek. I was going to argue that everyone else had brought a crapload of stuff with them, but I knew they had food and stuff for the party as well as all the tents and camping equipment.

Just before we all got in the car, Mum pulled me to the side. "You have a good time, and I trust you to be careful."

Hugging her was getting easier, so I gave her a brief one. Earning her trust back wasn't easy, and I knew that she worried and had doubts, but we'd get there.

"I'm proud of you, Tegan," she said, her eyes welling up.

I didn't feel proud of myself, not yet. I was still in a place where I didn't want to be, but I could almost see a way forward. Even now I spent most of my time running away from the things that were hard, and I still had a lot of anger over so many things.

"Thanks," I muttered, not feeling worthy of her pride at all.

"Look after my daughter, and make sure she doesn't get lost!" Mum said to Kai.

He laughed and blocked my arm when I tried to slap him. I would not get lost...well, unless everyone else did, too.

"I'll bring her back in perfect condition."

We set off for the camping site. Carly, Elle, and I were travelling in Kai's car with the bags of everyone's clothes, and his parents were taking the rest of the things we needed. The whole way, I gossiped with his sisters, much to his annoyance.

I turned in the seat, so I could see them in the back as Carly told us about this guy she'd just started seeing. Kai was interested then. I had a feeling that he was an incredibly protective brother, especially after Isaac had died.

"What's his full name, Carly?" Kai asked through gritted teeth after Carly had first answered with Alex's first name only.

"Do you need his full name?" I asked.

The dark look he shot me answered my question.

Carly signed. "Alex Jackson. Don't look him up though, please."

Kai promised nothing and changed the subject. "You coming fishing tomorrow, Tegan?"

"Boring," Carly and Elle chanted at the same time.

"Yeah, what they said. I don't like fish. They're wet and slimy."

"You're weird," he mumbled under his breath.

I glared at him, which just made him chuckle. *Prick.*

save me

"You can do the woman bit then—cook and clean." He held his arm up and was laughing before he'd even finished the sentence, knowing what was coming.

I knew I shouldn't retaliate because that was exactly what he wanted, but I couldn't hold it back. I swatted his arm twice.

We turned off the main road and headed down a dirty track, signposted for the campsite.

"So, Isaac loved camping?" I asked.

Kai's mouth kicked up into a small smile at the mention of his younger brother.

Elle was the one to answer, "He loved it. Carly, Kai, and I were always excited for our holiday abroad somewhere hot, but Isaac was all about the tents. It's all he'd want to do for his birthday, every year since he was three. If he didn't love it so much, we wouldn't be doing it now."

I felt a bit choked up that they were including me in such an important and personal weekend.

We found a space in the car park and started unloading the many bags from Kai's and his parents' cars. There was a lot, and I wasn't sure how we were going to lug them around in one trip.

"Kai, why don't you camp here? You know, *in* the campsite," I asked.

I grabbed my bag and looked around for another one that I could carry without it ripping my arm out of the socket. Kai took my heavy bag out of my hands and gave me two smaller, lighter ones.

"Because it's more private. We found it the second year we came. You'll like it there."

I really doubted that.

"Don't look so scared," he said with a chuckle as we all walked into the forest.

I walked as close to him as possible, trying not to freak out at every noise. I didn't mind the campsite because other people and cars were around.

"How far is it?" I asked.

"Come on, princess, how can you love all those horror films but be scared of the forest?" Kai said sarcastically.

"Um, maybe because I'm not *in* those horror films."

Melanie put her free arm around me. "It's really okay here. I was scared the first couple of days, too, but it's perfectly safe." She frowned at her son, who was laughing again.

Kai gasped. "Did you hear that?"

I pushed him. "Okay, go away!"

He walked ahead with his dad, laughing his arse off.

We finally reached a clearing, and I had to admit, it was really pretty. The river was clear, too, not that I was going to go in it. Thankfully, it was only three minutes from the public toilets.

We set up the tents near the trees, and Kai's dad collected wood to make a fire. I would be sharing a tent with Kai. Elle and Carly had a small one each, and Kai's parents had the biggest one with two separate rooms. On Isaac's birthday tomorrow, Melanie's parents would be coming, too, and apparently, they'd end up sleeping over.

The fire that Jason lit seemed entirely too close to their tent, but no one said anything, and they had more experience than me, so I kept quiet.

Kai chucked our bags in our tent—literally—and wiggled his eyebrows. I wasn't sure if he was joking about us getting down to it or not, but something stirred inside me that had me breathing quicker and biting down on my lip.

I texted Mum to tell her I hadn't gotten lost—yet—and that I would be turning my phone off, so the battery wouldn't die, but I'd check in again later tonight.

"Get some water boiling, Jason. I need a cuppa," Melanie said, unpacking a saucepan and stackable camping mugs.

I loved the dynamic of their family, how close they were, and that they genuinely enjoyed spending time together. That used to be my family.

Kai shook his head and opened a beer from the cooler, passing one to me, too. "Come on, Mum, it's beer time."

save me

"It's too early for me. I'm getting on a bit now," Mum replied.

He shrugged and then threw his arm over my shoulders. "Well, that's true." It wasn't really, she was only in her forties.

I sank into his side and sipped my beer, loving camping so far; although that could purely be because it hadn't rained yet.

After dinner, which was barbeque, we sat around the fire, wrapped in blankets, and we roasted marshmallows. It was actually pretty perfect.

"So, you okay now?" Kai whispered in my ear as he wrapped his arm around my waist.

I looked over my shoulder and rolled my eyes. "I'm fine. No bears yet."

He smiled, and I got lost in the orange flames reflecting off his dark eyes. He was gorgeous, no doubt about that, and he had such a good heart. Kai was someone you could spend a solid eighty years with and still not get bored.

Just after eleven at night, we all decided to go to bed. Isaac's birthday was hanging over everyone, and even though they were all about celebrating his life, it was plain to see that they still found it hard to stay so positive.

I followed Kai into our tent, and we kicked our bags down near the opening. The temperature had dropped dramatically, and it was cold inside the tent. I stripped down to my underwear and stole Kai's T-shirt.

Screw freezing to death.

I pushed Kai over and got inside his sleeping bag, too. He had a double, but it was a small double, so we were packed in pretty tight. That was fine by me though. I didn't mind being squashed up against his toned and tattooed body.

We lay down, and the rain started coming down heavy, hammering on top of the tent. Well, at least the sky had waited until we were inside before it peed down.

Sighing, he wrapped his arms around me, letting one slip up the back of my shirt. His fingers trailed over my skin, giving me goose bumps and making me hot and achy. I felt every featherlight touch right where I wanted to feel it, and I couldn't

371

stifle a moan as his fingers glided just above the top of my thong.

His breathing became heavier, and his other wandering hand crept around to the front. I almost combusted when he rubbed me through the thin material. His lips found mine just in time to muffle my groan. I arched into him and trailed my hand over his defined chest.

I wasn't sure what made him snap, but his hand left where I wanted it the most, and he rolled on top of me, ripping my thong off. He didn't even bother taking his boxers all the way off, and to be honest, it was awkward in the sleeping bag and would just have taken too long anyway.

He sealed his lips over mine in a hot and heavy kiss that made my toes curl and heels dig into his backside in a bid to get him to enter me quicker. Thrusting forward, he sharply entered me, and the days of pent-up sexual tension burst into a frenzy of desperate sex that wasn't at all sweet and romantic but was exactly what we both needed.

I clamped around him and fisted his hair, tugging hard.

My moans were rolling into one as I lost control. All I could focus on was how incredible his skin felt against mine.

"Fuck," he growled against my mouth.

He went faster until all I could do was hold on. I shattered around him, shamelessly crying out.

I bit down on his lip as wave after wave took me somewhere I'd never been before. This time was different. Yeah, something was definitely different, and nothing had ever felt so good before.

Groaning, he thrust hard once more and then stilled, pouring into me and kissing me like it was the last time he'd ever be able to kiss anyone again.

I fell asleep shortly after he curled me up in his arms again and planted the softest kiss on my forehead.

Tegan

"MORNING," I WHISPERED AS I rolled off Kai's perfect begging-to-be-licked-and-bit chest.

"Morning, princess."

"You all right?"

He nodded, kissed me for less than a second, and got up.

What is that? Is it something I've done, or is it Isaac? Either way, I hated him being upset and seeing the light in his eyes dull to nothing.

I awkwardly got dressed in the small tent and followed Kai outside.

The atmosphere was different today. Kai's family smiled and talked about Isaac, but I could see and feel the sadness. Kai barely said a word all morning. He pulled me onto his lap and laid his chin on my shoulder as I silently listened to stories about his little brother.

On a few occasions, Melanie looked like she was going to cry, but she'd told me that she wouldn't let herself cry on

Isaac's birthday. It was supposed to be a happy time, and she could wait until she was home. I was in awe of her strength and her determination to make his birthday a day to celebrate, having known him for just six short years.

I couldn't hold back the tears when Melanie talked about Isaac's obsession with the Army and his love of the dog tags Kai now wore. The entire time, Kai gripped them in one hand and held me with his other arm. I loved how much he loved his little brother.

"Walk with me?" Kai asked once Melanie had finished her story.

I got off his lap, and then I let him take my hand and lead the way.

"How are you doing?" I asked when we were out of earshot.

"I'm all right," he replied tightly. "Better, having you here." He squeezed my hand that little bit harder and rubbed his thumb over my knuckles.

I was glad I was here, too. I wanted, needed, to be there for him. "Good."

We walked deep into the woods, and usually, I'd be concerned, but Kai seemed to know where he was going, so I didn't worry.

"I wish I could've met Isaac. He sounds like an awesome kid."

"He was. Annoying as fuck, but I loved him like mad and would've done anything for him."

"You were a great brother to him, Kai, and I know you feel guilty over what happened, but I don't believe he could've ever been mad at you for a second."

"I don't know. When everything was explained, sure, I believe that he understood there was nothing I could do, or I would've done it. But I fixed things, always had. I was the one who'd mend his toys and take his floating fish to the vet and bring it back healthy. When Mum told him he had poor blood, he said..." Clenching his jaw, he blinked hard and took a deep breath. "He said, 'That's okay. Kai will fix it,' and I'd never felt so utterly helpless as I did in that moment. I knew then that he wouldn't make it. I could fix most things, but I couldn't fix his blood."

The pain in his voice cut me open. My heart hurt for him. I wiped a tear, unsure of what to say. It was so unfair that Isaac had lost his life; he was just a child.

Guilt over what you couldn't control was something I had firsthand experience with, so I couldn't preach too much to Kai and make myself a hypocrite.

"I'm sorry, Kai," I whispered, swallowing the ache in my chest. "It was a horrible, terrible, and devastating situation."

"Yeah," he replied, bringing us to a stop. "Tegan, I love that you're here and that you want to talk about Isaac and help, but can we please talk about something else? I just…I need to not think about it for a bit."

I hugged him because he broke my heart. The way he held on to me made me hurt for him. "We can talk about whatever you like."

Burying his head in my hair, he replied, "Thank you, princess."

He abruptly pulled back, and his mouth covered over mine, fiercely kissing me, as he fisted my hair. I gasped into the kiss and wrapped my arms around him once the initial shock had worn off.

His mouth was urgent, tongue practically fucking my mouth. I was all worked up and ready to screw his brains out in less than ten seconds.

"Kai," I said as he broke out of the kiss to lick and bite my neck.

He groaned and lifted me with one arm before sinking us to the floor. *Jesus.* I was left hyperventilating on the forest floor as his lips and teeth grazed over the sensitive skin below my ear.

"Kai, what are you doing?"

He groaned and pressed his forehead against mine. His eyes were wild. "I need you, Tegan," he whispered before kissing me again.

I held him closer to my body.

Kai wasn't in the mood to take things slow. He got to work on my jeans, undoing the button and tugging, until I stood up. He slid them down my legs and sat up straighter. He held my hips as I tried to sit back down.

Shaking his head, he said, "I want to taste you."

My legs trembled at the thought, and I felt like I would spontaneously combust, which—let's face it—would be disastrous in the woods. My thong was the next thing to go. Kai peeled it off, trailing his fingers over my skin as he went. His touch had my head rolling back.

"Kai," I whimpered.

The cool air felt amazing against my overheated body. His lips connected with my inner thigh, and I moaned.

"Please."

Two minutes ago, he was out of control, and now, he was torturing me.

He licked up my leg and attached his mouth to my clit. Crying out at the sudden pressure of his tongue, I arched my hips into his face and gripped his hair. If he kept that up, I was going to collapse soon.

I ached almost instantly, desperate with the need to come. His tongue lapped at me, swirling around the bud and dipping into my core. I burned. Fucking *burned*. I was so close, making too much noise for where we were but totally without shame

"Kai," I said. "Fuck." My body shook.

He sucked on my clit, and I came apart on his mouth, clenching around his tongue as he rode out my orgasm.

The very second I let go of his hair, he ripped open the zip on his jeans and got them down. Not taking his eyes off me, he pumped into my hand..

Jesus, that was hot.

"Come here," he said. His voice was so low and so husky that it didn't even sound like him.

He continued pumping until I straddled his hips, and he guided himself inside. His eyes rolled back, and I moaned as he filled me. I bit my lip, still oversensitive from coming just seconds ago.

"You feel so good." He kissed me again. One of his hands was in my hair, tugging lightly, while the other wrapped around my back and guided me to the rhythm he wanted, which was fucking fast.

I raised my hips up and slammed down as he pulled me onto him.

I bucked harder as I felt another orgasm building. Kai groaned into my mouth and thrust his tongue inside, fighting against my own. His fingertips bit into my scalp and hip. It didn't hurt. It would probably bruise, but it felt oh-so bloody amazing.

Tearing my mouth away from his, I cried out as my orgasm hit me like a tidal wave, washing over me again and again.

Kai grunted, burying his head in my neck, as he slammed me down hard and came violently. "Fucking hell," he panted.

Yeah, that was about it. That was probably the best sex I'd ever had.

I was seeing dots dancing in front of my face and collapsed against his chest. Kai held me, stroking my hair and T-shirt-covered back, for many minutes.

I pulled back when I started to get cold, and I kissed his swollen lips. "We should get back. Your grandparents will be here soon."

"Mmhmm," he mumbled.

Laughing, I carefully got off his lap and put my underwear and jeans back on. "Come on."

He watched me get completely dressed, enjoying the show, before he moved.

Pervert.

When we got back to camp, his grandparents were already there.

Everyone was sitting around and cooking on the fire. We'd been gone for hours and missed helping set everything up. Green balloons were hanging from the trees, and birthday banners were taped to the tents. A large cake was on the small table where the other food was starting to pile up.

His family didn't seem surprised that we'd been gone so long, and I felt my cheeks heat. It was probably obvious, especially since Kai had a stupid, satisfied grin on his face.

"So, this is Tegan!" his nan said as she hugged me.

"Yes, Nan, this is Tegan," Kai said, introducing me to her and then his grandad.

The night was spent eating lots of food and enjoying more stories about Isaac. There were loads, and by the time everyone went to bed, I felt like I knew him, too.

I was so humbled that they'd allowed me to be a part of their family tradition. It was such a personal and important one, and they'd welcomed me in, like I was a part of the family. I kind of loved them all pretty hard for it.

In the morning, we ate a quick breakfast of sausages and eggs and then packed everything away. I didn't want to leave. It was so nice, being away from reality in a bubble.

"Why don't you all go ahead to the cars? There's something I need to do with Tegan," Melanie said.

What do we have to do?

Kai looked at me for a second before walking off with his dad and sisters. He so knew what was happening.

Why didn't he bloody tell me?

"What are we doing?" I asked.

She pulled out a red rose from her bag and led me toward the river. That didn't help at all.

"I want you to let this rose go in the river." She handed it to me.

I blankly stared at her. *Right, I could do that…but why?*

"All right…"

"The rose represents your dad and the guilt you're holding on to. You need to let it all go and say good-bye."

The rose suddenly weighed a hundred pounds, and my hand tightened around the thornless stem. My heart raced.

I can't do that.

"What happened was a tragedy, Tegan, but it wasn't your fault, and there is nothing you could have done to stop it. You couldn't have possibly known what was going to happen. No more guilt, Tegan. *It wasn't your fault*," she repeated, emphasising her words.

I blinked back the tears and shook my head. "I don't want to say good-bye."

"I know, sweetheart, but saying good-bye doesn't mean that you're forgetting him or that you love him any less. Saying good-bye just means that you're moving on with your life. He'll still be a part of it. You are allowed to be happy. I'm not going to pressure you to do this because it has to happen when you're ready."

She obviously thought I was ready. Sometimes, I thought I was.

Here goes...

I took a deep breath and moved closer to the edge of the river. *I'm allowed to be happy.* I held my breath and closed my eyes. *I can do this. I can let him go enough to release some of the pain and guilt and be happy. He will always be my dad.*

At the same time as I let go of the rose, a single tear rolled down my cheek. A sob left my throat, and my eyes flew open to see the flower falling in the water and gracefully floating away from me. It hurt, but it also felt like a huge weight had been lifted, and I could breathe properly. I finally understood what I couldn't grasp before; saying good-bye didn't mean I didn't love him.

I clenched my jaw as I stood up out of the water for the first time since he'd died. I was no longer drowning. The fog lifted, and I could see everything so clearly—everything I'd done, how I'd treated people I cared about. Guilt over my dad was replaced with guilt over everyone else in my life and shame for how I'd let myself get so lost. I could handle that though. I was stronger. I could face everything and, hopefully, put it all right.

With a deep breath, I looked up to the sky through my tears and whispered, "Bye, Daddy."

Tegan

TAKING A DEEP BREATH, I rang Lucas's doorbell. My stomach was rolling over, and my palms were sweaty. I'd never been so nervous as I was to see him again after everything that'd happened.

It'd been almost two months since I'd last seen him, and I missed him a lot. Summer had been fun. I'd spent most of it with Kai when he wasn't at work and Sophie. My mum and Ava were also featured a lot, and I was happy that we could hang out like a normal family now.

My final year at sixth form was about to start, and I wanted to be able to concentrate without any mess. That meant doing something I'd wanted to do for a while—sorting things out with Luke once and for all.

He opened the door after what felt like an hour and looked at me with no emotion whatsoever.

Oh God, I've really screwed up.

"Hi," I whispered, playing with the sleeve of my jacket.

"Hi." He stepped to the side. "Come in."

"Thanks." Once inside, I slipped my shoes off and turned to him.

His emotionless expression made my heart ache. His eyes that had once shone for me were empty.

"Luke, can we talk somewhere?"

"Everyone's out. Come through to the living room."

The fact that he'd said the living room and not the bedroom didn't look great for me even though that might be for the best. Lucas sat on the single seat, meaning I had to be on a separate one.

Can he not even be within two feet of me anymore?

Lowering myself onto the seat, I asked, "How have you been?"

His eyebrows shot up. "Not great at first...but okay now."

Okay now was good, I guessed. I didn't want him to be unhappy.

"What about you?"

"It's been hard," I admitted honestly. "I've missed you."

He sighed. "I've missed you, too. So much."

Here was the headfuck part. We were doing okay but missed each other. I wasn't sure if that meant we were just stronger as individuals and could make a relationship work, or we'd changed, and we were better off apart.

"Have you worked through everything?" he asked.

"You can say his name, Lucas. I'm really okay now. Well, not completely, but I'm getting there."

"That's really great." He smiled, looking genuinely pleased for me. "So, Kai's mum has been helping?"

"Yeah, she's been amazing. I don't know what I'd have done if I hadn't had her. But it was you letting me go that finally gave me the freedom and the shove I needed to face up to everything. I owe you so much."

Lucas and Kai—I owed them both my life. Before them, I hadn't been going anywhere, not anywhere good anyway.

He shook his head and leant back, throwing his arm over the back of the seat. "You don't owe me anything. I'm just glad you're facing it and that things are getting better for you. They are, right?"

"Yeah. I can talk about Dad, visit his grave, and look through family pictures. It's nice to remember the good things and feel happy rather than feeling despair and loneliness."

"Good. Seems like everything's pretty much perfect now." He frowned as he realised how that sounded. *Perfect* wasn't the right word to use. "Sorry. You know what I mean though."

"Yeah, I do. Things are good…apart from us."

His jaw tightened.

We needed to sort this mess out. He was so important to me, and I hated us not talking. There were things I needed to say, about a million apologies I needed to make. It was embarrassing. Facing up to the things you'd done wrong wasn't easy, but I could see things clearer now. I knew what I'd done wrong—and not just to Lucas—and I was more than ready to make it up to the people I'd hurt.

"So," I said, biting the inside of my cheek, "how do you feel?"

"I…" He paused and sighed. "I do love you, Tegan, but I don't know. Everything was so quick."

"Way too quick," I agreed.

There had been no getting to know each other properly; we'd just jumped straight into a serious relationship and assumed everything would magically work out. We hadn't really been ready for it—me especially. Our expectations had been those like a child's who still thought fairy tales were real. Life didn't happen like that. People made mistakes, and relationships—*any* relationships—took work.

"You were right, Luke. I did need to sort myself out before I could be with anyone. I'm so, *so* sorry for how I acted and for the things I said. I know you were just trying to do the best thing."

"It's okay. I knew you wouldn't see it how it was right when I broke it off. I expected worse actually. I deserved worse."

"You didn't. But what did you think I was going to do?"

He grinned. "Beat me. I think I got off lightly."

It was nice of him to make light of everything, but we both still knew I had been a bitch.

"I'm sorry for the yelling. No matter what you say, you really didn't deserve that. So, what happens now? What do you want?"

"We don't work together, do we." It wasn't a question.

Deep down, we both knew we didn't.

"No," I replied, "we don't." My eyes started to sting. *Keep it together.* I really didn't want to ugly cry in front of him. "I don't want to lose you though."

"I don't want to lose you either." He got up from his chair and moved next to me, wrapping me up in one of his arms.

That was better. I needed him to like me enough to touch me.

"There's just too much to make this work, and I think we'd both end up hating each other if we forced it. I was unsure until we just talked but I think we're better as friends," he said.

That was what I thought, too, and what I wanted, but it was still hard to agree that we were never going to get back together.

"I'd really like the friend thing."

"Good." He leant over and kissed me softly for one second.

I knew that was it—the good-bye kiss that officially ended our relationship once and for all. I gulped and blinked rapidly, trying to stop myself from crying. Even though it was a mutual decision, it still royally sucked.

When I composed myself, I smiled at Lucas. "What else has been going on then?" Friends would ask that, right?

"Not much. Been racing a lot."

"Do you ever race for anything?"

"It's not *Fast and the Furious*, Tegan."

"Well, I don't know," I said. "It just seems pointless to do it for no reason."

"There's a reason. You race for the biggest balls."

"Lovely," I replied, turning my nose up in disgust. I wished I'd never asked. "Can I come again?"

"Wanna perv over the Lamborghini?"

I nodded. That car was amazing. "And you can take me out in it again, and let me have a go. Danny doesn't need to know a thing."

"Yeah, that's not gonna happen."

I laughed and lay back in the sofa.

This is going well. The friend thing is going to work.

"I should get going," I said after forty-five minutes of chatting.

"All right." He got up with me and walked me to the front door. "You sure you don't want me to take you home?" he asked.

"Thanks, but I already have a return bus ticket."

"Okay, I'll see you soon."

We exchanged a hug, and I kissed him on the cheek. It felt normal and finally uncomplicated.

"See you later, Tegan."

I turned around and said, "Thank you so much, Lucas."

"For what?"

"For saving me."

He nodded, and his lips pulled up into a genuine smile.

Thank you seemed so small compared to what he had done for me, but I hadn't known what else to say. There was nothing huge enough to describe how grateful I was to him. He'd let me go, despite not wanting to, so I could concentrate on getting better.

Walking away from Lucas felt odd. We were one hundred percent over, but I felt fine about it. I wanted him in my life, but friendship was all we were supposed to have, and I was so lucky that we'd managed to get past the crap to be friends.

"How did it go?" Mum asked the second I stepped through the door.

"Good actually."

"Really? That's great. What happened? What did you decide to do?"

I held my hands up. "Can I get properly inside the house before you start the inquisition?"

Mum waited until I was sitting down before asking, "So, what happened?"

"We talked about what we wanted and realised we just wanted to be friends. That was about it."

"That was it?" Ava said flatly.

"Okay, no, but that's all I'm going to tell you." I grinned smugly and reached for the bowl of peanut M&M's. They already had the junk food laid out, anticipating me needing a shit-load of sugar. "I think things are going to be okay. I'm determined to work on fixing it, like I am with you two."

"It's fixed, Tegan. We're family. You're my *daughter*, and I will never stop loving you. No matter what you do or how big of a pain in the arse you become, our relationship will always be fixable. I will always forgive because that's what you do when you're a mother."

A few months ago, I wouldn't have believed that. I hadn't been close to them, and I'd barely felt like family, but that'd changed. It wasn't just what you did when you were a mum; it was what you did when you loved someone. And I loved them both so much.

"See, baby sis? Everything is fine, so stop worrying and feeling guilty. It's done. You've apologised a thousand times, and you've changed your life. We forgave you a long time ago."

"Thanks, Ava," I said.

She smiled and added, "So, you're really not going to spill? It's a girls' night; it's like compulsory."

I rolled my eyes even though she did have a point. But I'd only just started joining in on their girls' nights, so I didn't feel compelled to spill all.

"If I feel like it later, I'll tell, okay?" I said.

That was the best she was going to get because, frankly, it was private, and that was how I liked it.

Tegan

I MET LUCAS IN the café halfway between our houses. We'd been meeting every week since we'd made peace last month, and it was really nice. It hadn't always been easy, but we wanted to stay friends, so we both put the effort in.

The first time we'd decided to meet, he'd offered to pick me up and go somewhere local to me. I didn't mind when we were together, but we were trying to redefine boundaries, so it didn't seem right—him going right out of his way to see me.

It was still the early days, but last week was the first time that there had been no awkwardness at all, so hopefully, that part was done. There was now less than two months until Christmas, and everyone was starting to get in the spirit of the season.

Kai's birthday was the twenty-ninth of October—two days away. We were going to have a small party at his that I'd planned, and I wanted to invite Lucas, too, since Luke and Kai were talking.

"Hey," I said, sitting down at the tinsel-decorated table he'd chosen. There was a latte waiting for me, too. "Thanks."

"How've you been?"

"Good. You?"

"Yeah, I'm fine." He ignored his phone as it buzzed once in his pocket. "Sixth form still going well?"

"Ugh, it's going."

He laughed. "No university plans then?"

"No," I replied. "I think I'm pretty much over the learning thing now."

"So, what's the plan?"

"Kai thinks I should open a music shop," I said, rolling my eyes and taking a sip of my latte.

"What's wrong with that?"

"That was Dad's dream. I don't want to do it without him."

"Do you honestly think you'd be doing it alone? That he wouldn't be right there with you?"

"I don't know."

It was something to consider. I certainly had enough money to start up a business; Dad had made sure of that with his three life insurance policies. I knew the amount now. My eighteenth birthday was only a few months away, and on that day, I'd be two hundred fifty thousand pounds richer.

His phone buzzed again, and I saw him squirm in his seat.

"You don't need to make a decision yet. How's Kai?"

Kai and Luke were fine now; all they'd had to do was give each other a chance. It was less awkward—them talking at first than me and Luke.

I narrowed my eyes and put the oversized mug down. "All right, what's going on?"

"What do you mean?"

"Don't play stupid with me. You're acting weird and ignoring your phone. Spill, Lucas."

He opened his mouth and closed it again.

"Oh, okay," I said, realising what was going on. "Tell me about her."

Frowning, he replied, "I don't know if that's a good idea."

"I thought we agreed to be friends."

"We did."

"So, what's the problem?"

"Really, Tegan? You were my first serious girlfriend. We've only just gotten to a stage where things are comfortable between us, and you want me to talk about this?"

"Yeah, I do. We talked about this, about what we really were. I loved you, Luke, but you know, because you said it first, it wasn't real." I'd loved him, that much I was sure of, but it was as a friend and someone who was so important to me. "I'm not just any ex, so please don't treat me like one."

The corner of his mouth kicked up. "I do love you, shorty."

"Good. Now, tell me about her." I held my finger up as he opened his mouth. "No, let me guess…Annie?"

"All right, Sherlock. Yeah, it's Annie. We're not together."

"You don't have to explain yourself to me. I know I've only met her once, but I liked her."

"We've been hanging out more."

"You like her."

Avoiding my eyes, he replied, "I do. We've been out before, as you know, but this time seems different."

"You're both older, and one of you isn't fucked up."

He laughed, and I felt the tension melt away.

"You weren't that bad," he said.

"You're too nice."

"So, you're not seeing anyone?"

"No. I've gone off men."

He smirked. "Really?"

I could tell what he was thinking—Kai. Honestly, the guy turned me on so much that I wanted to keep him locked in the bedroom, but I couldn't even think about being in a relationship.

"Maybe not forever, but right now, I'm working on myself and rebuilding a relationship with Mum and Ava. I hurt them for a long time, and the old me wouldn't have done that. I think I've got about another five hundred cupcakes, lots of apologising, and doing housework before I'll consider forgiving myself for how I behaved."

"You're too hard on yourself."

"Maybe, maybe not."

"Why haven't you made me any cake?"

I grinned and picked my latte up again. "I don't feel that bad about you."

"Oh, thanks," he said sarcastically. "I'm proud of you, Tegan."

"Thank you. Hey, I know you and Kai have been getting on a lot more. His birthday is coming up, and I wanted to know if you'd like to come. It's at his, and you can bring Annie if you want?"

"When is it?"

"Saturday."

He thought for a second and then nodded. "Okay, that'd be nice actually."

I thought so, too.

I smiled. "Cool. Wanna finish this and take me to the track?"

"Annie won't be there today."

Damn, he can see right through me. I shrugged. "Well, I'll just have to watch you race then. Honestly, Luke, you deserve to be happy, and if she makes you happy, then go for it. And text her back. You're being rude."

Kai

IT HAD BEEN AROUND four months since Tegan and Lucas had sorted things out and realised they were and would always be better as friends. They were both doing good and getting along, and I was going fucking crazy. *How much time is long enough to give someone after a breakup?* I wanted to pour my heart out to her about two months ago.

But I cared about her more than I cared about myself, so I could wait until I knew she was ready for a relationship. There was no way I'd jump into anything with her and risk it getting fucked up, like Lucas had. I understood what she'd been through and that she needed to sort herself out first. She'd done that now, so it must be the right time. And I wasn't sure how much longer I could go on having blue balls.

Tegan waved her hand in front of my face, snapping me out of it. "Hello? Where were you?" she asked.

My eyes went straight to her chest and snapped back up. *Fuck, that is a perfectly tight top.*

Don't jump her.

I replied, "Sorry. So, what film did you pick?"

It was early February and absolutely freezing outside, so instead of going out, we'd spend a lot of time at mine, having movie nights.

The corner of her mouth turned up in that little half-grin that meant she was hiding something. Her hands were behind her back.

I groaned as I realised what she had picked. "No way, Tegan. Come on, not again."

She flopped down on the sofa next to me, practically on top of me, and pouted. Her breast was pressed against my side. *Yeah, we are watching that again.*

"Please, Kai?"

"Fine. But no more this week," I said a little breathlessly.

She grinned triumphantly and got up. Well, I guessed I didn't have the same effect on her as she did on me. I was ready to strip her clothes off and take her on the sofa.

The start menu for *Magic Mike* appeared on the screen. I died a little more inside, and Tegan pressed Play. We had a pact that she'd never tell anyone I'd watched it if I didn't complain about how unhealthy her perverted little mind was.

Sighing, I pushed myself up. "I'll make popcorn. Sweet or toffee?"

She thought about it hard, as if she were deciding something life-changing. "Sweet, please."

"Tough decision, was it?"

"Bite me, Kai."

Don't tempt me.

Memories of biting her collarbone while she had been beneath me flooded my mind. I took a deep breath and went to the kitchen.

I threw a bag of cinema sweet popcorn in the microwave and grabbed a couple of Cokes from the fridge. When the popcorn was ready and I couldn't hold off on watching that fucking film again, I went back to join her. Tegan was lying on the sofa with her feet up, like she owned the place.

"Thanks," she said, grabbing a handful of popcorn and leaning against my side.

I put the Cokes on the floor in front of us and wrapped my arm around her. She moved straightaway and let me pull her closer against my body.

"You missed the first couple of minutes. Want me to rewind it?" she asked, surprisingly managing to keep a straight face.

"Oh, I think I'll be all right."

She giggled quietly and snuggled closer. "Good. We can watch it again on Monday, and I'll go for popcorn."

I smiled sarcastically. "So thoughtful."

Her body shook lightly as she laughed, but she didn't make a sound.

The past few months had been the same. She'd come over and stay until late or sleep over if Alison was cool with it, which she usually was since she trusted Tegan again. I was beyond ready for more than flirting and innocent hugs. I wanted to hold her and kiss her and throw her down on my bed and make sure she couldn't walk properly the next day. Since the camping trip, we hadn't slept together again, and the sexual tension was building. It'd been a *long* time.

She was getting better every time I saw her. Her smiles were bigger, brighter, and made her eyes shine. I saw more and more of who she was every day, and I loved that person, too.

Once the shit movie was over, we went to bed. When she slept at mine, she'd stay in my room, dress in my T-shirt, and lie all over me, not that I minded in the slightest. In fact, I was ready to make it a rule.

Flopping down on my bed, she pulled the quilt over her, covering up her toned legs. I flicked the light off and got in beside her.

"I can't wait to see your grandparents again tomorrow," she said.

Neither could I. Although I was shitting myself, my family knew exactly how I felt about her, and I just prayed they'd keep their big mouths shut.

Tomorrow was my nan and grandad's anniversary, and Mum had insisted that I bring Tegan, so everyone could see her future daughter-in-law—her words, not mine. She'd better fucking not say them in front of Tegan either.

Tomorrow could go two ways, and I really hoped it was the way that would end up with Tegan being my mum's future daughter-in-law and not end with her running for the hills.

We'd be staying overnight *with* Alison's permission. The only rule she'd stated was that, if Tegan had a drink, it would have to be in moderation. That was fine by me. Plus, without a no-sex rule, I was definitely trying my luck.

Kai

I WOKE UP TO Tegan kissing my chest. *Shit!*

She looked up and smirked. "Finally! I've been trying to wake you for ages. We have to go in half an hour, so have a quick shower. The bacon sandwiches are almost ready."

She jumped off the bed and skipped out of the room. *Fuck, she is perfect.*

We pulled up at my nan's forty minutes later, and I groaned as Nan came running out of the house. This was going to be painful. Nan wasn't exactly subtle.

"Kai, there's my little man," she gushed as she pulled me into a huge bear hug.

Well, that is just great. I could hear Tegan laughing quietly behind us.

"Tegan, we meet again. Come here and give me a hug."

Oh, kill me now.

Tegan had met them when we went camping, but there had been no time for them to get to know her since it was all about Isaac. This time could be about me and her—not that there was an official me and her. I was working on it.

Thankfully, Mum came out and pulled my nan inside.

"Come on, little man," Tegan teased, walking inside, ahead of me.

"Don't start, *princess*," I whispered in her ear, making her laugh.

Why can't I have a normal family?

We walked inside, and Tegan slammed back into my chest. I looked around to see what was wrong, and Nan's dog, Milo, was sitting in front of us. He was a Great Dane and bloody massive, but he was the softest dog in the world.

"Scared of the puppy?" I asked her. *My turn to be smug.*

"*That* is not a puppy!" She pushed back hard into my chest.

I laughed and moved in front of her. "Come on, Milo," I said, leading him into the kitchen.

She didn't follow me, probably because she was scared of the dog.

"Can you get Tegan? She's scared," I said to Mum as I made Milo sit on his bed in the kitchen until she got inside. *Dramatic woman.*

She walked in behind Mum and grabbed my arm, making sure I was between her and the dog. I wrapped my arm around her waist and reintroduced her to my grandad.

My uncle, aunt, and my cousin, Rylan, would be here soon. He was barely a teenager but had already turned into a horny sex-pest.

Tegan listened politely as Grandad told a story about working in coal mines when he was in his twenties. I could recite those stories in my sleep. Nan batted his arm with a wooden spoon, trying to get him to continue helping with making lunch and to stop talking to Tegan because he was "boring" her. She didn't look bored. She was laughing and had been asking questions, which was absolutely the worst thing to do because it'd encourage another story out of him.

After my grandad had covered his first year on the mines, the rest of the family arrived. Rylan's eyes immediately fell on Tegan, as I'd thought. He was a weedy little thing who had just started exercising and thought he was a fucking bodybuilder already.

"Well, hello," he said, brushing his boy-band hair out of his face. "We've not met before, have we? I'd definitely have remembered you."

Tegan arched her eyebrow.

She pressed closer to me. I could handle Ry being around if she was going to get all feely.

"This is Tegan. Princess, my cousin, Rylan."

"Hi," Tegan said, grinning in amusement, as Ry kissed the back of her hand.

I bit my tongue. Thank fuck I had been more interested in getting high or wasted than being a teenage twat like him.

"How old is he?" she asked once he'd left to get a drink.

"Thirteen, almost fourteen if it helps. I think he likes you."

"Lucky me," she said sarcastically, rolling her eyes. "He's not my type at all. I don't do toy boys or underage."

"Yeah, I forgot you liked older men."

She smiled shyly, and then her eyes widened. "Kai, your nan's downing cocktails!"

I looked up to see Nan finishing her drink, and then she started to make another bowl of some pink crap.

"Yeah, my nan's not exactly the normal, stereotypical chain tea-drinking, jumper-knitting Nan."

"I can tell," she replied.

I wasn't sure if she was horrified or impressed. The latter probably.

Nan caught her eye and waved. "Tegan, come and have some of this, love."

Stopping Tegan from getting fucked up on booze tonight was going to be difficult.

She walked over a little too eagerly and started drinking with Nan, Mum, and Aunt Sandy.

Well, at least she's not afraid of the dog anymore.

Two hours later, and Tegan was tipsy. Besides me and Ry, she was the soberest one here. My family liked to *enjoy* their time together.

We'd moved into the living room to sit on the sofas, and I had Tegan curled into my side, listening to my nan tell yet another fucking story about me when I was a kid. I'd prefer to listen to how my grandad had rescued a cat from the coal mines for the millionth time.

When Nan was disturbed by Grandad telling her the cookies were burned, she leapt up. I wasn't convinced she was even baking cookies.

Tegan turned to me. "Your family is awesome, and I can't believe how cute you look in a dress!"

I glared. Two. I was two, and I'd pretty much just worn whatever was put on me. Very soon, I would be burning that photo album. "Never mention it again."

She laughed and snuggled closer. "But you didn't look bad. Pink is definitely your colour."

"He looked gorgeous, didn't he?" Nan said, coming back into the room.

Grandad was nowhere to be seen, so he was either rescuing cookies, or she'd murdered him for making it up to get her away from Tegan. Both options were entirely plausible.

I need a new family.

Tegan, slightly happier and more touchy-feely from the alcohol, laid her head on my shoulder. "You're my favourite, you know?" she said.

I forgot how amusing she could be when she was drunk. "Yeah? I'm your favourite what?"

"Everything, silly."

I'd take that.

"You're my favourite everything, too," I whispered into her hair.

She tilted her head, smiling up at me, and for the first time, I saw some light in her eyes. It took my breath away. There was no sadness at all.

Fuck, I wanted her bad. Wanted to bury myself inside her and kiss her until we couldn't breathe.

I had it bad, and I was getting impatient.

For a second, I was sure she was seeing everything. She stared back, eyes becoming more intense with every second.

I was going to kiss her, and she was going to let me.

"So, babe, you staying here tonight? You can sleep with me if you'd like," Ry said, sitting on the other side of Tegan.

Well, he had the balls to come straight out and ask.

She frowned and looked away from me. Nan laughed, sticking her thumb up. Thank God, Tegan wasn't looking in her direction.

"I'm good, thanks. You're a little young for me."

"It's not about age; it's about experience. Answer me something, honestly?"

Tegan rolled her eyes but nodded.

"Would you really rather be sitting with Kai or me?" he asked confidently, obviously expecting her to say him.

Why he was so cocky, I had no idea. Although, at school, he probably had the girls eating out of his hands.

"Kai," Tegan replied.

That was the right answer.

"Oh, that's cold, babe," he said, shaking his head and walking back to his seat.

I didn't think I could be a teenager now, not without hating myself with a vengeance.

A minute later, Ry came back and sat in front of us. He'd thought of his comeback. "Hmm, why does it feel like the most beautiful girl in the world is in this room?" he said, smirking at her. Laughing, he added, "Okay, okay. Apart from being sexy, what do you do for a living?"

Now, I wasn't sure if he was just joking around now.

"Do any of these ever work?" Tegan asked.

Shoving his shoulder, I said, "No, they don't, do they, Ry?"

"You won't be able to resist me forever, babycakes."

I was pretty sure *babycakes* had put him securely in the do-not-touch pile.

Two hours later, and Tegan was still tipsy, but she'd not taken it past that. We excused ourselves and went to bed when my aunt and uncle did. Mum and Nan were still going strong. If Carly and Elle were here already, they'd probably go all night.

"Sleep naked with me," she said as I closed the door to the spare room behind us.

I watched, hard as hell, as she removed her top and unbuttoned her jeans.

Not needing to be asked twice—or once, really—I followed suit and stripped. When she was down to her underwear, she stopped, and the air thickened.

We'd seen each other naked plenty of times. All I had to do was close my eyes, and I could see every smooth curve of her milky skin.

Her eyes never left mine as she reached around and unclasped her bra. Her breathing was heavier, matching mine. I stood to full attention, straining against my boxers. Her breasts fell free, and I had a hard time refraining myself. I wanted to caress every inch of her skin, roll my tongue over her puckered nipple, and mouth her to an earth-shattering orgasm.

Shit, I might be hornier than Rylan.

"You're so beautiful," I said, taking a step closer.

I reached out for her, and she stepped into my embrace, running her hands up my back. My hands glided over her skin and landed on her supple breasts. She moaned and arched into me when I rolled her nipples between my thumb and finger.

She hooked her fingers under my boxers and pushed them down. I sprang free, only to be caught in her eager hand. I gasped as she gripped my cock, sweeping her thumb over the head. I kissed her hard, invading her mouth.

save me

She pulled, squeezed, and raked her nails over my skin until I was ready to fucking come all over her stomach.

"Tegan?" I said, gripping her wrist and stopping her from getting me off. I wanted to punch myself.

She bit her lip. "What?"

I wasn't sure what actually.

Laughing, she pulled me over to the bed and shoved me down. After removing her underwear, she climbed on the mattress. I held my breath as she lowered her body over me, and her mouth sealed over mine.

I loved her so fucking much.

Kai

"LET'S GO, KAI!" TEGAN shouted from the front door.

We were going to a stupid party at the social club, and everyone would be there, including my parents. Only two weeks had passed since we were at my nan's, and I had wanted to shield her from the crazy that was my family for longer, but unfortunately, I couldn't control where they went.

In those two weeks, things had changed on an unspoken front with Tegan. There was more to everything we did. Cuddling up on the sofa to watch TV meant more, kissing her meant more, sex was a hell of a lot more. Neither of us said a thing, but we both knew our relationship was changing. Or I was way off the mark, and things were about to get real bad for me.

"I'm ready," I said, and she pulled me out of my house.

I locked up and we walked towards Lucas' waiting car.

Lucas was—drum roll—actually a pretty decent guy. We'd spoken a fair few times since he'd broken things off with

Tegan, and we got along well now, much to Tegan's amusement. She was smug about the whole thing, saying all we'd needed to do was give each other a chance. Smug as she was, she was completely right. Luke and I hung out occasionally, and he'd even gotten me a go in a sweet Lamborghini.

Tegan and I got in the back.

"Hey," I said to him and his girlfriend, Annie.

Tegan was actually the one who had encouraged Lucas to ask Annie out. He had been unsure, and I thought he had still felt a little burned from how things had ended with Tegan. When your last relationship went to hell, it would make you hold back a bit.

"Hey," Luke replied. "Ready to get shitfaced?"

So, Annie is driving home then.

"Hell yeah!" Tegan said, grinning at me.

Oh, I was so up for that. She would get out of control when she was horny and drunk, and I was well up for wild sex.

We arrived five minutes later and got out of the car. Tegan and Annie walked off ahead.

"Bring our drinks over, we'll get a table," Annie said over her shoulder as we entered the club.

Lucas saluted and muttered, "Demanding." He didn't mind really though, he was crazy about Annie.

We sat at a table, not near my parents. They were with their friends anyway, so I wouldn't get the third degree for ditching them.

We took it in turns to get drinks and I think Tegan is fully committed to getting drunk because she's been having doubles.

"Right, my turn," Tegan said. "I'm tipsy so no one change your order because I'll just forget. You're getting what you've been drinking." She got up and walked a little too carefully over to the bar.

Lucas shook his head, flopping his arm over the back of Annie's chair. "Come on, man, just tell her already."

save me

He'd grown bored of my lack of telling Tegan how I really felt. I didn't think there was a single time that I'd seen him when he didn't give me shit for it, the bastard.

I had enough alcohol in my system to tell me that blurting it out now was a good plan. "Yeah, I should, shouldn't I?"

He nodded his head.

"Right. Okay. How?"

He shrugged. "Dunno, but be *really* obvious about it. You're gonna have to spell it out for her 'cause she's kinda blind when it comes to your feelings for her."

Right. She'd said to Lucas once that she didn't think I wanted more with her. *Seriously, how stupid?*

"Spell it out?" I wasn't going to tell her over a game of Scrabble. "Or sing it," I said, looking over at the karaoke machine. I knew I didn't have a cat-being-strangled voice, so I could pull it off easily.

Lucas's eyebrows lifted higher than they looked like they should be able to get. "Part of me wants to stop you, but the other part *really* wants to see you do this," he said.

Tegan came back a few minutes later, carrying a tray of drinks.

Everyone was here—my parents, Alison, Ava, Lucas, Annie, Elle, and Carly and her boyfriend, whom I had yet to threaten death upon. They were all going to witness this—and possibly film it, too.

Well, it's now or never.

"Back in a second," I said to Tegan.

I walked toward the DJ. It was surprising, even to me, when I still thought it was a good idea as I put my request in. Jim Beam was dangerous, and Jack Daniel's was a confidence-boosting prick.

My gut twisted around with nerves. *Please let this work.*

"And next up is Kai singing to a girl…" the DJ said.

Thankfully, he'd followed my instructions and not announced the song or the girl. If Tegan didn't know it was to her, then I would just plain give up on women altogether.

I didn't need to worry about giving up on love for long because, the second she looked at me, her pretty green eyes widened. Then, I got the I'm-going-to-kill-you look. She wouldn't though. She would be randy as fuck later, and I knew she wouldn't sleep around again.

I took the microphone and said, "Apparently, I have to be more obvious here, princess, so here goes…"

The music started.

I sang her song – "Just the Way You Are" – to her, and although I knew I would be getting kicked, I also knew it was having the desired effect on her. Her eyes never left mine, and I thought I also saw them tear up.

In that moment, as she stared at me like I was the only man on the planet, I knew we had something real and something lasting. I would do anything for her, even make a tit out of myself in front of a packed bar.

Right then, nothing but her, nothing but *us*, mattered.

I'd just started the second verse when she made her way over to me. I wasn't sure what to do—stop singing, keep going, protect my manhood. She shoved my arm aside, and the mic fell to the floor.

Gripping the front of my shirt, she yanked me forward, and her mouth smashed against mine.

Fuck yeah!

I kissed her back, holding her close and lifting her slightly off the ground. In the background, I could hear cheers and wolf whistles from the crowd, but it was muffled by the sound of my heart.

Her lips were so soft yet so rough against mine. It wasn't a sweet kiss; it was months of pent-up frustration and want. It was a promise and absolutely everything that was right with this fucked up world.

I loved her, plain and simple, and I was going to go on loving her until the day I died.

She pulled away first. "I love you, Kai," she whispered.

I stopped breathing.

save me

I pulled her closer and pressed my forehead against hers. Everyone else disappeared, and it was just us.

"I love you, too, Tegan, so much. I promise, I'll do everything I can to make you as happy as you make me."

"You already do make me happy. I'm just sorry it took me so long to realise that you're it. You're everything."

I moaned and kissed her again.

"So, I love you, but you're still in *so* much trouble for doing that in front of everyone."

Grinning, I replied, "Sorry. I just needed to tell you."

She deadpanned, "You never thought to just *tell* me?"

"Yeah, I know. Well, before you kill me, do you want to be officially mine?"

She rolled her eyes, wrapping her arms around my neck, and the subdued cheers started getting louder again.

I was pretty sure I heard a couple of people say, "Get a room."

She looked happy, real happy, and that was all I needed. Until Tegan, no one else's happiness had meant so much to me since Isaac.

Kicking her eyebrow up, she replied, "Yeah, go on then."

Stroking her bottom lip with my thumb, I lowered my head to whisper, "The things I'm going to do to you tonight."

Tegan

I SLOWLY LOWERED MYSELF to the grass beside Dad's grave. "Hi, Dad," I whispered.

Visiting him was easier, but it would never be easy. I still missed him more than ever, and I knew that would never go away.

Mum squeezed my shoulder from beside me. It was my eighteenth birthday, and we'd decided to make a tradition of visiting Dad on birthdays. Mum and Ava had followed me here, ready to celebrate me becoming an official adult. I hadn't felt like a child or teenager for a long time, but I had finally grown up enough to be classed as an adult. It had nothing to do with age.

Ava poured pink bloody champagne into three plastic champagne flutes and handed them out, a tradition that Dad had started once we'd turned sixteen. Before then, it'd been pink lemonade for breakfast for his girls.

We were all wrapped up in thick coats, hats, scarves, and gloves. It was February 20, and last night, a few inches of snow had fallen, but there was no way I wasn't going to spend at least a small slice of my birthday with Dad.

Ava raised her glass. "Happy birthday, Tegan."

"Yes, happy birthday, love," Mum added.

I smiled, genuinely smiled. "Thank you."

"Your dad would have been very proud of you both," Mum.

Gulping down the emotion, I smiled at Mum as I finally realised she was right. I had been a screwup for a while, but I'd faced up to what I'd done wrong, put things right, and grown.

"He would be proud of you, too," I said.

I wasn't the only one who had been through a rough time and made it out as a better person. Mum didn't take any crap from me anymore.

"Thank you, honey, but I made so many mistakes after he died."

"Oh, hell no!" I said. "I totally call that one. I was a big mess, a complete bitch, and I made so many *big* mistakes that make me cringe every time I think about it."

Ava laughed, tapping her acrylic nails on her cup. "That's true; she did mess up a lot."

"Thanks, Aves."

She shrugged. "We're here together now. You've more than made up for it, and we're happy. That's all that matters."

I was happy now. Occasionally, I still felt myself being pulled under by guilt, but I wouldn't let it consume me.

"Yeah. So, what's next?" I asked.

Sipping my champagne, I willed them to spill all about my surprise party. They weren't good at secrets. I'd found out about it two weeks ago.

Ava smirked. "Don't you want to spend the day with Mr Perfect?"

Perfect, Kai was not, no one was, but there wasn't another person in the world whom I wanted to drive me insane more than him.

save me

"He's picking me up at six. We have loads of time until then."

"Why don't we go home, watch some movies, and have a pampering birthday until six?" Ava said.

That was all great, if she hadn't already pampered me last night. I'd had a face pack and hair treatment, and my fingernails and toenails had been painted. They were clearly running out of distract-Tegan ideas.

"Sounds good," I replied, trying to refrain from jumping up and down and telling them that I knew what they were up to.

"Okay, cake time. You know your dad hated waiting for cake," Mum said, smiling, as she unwrapped the cake from the foil and handed a slice to me and one to Ava. She placed a slice on the ground for Dad and started eating hers.

When it was Dad's birthday, we'd have to do the cake first because he couldn't wait. He had been such a big kid, and it was those little things that I missed the most.

"Oh!" Ava said. "Do you remember when you wanted the biggest birthday cake in the world, and Dad spent two days making cakes and stacking them on top of each other? It was so high and almost reached the ceiling."

I laughed as I pictured the huge wonky, bright pink cake. He'd had to put kebab sticks through the middle to stop it from all falling over. There was nothing he wouldn't have done for the people he loved.

"Thanks, Dad," I whispered.

"So, we talked about what to get you for your eighteenth," Mum said, putting her drink on the ground and turning her body to face me. "Dad wanted to get you a car. Actually, he wanted to get you a Ferrari, but I put my foot down there. Tomorrow, I'm taking you car-shopping!"

My mouth hung open. "You're buying me a car?"

"One rule though—you're not getting anything too fast," she said.

I nodded, practically squealing with excitement, and gave her a hug. I was going to get a car. I hadn't been in the right place to worry about learning to drive, so I was behind and had only had a handful of lessons so far.

"I promise. Thank you!"

"You're welcome. Let's head home, girls."

I got a text message on our way back to the car with three words that made my heart rocket.

I love you.

Kai could say it a thousand times a day, and I still wouldn't get bored of hearing it.

I tapped back a message and got in Mum's car.

Love you, too.

Love didn't seem like a strong enough word to cover what I actually felt for him.

The whole way home, I strained to keep a straight face. With every not-so-secret look Mum and Ava shared, I felt laughter bubble that little bit higher. But I didn't want to ruin it for them; this was obviously something they had put a lot of effort into. I'd just gasp and hug them when I walked inside, and people yelled, *Surprise.*

Mum pulled into the drive, and there wasn't a single car in sight. I tried to peek through the window, but it was light out, so I couldn't see. Either the guests had done a good job of parking out of the way, or they were pulling a double bluff, and there was no party.

They let me go ahead to the front door, and I wasn't sure if that was part of the plan.

In less than ten seconds, I was doubting myself and dissecting everything they had been doing.

I opened the door, making a little more noise than usual, and a chorus of "Surprise!" made me jump even though I'd bloody known it was coming.

I fake gasped and turned around just in time to catch Mum and Ava as they tackled me into a hug.

"Happy birthday," they said, kissing my cheek.

save me

"Thank you."

I turned around and hugged my grandparents, aunts, uncles, and cousins as a conveyer belt of guests wished me happy birthday. Holly and James stayed back a bit, both cooing over baby Jax. I'd held him only a couple of times and completely freaked out at how fragile he seemed. I could wait until he was a little older.

Turning around, my heart stopped as Kai stood in front of me. He looked so gorgeous in ripped jeans and a black shirt with the sleeves rolled up, revealing his forearms. I very quickly closed the distance and wrapped my arms around his neck. He had me melded to his body in an instant, not happy to have even a centimetre of distance between us. That was fine by me. The next thing to hit me was his scent. First thing in the morning before the rest of my senses caught up to the fact that I was awake, I would smell him. It was so comforting that it made my heart ache.

Without saying a word, his lips sealed over mine, and he kissed me long and slow. His tongue probed my bottom lip, teasing.

He pulled out of the kiss, pressed his forehead against mine, and breathed, "Happy birthday, princess."

Tegan

IT HAD BEEN SIX months since Kai and I officially got together, and we were celebrating our half-year anniversary and me leaving sixth form. It'd taken a lot of work, but I'd finished school and gotten good grades, and I was looking forward to the future with Kai. I was proud of how far I'd come and what I'd achieved.

I was with the guy who had wanted regular sex on his motorbike and considered it romance. He'd told me he wanted me through karaoke, so I hadn't held up much hope for traditional romance.

"Where's he taking you?" Ava asked.

Mum sat on my bed, too, watching me pack a small suitcase.

"I have no idea. It could be anywhere. Do you two know?" I was pretty sure they didn't because they were awful at keeping secrets.

"No, he's not told us," Mum replied, avoiding eye contact.

"He so has. You're not going to tell me though, are you?"

She shook her head.

"Will it make me mad at him?"

Ava laughed. "Not this time."

So, he really has planned something traditionally romantic? I wasn't convinced. Whatever he'd told them, it was all lovey, but obviously, he wouldn't have told them if he were taking me to a sex dungeon for the weekend.

"You know, neither of you is very helpful."

"He's planned something nice, and you both deserve nice, so relax and enjoy it," Mum said.

Oh, I was sure I would enjoy it—romance or sex cave— but again, I didn't like not knowing what I was doing.

I held my hands up. "Okay, fine, I'm chilling out. What do you two have planned for the weekend?"

That was one thing that hadn't changed. Mum and Ava were still so close that, sometimes, I would feel like a third wheel. But it was better, a lot better. I would make an effort to join in and not let self-doubt convince me they didn't really want me there. They did, and I wanted that, too. I'd never worried about my relationship with them all that much because I was always with Dad, but now, I realised how important they both were to me.

"Cinema and shopping," Ava replied. "We'll be here when you get home on Sunday though. Can't miss the Sunday roast. Kai will stay, right? We assumed, since you were here, he would be. You know, since you never leave each other's side."

I waved my hand around the room. "He's not here now, is he?"

"Give it a minute," Mum said dryly.

All right, so Kai and I barely spent a night apart—besides one night a week when Mum, Ava, and I would have a girls' night. I didn't care what anyone thought though. I wanted to be with him the whole time.

"You can't use that. He's due here soon anyway."

They both smiled.

save me

They were happy now, too, but Mum was lonely. I could tell sometimes that she was thinking about her future. She didn't want to see anyone else, not now, but she found it hard to think about spending her life alone, especially once Ava and I moved out. I felt such fierce loyalty to my dad that a selfish part of me didn't want her to be with someone else, but that was the part that I was working on exorcising. I wanted my mum to be happy again, and if that meant she eventually moved on with another man, then I would support her, no matter how hard or strange it was.

"He's always due here soon," Ava said, lifting an eyebrow.

"Oh, stop teasing her. It's sweet. You remind me of how things were with your dad in those early years."

"What? Then, he started to piss you off?" I said, dodging her arm as she tried to slap me for my choice of words.

"Honey, they all start to *annoy* you after a few years. You know they're the one when you still want to be around them anyway."

I already knew that about Kai. The guy had sung to me in front of a packed bar, and I hadn't killed him. I was sure I could overlook petty, annoying things he did, like leaving socks lying on the floor by his bed.

"You want that again?" I asked her.

We'd not had that conversation yet. Ava and I had spoken about it before but never to Mum.

"Don't be mad at me. I know it's too soon, but we want you to know that you never have to be scared of telling us if you do."

She stood up and hugged me, holding one arm out for Ava. Group hugs were something I was slowly getting used to as well.

"Thank you, both of you. Right now, I can't even imagine being with another man, but perhaps, one day, if I feel differently, it's good to know that I have your support, or I'd be worrying."

She would be worrying about my reaction. I was the one who went off the deep end. Ava was normal.

"I've not handled a lot all that well," I said, breaking out of the hug. "But I'm stronger now, so you really don't have to worry about me."

"I know," Mum replied, tucking a lock of hair behind my ear.

"Party's up here then," Kai said, walking into my room.

I wasn't ready for him, not at all prepared for the massive jump in my heart rate. I turned and locked eyes with the guy who meant everything to me.

I stepped into his arms because, if we were around each other, we had to be touching. Apparently, that would stop once all the annoying things kicked in.

"Hey, I'm almost done packing."

He kissed the top of my head. "You won't need clothes."

At first, my mum had slapped him when he made comments like that, but now, she laughed and, more disturbingly, sometimes joined in.

This time, she laughed along with Ava. I didn't though because it was entirely possible that we were going to a sex dungeon.

"Hurry up then. The sooner we get there…" He trailed off, kissing the side of my head.

Wisely, he didn't finish the sentence, but Mum still laughed again.

We arrived at a tiny cottage in the middle of nowhere. We'd been driving for almost three hours, and we were, apparently, somewhere near Sherwood Forest in Nottinghamshire.

It was pretty, and I'd made Kai promise to take me to the forest, so I could see where Robin Hood had done his thing.

I got out of the car, a little bit in shock. The cottage was so small and quaint that I wanted to buy it instantly. It was just too cute.

save me

"Kai," I said, taking his hand as we walked inside. This was not a sex dungeon.

I ran my fingertips over the ivy growing up the walls as Kai opened the door. "Come on," he said, pulling me inside.

Downstairs, there was only a living room and a small kitchen/dining room. A fireplace took almost all of one wall. Upstairs, there was a large bedroom with a four-poster bed and a bathroom with the most gorgeous roll-top bath.

I turned to him and held my hands up. "What…"

"You wanted romance, princess."

Yeah, but I hadn't thought I'd get it. I wasn't the romance type, but the harder I'd fallen for Kai, the more I wanted the occasional moment where things were so sweet that I half-wanted to puke.

He reached over me and started to run a bath.

"What are you doing?" I asked.

"Laying a carpet," he said sarcastically.

There's my Kai.

"Funny."

"I'm going to get our bags from the car and bring the massage oils and bubble bath up here. Then, I'm going to romance your tits off. When I get back, be naked and in that tub."

I made it my mission to get him to say something romantic this weekend, too.

When he disappeared out of sight, I stripped my clothes, laid them on the little wooden chair, and stepped into the ankle-deep hot water. I tipped the complimentary bubble bath in because I wasn't sure how long Kai would , and I wanted lots of bubbles.

"Close your eyes, Tegan," Kai called through the door.

"What? Why?"

"Trust me. Lie back, and close your eyes."

I did what he'd said and lay back in the water that just reached the top of my belly.

He poured something in the bath, which I assumed was more bubbles, and grazed my leg when he swooshed the water around. "Keep them closed until I say."

The next thing I heard was tiny little thuds, lots of them, and I was pretty sure I heard his belt hit the floor. I didn't know if he'd planned it to be such a turn-on, but it was. There were no handles on the bath for me to grip, so I focused on trying to keep my breathing even.

Lavender. I could smell lavender. I wanted to open my eyes so bad.

"How much longer?" I asked.

I sensed his smile.

He turned the water off when it was just above my breasts. "Not long." His voice got further away, and when he said, "Okay, open," I knew he wasn't in the room anymore.

My mouth fell right open when I saw what he'd done. He'd lit candles on the windowsill, scattered rose petals on the floor, and had three bottles of massage oil beside the bath.

He was taking this romance thing seriously.

"Kai?" I called. *Am I dreaming this?*

The door opened, and I burst out laughing. No, I definitely wasn't dreaming. Kai stood completely naked, besides his dog tags, obviously turned on as well, holding a long-stemmed rose between his teeth.

He held his hands out to say, *Well, what do you think?*

"I love you," I said, still laughing at how ridiculous he looked.

Opening his mouth, he let the rose fall to the floor. It reminded me a little of how I'd let go of my dad, but I didn't dwell on that because I hadn't told him or anyone else exactly what had happened, just that I'd said good-bye.

"So, top marks?" he asked, waving his hand toward the candles.

"Hmm, top marks once I see how good you are at giving massages."

He pointed at me. "Sit up I'll show you."

He got in behind me, pulled me right back against his chest, and wrapped his arms around me.

I loved it, loved him, and loved how safe I felt when he was with me. He was my peace, my happy ending, and when I had Kai, nothing could kill me the way it had when Dad died. We could go home right now, and this still would be the best day of my life.

Planting a kiss on my shoulder, he said, "Sit forward."

He reached over and poured some oil onto his palm. When his hands touched my back, I closed my eyes. He worked slowly, rubbing every inch of my back and shoulders, with a touch that was both soft and firm. I was in heaven.

"I love you," he whispered, kissing my neck. "I don't say it enough, I know that, but never doubt how much you mean to me. Even after I made my peace with Isaac's death, I was hardened to emotion, but you changed that. I have never loved anyone so much or so hard. I'd do anything for you."

I felt a tear trickle down my cheek. "Kai..."

"Shh," he whispered. "You want a mushy moment, so don't stop me because I'm on a roll here."

I laughed, still crying. He ran his hands along my arms and curled his chin around the base of my neck.

"You make me a better person. You make me want to settle down and do all of the big commitment and responsibility shit I've avoided for so long. None of that scares me anymore because it'll all be with you. I know things won't always be easy, but I promise you, I won't ever give up on us. I'll fight to the death to give you the life you deserve, and I'll try every day to make you happy."

"You don't have to try to do that," I said.

"You're my world." He gripped my hands and murmured against my neck, "Marry me, Tegan."

I froze. That, I'd expected even less than the bath surprise.

"So, I pour my heart out for five minutes and propose, and you can't even say one little word?" His lips brushed my ear. "That word is *yes*."

I closed my eyes, tightening my grip on his hands. A sob escaped my mouth, and I knew it was pointless to even try to stop myself from getting all emotional and blubbery.

Awkwardly turning around, I placed my hands on either side of his face and kissed him. "Of course I'll marry you. There's no one else I'd want to spend the rest of my life with."

His smile was so pure and so genuine that it made my heart skip a beat. I was determined to give him everything he deserved, too. We'd both made mistakes, but we were going to be happy. We deserved happiness.

I managed to squeeze my legs on either side of his and mould our bodies together.

"I tried to find a ring, but none of them were pretty enough for you."

I loved what he saw in me. "Let's find one together— something that's perfectly imperfect, something that's *us*."

"Hey, I'm the one doing the mushy stuff tonight."

Grinning, I added, "Fine, get me the biggest diamond the shop has."

"I love you, Pennells."

"Love you, too, Chambers. Forever."

He kissed me until the bath water ran cold, and our fingers looked like prunes.

epilogue

Kai

"ARE YOU NERVOUS YET?" James asked, handing me a beer.

It was eleven in the morning on my wedding day, and I was about to drink my third beer.

Tegan and I had been together for three years now, and I'd proposed to her about six months into the relationship. We'd finally saved enough to have the wedding we—*she*—wanted.

Lucas pushed the plate of sausages and bacon we had ordered to the room toward me. "Nervous about screwing up the words?"

"Or saying the wrong name?" Adam added.

"Oh, fuck's sake, now, I'm going to! Tegan. Tegan. Tegan."

My arsehole best man and ushers laughed.

She would kill me. Worse, she would do something to my dick that made my eyes water from just thinking about it.

Tegan Zoë Pennells.

The fucking Registrar was going to say it first anyway. All I would have to do was repeat.

"Are you not nervous that she won't turn up?" James said, smiling around the neck of the bottle.

That was one thing I was sure of; she now knew exactly what she felt and what she wanted.

Since clearing her head and turning her life around, she'd been left with a lot of guilt. Her guilt over me had been completely misplaced. I had known the score. She'd been clear about what we were and what she wanted from me. I'd told her that she had nothing to be sorry for, but not too often, I really enjoyed the make-it-up-to-you blow jobs.

"No. There's no way she won't be there. Anyway, you fuckers are supposed to be *supportive*."

"Hey," James said, "we are. Drink your beer."

Lucas shoved the plate even closer. "And eat."

I ate and had another beer, and then it was time to get married. James, Lucas, and Adam escorted me to the ceremony room where the Registrar, my parents, and Alison were already waiting.

"Are you ready, Kai?" Alison asked.

"Is anyone ever ready for Tegan?"

She laughed and shook her head. "You'll look after my daughter, won't you?"

"We're just down the road, you know."

Tegan hadn't wanted to move in with me until we were married even though she stayed at mine most nights. She needed as much time as possible with her mum and sister. They'd finally gotten a good relationship where she didn't feel like a third wheel, and I knew that, when she moved away, she wanted good memories of living with them.

"I know, I know. I'll miss her though. She's my baby."

I grinned. "Soon, you'll have plenty of grandbabies to keep you busy."

"Promises, promises," she muttered playfully. Then, she took her seat beside my parents.

Honestly though, Tegan and I were in no rush to have children. Tegan couldn't keep a goldfish alive, and I'd probably put a nappy on upside down and inside out.

Our guests started to arrive. We had forty people, and it was only close family and friends attending, the people who meant the most to us. Although she'd invited practically the entire town to the evening reception.

Alison had asked if Tegan wanted her or her grandad to walk her down the aisle, but she'd refused both. I thought, if it couldn't be Simon, she didn't want it to be anyone, so she was walking alone. I hated that thought, but I knew, when she left that ceremony room, it would be with me. She wouldn't have to do that part on her own.

I watched the room fill up with people who were smiling a little too much at me. It was one of those *eek* smiles, like I didn't understand how much of a big deal it was to get married.

My mum was the last person to sit down because she'd been talking to everyone about how happy she was, and she was already crying. I'd expected tears, but I'd thought she'd at least be able to hold off until we were saying our vows.

An acoustic version of "Wherever You Will Go" by *The Calling* started playing, and I knew this was it. I was so ready to make her Tegan Zoë Chambers that it was unreal.

Elle, Carly, and Ava walked down the aisle, one after the other, and all looked stunning in full-length chocolate brown dresses with wild orange and white flowers. I took a deep breath as Ava reached the point that meant the next person had to walk. The next person was my bride.

Tegan walked through the door, and I felt like I'd been hit in the gut by a sledgehammer. She was everything I wanted. Every imperfect part of her was perfect to me.

Her dress was all lace and strapless with a matching chocolate-brown sash around her waist. Her hair, hair that I loved tickling my thighs and chest, was curled loosely down her back.

She walked toward me, green eyes glowing and never leaving mine. The hand that didn't hold her flowers was wrapped around the necklace her dad had given her for her sixteenth birthday.

I was so proud of her that I could've fucking cried. I felt my throat tighten, and I cursed Mum for her overemotional genes.

Tegan smiled wider the closer she got to me, and I wasn't sure if she was amused that I was gawping at her like an idiot or if she was just as happy as I was. It was likely to be both.

She reached me, and I felt like asking her to go back and walk again because I needed a minute.

"Fancy seeing you here," she whispered.

Fuck rules. I kissed her.

The Registrar cleared her throat, and when I pulled back, she kicked off the ceremony. We'd chosen to stick with the words provided—and when I said *we*, I meant *she*—because, after telling her how I'd felt through karaoke, she didn't trust me not to embarrass her again. *Smart girl.* She'd also vetted my speech.

The ceremony seemed to take no time at all. We had no extras, no songs, and no readings, so in less than twenty minutes, we were married, and I was kissing my wife. Tegan put her hand on my chest to push me away.

That's my wife!

I tucked her under my arm as the Registrar announced we were Mr and Mrs Chambers, and the applause lasted until we left the room.

Nothing had ever felt as good as when she was announced as my wife. I felt safe, happy, and secure. As long as I had her, we'd be fine. Whatever the world lobbed at us, we'd get through it together.

"What do we do now?" I asked before kissing her.

I knew we had to have a million photos taken before we'd get fed, but I wasn't sure where all that was happening and where we needed to be. All I wanted was to go to our room, so I could peel that white dress off her.

"Gardens for drinks and photos," she replied, leaning into me. "I could really do with a drink right now."

"Drowning your sorrows already, baby?" I asked, tightening my arms around her.

Biting her lip, she nodded. "Mmhmm."

I was about to kiss her again, but people wanted to fucking congratulate us. It felt like an eternity before we got any time alone again. After photos, we talked to our guests, and then we were called for dinner.

But, as everyone chatted among themselves, I managed to throw my arm over her chair and speak to her in private.

"I want to get married again," she said.

She looked so happy that it made my heart ache.

"Can you at least wait until this one is over?"

She pouted. "I'm not sure. I loved marrying you."

"Are you getting all mushy on me?"

"I think so. Payback for your romantic proposal," she replied against my lips, making my dick stand to attention. "Do you have a problem with that?"

"Not as long as you still want me to do all those things to you that make you scream and turn you into a nympho."

Her eyes blistered. "I'll always want you to do that."

"Good. Then, you can say whatever the hell you want."

She smiled. "I love you, Kai."

"Back atcha, princess."

"This should wrap up in about ten minutes. Want to spend the two hours between now and the evening making me scream?"

I cleared my throat. "You're sitting on my lap, and I'm doing that thing with my fingers."

Raising her eyebrow, she replied, "Oh, I know you are."

acknowledgments

FIRST, I NEED TO SAY thank you to Kirsty for cheering me on when this book wouldn't end! Your love for Kai made me love him more, and then, BAM, he gets the girl.

Thank you to my ladies who I know I can always count on. Zoë, Chloe, Rachel, and Hilda, you ladies are rock stars.

Finally, thank you to the most fabulous editor. It's such a pleasure to work with you, Jovana. I always look forward to receiving my manuscript back and seeing how you've made it sparkle.

Made in the USA
Columbia, SC
13 November 2017